IN A FLASH TONI
RECOGNIZED THE TRUTH

Not only was she in love with the man standing near her, she wanted him with a hunger so strong it threatened to invade her carefully guarded heart.

She had no time to resist the mad burning desire. For Mark covered the space between them and was close to her—so close she found it impossible to breathe.

"Did you miss me, Antonia Cameron?" The voice was husky, powerfully seductive.

"Certainly not," Toni shot back with a passionate need to hide her new knowledge until her reeling senses had time to recover. "I've been much too busy working even to notice you were gone."

"Really? Let's see, shall we?" With a low and gentle murmur Mark reached for her, his eyes gleaming with his intent....

JESSICA LOGAN
is also the author
of this SUPERROMANCE

20—JOURNEY INTO LOVE

This title may be available at your local bookseller
or by writing to:

Worldwide Reader Service
1440 South Priest Drive, Tempe, AZ 85281
Canadian address: Stratford, Ontario N5A 6W2

JESSICA LOGAN
PROMISE TO POSSESS

A SUPERROMANCE FROM
WORLDWIDE
TORONTO · LONDON · NEW YORK · SYDNEY

Published August 1982

First printing June 1982

ISBN 0-373-70027-X

Printed in U.S.A.

CHAPTER ONE

THE WIND WHISTLED out of the northeast, singing through the rigging overhead. Toni raised a gloved hand, tapped her hard hat firmly and glanced up. The derrick towered impressively, a good two hundred feet above the floor of the drilling rig. Three quarters of the way up, the footboard was empty of the ever present occupant required during the actual drilling.

The arc of deep blue sky was truly unusual for a February day on the North Sea. The wind whipped froth off the sharp swells of the moving water. As the girl listened, the waves slapped against the vast hollow legs of the drilling platform, but the hiss of the spray thrown up by the wind was lost in the sound of the machinery.

All this was a part of Toni's complete satisfaction with life. It was six months since she and the seismic team had decided this was the place to drill. In this rough and unfriendly sector of restless water, the team had struck, capped and controlled a high-production oil well.

Offshore operations engineer for Empire Petroleum, Dr. Antonia Cameron, geophysicist-paleontologist, flirted with complacency in the knowledge of a job well done. Where were the scoffers now who thought a woman couldn't do it? She *had* done it the first time around, easily and efficiently.

"And pride goeth before a fall, Toni, my girl," she reminded herself, a quick smile dimpling her browned cheek. She pulled off her hard hat and rubbed her gloved hand through thickly smooth black hair, which glinted in the sun as the wind caught it to whip it in attractive confusion around her face. A slim and eye-catching figure in boots, jeans and a short sheepskin coat, Toni Cameron had lived around oil men all her life. The admiring glances of the roustabouts and pipe fitters escaped her notice entirely. Nor did she see the intent and interested gaze of the tall man lithely propped against the wall of the superintendent's shack.

High overhead the giant crane moved under the sure touch of the operator, Ian Taylor. An enormous load of well casing, balanced nicely at the end of the taut chain, dipped over the edge of the platform, then disappeared. Toni knew the unused casing was being lowered to the deck of a ship riding the restless sea far below. The cost-conscious corporation that was responsible for controlling operations was transporting the material to a site where it had an immediate use.

Ian was an artist when it came to handling the unwieldy gigantic machinery. Giving in to an impulse, Toni moved to the edge of the platform, grasped a guy wire in a gloved hand and watched as he lowered the heavy casing onto the heaving deck of the ship with the precision of a master craftsman. She grinned up at him, flipped an appreciative thumbs-up signal, then turned to go toward the superintendent's shack.

Several hundred yards away a movement in the waves caught her eye. Toni stopped, booted feet widespread, to watch a large seabird skimming the water. A pelican or a puffin, she decided, unable to determine which because of the angle at which it was flying. She concentrated on the bird's ungainly flight, for the moment forgetting where she was.

She did not relate the sudden hoarse shout that went up as anything concerning her. Nor did she see the man leaning against the wall of the shack launch himself toward her.

He hit her with a flying football tackle, expertly executed, as one hundred eighty pounds of hard muscle hit her. His shoulder crashed into her below the waist, his superior weight driving her down into the safety of the rough decking of the rig. His arms closed around her upon contact. He rolled as they hit the deck. The massive swinging hook of the returning boom skimmed over them with bare inches to spare.

Toni's breath left her battered body with a rush that caused her senses to reel. Rage, resentment and a sense of unreality boiled up in her, but she was incapable of expressing a thing. She lay on the scuffed flooring of the deck, stunned, fighting for breath, frightened into speechlessness.

The man's body pinned her down. With his face buried in the curve of her neck, his breath was a rasping harshness against the coolness of her skin, exposed by the folded back lapels of her short sheepskin jacket. Arms with the strength of steel held her closer than any man had ever held her before.

Recovering a little, and aware of the gathering crowd, Toni moaned a faint protest, then tried to move. The reaction of her captor was immediate. He raised his head, stared down at her with eyes as cold as the wintry North Sea. His body, taut, unyielding, pinned hers to the deck with a hard ruthlessness. He was furious.

"Just what in God's name were you aiming at, you little idiot? Trying to get your fool brains splattered all over the place? Damn it to hell, woman, you need a keeper. Who was the irresponsible half-wit who allowed you aboard a working oil rig in the first place?"

Toni stared up at him in angry disbelief. Surely he knew her name, and that she was in charge of the operation here!

"How dare you speak to me like that? Let me up this instant!"

"I'll let you up when I am good and ready!" The husky declaration grated on her alerted senses. His voice dropped, hazel eyes blazing. "I've a good mind to teach you a lesson you will never forget!"

Toni stared up into the determined male face so close to hers and was suddenly very uncertain. Stillness washed over her. Every nerve she owned was screaming a warning note, quivering with subtle awareness that she had spent years keeping locked away in the depths of her subconscious. Frightened now on that deep and unexplored level, Toni's attack retreated.

"We're attracting some very interested attention," she whispered softly, clutching at any straw that might distract her rescuer from the leaping purpose she read in his eyes. "Please let me go now. I'm very grateful for your quick action. Thank you very much."

It worked. She felt the hard tension flow out of him, leaving the muscular length of him pliant against her. Amusement softened the fire in his eyes and deepened the crease running down his cheek, emphasizing the strength of his determined-looking jaw. A dark brow hooked into the unruly thatch of tawny hair being whipped around by the breeze.

"Okay, Dr. Cameron." So he did know who she

was! "I'll let you up if you'll promise to keep your competent brains in that attractive little head of yours. Promise?" His drawl slurred his syllables in a manner Toni found vaguely irritating. She nodded at him wordlessly, trying to assess her dislike of the man.

Never had she been so grateful for anything as she was for the moment he rolled away, freeing her from his pinioning control.

Ian Taylor reached down and pulled her up from the deck. "My God, Toni, what got into you? I thought I had you for sure. If it hadn't been for Anders here...." A shudder raced through his usually stolid Scottish frame.

Toni reached up a gloved hand and touched his worried cheek. He must have broken all records getting down to the deck from the cab of the derrick. "I know, Ian. I'm sorry. Forgot myself."

"Well, you bloody well better not be so foolish again." He rapped the words out with punishing scorn. Toni felt like a schoolgirl caught out in a mischievous prank. It was a new and uncomfortable feeling that did not sit well with her usual cool competence. She shot a look of intense dislike at Anders, blaming his caustic censure for the main part of her discomfort. He smiled up at her, amused. Toni's dislike flared.

"I've never known you to do anything so stupid before," Ian plowed on, ignoring the danger signals.

"I've promised Mr. Anders I shan't be so dumb in the future." Toni's frosty announcement crackled with distaste for the man still sitting at her feet.

Anders had dropped his head. Arms resting on his drawn-up knees, he let his strong hands hang loosely between them. The color had returned to the clear bronze of his skin, but he looked quite exhausted. Wondering why, Toni regarded him curiously. As if feeling her eyes on him, Anders lifted his head and stared solemnly at her. Toni caught her breath, her aversion blazing down on him.

The cold challenge of his angry inspection told her clearly he was resisting a full-grown impulse to issue punishment with proper force to proper places. He wouldn't dare! Toni fixed him with a cold little smile as he came to his feet with a deft flexing of powerful muscles.

"Good show, Yank. Allow me to thank you for all of us," Ian said, shaking the American's hand and grinning down at Toni. "This little lady is sort of a good-luck piece for us. A well-shaped rabbit's foot, you might say." Toni shot him a look of disdain, saw the real concern in his bluff face. "We wouldn't want anything to happen to her."

Color wavered in the girl's face. Unaccustomed to calling attention to herself, Toni could have done without being the center of it now. And she most certainly could have done without the devastating examination of the tall American. He was staring at her as though committing her features to memory.

She scowled up at him, then turned her back on the men, intent upon escape. It irritated her to have acted so carelessly, especially in the presence of the complacent superior Anders. She owed him a real debt of gratitude, of course, but now that she had come to notice him she doubted very much whether she could ever come to terms with his air of arrogant authority. He was just the sort who would think a woman's place was in the kitchen, cooking up goodies for his delight! She grinned at the thought, for she must have been quite a surprise to him. Determinedly she headed for the shack, but he followed her, a long arm reaching to thrust open the door as she approached.

Toni glanced up at him as she passed through the doorway. He had gone oddly pale as he tackled her there on the deck of the rig. It had almost been the pallor of one very intimately concerned with a cherished love, a member of one's family. Toni had noticed it, wondered about it, then pushed the absurd thought aside. This man was a complete stranger to her, as she was to him. His concern could only have been that of the casual observer who had jumped to her rescue.

"Thank you, Anders," she murmured. His hazel eyes lit up, danced with golden flecks as he smiled.

"You are welcome, Miss Cameron," he drawled in a low voice. His smile deepened, causing his face to crease with undeniable charm. There was a devil somewhere in this man, Toni thought briefly, dismissing him from her mind.

Clive Atkins, the civil engineer in charge of production now that the oil well was in place, looked up from the papers he was studying and grinned at her, his face a wealth of wrinkles.

"Well, then, Toni my love, what have you decided?"

Atkins was an old and trusted friend. She had known him since she was a child. He had worked with her father and had been on the rig where the accident costing her father and her fiancé their lives had occurred.

It was Atkins who had come to the university to break the news of the tragedy to her, who had stayed with her until she accepted the fact that the men most important to her were gone forever.

He had consoled her, counseled her, kept her at her studies and given her the will to succeed when she came close to being broken. And Atkins had sponsored her since university, bringing her along, showing her the practical applications of her knowledge and intelligence, stiffening her confidence in herself and guiding her advancement with Empire Petroleum. It was as much due to his wise and constructive advice as to her own effort and skill that she had been made E.P.'s first female offshore operations engineer.

And now this fabulous offer from United Petroleum of California had materialized. Swift on the heels of having the first wildcat she had ever spudded become an overwhelming producer, the heady offer to join United's exploration team was a dream come true.

Of course it meant leaving Scotland and her mother and grandfather. And Rob, her younger brother. But Rob was busy at the university and wouldn't miss his older sister too much. And mom and grandfather were both well aware of the suitcase existence of oil workers. Grandfather Cameron had been an oilman all his adult life, wildcatting all over the globe. His only son, Antony, had followed in his footsteps, marrying Joan Lutman, daughter of a paleontologist working the Riyadh syncline for some of the first discoveries in Saudi Arabia.

Yes, her mother and her grandfather would understand her leaving the security of Empire Petroleum for the promise of United Petroleum. Come to that, they would even understand her desire to visit the States and see how the other half lived.

Suddenly she realized she had forgotten the American behind her, and had failed to notice the stillness in his eyes as he awaited her answer to Atkins's question.

She did not see the quickly masked flare of triumph when she told her old friend she had decided to accept the offered terms.

"Right. You'd better get cracking, then." Atkins rounded the counter that served as a desk and grasped her slim shoulders in very large and gentle hands. "That chopper will be in from Aberdeen in less than two hours. You are supposed to be on it, according to my instructions, if you are going." He engulfed the slim girl in a massive bear hug, then dropped an affectionate kiss on her silky black hair. "Damn it, I'm going to miss you, Toni." His eyes glistened as he released her. Catching her hands as they slid from around his burly form he squeezed them affectionately before dropping them.

"You are leaving, too, Anders?" Atkins glanced at the impassive astute face of the American.

The big man nodded. "We're ticketed on the morning flight out of Heathrow to Dallas, same as Miss Cameron. We'll all be part of the same team, I understand. The company wants us on site within the week."

Toni gasped as she turned to face the bronzed harbinger of doom. Her hastily made plans to go home before leaving for the States were in jeopardy. She stared at him with undisguised hostility. "Oh, I couldn't possibly leave tomorrow morning!"

Anders looked at her thoughtfully, a muscle twitching in the left side of his lean face. "Loose ends to tie up, Miss Cameron? A boyfriend to say goodbye to, perhaps?"

Toni flushed slightly at the caustic overtone in that lazy drawl, but returned the penetrating regard of those glinting hazel eyes with a mounting displeasure that turned her own gaze into a stormy deep blue.

"If it were something of that nature, it would be of no concern to you!" Her crisp voice brooked no argument. She was not the least inclined to explain that Jock Cameron was her disabled grandfather. Toni Cameron had not spent most of her young years controlling the bumptious males with whom she had come into contact to no avail. Her tongue and temper, once aroused, were something of a legend among the men on the oil-rig crews. Always the lady, she had a reputation for being able to tear a strip off any man who trespassed in a manner that left that unfortunate male wishing for wisdom, discretion and considerable distance from the lady he had roused. Few possessed the temerity to try again once tackled by her.

Busy getting things in shape to turn over to the permanent crew, Toni had paid little attention to the man before her during the past week. He had been aboard the rig. She knew he and the five Americans with him were here to study the methods by which this newest well had been located. All her contacts with them had been straightforward business, zeroing in on techniques and equipment usage. Each contact was brief because of her concentration on the job at hand. Anders's questions had been intelligent and concise. She recognized him to be a working geophysicist with a comprehensive grasp of his job. That he was probably an excellent manager of men as well as materials, she had gained from his manner of conducting himself. But she hadn't thought further on it. He had certainly come to her attention today, however.

She noticed him once more. The man had the most incredible lashes she had ever seen on a male. And he stood there, making no attempt to hide the amusement in his hazel eyes as he watched her.

Mark Anders. Most assuredly an attractive male specimen, if one cared for the rugged domineering type. Accustomed to having his own way, she judged. And able to exert masses of charm if he wished. Well, he could exert his charm elsewhere. She would have none of it.

Toni's chin came up, and she swung away from him to face Atkins. "Clive, I really didn't bargain to go so soon. I cannot leave without going home. Jock would never forgive me. And I must see mother.... Think you can fix it for me?" The smile she gave him would have melted ice.

"Leave it to me." The older man glanced reflectively at the man behind the girl. "Go on and get your things ready. You'll want to catch that chopper. Just how do you plan to get to Edinburgh?"

"I'll manage!" Toni left, flipping a farewell to Atkins, refusing to glance at the man standing beside him. But she spent the next several hours being very, very ably managed by one Mark Anders.

She dashed out to the big copter as it hummed on the rig's pad. Handing her case up to be stowed, she slipped into the required life vest and boarded, Anders on her heels. He cocked an inquisitive eyebrow at her as she slid into a window seat.

"Mind if I sit here?" He folded that muscular length of his into the bucket seat beside her as he took her indifferent lift of shoulder to signal agreement.

"I couldn't help overhearing your discussion with Clive, Dr. Cameron." He opened the battered attaché case he had positioned on his knees, rummaged in it, then dragged out a sheaf of papers. "I have business in Edinburgh tomorrow. There will be a car ready for me when we reach Aberdeen. If you would care for a lift, I would be more than happy to take you down with me."

Toni studied him carefully. He was politely attentive, nothing more. Accustomed as she was to the rough camaraderie of oil crews, she found it easy to accept his undemanding offer. "That would certainly solve my problem. Thank you very much, Mr. Anders. It is most kind of you to offer."

"Not at all. Glad to be of service."

He turned away, then swung back to face her. "We are going to be working on the same exploration team. My name is Mark. Mr. Anders was my dad." His voice was quiet, his face suddenly impassive as he carefully watched her.

"All right, Mark." Toni wondered briefly at the intensity of his tone. It was almost as if he had some added reason for a more personal form of address. Ridiculous, of course. "I'm Toni to most people with whom I work."

"I prefer Antonia. Suits you."

He did have a nice smile when he was trying to get along, Toni mused. Ignoring her then, he got to the task of sorting through the papers before him. Toni opened her paperback, pushed a disturbed consciousness of him away, and read.

And so, some hours later, she was traveling in a powerful black Jaguar. Hurtling through the night under the skillful guidance of Mark Anders, the car was swallowing up the country roads at a tremendous rate of speed. Toni wondered idly about the man behind the wheel. Somehow he did not fit the pattern of the run-of-the-mill oil worker. She stole a guarded look at him.

Muted light from the car's instrument panel lit the

lean planes of his face and threw up dark contrasting shadows that brought his wide forehead, firm mouth and square jaw into fine relief. The crease cutting a path from the high cheekbone to the jaw on the near side of that determined face was blatantly masculine. His deeply bronzed, wind-roughened hair was as shaggy as a lion's mane, she found herself thinking. Kurt had been darkly handsome in contrast.

No, Mark Anders was not her cup of tea at all. Thank goodness. No man had interested her since the tragic fall of her fiancé into the icy waters of Cook Inlet in Alaska four years ago. A new relationship was the last thing she wanted or had time for.

The thought of the tragic death of Kurt Grady and her father intruded now, pushing away the girl's growing awareness of the intense vitality of the man seated beside her. Had their bodies been recovered, the nightmare aspect of the fall, from a faulty work basket high above the offshore drilling rig, might have lessened, she supposed. Neither of them had been found. The whole bizarre incident had left a wound that never seemed to heal. And the horror of the accident still wakened Toni some nights, arousing an aching knowledge of irreplaceable loss. Sadness washed over her now. Foolish, she knew, and even morbid. But she did miss them so. No one else ever seemed to fill that giant gap.

The man beside her heard the small sigh and turned to her, his expression hidden in the dark. "Are you tired, Antonia?"

"Yes. Yes, I am rather. It has been a hectic week." She smiled faintly, liking the way her full name sounded on his lips.

"Hang on a minute. I'll put your seat back down

and you can catch forty winks.'' He reached across her, fumbled a moment with the side of her seat, and the back lowered smoothly into a comfortable incline. With a quick twitch he jerked a soft car blanket from somewhere in the back, then spread it over her with smooth efficiency. Toni snuggled gratefully into the soft leather, pulled the covering close and shut her eyes. Her murmured ''thank you'' was barely audible.

''Sleep tight!''

The colloquialism caused her mouth to lift in a quick smile. She settled down then and drifted off to sleep in moments.

Toni awoke abruptly some time later. She was conscious of warmth, discomfort, strangeness. An unidentified weight held her firmly in place. Gently stirring air moved faintly, sweetly, against her cheek. It was sleepy curiosity that caused her to turn her face toward the source. Her heart lurched as she opened her eyes to the shock of a man's peacefully sleeping face within inches of her own.

Sun-bleached lashes traced a golden smudge against the darkness of his lean tanned cheeks. He was turned toward her. His head was pillowed on his sheepskin-clad left arm. His right arm was resting in a firm curve around her slender body, under the warm car blanket he had so thoughtfully provided. The indomitable Mark Anders was sleeping next to her in an intimate closeness that was very disturbing, she found.

Even as she reacted to the weight of that muscular restraint around her person, Toni was faintly amused at the curiously vulnerable cast of the man's features in sleep—rather like a small urchin's, worn out by the pursuit of mischief and caught off guard by a well-earned weariness, she decided wryly. It was a look that would cause almost any woman, seeing it on his dark face, to have an instant desire to mother him.

But she knew that her own undefined but nonetheless strongly felt antipathy for the man was her best protection against that appeal, so she wafted a small paean of thankfulness heavenward as his lashes stirred.

Toni was instantly trapped. She drowned in the brown green depths of those eyes so close to hers. Without moving, he teased and seduced her with a sure projection of male personality. Tension built between them with the swiftness of a gathering charge of lightning. Her eyes softened to blue velvet, lips parting in startled protest at the potency of the challenge in that masculine gaze.

Mark's smile was gentle as he closed the space between them, his lips like silk as they touched her trembling mouth.

The lightning struck then, leashed tension flashing through Toni's responsive being in a flame of awareness that left her weakened, yet hungry for more of the exquisite promise latent in those demanding lips. She moaned a soft protest against the stirring glory of his kiss. Wrenching herself free, which tumbled the soft warmth of the car blanket to the floor, she sought to shatter the intimacy of the moment she was sharing with this disturbing stranger. She went rigid in outrage for an instant, anger a bitter taste in her mouth. Then common sense came to her rescue and she was back in control.

Why on earth was she overreacting to this arrogant man? And besides, it wasn't as if she'd never been kissed before! Reacting crossly to the muscular arm pinning her to the seat, she managed to do a decent job of ignoring the niggling thought that she had never been kissed with similar intensity before.

"Couldn't resist that. . . ."

The deep drawl was entirely unrepentant as the big American acceded to Toni's fidgeting and removed the arm encircling her waist. He stretched himself, the confines of the car doing little to mask the easy grace of his lithe body. No apology was offered as he touched the control, righting his seat back. After shrugging his sheepskin down into a comfortable position he turned to look at her, rubbing his large hand across the rasp of his unshaven face, eyes slumberous. He reached a long arm across her alerted body; then his fingers were seeking her seat control. Hazel eyes teased her, warm with laughter. Toni felt an answering warmth in spite of herself. She tensed as he fumbled with the elusive control, and schooled herself to stillness as his arm rested briefly on her leg. It was a bit more difficult to hide her response to that light touch from herself, however. A surge of feeling she could not define made her catch her breath, which caused those searching eyes to narrow intently as the man watched her expression.

"Where would you like to go, Miss Antonia Carla Cameron?"

Carla! His mention of her middle name was the last straw! How could this impossible man have found it out? More to the point, why had he even bothered? He could have heard Clive mention it, she supposed angrily, but it wasn't likely.

"I think we'd best be on our way. We are about to be officially noticed." Those quiet words were bland, as was the dark face turned to her. Toni took note of the car's position on Princes Street. The castle was an aggressive bulk looming nearby. Mark must have parked alongside the pavement sometime during the night with a blatant disregard for posted regulations. But the purposeful approach of a traffic warden gave promise of quick attention to those rules.

Willing her aroused temper down, Toni gave clear instructions as the powerful car roared into life under expert hands and pulled away from the curb. The warden glanced in at the pretty passenger, then sketched an impudent thumbs up at the fortunate male who drove away. Mark chuckled good-humoredly, the deep sound pleasant.

Toni considered him bleakly as her sense of outrage grew. "If you will just let me off at the bus depot, I can catch one that passes my home. It's just along here. They will be starting the early-morning schedule soon." She felt a measure of relief that she was about to put some distance between herself and the man behind the wheel.

"Why not let me drive you home? It's just going on seven, so I won't be able to attend to business for hours. It would please me to deliver you to your door, and I'm sure it will save time for you." His bland politeness put the reasonableness of his request on an innocuous level Toni could not fault.

"Well. . . all right. If you're sure you don't mind."

"I assure you I'm pleased to do it." He turned that tawny head of his, and white teeth gleamed against the deep tan of his skin as he smiled gently at her. "Are you hungry, Antonia?"

"I am, but why don't you come home with me to breakfast? It seems the least I can do to repay your kindness." Toni had an odd reluctance to issue the invitation, but felt she must.

"I would enjoy that. Thank you." He was silent a moment. "Will you see Jock while you are home?"

Startled, Toni glanced at the dark impassive profile.

"Jock?" she exclaimed, completely bewildered.

"I believe you said you could not possibly leave Scotland without seeing him."

"That's true." Toni recalled her brush with him in Clive's office. Odd that he remembered. "Jock is my grandfather—Jock Cameron. My mother keeps house for him. He would not understand if I went without talking my plans over with him first."

Mark smiled down at her, a glint in his eyes she could not define. "He will try to influence your decision?"

"Not at all."

Toni settled back comfortably, intent on the familiar rolling countryside as the car left the city behind and moved rapidly toward her own valley and the delightful stone cottage that she had known as home all her life, no matter where she found herself. His face still and thoughtful, the man beside her concentrated on his driving. If he was waiting for her to explain further about her grandfather or her need to discuss decisions with the old man, he waited in vain. For Toni had lost herself in the glow of anticipation she always experienced as she returned to Dawn Cottage.

Warm, gray, welcoming, the cottage was lovely in the early light. Nestled in a hollow, it presented a view of slate-shingled roof and homey gables to the travelers as they stepped from the car. Toni stood for a long moment, breathing in the crisp air, resting her eyes with gladness on the wooded hills rising as a backdrop behind the picturesque dwelling. Smoke curled from the square chimneys, speaking an invitation to warm oneself beside a wide hearth. A graveled walk beckoned one down to the paved courtyard, which seemed to be waiting for summer sun and lounge chairs. The great trees spreading bare branches above the roof seemed, even in their bareness, to offer strength and protection to all who entered this peaceful domain. Roses empty of branch and bud were waiting in neat beds for their time of flower.

"It never changes." Her glance shared with the stranger at her side some of the feeling she treasured for the only real home she had ever known.

His smile was gentle. "You love it, don't you? I can see why."

Her smile came then, dimpling her cheek, lighting her eyes with an infectious gaiety. She left him and skipped down the steps to the patio with the sure-footed abandon of a child. Mark's long strides brought him to her side as she reached for the old brass knocker and banged it impatiently. Somehow, and most strangely so, it now seemed fitting that he was with her....

CHAPTER TWO

"ANTONIA!" Velvety eyes as blue as the girl's misted as Joan Cameron folded her offspring into loving arms. "I wasn't expecting to see you for weeks."

"I know, mom. Clive is finishing up for me. I'm going to Texas."

"Texas! Whatever for?" Even as she asked the question, Joan turned her attention to the smiling man looming behind her daughter. Her eyes widened, and she touched the neat chignon confining her dark hair with a feminine instinct.

"This is Mark Anders, mother. My new boss. He has business in Edinburgh today and offered to drive me down."

"Thank you, Mr. Anders. I see little enough of this child of mine. Won't you come in, please?"

"Mark, if you don't mind, Mrs. Cameron." His smile was charm itself, Toni thought rudely, guaranteed to captivate and reassure any female under ninety with whom he came in contact.

"And I am Joan." She offered him flour-dusted fingers. "Please excuse my appearance. I'm just getting breakfast." Mark's answering smile soothed Joan's doubts about her appearance.

"I've asked...Mark to join us for breakfast." Toni was surprised at the tartness of her words and her reluctance to use his first name, but it would be foolish not to, since they were going to be working together, as he had said.

Joan shot a keen look at her daughter, then glanced back at her companion as she closed the door. Mark winked at her as he shrugged out of his sheepskin, and Joan smiled, the corner of her mouth dimpling.

Trust him to know how to get around her mother! Toni hung her own jacket on the rack and went toward the kitchen, looking for her grandfather.

Her own dimple sprang into being as she wrapped warm arms around the old man who was confined to a wheelchair. Finally she struggled out of his bear hug and sat back on her heels. "How are you, Jock Cameron?"

"No complaints, lass, now you've brought sunshine to this gray winter's day. And who might yon laddie be?"

Toni introduced the two men.

"I'm just a stray she brought in from the cold." Mark's smile was easy. Cameron looked him over carefully as they shook hands.

"Toni, show Mark where he can wash up, then you set a couple of places at the table, please. I'll just finish these biscuits." Joan went back to her preparations for the meal.

"My shaving kit's in the car." Mark ran his hand over his stubbly chin. "Would you mind. . . ?"

"Certainly not," Joan replied, smiling again. "You'll be needing a shave if you are to see to business. Just make yourself right at home, Mark."

"Thank you, Joan." He ducked under the low lintel and followed Toni down the wide passageway. "I'll just get my stuff."

Toni waited for him as he dashed out into the brisk

morning air without bothering about his jacket. She watched him come back down the long steps, his broad-shouldered figure moving with an easy grace.

A charming man, she admitted grudgingly. Without asking, she knew her mother liked him. And she had seen approval in Jock Cameron's shrewd appraisal of him, as well. She was rather the odd person out in the Mark Anders's Admiration Society, but she just couldn't help the natural antipathy his type of personality aroused in her.

Oh, well. She shrugged to herself as he came back to the door. Mark looked at her, his eyes glinting with amusement and something else as his hazel glance met her blue one. He didn't say a word as he followed her.

"Just through here." Toni snatched a fluffy towel from the linen cupboard, added a facecloth and thrust them at him rather unceremoniously. "You'll find soap and everything you need in the bathroom."

"Thank you, Miss Cameron." His eyes gleamed under those absurd curling lashes of his, and Toni had the distinct impression he was teasing her—or worse, laughing at her with a secret amusement of his own. Chin in the air, she threw him a glance meant to chill. Water gushed as he prepared to shave, but Toni was sure it was the sound of a quiet chuckle that followed her down the passage.

"Tell me of yon well, lass."

Answering Jock's eager knowledgeable questions gave her definite relief from the tension that bothered her every time she was in Anders's disturbing presence.

They were deep in a technical discussion when Mark dodged back through the low doorway. His nostrils twitched in appreciation as he savored the delicious aroma of Joan's efforts.

Toni ignored him and carried on with her explanation of the new onboard computer that had been used in siting the well. Her grandfather, old wildcatter that he was, had a sharp interest in the techniques. He shot two or three questions at Mark, found out the big American knew what he was talking about and included him in the discussion. Before breakfast was finished, Jock and Mark were talking as if they had known each other all their lives.

Toni was helping her mother with the washing up when the two men fell silent. She glanced up from the cup she was drying. Her grandfather had his wheelchair pushed back from the table. Mark, long legs outstretched, was staring at the scruffy tips of the boots he had crossed at the ankles. Wide shoulders braced against the back of the chair, his face looked unutterably tired. Jock was considering the younger man's brown and weary features.

"Laddie, how long has it been since you had a good sleep?"

Anders glanced up, startled by the concern in Cameron's gruff tone. "I left California a week ago, sir—just after we heard Antonia had been successful and brought her well in. We'd been watching the efforts in the North Sea because United Petroleum thought the same techniques could be used to open their new project in the Gulf of Mexico. They sent out a team to check it out. I'm part of the team. Been too busy to get much sleep, though. I reckon it can wait until we get to Texas."

Had he worked all that much once he came aboard her rig? Toni couldn't remember. She had a vague awareness of his constant presence during the times she had been on duty, but she had paid little attention to him until he had tackled her with such bruising efficiency. She felt her color rise, and turned hastily to the business of stacking away the clean dishes. Her mother watched her with a smiling kind of curiosity.

"What time did you get ashore last night?" Jock asked. Mark told him and her grandfather nodded. "Drove all night to get to Edinburgh, noo doubt?"

Mark laughed and glanced at Toni. "I was grabbing forty winks when the traffic warden came along and Antonia woke up." His deep voice trailed off, and he watched with interest as a rosy hue crept into Toni's traitorous cheeks.

"I have to go pack a bag, mom," she mumbled, and left the room in undignified retreat.

She ran up the stairs to the storage room under the gables and retrieved her suitcase. Usually she didn't bother with one, as she was content to stuff her belongings into the soft-sided oblong roll she called the Sausage. But going to the States seemed to call for a little more.

Not much more, she decided after she returned to her bedroom, which was on the ground floor, as were all the bedrooms in Dawn Cottage. Toni loved the room she had occupied all her life—when she was home.

She closed the door on the muffled conversation and laughter drifting to her through the central passageway. Her family certainly seemed to be enjoying Mark Anders. Well, let them get on with it. She wasn't about to be taken in by all that...that smarmy amiability of his. A bit shocked at her unusual feeling of aggression, she plunked the case on her bed and proceeded to sort through her wardrobe with real zest. She was about finished when Joan tapped on the door and came in.

"Are you all right, dear?"

"Just finishing, mom." Toni fastened the case and struggled a moment with the leather straps encircling it. "There!" She placed it on the blanket chest at the foot of her bed. It didn't weigh much.

"Are you sure you have all your things?" Joan crossed the room and sat on the bed. She had long since given up supervising her independent daughter's needs.

"I'm going to be based in Galveston. According to Clive, I should find it quite warm even at this time of the year." Toni recognized her mother's concern and appreciated Joan's effort to let her run her own life. "Don't worry about me, mom."

"Well. . . yes. I try not to interfere. . . ."

Toni dropped down beside her and hugged her. "I understand how hard it must be to have me for an only girl. But I wanted dad to be proud of me. . . and you and granddad, as well!"

"Oh, Antonia! I couldn't ask for a better daughter. And your grandfather was ecstatic when your wildcat came in! I expect you know that." She smiled a misty smile at the face so like her own. "Your dad would be strutting like the cock o' the walk if he were alive! And Rob is as proud as anything, too. We had a letter from him yesterday. You and the well are all he wrote about. Pages and pages. You'll have to read it."

"I wish I could see him, but I won't have time. We take the overnight train today because we are due to fly from Heathrow tomorrow, I understand."

For some curious reason, the pause that followed

was full of some odd expectation. "I like your Mark Anders." Joan finally filled the brief silence abruptly.

"He's not my Mark Anders!" Toni left her mother's side and stalked to the window. "I hardly know the man." Her protest was very cold indeed.

"I've gathered that." Joan's dry comment sailed over Toni's head. Her daughter stared blindly out at the familiar scene.

"Sorry, mom. I didn't mean to snap at you, but the man is so insufferable. I just can't seem to tolerate him!"

"Has he made improper advances to you?" Joan sounded surprised. "He doesn't seem the type."

Toni's face flamed. Mark's gentle teasing kiss had affected her more strongly than anything in her recent history. But in no way could it ever be classed as an "improper advance," and she knew it.

"Don't be ridiculous, mother. Improper advances went out when women's lib came in. And anyway, he wouldn't dare!"

A keen look at her child's flushed and grim face assured Joan few men would indeed dare in that particular direction. "Has he been rude, then?" she persisted. "He seems to be such a gentleman. . . ."

Toni laughed ruefully. "I've been shockingly rude to him, but no, he hasn't even tried to get his own back yet. Though I expect he will. I haven't been overly impressed with his meekness."

Joan chuckled her agreement. "Shame on you, Antonia. Say, will you run down to the village for me? I've asked him to stay for dinner and I need some things." She pulled a short list from the pocket of her sweater. "You can take the car."

Toni masked her annoyance at the thought of having to watch Mark charm her family around his finger again today. She took the list. "I'll walk. I need the exercise. Besides, it will give me a chance to do some visiting."

As a rule she tried to keep in casual touch with the few people she knew. Postcards, notes scribbled about her latest adventure and brief and informal visits when she was in the area all served the purpose. Frankly, she had not thought to go to the village this trip home, but she went gladly, although she knew she was trying to avoid any closer contact with the disturbing male who had so blithely installed himself in her home. *Coward,* her innate honesty shouted.

With an impatient shake of her gleaming black head, she ignored the charge and visited village shops with a determined effort. She chatted and laughed with the folks she had known most of her life. It was a good three hours later when she went down the long steps to the cottage door and let herself in.

The house was very quiet. The door to her grandfather's study was closed. She supposed Mark Anders was in there, talking to the older man. The sleek black Jaguar was still parked at the top of the steps, where he had left it on their arrival.

Joan was not in the kitchen. A fire glowed in the big fireplace and the kettle sang merrily on the hook above it. Toni smiled as she deposited her load on the scrubbed table.

Her mother was a hopeless romantic. She loved to hear the sound of the kettle as she read or worked around the kitchen. Rob always teased her about catching a cricket and caging it so she could have one of those to listen to, as well. Not that her brother was any better, Toni thought. At twenty-one he was just as inclined toward magical solutions to life's more resistant problems as their mother was. Toni knew herself to be the practical, hardheaded member of the Cameron family.

And it's a good thing I am, she told herself. She opened the kitchen door and looked out onto the enclosed entryway. Joan's bicycle was missing. Her mother had probably gone down to MacCall's. The neighboring farmer supplied them with milk, butter and eggs.

Toni removed her coat and took it back down the passageway, her feet quiet on the thick runner stretching the length of the hall. Reluctant to interrupt Jock and Anders, she went to her room with the thought of checking on the clothing she had decided to take with her. She was all the way into the familiar room before she saw the male clothing neatly folded on the chest at the foot of her bed. Boots stood at the near edge of it.

Mark, lying on the side that was turned toward her, was sleeping peacefully on her pillow, the long line of his body molded by the drift of bedclothing tucked under his chin and around his powerful shoulders. Toni, motionless yet poised for flight, stared down at him, startled, her heartbeat hammering.

What on earth was he doing in her bed? And why was he sleeping instead of attending to his supposed business in Edinburgh? She found her answer in a large brown envelope that stuck out from under the pile of clothes. Whatever the nature of the correspondence it hadn't taken him very long to fetch it, she mused, for he was certainly in a deep sleep and had probably been there for some time.

But he stirred then and turned, his bronzed handsomeness an alarming contrast to the snowy whiteness of the pillow under his leonine head. Toni gave in to cowardice and ran.

Never had she felt less competent to deal with rioting sensations that were swamping her usual common sense. And never had she felt less inclined to examine the roots of those ridiculous and very upsetting sensations.

TONI AWOKE THE NEXT MORNING safe in the self-contained, first-class railway compartment in which she had slept from Edinburgh. The train was still. The hypnotic pulse of the turning wheels had long since ceased. Fleeing south through the deep night, the famous Flying Scotsman had arrived in the very early morning at King's Cross, and now stood quietly in the vast and echoing station, while passengers who wished to slept undisturbed.

Toni yawned, stretched with the supple grace of a cat and reached for her wristwatch. Half-past seven. She swung shapely legs to the floor and set about her morning ritual in the tiny compartment, then re-packed her case. Her breakfast tray arrived at exactly eight o'clock, and she accepted it from the attendant who knocked discreetly.

She had just finished when knuckles again rapped against the compartment door. Knowing it must be Mark, she felt an unwelcome breathlessness touch her, and her brows knit crossly. She shrugged off the momentary sensation and opened the door to a completely transformed individual. Gone was the jeans-clad, rough-haired working man. In his place stood a perfectly tailored, urbane man of business. The expensive material of his dark suit fitted his broad shoulders without wrinkle or strain and emphasized his narrow waist. The lighter shade of his silky shirt was enhanced by the beautiful well-toned tie. Gold winked from the cuff link exposed on his arm, over which a black Burberry coat was carelessly thrown. That, too, would fit him to perfection, Toni knew.

Even his shock of tawny hair had been tamed and lay in neat waves against his well-shaped head, just touching the collar of his immaculate shirt. Wide sideburns neatly defined the lean face. Mark's left eyebrow climbed into that characteristic canted hook as he looked down and gauged her astonishment. He grinned, his teeth flashing against the brown of his face.

"Good morning. I've surprised you, Antonia?"

"Yes...well...." She leveled a mischievous twinkle at his imperturbable hazel eyes. "I wasn't aware Cinderella had a male counterpart."

Mark laughed. "Come. Our chariot awaits without."

He reached past her, swung up her case, then stood aside, allowing her to pass. Toni preceded him down the narrow aisle toward the door, wondering how he had managed the change. The suit in which he was so elegantly attired was not the sort one carried in the small case accompanying him from the drilling rig to Edinburgh.

The probable answer awaited on the long platform stretching the length of the train. Obviously there to meet them, a man came down the platform, impeccable in a chauffeur's uniform with a peaked cap under his arm. He grinned a salute, then took Toni's bag.

"Hope I picked up the right stuff, Mark." It was

obvious his reference was to the perfectly matched clothing Mark was wearing so well.

"Absolutely top of the class, John. I've dazzled Miss Cameron with my sudden transformation from roughneck to dandy." He introduced the man cheerfully as John Gann. John was cockney in accent and manner, but perfectly at home with the bantering American. "John is a permanent member of United Petroleum's London staff," Mark explained as Toni hurried to match the long strides taking him along the platform to the barrier. John followed with the luggage.

"I didn't know United Petroleum had a permanent staff here."

"It has." He handed the guard the tickets he held, then led the way through the bustle of early-morning commuters toward the parking lot. "Offices, staff, executive suite for visiting potentates at the Park Lane Hotel—the lot. I have my own pied-à-terre in Belgrave Square." He stopped abruptly and stared out the window. "It's very wet out there!"

Toni, following his swift footsteps doggedly, was determined to keep up with him. But his sudden change of pace caught her off guard, and she careered into him at speed, her handbag flying through space. It emptied itself neatly as it landed with a thud against the near wall.

Mark caught her to keep her from falling. One arm was a band of steel around her slim waist, while the other hand pressed her flushed cheek into the smooth wool of his suit jacket.

Unbidden, the memory of his arms around her in the middle of the North Sea returned. Angrily she thrust the thought away, in no way ready for the idea that she might learn to enjoy the feel of powerful arms around her. For a moment she was intensely aware of the muffled thud of his heart. Feeling smothered, she wrenched free of the firm hand supporting her with such calm determination. Glaring up at him, booted feet spread in fighting stance, she looked ready to battle.

Mark grinned, amusement in his unrepentant hazel eyes. "I am sorry, Antonia."

"Sorry!" There was no question she was tossing aside his apology as worthless. "You charge through this crowd as if you were running a race, then stop in front of me with no warning. Then you hold me as if—" Toni choked up, acutely aware that she had been about to say "as if you had the right."

What was wrong with her? After all, he had saved her from grievous bodily harm, taken her to Dawn Cottage with admirable dispatch and been most gentlemanly at all times. What was it about him that triggered such definite negative emotion?

"As if?" The man's cool teasing drawl dared her to finish her uncompleted sentence. She glared at him.

Irrationally angry, she began accepting her bits and pieces from assorted people who had retrieved them from the wide area over which they had scattered. Murmuring her thanks, she jumbled things back into her handbag. As a result, all the hurriedly assembled belongings would not fit. Toni struggled, glanced up at Mark's interested face and lost her temper completely. He was responsible for the mess. It was too much that he was amused by it!

She was sputtering as she reached for the expensive leather folio in which she carried Kurt's last photograph. He had given it to her just before he kissed her goodbye to go on the assignment that had cost him his life. A professional studio portrait, the miniature was a fantastic likeness of the man who had asked her to marry him.

He had written "Love me forever, as I love you," across it, signing "Kurt" with the flourish so characteristic of him.

Her fumbling fingers knocked the folio from the hand of the stranger who held it out to her. It flew open and fell at Mark's feet; he quickly bent to retrieve it.

He glanced at Kurt's laughing handsome face. As she recalled the incident later, Toni was sure Mark's alert hazel eyes must have read the message written there in Kurt's bold hand.

His strong fingers closed on the soft leather of the folio. As he flipped it shut his eyes sought hers, held them.

Time stood still for Toni. The station and the background noise blurred. She became aware only of the man who knelt at her feet. She saw the skin tighten over his lean cheekbones. The crease that ran down the length of his face deepened and hardened. His lips thinned in a ruthless line. Somehow she found herself unable to drag her eyes away from his. Breath held, she had the sensation of drowning in icy hazel depths. Crouched, perfectly balanced on his heels, shoulders seeming even wider in his foreshortened pose, he epitomized an aggressive male hunter. For a timeless instant every nerve in Toni's lissome frame became attuned to the challenge of the man, the nature of the challenge unknown but disturbing. Her whole being tensed in antagonistic anticipation.

Then he was on his feet, breaking the electric awareness, seemingly oblivious to Toni's small gasp as she accepted the soft leather keepsake from him.

"That everything?" The question was brusque, his deep voice harsh. "Let's go, then," he added at Toni's bemused nod.

Wordlessly she followed him through the damp parking lot to a luxurious Rolls. John had the cases in the trunk and was holding the wide door open for her. Mark rounded the car, depositing himself beside her as John closed her door.

"Miss Cameron's hotel first, I think, John, then on to the office. Jeffers is expecting me." Mark gave the order as the big car purred into action under John's hands.

Toni looked sharply at her companion. "I thought we were to go to Heathrow to catch an airplane for America."

"We were and we will." The lazy drawl sounded cold, almost bitter. "Something has come up that I must attend to before we leave. You will be staying in the corporate quarters for a couple of nights."

"Surely I don't need to delay my departure even if you are needed here. I am quite capable of getting on and off planes." Her protest was strong and tart. Toni knew without a shadow of doubt that she did not wish to stay in London in the company of the man beside her. Not for even a little while. And certainly not for a "couple of nights" in the corporate quarters! What was he playing at? Forthright, she asked.

"I assure you I am telling you a straight fact, Antonia. I have matters to attend to here." He paused, continued bluntly. "U.P.C. has made up its corporate mind that we are to travel together. So you and I are stuck with each other, no matter how we feel." A quick lopsided grin flashed, disconcerting her further.

The anger she had felt at King's Cross still latent, Toni protested in hot displeasure. "It is my understanding that I have been employed by your company as a working geophysicist. Am I not correct?" He nodded. The grin stayed, but his eyes narrowed. "I must point out, then, that my tasks must surely be concerned with the techniques of locating new sources of oil. Am I still correct?"

"Still in the ball park, as we would term it." His face became unreadable, but the hazel eyes still glinted as he masked them with those long lashes of his. Toni repressed the tingle engendered by his look. She scowled at him as she wondered if he was aware of the effect he had on people. That wicked, crooked little-boy grin of his! It was so potent, so disarming.

He must know, she decided. He had used that same charm on her mother and grandfather. They had succumbed without an attempt to resist or see through it, and almost instantly treated him as part of the family. How had he managed it? Her family was friendly, but usually not so prone to accept strangers with such open arms.

She smiled at him now, trying for an impression of cold grim logic. "If I'm correct in my assumptions, let me assure you London does not have the proper geologic substructure to warrant a geophysical search for oil beneath its streets. We won't find any here. So let's stop this silliness before it starts. If you must stay here, fine. Stay. I'll just get on to Texas and my job. I am quite capable." Unaccountably, Toni felt the swift rise of color his sardonic change of expression caused. She frowned and tried unsuccessfully to suppress the blush.

Mark's left eyebrow shot up now as he watched her. "Relax, Antonia." Harshness had vanished; the lazy drawl was amused, deeply musical. "U.P.C. is paying the freight and calling the tune. You are under contract to them so your working time belongs to them. I'm afraid the corporation will refuse to understand if you insist upon treating their request as silly."

Toni, who should have been enjoying the smooth passage of the powerful car down Great Russell Street into Bloomsbury, gave up the inclination to plunge into nostalgia and turned to her opponent, battle flags flying. Important as this area had been to her during her university days, reminiscing could wait. There was no way this obnoxious individual was going to tell her what she could and should do! She managed to marshal all the animosity she had felt during the past two days into one searing blast.

"The corporation can take its request and stuff it!"

Unused to swearing, or being rude for that matter, Toni felt the red flame of her flush and stared stonily ahead. She knew very well she had overreacted shamefully to Mark's infuriating announcement, but she felt totally unrepentant. The only sound in the big car came from the outside as John tackled the intricacies of crossing New Oxford Street for the relative safety of Shaftesbury Avenue. All the way up to the entrance of the luxurious hotel overlooking Green Park, Toni maintained her fixed interest in the scene through the windshield in front of her. Not once did she glance into the face of the man seated beside her.

Had she done so, she would have surprised a thought-ful, almost tender expression on his lean features.

Skillfully dodging traffic, John guided the big car across Piccadilly, then slipped into a parking place. On the curbside of the Rolls, Mark uncoiled his lean length and was at her side of the car before John could manage it. The chauffeur shrugged as he turned his attention to the bags in the trunk.

"Shall we go in, Antonia?"

"I seem to have Hobson's choice, haven't I?" she snapped crossly, while thrusting her booted feet into the busy street. Mark placed a protective hand under her right elbow, putting himself between her and the oncoming traffic. Toni, in no mood to accept a chivalrous gesture from him, wrenched away—and stumbled over the uneven curb.

Mark caught her before she fell. For the second time in less than an hour she found herself captive in strong arms. He watched her solemnly, a devilish glint in his quiet gaze.

"This could get to be a rather pleasant habit" was his infuriating comment.

"Let me go."

"Mind your manners, Antonia. Say 'please.'" His face unreadable, his eyes intent, Mark stared down into the furious small face that was mostly blazing blue eyes. Toni struggled to free her arms, wanting to slap him in the worst way. She was suddenly, intensely aware of the hard muscled length of the man and of the ease with which he held her.

"Please let me go!" she gasped, unwilling to prolong the strange erratic sensations racing along her nerves as she was forced to acknowledge the masculine strength latent in him. Grinning, he released her.

"You are no gentleman," she lashed out at him as she fled toward the door through which John had already disappeared with her case.

"Am I not?" With a long-legged stride, Mark was at the door to open it for her before she could reach it on her own. "Well, I can rectify that. This way, please." Again firm fingers fastened around her elbow. Unwilling to struggle with him in the elegant lobby of this obviously expensive hotel, Toni let him lead her down a short passage to the elevator.

Standing near the open gates, John handed her case to a bellhop, then turned to his employer. "I'll need to tend to the car, Mark."

Mark nodded at the older man. "Go ahead. I'll be down as soon as I get Miss Cameron settled in."

Toni refrained from comment. She stepped into the elevator and seethed. So Mr. High and Mighty Anders would see her settled in, would he?

He glanced at her smoldering expression, that objectionable glint sparkling then quickly masked as he turned to the man carrying her case and began talking about soccer with him. The easy conversation continued as they left the elevator and crossed a beautifully decorated hallway to the door of the suite the corporation apparently kept in readiness for visiting VIPS.

Listening to the male chitchat Toni admitted to herself how good Mark was with people. The ease with which he had recalled some of the glory days of early oil exploration with her grandfather, had spoken to her mother of the Scottish poets—a passion of Joan's—and was now discussing the intricacies of soccer with a man obviously a rabid follower of that rowdy sport, put her quite off her stride. Give the devil his due, she told herself, Mark was a master at drawing others out, at assessing strengths of personality and personal interests, and using those interests to put strangers at their ease.

What did he see as her strong points, she wondered idly as she passed through the politely held door and into the truly beautiful lounge of the corporation suite. It would be interesting to find out, she thought a little grimly, her anger forgotten as she considered the intriguing possibility of monitoring his efforts to charm her as she had seen him charm others.

Forewarned is forearmed! A dimple flashed, which was instantly disciplined. Toni crossed the thick creamy carpet to gaze across the acres of Green Park, lovely even now with the bare branches of the trees weaving intricate patterns against the gray morning sky. Her natural good humor restored, she listened to Mark dealing efficiently with the hotel employee, then she became alertly conscious of the sudden quiet as the massive door swung shut.

"Will you be able to put up with this for a couple of nights, Antonia?" The easy drawl sounded mocking, to say the least.

Toni, framed in the wide expanse of the sparkling glass picture window, looked part of the pleasant scene as she turned. She took her time, glancing deliberately around the beautifully appointed room. It was color coordinated in a soothing palette of golds, cream and warm browns, blending good antique pieces with the frankly modern comfort of sofas and couches. Flowers in a lovely arrangement brightened the surface of the chest standing elegantly against one wall. A fragrant bowl of white hyacinths occupied pride of place on one end of a low table running the length of the enormous sofa, the deeply rubbed, gleaming surface of the warm wood reflecting back a soft image of the flowers. High creamy walls supported the ceiling, its exquisite pattern standing out in rich gold.

Aware of shining eyes watching her, Toni sighed and glanced up into the quiet face. "You must be joking. U.P.C. does very well by its visiting dignitaries. This is lovely." Her dimple appeared, then quickly vanished. "What will happen when they discover a roughneck wildcatter has occupied this hallowed ground?"

"Just don't leave oil on the sheets and we are probably safe." His grin flashed, a slash of white teeth in the dark brown of his face. "The bedroom's through there, with the bath." He waved a long arm toward the partially opened door to the left. "Make yourself at home. Duty calls. But I'll be back in a couple of hours to take you to lunch." Moving toward the door he paused, hand on the knob, and glanced back at her. Then he was gone, the door closing behind him.

Refusing to dwell on the thought that he in some way represented a threat to her ordered and entirely satisfying way of life, Toni shrugged impatiently, then went to explore the luxurious quarters. Crossing the beautifully furnished bedroom, she stopped with a small sound of delight at the entrance to the bath.

Sunken, tiled and golden, the bath itself looked big enough to accommodate a small swimming party. Huge bath towels hung from heated rails. The accompanying shower was a dream come true after the cramped facilities aboard the oil rig.

Toni sighed with the sheer luxury of it all and shed her clothes on the spot. With reckless abandon she splashed a fragrant bath oil from a selection of delicate bottles standing on a recessed shelf of the vast tub. The sound of the water rushing from ornate faucets was pure bliss.

Stepping into water made silken by the oil she had splashed around with such disregard for expense, Toni wondered briefly whether the hotel itself provided such luxuries for favored guests? Perhaps it was part of U.P.C.'s treatment when softening up visiting dignitaries. The thought made her giggle. No matter. It was sheer ecstasy to relax in the tub, almost totally weightless and mindless, the warm scented water infinitely seductive.

It was some time later when Toni became aware of an insistent thumping of a fist on the door of her suite. Vaguely aware that it might have been going on for a while, Toni reluctantly left the bath. Wrapping a huge towel around her body sarong-style, she made for the door, running her fingers through her damp hair.

"What is it?" she asked sharply.

"John, Miss Cameron. I'm to see you get this."

Even through the thick door his voice was unmistakable. Toni clutched her towel and opened the door a crack. John was standing there, neat and efficient-looking, a fur draped over his arm. He smiled quietly.

"Sorry to get you from your bath, Miss Cameron." He thrust the soft bulk of the fur through the door into her hands. "Mark gave me instructions to deliver this to you. Thank you, miss." Then he was gone.

Toni stared at the exquisite mink coat. She pushed the door closed, controlling her towel as well as could be expected. A rising sense of outrage boiled up and managed to do great damage to her short-lived feeling of well-being. Just what did Mark Anders think he was up to, she wondered as she drew a deep breath to calm the storm within.

CHAPTER THREE

THE QUICK BURR OF THE TELEPHONE cut into the room's silence. Toni jumped, nerves unexpectedly quivering, then advanced somberly upon the noisy instrument, throwing the mink across the back of the nearest couch. There was little doubt in her mind as to the identity of the person calling.

"Hi." No mistaking that lazy drawl. "Thought I'd best let you know that John is about to deliver a coat to you."

"A coat?" she played up grimly. "Why should he be about to do such a silly thing?"

"Company business. I'll explain when I pick you up. Won't be able to get away for another half hour. Can you wait? Wouldn't want to starve U.P.C.'s newest employee."

"Company business, you say." Toni deliberately ignored his attempt to bypass the issue. "I am not an idiot, Mark Anders. What kind of company hands out gorgeous mink coats to new employees—or supplies them with these kind of quarters, come to that?" Winter ice was definitely much warmer than Toni's sharp voice.

"So John has been there." His tone was calmly dismissive. He did not wait for her answer. "I've explained that it is company business." The American drawl was suddenly most precise. "I will give you the details when I get there. Be ready. See you." And he abruptly broke the connection.

Toni, exasperated, stared at the instrument in her hand with blank hostility. Such bossy arrogance! What on earth was going on?

Dropping the offending phone onto its waiting cradle, she clutched her makeshift sarong firmly about her and headed for her clothes, determined to get to the bottom of Mark Anders's little game before the day was much older.

Her whole being seemed to react against the tacit inexplicable threat that he represented. A little wildly, she wondered what exactly it was she was resisting. Unable to come up with a pat answer, she decided she had best be ready when he arrived to take her to lunch. Ready in more ways than one, she assured herself. Just let him try some high-handed scheme!

Curling her bare toes into the rich carpet underfoot, she went into the bedroom, dropping the towel around her slender ankles as she reached into her case for her underthings.

It was then that she saw the expensively wrapped package resting on the dressing table. Small and neat, it had been placed on a square white card, her name clearly visible on the front. Toni picked up the card, her attention caught by the bold lettering. Knowing whose writing it was before she turned the card over, she stared at Mark Anders's distinctive signature.

She slid a nail under the edge of the thick paper in which the package was wrapped, even as she realized that the wise thing to do was to hand it back unopened.

"Curiosity will get you yet, my girl," she murmured with grim amusement.

The expensive paper concealed an exquisite box, in which rested an equally exquisite crystal bottle of amber-colored liquid. Unable to resist, Toni tried the perfume on her wrist. The fragrance was wonderful. She sat down on the dressing-table bench, turning the lovely bottle in her fingers. Glancing up and noting her bemused expression in the mirror, she smiled ruefully.

Mark Anders. How did one deal with such an unexpected man? He had been driving most of the night before last. All day yesterday he had been at Dawn Cottage, most of the time fast asleep in her bed. Then all last night they had both spent on a train thundering through the dark. Most certainly there had been no free time for him to go shopping this morning.

How had he managed to obtain such an expensive bottle of perfume and have it delivered? It couldn't have been anything but a last-minute purchase, since she was only in London on a hasty last-minute decision. Or at least, that was her understanding. But obtain it he had. More to the point, why was he bothering?

Thoughtfully Toni turned her back on the gleaming crystal bottle and slipped into dainty panties and bra. She unpacked her case, hanging up the few items she had with her. The more intimate essentials went into the top drawer of the enormous dresser, while her few cosmetics were neatly assembled on the dressing table beside the perfume.

Dumping out the contents of her handbag, she reinstated it to its usual order. Slowly she picked up the leather folio protecting Kurt's picture and opened it, her gaze pensive. Looking at the handsome face, she welcomed the feeling of warmth and love the sight of her sweetheart's photo stirred in her even after this length of time.

That love crept around her, enfolding her in a cloak that protected her from the frightening necessity of ever again having to live through such a traumatizing shock. Toni Cameron had no real perception of the depth of that shock to her personality, nor did she probe her readiness to accept male companionship only if it did not threaten to intrude upon the island of safety that she had withdrawn to at the loss of her beloved father and fiancé.

"Oh, Kurt, I miss you so...." Whispering the words on a sigh, Toni felt the prick of tears and the sudden tightening of her throat.

She snapped the folio closed impatiently. Loving Kurt Grady as she had, missing him still as she sometimes did, it had been ages since the thought of him brought tears to her eyes. Why today? The answer did not come. Picking up the scented bottle with a sense of defiance, she sprayed a fragrant veil around herself. Glorying in the exquisite consciousness of luxury, she dressed in the only outfit she had with her that was in any way feminine.

The warm brown tweed of the fitted skirt looked rather stunning teamed with its toning turtleneck cashmere, especially when she pulled on the dark brown leather boots she had worn on the way down from Scotland.

She tied a slim silk scarf done in the color of her skirt under the soft roll of the sweater, and slipped on a suede vest. Upon inspection, she decided she would do for the projected luncheon. It was a good thing one could wear almost anything in London now and still not be thought gauche.

Expecting to go directly from Scotland to Heathrow and then be on her way to Texas, Toni had packed only essentials—a few skirts and several outfits of jeans and sweaters. She did have some fairly nice blouses with her—and of course that outrageously expensive suede pantsuit—but really nothing she would feel comfortable in around town except her present outfit.

She had deliberately determined to travel light, planning to spend part of her fabulous salary to outfit herself completely once she was in the States. Having always bought her clothes off the rack, she was confident that the stores in America would prove quite adequate for her needs. She dressed well, but she had neither the time nor the temperament for affectation.

Feet on the ground, assured of her own worth in her job, she took any flattery with more than a grain of salt, answering it in the same vein of good-humored banter that it was given. She respected each man for the contribution he made to the team, and expected and received the same sort of respect for her own efforts.

It had never occurred to Toni that she might be more than ordinarily pleasing to the eye. Mirrors were something she combed her hair into proper order by or used when she wished to put on lipstick, which did not happen too often, either. She really had no conception of her sweet striking beauty.

Perhaps it was due to the fact that she had spent her formative years miles away from any children near her own age. Most of her life had been lived in the company of the adult male, with little feminine influence. As the Camerons moved from site to site, even Joan had been almost a background figure in contrast to the working oilmen seeking her father's companionship and advice. Toni had become used to hard living, treasuring the rare stopovers at Dawn Cottage. Most of the places her grandfather and father worked were extremely remote, lacking in many amenities.

Even her education had been different from that of most of her contemporaries. Her mother had been a school teacher, leaving the profession to follow her husband around the world. So she saw to Toni's early education, laying an adequate foundation for the rigorous demands of her grandfather and father as they taught the girl disciplines that were later to assure her a place at the University of London.

The summer before she was to start university, Kurt Grady had come into Toni's life—in the back of beyond of Turkey. Handsome, intelligent, Kurt had wooed her and finally won her as only an unaware, sensitive girl can be won by a man intent on the first awakening of her sensual nature. Grady had been an experienced man, using words, small gestures and undemanding contacts because he had found himself deeply in love with the daughter of his superior and willing to wait for her.

Toni had blossomed, but she never believed Kurt was first attracted to her because of her beauty, no matter how many times he repeated it. As far as she was concerned, it was just a part of the chat men thought women expected of them.

She used little makeup, just a toning lipstick and on occasion a touch of eye shadow. Her brows were black and finely arched. There was nothing she knew how to do to improve them. Her lashes were reasonably long and had a nice curve to them, she thought, whenever she noticed them at all. She kept her silky black hair short because it was convenient to wear it that way. She realized she was slender and that she fitted her jeans fairly well. She had no idea how good she looked even in the rough clothes she found most suitable for her job.

At twenty-seven, unable to forget Kurt, she did nothing to attract male attention. Her days were filled with casual male contact. She did go on the occasional date, and enjoyed parties, films, plays and dancing. She was a good violinist, playing often for her own enjoyment in the quiet of her own quarters.

She had learned to fend off any encroaching male involvement before an escort could get started, always well in control of the situation.

Toni was firmly in control once again, her sheepskin flung over the end of the nearest chair, when Mark knocked. She had not touched the mink since draping it over the couch before answering the telephone.

Opening the door, she gazed up with laudable calmness into the man's quiet face. Mark was well over six feet tall, forcing Toni to tilt her sleek black head back in order to meet his eyes squarely. He looked down on her impassively, that glint of devilment lurking in his eyes. She watched his nostrils flare, then narrow, knowing he was savoring the scent he had given her. She found herself wondering if he always gave the same scent to all the women he knew, and how many that might be, then dismissed the thought as she had no wish to tread on such dangerous ground.

He grinned, almost as if he had read the direction in which her mind had strayed. "Ready to eat, Antonia?"

"Yes, I am, thank you." Very deliberately she reached for her sheepskin. But Mark crossed the room swiftly, took up the sheepskin and substituted the mink with a smooth economy of movement.

"I think not." His amusement only increased her flare of temper. "This was sent to you to be worn while you are in London. Company policy demands the employees look a credit to them."

Toni drew herself up to her full height, her face a vivid expression of denial. He didn't give her time to say a word.

"Let me assure you that the coat is not yours, Antonia." There was no denying the mockery in that deep drawl. "I'm fairly well known in circles that really count, as far as the well-being of the corporation in this country is concerned. In order to maintain a certain importance, a kind of, er, front, if you will, must be, er, catered to." He dropped the luxurious coat around her slim shoulders. "Unfortunately, due to a sudden need for my presence in London, you have been delayed in your own departure. The corporation realizes you were expecting to go straight to your job in the States. You can't be expected to have with you the sort of clothes needed if you are to represent said company. So they are supplying them—no cost or obligations. That means...no strings attached," his deep voice mocked. He stepped back and regarded her slender form wrapped in the expensive fur, his eyes gleaming with an inner satisfaction.

"They do expect you to represent them. Tonight. There is to be an exclusive reception for some extremely influential oil sheiks. That is why you must wear the coat. And that is why, once I've fed you, I'm taking you shopping."

"Shopping!" The word was a strangled protest.

"You are stark raving mad if you think your company will want to buy clothes for me!"

"Nope. Strict orders. Let's go eat." He scooped up her handbag from beside her discarded sheepskin, then escorted her firmly out, closing the door behind them.

Incredibly, Toni found herself moving at the impossible man's side, getting into the waiting elevator and crossing the sumptuous lobby once they reached the ground floor. Mark paused on the steps outside. He turned her gently toward him and met her snapping blue eyes with imperturbable good humor.

"Shall we walk? It's just over the road in Knightsbridge. We could go through the park."

His amusement lurked, masking a deeper reaction Toni could not define. "Yes, please. A walk would do me good."

How did he do it?

The silent question in her mind, Toni studied the lean brown face opposite her and tried to answer the question for the umpteenth time. They were seated in a pleasant small restaurant just off Sloane Street, the remains of the excellent luncheon between them on the polished chopping block used as a table. Meeting her eyes, he smiled that crooked smile she found could so disturb her senses. Toni dropped her lashes and studied the remains of the coffee in the mug she held. Come to that, many things about the man across from her disturbed her. In the past two hours she had chattered away to him with all the reserve of a schoolgirl. It had been easy to respond to his lazy questions about her life, her family, her work. Her reticence had vanished without a struggle. How had he managed to break down her reserve? Somehow he had made it seem natural to confide in him.

Realizing this, Toni looked up, and searching his face for signs of guile, found none. Surely no woman could object to the intent willingness to please that her escort managed to project. And no female in her right mind could object to his attentiveness. She was suddenly aware of the fact that he had not mentioned the reception she was expected to attend. With her usual directness, she asked about it. "Shall we get back to U.P.C.'s expectations, please? I've already told you I understood I was hired as a working—"

Mark interrupted, anticipating her pointed remark. "As a working geophysicist. I know, and you are, of course. That's why they want you to do this job for them." He pushed the crockery to one side and leaned forward. "The reception this evening is extremely important to U.P.C. The Arabians are here because U.P.C. has made a discovery that could be important. It could be especially important in the Mideast. If U.P.C. can convince them and get a jump on contracts, it could mean millions. It is my contention, the corporation's as well, that there is a tremendous gap between the amount of known reserves of oil in the world and the potential. Perhaps, by relating a detailed geological history of any given region to what we know of the occurrence of oil, we can discover vast unknown fields."

"What techniques do you think will be most effective?" Toni was curious, since the discovery of new areas for producing wells still required the kind of rarefied combination of skill, luck and Russian roulette that even the most successful operations were forced to rely upon.

"We have to analyze the detailed history of the region, relate it to the actual physical nature of the rocks, study the tectonic history of the basic architecture and the basement structure of those rocks, and tie it all together with a computerized profile. This profile should allow us to project the conditions known to be necessary for oil entrapment." In a few swift words he sketched the geological events responsible for the north-south layering of rock that had set up the great oil fields of Arabia. Toni listened, enjoying his concise summary and professional grasp of the area he discussed. "Understand what I am talking about, Antonia?"

"Yes, I do." She was excited by the prospect he had so ably outlined. "You mean that most of the producing areas are confined to a comparatively small spot on the peninsula. If conditions forming that spot can be traced through stratigraphy and tectonic pattern, there is a good chance conditions producing those fields are much more extensive than we now believe."

"Full marks, Dr. Cameron." Toni could not suppress the inward glow sparked by his approving regard. She smiled at him. "U.P.C. thought it a good idea to have you put in the picture so you could explain it tonight."

"Why me particularly? I can see what U.P.C. has in mind, but...."

Mark met her level gaze frankly. "The corporation thinks you have the best chance of attracting the Arabians' attention. Your combination of brains, beauty and expertise can't be beat." His slow smile teased as it took in the fresh color that wavered in her cheeks at the offhand compliment. "The sheiks are a sophisticated bunch, hard shelled as they come. We are count-

ing on your ability to get their interest and curiosity
aroused. I'll be there to convince them that U.P.C. is
the outfit to handle the exploration, once they come to
see the possibilities.''

Toni grimaced. "I'm to be used as some sort of...
shill?'' She stumbled over the word as she shot him a
look of disgust.

"Not at all!'' He sounded horrified. "It's just a
matter of showing them the potential, then convincing
them U.P.C. is qualified to do the job. It is important
to the well-being of the corporation. Will you give it a
shot?''

Toni searched his expression thoughtfully. His sincerity seemed obvious. She sighed and gave up. "Well,
as you say, my working hours belong to the corporation.''

"Thanks, Antonia.''

His eyes warmly approving, he stood and held the
fur for her. Toni felt her heart skip a beat as he
wrapped it around her. She thrust her hands into the
silken pockets, and noting the little blond cashier's instant response to his easy charm, watched him pay the
bill.

He certainly knew how to lay it on without any apparent strain, she thought crossly. Women probably
fell for him like tenpins. Even she had fallen victim,
she remembered ruefully. When had she ever talked
about herself as she had during the lunch hour just
past?

Mark came toward her, then he paused a moment,
his keen eyes searching her face as he dropped coins
into a pocket of his superbly fitted trousers, and
smoothed bills into the supple leather wallet he held so
carelessly in strong brown fingers. His expression

changed as he watched her. The teasing light she was so often aware of turned into an unexpected wariness as his lean face tightened.

For an instant Toni was sure she glimpsed implacable resolve. He had the look of a marauding male who knew just exactly where he was going and how he planned to reach his goal. His masculinity seemed to challenge her in a way she had never before experienced, sending a chill of real apprehension coursing through her. She vibrated unexpectedly with a sudden awareness of herself, felt her color rise and dropped her lashes quickly. She was unable to sustain the intent glance that seemed to plumb the depths of her being.

"Let's go shopping, Antonia."

The satisfaction in the deep voice caused her to glance at him sharply, but his brown face was still, unreadable.

CHAPTER FOUR

NERVOUSLY TONI WATCHED MARK flag a taxi. Once in it, she tucked herself into the far corner, sure in her own mind that she must have as little as possible to do with the man beside her. Her heart still thudded in a silly rhythm quite unlike its usual pattern.

In some obscure way, she knew instinctively that her surge of awareness had been a brief moment of recognition of a knowledge as old as mankind. It had been a clear call of mate to mate.

That awareness frightened her. Accustomed as she was to dealing with strong and determined men, Mark's ability to stir unknown forces in her was something she neither understood nor welcomed. Never before had she been so conscious of one man's powerful masculinity.

She knew with an aching sense of betrayal that she had never felt as drawn to Kurt as she now felt to Mark Anders. Despising herself for her reaction to him, she sought refuge in the knowledge that she also harbored a passionate dislike for the man. This realization gave her a clear sense of relief. She took herself firmly in hand, managing a cool control as he handed her out of the taxi onto the pavement in front of the elegant portals of one of London's most exclusive couturier's.

Aware that he was watching her, she glanced at him

as the doorman held the exquisitely engraved plate-glass door open for them to enter.

She caught a faint gleam of satisfaction in those hazel eyes. It was the same expression she had seen in the restaurant, no doubt put there by his assessment of some reaction he had seen in her. Anger welled up. He had no right to arouse unwanted feeling in her! More to the point, his astuteness seemed a gross invasion of her privacy. And he most certainly had no right to look so insufferably complacent!

Once seated in a luxurious private room, Toni was a silent observer to the power of the man's charm and ability with people.

In the brief glimpses she'd had of the world of haute couture, all forward movement was as tightly orchestrated as the choreography of a first-class ballet. Nothing hurried or unplanned intruded upon that specialized atmosphere. But Mark ordered and moved the immovable with precision and speed. Lean face intent, he viewed the gorgeous array of gowns paraded before them, rapidly selecting three with an unerring eye for style and color. Toni was quickly enthralled. She found herself in a private fitting room, slender feet wrapped in beautifully made stiletto-heeled shoes that were little more than gleaming ribbons of leather. Lovely dresses were slipped over her head. Tutting, the fitters would twitch and pin, finally releasing her to view her image. Toni was captivated by the difference between a model dress and one off the rack. The shaping, the material and the luxury of individual creativity were a heady experience.

Mark assessed her appearance in each of the gowns he'd chosen. Toni stood in the last one, a shaft of silken loveliness. It moved as she moved, clinging and releasing itself in lovely harmony with her slender form. It was exquisite, personal in a way Toni had never known a garment could be. For the life of her she could not be indifferent to the gown and the way she looked in it.

Her dark head held at a proud and defiant angle, she stepped back into the private room where Mark Anders was waiting. Unaccustomed as she was to desiring to create an impact on the men she knew, Toni still wished Mark to be suitably impressed now. In some indefinable way she realized she would be hurt if he did not react pleasurably to her changed appearance. She wanted not to feel this way, not to want his approval, but found it impossible to be indifferent. And so her anger rose, and she came through the curtained archway with blue eyes darkened, color high, demanding his approval. She got it.

Senses alert, she heard the soft sound of his indrawn breath as she paused in the entrance. Toni looked at him sharply. The face under the thatch of russet gold hair was impassive, and the teasing light she so often saw in his eyes was replaced by one of quiet seriousness.

"I like that one, Antonia. What do you think?" He was playing the perfect gentleman, deferring to the opinion of his companion—as long as that opinion was the same as his, Toni thought sharply.

He looked so innocent, so straightforward, but she was suddenly certain the quiet currents in Mark Anders ran very deeply indeed. What would it be like to plumb those depths? The errant thought caught her unawares, and she thrust it away with indignant haste.

Toni took no part in the discussion following the

selection of the golden gown. Using his formidable charm, Mark persuaded the head of the couture house to have the dress ready and delivered to Toni's hotel in time for the evening's affair. Even granting that the gown needed little alteration to fit perfectly, it was still unthinkable to expect a house with the reputation of this one to deliver on such short notice. But Mark got his way. Toni, returning from the fitting room in her street clothes, listened to the couturier assuring the tall American he could count on delivery. Naturally, she thought wryly. When did he not get his way? A small warning again tingled through her nervous system.

Mark caught her look, grinned. "You don't approve of me, do you, Antonia?"

Her color rose at his unexpected reading of her thoughts. "I neither approve nor disapprove of you, Mark Anders." Her tone was distinctly cool. "I don't know you well enough. And neither do I have the right."

"Do you not?" His left eyebrow crooked above lazy humorous eyes. Long fingers fastened themselves around her fur-clad elbow as he assisted her into the taxi awaiting them at the curb. "You continue to amaze me." And somehow the ambiguous statement held a strong thread of satisfaction.

With scarcely time to draw breath, Toni found herself in a softly lighted and very lush beauty salon. She was then washed, trimmed and polished to a fine perfection. Every hair lay in sleek and disciplined order. Her short and well-shaped nails were put in diamond-bright condition. Makeup was applied with a skill that transformed her natural beauty into a startling classic flawlessness without any detectable evidence of artifice. Toni stared at herself in the mirrored walls of the room. She found the sight a little hard to believe, and wished she had refused to go along with Mark's plan to glamorize her for the good of the organization. The image thrown back at her left her in no doubt about his success. She had not realized what specialized care could do for one's looks.

"The corporation may have made a big mistake," she told him as they rode toward Bowater House and the impressive company headquarters.

"How can they really expect me to go back to roughnecking after this kind of treatment?" she asked when they were alone in an elegantly appointed office that Mark used when he was in town. "I may decide I want to carry on, now that I've tasted all this forbidden luxury."

"The corporation knows exactly what it is doing, Antonia." His lingering glance caused her heart to skip disconcertingly. "Those guys from that there desert ain't never seed nuttin' th' likes o' you. An' when they cotton on t' the gray matter you got stored away in that there pretty li'l head, why, honey chile, they jist plain gonna flip outta their cotton-picking minds! They gonna eat outta yore grubby li'l oily paws—an' love it!"

Toni laughed merrily at his drawling patois delivered in a nasal resounding twang she recognized as indigenous to the region of the States known as the Deep South.

"Seriously, you will knock those desert sheiks dead, Antonia Cameron."

"Your kind opinion is appreciated," she said, laughing.

Toni knew she was being manipulated. But only this one time, she decided firmly. Never again would she let Mark Anders find himself able to use her, she vowed quietly. Then she paid strict attention to his concise explanation of U.P.C.'s thesis on the use of definitive geologic models of oil wells that were presently high producing in order to locate undiscovered deposits.

"U.P.C. has already figured out how to link the information fed into the computer from all sources into the building of such a profile. It should provide us with a much more accurate tool for pinpointing potentially high-producing fields, and we want to start in the Persian Gulf. We are going to use it in the Gulf of Mexico, as well, but we know more about the Persian Gulf. However, we need permission to try."

"That is what you are going to attempt to do at the reception this evening?"

"I have great hopes for the outcome of the reception," he answered calmly. "The men there tonight control the activities in the gulf. If we can interest them in this as a viable proposition, the corporation will have it made."

"You are gambling a great deal on an unknown factor."

"U.P.C. doesn't think so, and if I may say so, U.P.C. seldom misses a trick. So lay your doubts to rest, Antonia. If the corporation is content that you are the factor ensuring success, then rest assured, you are the factor. So just relax and enjoy yourself." The mischievous glint was back. "Yours is not to reason why," he quoted. His bright glance slid over her, again triggering that breathless response she hated so much. "The gamble is worth the price," he added softly. "I can tell."

"Well, as long as they know what they are about."

She was angry, uncertain because she found her uneasiness on the upswing once more. "Has U.P.C. enough of a financial base to support such an experiment?"

"It can be handled if the contracts are drawn up correctly. And they will be." He went on to explain the quality of the opposition. The company needed an extraordinary wedge in order to get a foot in the door and do it first, especially if the premise was as sound as they thought it to be.

Toni responded to the challenge of the situation with confidence, deciding she could only do her best. Nevertheless, she was uncertain about the wisdom of choosing a woman to present the idea to a group as traditionally entrenched in the concept of male superiority as a gathering of Arabian sheiks.

Mark finally called a taxi for her and sent her back to the hotel to rest before dressing for the evening's affair. Strictly black tie and extremely formal, it was to be held in the rarefied precincts of Claridge's.

What a strange and different day this was, Toni mused as she opened the massive door to the suite she occupied. She had the door closed, her back against it, before she saw the great mound of packages stacked upon the elegant coffee table. Large and small, of various alluring shapes, the boxes completely covered the surface of the long table. Elegantly black, they all bore the name, in massive gold block letters, of the couture house she had visited with Mark Anders.

Toni stared, aghast. Surely there must be some mistake. Taking off the mink, she hung it carefully in the closet recessed into the wall, then sat down and began opening. Thirty minutes later she sat still as a stone in the middle of the contents of those boxes: cobwebby underthings of silk, weighing no more than a whisper, sized to fit her perfectly; lacy tights; all the gowns she had tried on earlier, including the one chosen for to-night's reception; beautiful Gucci shoes and matching bags to complement each of the gowns; leather gloves as soft as silk.

Toni sat in the middle of the exquisite loveliness meant to soften a girl's heart, and felt hers turn to a block of ice. It was no mistake. She was as sure of this as she was of her own name. Who did Mark Anders think he was? And even more important, who did he think she was? A ridiculous teenager, to be impressed by the extravagant waste of his employer's money. Or perhaps an easy mark to be bought and brought to heel by gifts such as these?

Swiftly she packed all the offerings into their various boxes and stacked them neatly beside the door. She lingered long moments over the advisability of refusing to wear even the gown she had agreed upon, deciding finally that she must fulfill her commitment to go to the evening's function. The corporation's need had nothing to do with Mark Anders. She must be properly dressed. Yes, she would wear the lovely thing, then return it tomorrow along with the mink coat and any accessories she had to borrow if she was to do the task assigned her.

Toni was dressed, a figure of golden loveliness, when Mark knocked. She opened the door, her eyes blazing her anger at him. "You may remove these boxes and do it now or I shall not accompany you tonight."

One straight black brow quirked. "Not one step?"

"Not one step."

His glance rested appreciatively on her slender shape

so sweetly encased in the flowing gold of the gown, lingered on the shining midnight cap of her hair, drifted lazily to her sensitive mouth so firmly set, and finally sought the clear blue of her blazing eyes. He gauged her determination with consummate skill.

"If I may come in, I will call down for John."

Toni stepped aside and Mark went to the telephone, where he asked the desk clerk to send his man up. His face settling into a withdrawn and very thoughtful mask, he waited silently until John arrived. He loaded the boxes into the chauffeur's arms while issuing brief instructions, which Toni failed to hear because she was in the bedroom gathering up the little golden bag containing her evening essentials. She was surprised to find she was a little saddened to see all those beautiful things go. And perhaps she was a little miffed too, that Mark had not tried to persuade her to keep them.

"Why did you have all that sent over?" Curious, Toni could not help but ask the question. "Surely you must have known I could not keep them."

"I saw you in them today, remember?" His voice was deep. "They were made just for you. I didn't think anyone else should wear them. Only you."

Toni almost stopped breathing altogether. Her eyes searched the impassive face looking down into hers. He wasn't teasing now. She could detect absolutely no sign of laughter or devilment in him. The man was mad, she decided recklessly.

"I'm sorry if I offended you. Forgive me and let's get on with the job, shall we?" As he watched her, he seemed wholly absorbed in the expressions chasing each other across her mobile face. Suddenly he relaxed, reached for the mink coat and touched her arm. "Everyone makes mistakes. Even me, unfortunately!"

His chuckle was a comfortable sound, inviting her to join him in his own discomfiture. Toni removed his long fingers from her arm, unable to analyze her need to break even such casual contact with him, but smiled up at him as he towered behind her. She expected him to drape the coat around her waiting shoulders, but he gave a quick shake of his darkly golden head.

"I think not, Antonia." He reached beyond her and opened the door. "It's a shame to cover you with this before I must."

"You are rather gorgeous yourself," she said deliberately as they walked, counterattacking his provocative attitude with intentional challenge. The beautifully cut dinner jacket did set off his blond handsomeness to perfection. She cast a consciously bold and assessing glance across his breadth of shoulder as he leaned with casual ease against the wall of the descending elevator. Then she took in the contrast of his snowy ruffled shirt with his tanned skin, the elegance of the pants covering his long and muscular legs, then returned solemnly to the laughter in his eyes. "You would be spectacular with lace at your throat and wrists. Too bad fashion has changed!"

His laugh was quick and deep as the elevator opened. "Yes, and I will probably be in need of the dress sword of that period tonight." Seeing the puzzled expression she cast him, he grinned, ran his hand down her arm as they crossed the lobby and entwined her fingers in his. "Just to keep you from being carried off by a handsome, dark-eyed sheik," he elaborated.

Toni stopped at the door, the warning again singing through her as Mark held the coat. Thrusting her arms into its silken sleeves, Toni dared not look at him. His hands on her shoulders were deliberately caressing.

Toni surprised herself by offering no protest as they walked down the steps to the limousine, her hand recaptured in his warm grip. John opened the Rolls's door, saw them in, closed it and tucked himself into position. The packages were not in evidence.

Once in the big car, Mark turned to a quick briefing of the evening's activities, teasing forgotten. Toni breathed a sigh of relief, listened to his deep voice giving concise instructions and reassembled her scattered feelings.

By the time the limousine rolled smoothly under the portico at Claridge's, Toni was back in control of the situation and of her warring senses.

Two hours later Antonia Carla Cameron sat down amid enthusiastic applause.

"Absolutely top of the class, Antonia," Mark murmured in delight. "Superb!"

"Thank you." Toni's dimple flashed.

"Charming, Miss Cameron." The sheik seated to her left smiled at her in unqualified approval. "I cannot believe one so lovely as you could be so knowledgeable. What a beautiful surprise you are to me and to my countrymen."

The man was a handsome specimen of manhood. He was tall, almost as tall as Mark Anders. His perfect features were dark and exotic, classical in shape and proportion. He had black eyes that glowed at her with an intense and flattering approval.

Toni looked up at him, a little bubble of happiness she had never experienced before causing her eyes to shine. "How nice of you to say so," she murmured.

"Not at all. It is the truth." He smiled again.

Toni smiled back, intrigued by a sudden thought, too intrigued to notice the sharp glance she received from Mark. She was interested in the fact that she was suddenly finding it a very pleasurable situation to be the center of the attention of so many admiring men. And she dimly realized that she had been shunning such attention for years. She thought about it quietly now.

Of course, during her teens she had been a tomboy, who had needed every bit of her parents' firm restraint and guidance as they redirected her efforts to become "one of the boys." Then she had met Kurt Grady and become absorbed in her first and only love affair. At a time when she would normally have had a great deal of interest in the attentiveness of the men around her, she had already centered her world on Kurt.

The tragedy of his death, coupled as it was with that of her beloved father, had struck deeply and shattered her. It had become impossible for her to respond in the way most women are naturally happy to respond to any attractive, reasonably presentable male. Instead she had gone back to treating all men as she had when she was growing up. In spite of her family's efforts, she had finally become one of the boys.

Tonight she was suddenly and acutely conscious of the fact that she quite enjoyed the praise of these men. What had brought that unusual awareness to the surface? And why had it surfaced tonight?

Thoughtfully she sought the golden head of Mark Anders, her mind on the feelings he had aroused in her during the past few days. At that moment he met her assessing gaze with that mischievous grin of his. It slanted across his attractive face in the endearing manner he had.

"Here, Miss Cameron." The tall sheik was beside

her. A strong brown hand captured hers and folded it gently around a hard object. "A penny for them, as you say in your country."

"What?" Toni laughed, startled. "Oh, you mean a penny for my thoughts. Sorry. I was rather far away. But my thoughts were not worth anything."

"Ah, Miss Cameron...." His quiet protest was delivered with such sincere intensity that Toni inspected his handsome face with care. Here was a man who could be dynamite, she realized. He smiled at her with teasing, soft black eyes. "You have no idea how many men are in this room tonight who would give a great deal if it would only insure sharing the very least of your thoughts. I am one of those men. Will you have a coffee with me, please?"

That long dark hand of his was still wrapped firmly around her small one. His expression told her quite clearly that he could not imagine she would refuse his invitation.

"Yes, I will have a coffee, thank you—on one condition," she responded with mock seriousness.

"And that is?"

"I must have my hand back."

He laughed, raised it to his lips and brushed a kiss across it before he tucked it into the curve of his elbow to guide her toward a small deserted table.

"I am Prince Hussein Ibn Saud, Miss Cameron. I am a bedouin with sand in my boots, who has come to your shores from my country, Bahrain, to partake of your culture and commerce. I had not thought to meet so beautiful a lady while talking about oil." He seated her at the little table, then beckoned for service from an attentive waiter.

"Your English is faultless, and you may have your

coin back. I have no intention of sharing my thoughts."
Toni put it on the table, and saw then that it was gold.

"Is it because your thoughts were occupied with
Mark Anders?"

"Certainly not!" Toni's denial was swift, but not as
swift as the color that rose to her cheeks. The suave
man smiled softly, black eyes alight with approval.

"Forgive me for my assumption. I saw you looking
at him. I thought your involvement might be such that
I could be intruding if I allowed my interest in you to
show."

"I do forgive you, of course. But I wonder how you
came to make such a wild assumption." Toni sipped
her coffee and regarded him gravely. "Mark Anders is
an associate of mine. A new associate." She did not
elaborate further.

"I cannot tell you how happy I am to hear you say
so." His dark eyes shone with delight. "I am indeed
the most fortunate of men. For a moment I was fearful
I had discovered your existence too late—that Anders
had, er, assumed responsibility for your well-being,
shall we say?"

Toni repressed a giggle. "Surely you must know that
I am old enough to answer to no one in these days of
women's liberation, Prince Hussein?"

"Ah, yes. Women's lib." His shoulders lifted in an
expressive shrug. "We pay too little attention to it in
my sandy domain, I am afraid. Still, you are much too
desirable not to have some man intensely interested in
your well-being, Miss Cameron." He smiled at her, his
hesitation charming. "Forgive me if I err, but I
watched Mark Anders rather closely. I gained the impression he was the man."

"No." Toni's negative was unequivocal. She had no

inclination to examine the feeling behind the monosyllable. Finishing her coffee, she put her cup down, frowning at the idea that Mark Anders's attentive behavior that evening could have given the impression his interest in her was anything other than that of a co-worker.

He had stationed himself at her side and remained there all evening until now. His face had been quiet, observant, his eyes approving as she talked about U.P.C.'s new theory. Once her audience had recovered from the shock of learning she was indeed a working geophysicist, and a successful one at that, they had given her their undivided attention.

Proceeding to the business of understanding the concept, they had picked her brain with a vengeance, firing questions, absorbing answers. Enthusiasm had risen in the room as she showed them the real possibilities of the new techniques and the implications for future exploration. Toni had been conscious of Mark beside her, conscious of his pleasure in the success she was having, but that was all.

Evidently Sheik Hussein had misconstrued the reason for Mark's interest. Toni set him straight, politely but firmly. Hussein smiled at her and set down his cup as he leaned toward her.

"Then may I take advantage of the incredible lack of foresight on the part of your countrymen and others and ask you, as an uncommitted young woman, to have lunch with me tomorrow?"

Toni regarded him quietly. She found to her utter amazement that she was pleased with his restrained flattery, his elegant effort at flirtation. Surely few women had ever been asked to lunch by a handsomer man!

Hussein smiled at her. "I ask you to lunch only because I shall not be here later. To my sorrow, I must leave tomorrow evening for Bahrain." Those black eyes, soft as velvet, pleaded with her. "I truly must see you once more before that. Please?"

Somehow Toni had the distinct impression that the man before her rarely had to ask anyone to please him. She returned his smile.

"I would enjoy that." As she rose she found herself pinned by Mark's scrutiny, but she met his challenging scowl, then turned back to Hussein. "Shall we meet somewhere around half-past twelve? I have some things I wish to do in the morning. It will save me the trouble of returning to the hotel."

Mark was by her side as she completed making the arrangements to meet the sheik. Fur in hand, he asked her if she was ready to leave. He and Hussein cast assessing glances at each other as they said their good-byes. If there was tension between the two men, Toni did not notice it.

Her dimple flashing in amusement at herself, she walked beside Anders on the way back to her hotel. They were walking at her request. Quite simply, she needed the crisp February air to bring her back to earth. She decided she could become addicted to such a heady sensation of success and such lavish attention.

Breathing deeply, enjoying the rush of cold air into lungs too long subjected to cigar smoke, she slanted a glance up at her companion.

He grinned with wicked charm as he met her gaze. "Well, we did it, my love!" He captured her hand, enfolding it in strong fingers. "We make a hell of a team." Satisfaction rode gaily in his voice. The casual endearment was entirely offhand, his expression completely innocent under Toni's sharpening regard. "Old U.P.C. should be celebrating tonight!"

Toni smiled, a sweet contentment invading her senses—content with herself, content with this exceptional man at her side, content with the job of work she had done for him. It was extraordinary.

"They seemed convinced. Do you think they will go ahead with the idea?" she asked.

"I am sure. You knocked them dead. I knew you would." Complacency at his own good judgment laced his voice. "I just swept up the pieces after you shattered all possible resistance. After all, what sane man could resist a golden goddess speaking sense?" He laughed, squeezing the hand that was tucked in his. "I'm to see a committee appointed by them tomorrow, complete with lawyers and oilmen. We'll start negotiating contracts. And it is all due to the way you were able to present the concept to them."

"Glad I could help," Toni answered simply and was silent, surprised at the warm glow his approval caused.

They rounded a corner and headed toward the hotel in the near distance. Toni was aware of the comfortable silence, of the movement of her body sheathed in the silky fabric of her gown, of the luxurious feel of the mink wrap, of the warmth of the strong hand holding hers.

And gradually her awareness expanded to take in the essence of the man beside her. His height, his leanness, his lithe body, the grace of his movements as he shortened his stride to accommodate hers.

Her peace and contentment exploded. Toni sighed self-consciously and removed her hand, thrusting it into her pocket.

His left eyebrow shot up and the teasing look vanished, his face becoming thoughtful. It was some time before Mark broke the silence between them. Speaking casually, his soothing voice somehow forcing her to dismiss her self-consciousness as nonsense, he talked about their departure the day after tomorrow for the States, about testing the geologic model theory on an area in the Gulf of Mexico that U.P.C. owned and about the members of the exploration team she was to join. She responded quietly when necessary, finding it hard to concentrate on the words he was uttering, for she was listening instead to the deep musical quality of his speech.

Mark escorted her across the lobby, deserted now except for the man on duty behind the desk, and accompanied her to her door, becoming strangely silent as the elevator carried them upward.

At the door Toni searched the tiny evening bag she carried, her pulse fluttering under the golden silk at her throat. No key. Uncertain, she glanced up at her companion. Devilment glinted once again in the look he gave her as he fished the key from the pocket of his black Burberry. Reaching around her, he thrust it into the lock, then pushed the door open. She rushed quickly into the room, determined to be away from the threat he posed.

"Antonia." The deep velvet of the lyrical word halted her in her tracks, but she resisted the impulse to face him.

"Yes?" She was pleased with the briskness of her response.

"Look at me, Antonia. I've something important to ask you."

Well, she thought dryly, *what's the big deal? You've been kissed before, Toni Cameron.* The absurd thud-of her heart warned her she expected something quite different from any other time, any other kiss.

But she turned to face Mark, her eyes a deep and stormy challenge. He towered above her, elbow crooked against the jamb of the door, head resting negligently on his doubled fist, the upturned collar of his Burberry a frame for his sun-browned face.

"You look as feisty as a bantam hen defending her honor." Mocking laughter sparked in that direct gaze of his. "What's the matter, Antonia?" the lazy drawl teased adroitly. "Are you afraid of me?"

"You are the most outrageous man, Mark Anders. Of course I'm not afraid of you. I expect and trust you will remain a gentleman—" Her flow of wrath stopped as he reached out and slid a long and gentle finger across the softness of one raven eyebrow, down the sweet curve of her cheek and under her small chin. Toni could not have finished her sentence to save her life. Every nerve in her body stirred into life at his feathery touch.

"You ask a lot of me. At this moment I have absolutely no desire to remain a gentleman." Toni felt the seduction in his touch and in that deep drawl. A smile curved his firm lips, deepening the creases in his cheeks. She could not pull away from the magic of shared intimacy.

"You were absolutely superb this evening, Antonia. You enchanted those desert men. I want to thank you."

"I...I...." Toni took a deep breath and started again. "It isn't necessary to thank me, surely. Just a part of my job, wasn't it?" Had she enchanted him, as well? The question drifted through her mind, wraith-like, unsettling.

"We don't leave for the States until Thursday. Will you go to the theater and dinner with me tomorrow evening? Please?"

"Yes, if you would like me to." Anxious to break contact with him, to regain control of her treacherous impulses, Toni felt ready to agree to anything. And he was looking at her so strangely....

A timeless moment hung between them. But it shattered as Mark drew a ragged breath, his face settling into an impassive mask. Toni frowned. What had she seen in those keen hazel eyes?

"A word of warning, Antonia." His voice hardened. "Be careful in your dealings with Hussein. He's just divorced his wife of ten years. He's looking."

"I beg your pardon!" The magic of the moment vanished for Toni. "What a ghastly thing to say to me! Why do you think I might be remotely interested in the man's private life?"

Mark sighed. "I wasn't as concerned with your interest as I was with his," he remarked obscurely. "I can well imagine his wishing to whisk you away to his desert, the bride of a latter-day 'Sheik of Araby.'" His brown hand slid down, encircled the back of her neck and aborted her effort to jerk away from him. "U.P.C. would not enjoy having their latest employee lost to them. Hence my concern."

Toni inspected his innocent expression and hesitated, but her curiosity got the better of her. "Do you know why he divorced his wife?" Somehow such an action did not seem compatible with Sheik Hussein Ibn Saud's quiet air of contentment.

Mark grinned at her, shrugged dismissively. "Seems she was unable to have children, which is not easily foreseen. Hussein was heartbroken, I understand. He loved her, but he has a duty to leave an heir and apparently had little choice in the matter." He managed to give the distinct impression he considered the sheik's reason for divorce irrelevant. "He needs to find a suitable mother for his children."

Toni's backbone stiffened in outrage at his implication. Thumb under her chin he tilted her face up, inspecting her gravely.

"I wouldn't want you to get the assignment," he murmured. He kissed her forehead, then disappeared down the open staircase without a backward glance.

Toni watched his broad back, his thatch of dark gold as he vanished, wonder stirring secretly in the back reaches of her mind. It was just as well she had no need to analyze the unexpected feeling of deprivation nibbling at her. Surely she was not piqued because he had not properly kissed her good-night!

CHAPTER FIVE

TONI SLEPT LIKE A LAMB and awoke with determination acting as a balm for her nerves. She showered, dressed, then packed the lovely things she had worn the night before back into their boxes. She even included the vial of perfume. Draping the mink over the boxes, she called the desk and had a man sent up. Her instructions for the delivery of the expensive articles to U.P.C. headquarters at Bowater House were explicit.

Toni was quite pleased with herself as she went out to find some breakfast. She hoped the return of the garments and accessories would emphasize her disapproval of Mark's use of company money to further his own ends. Not for one moment did she think U.P.C. had any idea of the amount of corporation funds Mark Anders was willing to spend. She wondered how he justified such spending, acknowledged it wasn't her affair and shelved her curiosity.

After a good breakfast, she spent an enjoyable morning visiting with her old friend Marge Hansome, with whom she had roomed in college. Marge had married an engineer, Jim, and was now expecting their first child. The woman's exuberance was just what Toni needed to get her mind off the disturbing Mark Anders. They parted tearfully, resolving to keep in touch more often.

It was just one o'clock when Toni's taxi pulled up at

the exclusive restaurant in Mayfair, where the prince was waiting. He brushed her fingers with his lips in an enchanting gesture as his dark gaze registered approval.

Toni smiled back at him, encouraging him in a way she would not have done a week ago. They went in to a perfect luncheon they both enjoyed. Toward the end of the meal Toni became conscious of someone at her elbow. Hussein stood, a smile slashing across his classic features.

"Mark! I didn't expect to see you again before I left. Welcome, old friend. Will you sit with us?"

"Sorry. Linda and I have just finished. We must get back to the office. I have work to do before I call for Toni tonight. I would not want to be late."

Toni endured the challenge he seemed to issue so innocently as she quelled the quickening of her heartbeat. It was becoming more useless each time she saw him to try to stop reacting to his presence. She looked beyond him and fastened her attention on one of the most gorgeous redheads she had ever seen. The woman was willowy, shaped like a dream. She was much taller than Toni, the top of her glorious shock of red curls on a level with Mark's eyebrow. Toni's head barely reached his chin line, she realized with a swift feeling of inadequacy. As Anders introduced his personal assistant, Toni found herself staring at Linda Wells's perfect alabaster complexion. And never had she seen such beautiful eyes. They were long lashed, curving upward in the most arresting manner.

Yes, Linda Wells was a most beautiful woman. She stood behind Mark Anders and glowed with a radiance Toni resented quite irrationally. Mark's expression was unreadable, but Hussein's delight was easy to read as he bowed over the slender female hand so graciously offered.

"Sorry to intrude," Mark murmured politely, his eyes on Toni's skeptical smile. "I wouldn't have presumed ordinarily, but seeing you like this is most fortunate. Could you ring before you catch your plane, Hussein? There are a couple of points I need to clear with you personally. Linda and I will be working all afternoon."

"Most assuredly, old friend. You are sure we cannot talk here?"

"Unfortunately I need to refer to the papers our teams drew up this morning. If I can consult with you now it will save my flying to Bahrain to straighten it out."

There was an undercurrent of meaning Toni could not understand to the conversation going on between the two men. She was not sure the Arabian was aware of it, but she knew Mark Anders's tone was intentional. Thoughtfully she watched the tall U.P.C. man. Anders glanced down and grinned at her.

"I'll phone, then, as soon as I finish this most enjoyable luncheon with my lovely companion." Hussein looked fondly at Toni.

Mark put a lean hand on Linda Wells's shoulder, then moved it down to close around her perfectly groomed fingers. His face expressionless, he nodded. "We won't intrude any longer, then. Come, Linda. Back to the salt mines." He herded his gorgeous companion toward the elegant reception room, turned and glanced back at Toni over one shoulder. "See you at half-past seven, Antonia. Be ready."

Toni felt her color rise at the reminder. It wasn't so much the words he used as his tone of voice. She squirmed in silent rebellion at the hard possessiveness he took no trouble to mask as he flung the careless words at her. The Arabian prince watched her carefully.

"It is a coincidence. There are many places to have a nice lunch here in London. Yet we both chose to bring our beautiful companions to this particular place. Strange, is it not?"

"Yes, it is. I expect it just means you both like the quality of the food and service here." Toni's shrug was careless, concealing her own doubt—at least she hoped it did.

She remembered the previous evening. He had appeared at her side, the mink over his arm, as she made the arrangement to meet Prince Hussein here. He could very easily have overheard them. But to think he had come here with the beauteous Linda on purpose was to suppose he had some sort of a personal interest in her activities—that he was in some manner checking up on her. It suggested an involvement Toni was in no way ready to admit might be possible.

She sighed and made a definite effort to relax in the easy company of the man trying so skillfully to entertain her. He was a pet, and a very handsome, charming one, as well.

Hussein responded easily to the fun in Toni's eyes and kept her dimple winking with his wit. Toni teased him while keeping him firmly in his place. He accepted her treatment with cool ease. They enjoyed each other thoroughly and said their farewells with regret, Toni promising to see him again when time and circumstance allowed. She did not tell him she was leaving the next day for the States, as she recognized the danger of his attractiveness. A mild flirtation was one thing.

Anything more was unthinkable. She also recognized the relief she experienced as she bade him goodbye, getting out of his low-slung sports car at the entrance to Liberty's. She walked through the ancient archway, turned and flipped a hand at him, glad to be away from the pressure of his personality.

Really, his effect upon her was almost as bad as Mark Anders's. Almost. The difference was that she truly liked Hussein. He charmed and cosseted her in a way she could relate to very easily. Mark just annoyed her.

Content with her analysis, Toni spent the afternoon renewing her love affair with London. After squandering pounds on a lovely silk blouse she found in Liberty's, she hailed a taxi to Foyles and found a book of poetry she knew would please her mother, then drifted down Shaftesbury Avenue to Piccadilly and bought a tin of her grandfather's favorite tobacco from Dunhill's. She went to the post office by St. Martin's in the Fields and mailed the gifts, then watched a sidewalk artist out beside the National Gallery and generally enjoyed the day.

It was late by the time she reached the hotel. Mark was waiting in the lobby, rather spectacular in a black turtleneck sweater and black suede pants that fit like a second skin. A fine black suede jacket was slung carelessly over one shoulder as he came toward her across the lobby, his eyes narrowed.

"Enjoy your day?" He towered over her, his abrupt question curt. "Where have you left Hussein?"

Toni stared up at him and shrugged dismissively. "I have enjoyed my day. And I really cannot see that it is any of your affair where I have been or whom I may have left," she told him with some asperity.

He looked at her a moment, then nodded. "You are right, of course. It is none of my business. Let's not quarrel tonight, Antonia. Shall we call a truce and see if we can have a little fun?"

"That would certainly make a change," she retorted.

He grinned at her now, the devilment back in his eyes. "If you are willing to take the chance, it's time we left." He offered the statement calmly.

"Give me a few minutes to freshen up and I'll be with you," she replied politely, denying the quick response she had to the devilment that danced in his eyes.

"Five minutes, Antonia?" He laughed easily. "Then I'll be up to drag you out. Okay?"

Toni fled for the elevator and made it back down in less than ten minutes, her light makeup freshened, the Liberty blouse tucked into her skirt under her sheepskin.

"Game to ride the bus?" Mark challenged her as she joined him in the lobby.

"Certainly." Toni enjoyed riding the red London buses, but found it hard to believe the urbane man beside her shared the feeling.

"We'll have to hurry. There it comes." He grabbed her hand and ran toward the bus stop. Toni flew alongside him. They made it, piled on breathless with laughter as they climbed the narrow stairs to the top deck. The seat swayed as Toni collapsed into it, which caused Mark to come down hard beside her. His muscular frame mashed her into the corner and knocked the rest of the air from her lungs. Instantly solicitous, he put his arm around her shoulders, his breath sweet on her cheeks.

"Are you all right? Did I hurt you?" Concern creased his brown face.

"N-no. I'm fine," Toni wheezed, giggling and fighting for breath at the same time. He frowned, released her as she began to wriggle. He turned to the ginger-haired little conductress who had followed smartly on their heels up the twisting stairway. Toni regained her equilibrium as she listened to the exchange of pleasantries between the girl and the American. She watched him search the pocket of his fitted suede pants for change, watched the girl flirt with him as she responded to his teasing. *I must be the only one around with any immunity to his charm,* she thought with a fine disdain. But somewhere deep in her consciousness a suspicion that she might be less immune than was wise worried at her. She stamped the suspicion out.

Of course she was immune. She didn't even like the man. But how she was going to be able to work with him was still a mystery to her, one she had not yet explored in depth.

They left the bus at Charing Cross, clattered down Villiers Street and crossed the river by walking over the railroad bridge toward the theater. The play was a tongue-in-cheek comedy they both found extremely funny. Toni was rosy with laughter as they left with the chattering crowd. John met them outside the door and whisked them away in the Rolls. They were welcomed into an intimate restaurant somewhere in the back streets of Knightsbridge, where they dined royally. Mark's politeness was constant.

Toni, uneasy, drank too much of the excellent wine served because she was preoccupied with the need to keep herself very busy. Even so, by the time they returned to the hotel her usually reliable nerves were in shreds. As Mark followed her into the elevator, she clung to her slippery control, conscious that she seemed to be in a hazy state of mind. Probably brought on by a war between wine and wisdom, she thought wryly as she handed her door key to the man beside her.

"Aren't you going to ask me in for a nightcap, Antonia?" his lazy drawl teased, but he made no move to follow her or to delay her rather precipitate movement into the safety of the room.

Toni turned to face him, color wavering in hot cheeks. A hidden perversity battled her cool aloofness. It allowed her to take in his black-clad, arrogant length as he leaned one broad shoulder against the doorframe in what seemed a favored position of his.

"Sorry—" she flipped the word at him with a cowardly sense of relief "—there is nothing here."

The relief was instantly killed by the laughter in Mark's slanted glance. "With your permission...." He straightened and closed the door as he shed his black suede jacket, which he tossed onto the back of a chair. Then he crossed to the handsome chest against the wall and touched a button. A door sprang open to reveal well-stocked shelves and a supply of sparkling crystal. Toni gave up and dropped her sheepskin beside his jacket.

She plopped her overstuffed handbag on a corner of the low table and took the crystal glass from him, her nostrils twitching at the pleasant orangy aroma of the liqueur. She sipped it carefully. It was delicious, spreading nicely warming fire through her system.

Toni smiled and glanced up. She surprised such an intense and contemplative scrutiny on Mark's lean tanned face that she raised the glass in her hand in an instinctive gesture of defense. The gulp she took was careless in the extreme, for the liqueur struck back with a vengeance. She choked and spluttered breathlessly.

Through the sudden tears blinding her, Toni caught her companion's instinctive gesture of help. She moved hastily backward, compelled by a need to avoid his reaching hand, but she forgot the low table. She fell heavily over it, disheveled, gasping. The crystal flew from her hand and dispersed a glittering shower of expensive liqueur over Toni and the lush carpet.

Mark dropped to his knees beside her and caught her struggling body in strong hands. Unfortunately her silk blouse had not been constructed to withstand the stress generated by his powerful arms. Buttons flew. As his arms engulfed her Mark was still with an intenseness that immobilized Toni. She became poignantly aware of the thud of his heart against her silk-clad back, of the hard feel of the muscular arms around her body. Her senses were swamped by the mingled scent of tobacco and leather, and his subtle, entirely male fragrance. A hypnotic lethargy held her enthralled as his hands moved soothingly over her satiny skin, which was bared by the abrupt departure of her treacherous buttons.

Toni's breath caught as those seductive fingers touched where no man had touched before. She squirmed in an abortive attempt to escape. Mark laughed as he turned her around and sank with her to recline on the carpet. His eyes gleamed with a hunger that demanded immediate attention.

"No!" Toni spat the word in a terrified attempt to distract him from his very evident intentions.

"Oh, yes, Antonia. Yes...." The whisper caressed her as he lowered his mouth passionately to hers. Toni struggled, determined to push him away. Mark swore briefly, tightened his grip and crushed her into the hardness of his body. His lips came back to hers with an insistent mastery not to be denied.

Toni lost the unequal struggle. A tide of sweetness washed over her, drowning her in depths of ecstasy. Without knowing it, she matched his passion with the fire of her own and concentrated the whole of her being on the seductive mouth exploring hers so expertly. She trembled with the desire aroused by the touch of his gently moving fingers as they wandered over her neck and shoulders, the swell of her breasts.

Under his sensitive knowledgeable hands, Toni was transformed as desire awakened and flamed. Passion struck deep, uniting flesh and blood and heartbeat into one pulsing whole, then tossing her high on a wave of unbearable delight. Soft arms around the strong column of his neck, she moaned with the sublimity of his seduction, melding herself into his masculine body.

Mark's breathing rasped. For a moment he took in oxygen like a drowning man, then went back to the awakening woman in his arms. Toni welcomed the deepened sensuality as his mouth claimed hers, dimly aware of the thunder of heartbeats. His? Hers? What did it matter? The sensuality existed, a part of them both. In seconds Mark had taught her the meaning of being a woman, the meaning of response to the call of the male. Toni trembled with the beauty, the sheer poignancy of awakening desire. Hungry for more, she matched his passion with her own, aware only of his gentle expert exploration.

She sighed as Mark raised his leonine head and shifted her slightly. He moved, brushed seeking lips over her closed eyes. Tenderly, softly, his mouth sought the rounded silkiness of her breast, the thrusting hardness of glorious pink nipples. The jolt of his invasion tore through Toni and shattered her last defenses. She murmured his name incoherently as she laced feverish fingers through his golden brown hair, intent on returning those demanding lips to hers.

Mark nibbled the sweet nipple under his questing mouth with white teeth in a tender refusal to be distracted. His gentle punishment caused Toni's eyes to fly open... and settle upon Kurt's photograph, spilled from the handbag she had knocked to the floor in her tumble.

Toni stared at it, going rigid with shame and disgust at herself. What was she doing? What was she thinking of? What kind of a woman was she, to act this way, to respond in such a manner to a man she had known less than a week?

"Oh, Kurt!" The words were torn from her throat. Completely wretched, she turned as rigid as stone. Mark raised his head. His eyes raked her white face as he sought to understand her panicky withdrawal. Face bleak, he made no attempt to detain her as she wrenched herself out of his arms and fled into the bedroom. The door slammed behind her.

He knelt where she had left him for a few moments. Pain and frustration marred his strong features, turning his eyes opaque and lifeless. Gradually he focused on the pictured face in the folio on the floor. He rose then, stooping to scoop it up.

The oath he muttered as he snatched his jacket and left the suite was not pretty. Nor was it meant to be.

CHAPTER SIX

TONI STRUGGLED FROM SLEEP the next morning to a flaming headache. Her aroused senses had refused to allow her to relax in the comfort of the bed. The wine had its turn, too, as it added nausea to her upset. And the disorder of the bedcovers attested to her subconscious effort to escape the knowledge that she was capable of a passion that demanded fulfillment—when that demand came from Mark Anders.

Toni was deeply disgusted by her reaction to him. What had come over her? Whatever it was, it had certainly put paid to her cherished belief in her ability to control the intentions of the men with whom she worked.

"Oh, damn and blast!"

She stumbled out of bed and into the shower. Dressed in her suede pants and boots, she threw on her cashmere sweater, jerked a comb through her black hair and scuffed moodily into the sitting room, straightening it up with shaking fingers. After she telephoned, room service delivered a pot of tea and two aspirins.

Toni sat staring into her cup with a calm born of desperation. It was essential that she come to terms with her unforeseen physical response to the lure of Mark's sexuality. If she could not do it, life would become untenable and she would have no business going to the States, where they would be in constant proximity.

He was contemptible, she decided, anger causing her blue eyes to smolder stormily. It was inexcusable that he had taken advantage of her vulnerability in such a manner. Really, he had no depth of character at all. If he had been gentlemanly, had allowed her a little time to recover, she would have been more herself, more able to reject his assault with a withering scorn even he could not have laughed off.

But as she remembered her reaction, her awakened passionate need struck deeply. She longed to experience again the intense excitement of being in Mark's arms as he kissed and caressed her. Toni squirmed and drank her tea in an effort to ignore her new knowledge. She soldiered on to the crux of her problem, fervently hoping that she had only responded to his onslaught because she had been weakened by too much wine, a bad case of nerves and a cruel lack of breath.

Nevertheless, she knew very clearly that the easiest way to insure her own peace of mind was a refusal to go to the States. Toni mulled this over, teacup arrested in taut fingers. Set against her very real desire to throw her contract in his lean and arrogant face were the benefits U.P.C. was supplying. It really was a dreamy contract. They were offering her a house complete with housekeeper and gardener. A company car was to be at her disposal, use unlimited. She was to get a salary impossible to match elsewhere at her present level of experience, and she would have the opportunity to work with the very latest of computerized equipment—something she really wanted to do. She balanced these advantages carefully against the fly in the ointment, Mr. Mark Anders. She decided she would be a fool to refuse to honor her contract.

Surely she was in control of her own emotions? Come to that, her emotions were not involved. It was only that she had this inexplicable and very unwelcome response to that blatant male charm of his, a response that was wholly physical. Surely she could handle that!

The teacup rattled with the force with which it was replaced in its saucer. Toni ran distracted fingers through her hair and reached for the telephone. She had a sudden need to hear her mother's quiet and sensible voice.

Joan was clearly puzzled at the strain in her daughter's slightly strangled salutation. "What is bothering you, love? Are you...in trouble?"

Toni's oversensitive nerves picked up the hesitation in her parent's question. "No, mother. Of course not." She hesitated. "I just wanted to let you know I was leaving for the States today...and to tell you and grampy goodbye for a while."

"Yes. Well, I did know you were leaving today."

"How did you know that?" Toni was sure her mother should have expected that she had left the U.K. on Monday, straight after the overnight trip down on the train. That was three days ago. "How did you know I hadn't gone already—that I was to go today?"

"I just knew." Joan's flat statement brooked no further questioning.

Toni, quite accustomed to her mother's gift for knowing the whereabouts and condition of those she loved, did not press for an explanation. She spent several satisfying minutes chatting with her parent and grandparent. Tension flowed from her with the easy conversation.

"Antonia...." Joan's tone commanded her daughter's instant attention as Toni was about to break the connection. "Don't waste time fighting your heart, my dear."

Toni stared at the phone in her hand. "Mother! I don't understand you. What...?"

"You will, Toni. You will." Joan hung up then, her soft chuckle replaced by a discordant buzz. Toni set the phone down, her eyes thoughtful as she went to answer the rap on the suite door. John was there. They needed to hurry to the airport. Mark would meet them there, the chauffeur said. He had been called away on urgent business.

They had been at Heathrow for some time with no evidence of Mark, when Toni decided to go look for a bun and a cup of tea, the rumble in her midsection reminding her she had eaten no breakfast. She crossed the upper lounge assigned to passengers awaiting flights and headed for the restaurant. Passing close to a window with a view of the ground floor of the busy terminal, she halted in midstride as she caught sight of Mark.

He came through the glass doors below, head down as his wide-shouldered frame split the crowd with the same efficiency a ship's prow has as it slices through water. A lord of creation.... The errant thought struck Toni as Mark's head came up. His eyes searched the glassed area above him as he looked for someone.

Me, Toni knew, but fled, her need for sustenance completely forgotten as her need to escape detection by those keen eyes took over. She blessed the blare of the announcement, which requested that passengers now board the Concorde. John had to move smartly to keep pace with her as she followed directions toward the plane. He was to accompany them on the flight at a telephoned instruction from Mark, he had told her when he picked her up at the hotel.

Toni was busy with her seat belt when Mark entered the plane. He stared at her a moment, his expression shuttered, then crossed to stand above her.

"Go away."

He inspected her gravely. He was still clothed in the black suede pants and turtleneck he had worn on their theater date, she noted. The jacket showed clear signs of dampness, as if its owner had dashed around in a rainstorm. And he really did not look as though he had slept.

It would serve him right if he hadn't after that performance last night, although she could not really imagine one of his obvious experience being upset by such an encounter. He very probably had not even given it a second thought!

Toni felt the heat rising in her face. She dropped her lashes, unable to sustain the intimacy of the eye contact between them. Damn the man! And damn her unwarranted response to his presence!

Mark watched her a moment, then sighed and dropped a sheaf of papers into her lap. "Some organizational procedures, Antonia. Look them over so you will know how we operate. A manual on the linkage of our computers is there. You will need to understand how we expect to feed the information you obtain into the system. It will be of immeasurable help to us in setting up the computer profile we hope to use when we position the rig."

He went back to sit with John. Toni applied herself to the papers, her ball-point flying as she made notes in the margins of the reports. Lunch came and went. She ate and enjoyed, her eyes on the papers as she continued to absorb the contents. She was entirely unconscious of hazel eyes across the aisle as they inspected her from time to time. When the captain of the aircraft strolled into the luxurious cabin she was still intent on her task.

"Ladies and gentlemen, we are about thirty minutes from our landing pattern at Washington, D.C." His blue eyes twinkled under the elegant peaked cap of his office. "I expect you all know we arrive there—or you could be on the wrong plane!"

Toni joined in the wave of laughter that greeted the statement. The sound of her pleasant chortle caught the captain's attention. He glanced at her and winked. Startled, she smiled as she joined in the fun.

"We hand you over to an American crew at Dulles. You will only be on the ground long enough to go through U.S. Customs. If that experience triggers frustrations, let me assure you that you will be in Dallas, in the great heart of Texas, in time for an additional lunch." He talked to all the passengers, but his gaze kept returning to Toni's smile and the dimple that chased in and out beside the sweet curve of her lips.

Toni laughed with the others, enjoying his witticisms with an easy appreciation. Neither she nor the dark-haired captain noticed the look of steely toughness that settled over the man seated across the aisle.

The captain left and Toni picked up her handbag, intent on renewing her lipstick. She rummaged busily in the cluttered bag. As she found the small cylinder, she realized with a pang that pierced her being that Kurt's picture was not in the purse. Stricken, she felt the blood drain from her face. She looked up in wild disbelief and caught Mark's scrutiny.

He came to his feet instantly. "Antonia, what is wrong? You are as white as a sheet." He bent over her, his voice rough with concern.

"Kurt's picture is gone." Her choked whisper was a sob of despair. "It must have fallen out of my bag last night in the hotel room." Toni did not remember seeing it when she picked up her handbag, but then she had been occupied with another problem. She cursed her carelessness as her velvety eyes accused the man bending over her. If he had behaved as he should have, she would not have tumbled to the floor last night and the photo would still be safe. She glared at him. How could she forgive him? Mark's face grew bleak as he watched her quiver with rage.

"Don't take it so hard, Antonia. It's only a picture."

"It is all I have of him!" she lashed out bitterly. Mark swore softly, then straightened.

"John is to return to London on the next flight back." He made the statement with a quiet contempt. "I'll have him pick the damn thing up since it is so important to you."

Toni stared at him, unable to understand the pointed bitterness of the statement. "Thank you, Mark." Determined not to be put off by the curt manner in which he made the offer, she ventured a tentative smile. "I would be truly grateful. It means a great deal to me."

Mark shrugged dismissively. "Right. I gathered as much. Who is he? Your lover?"

Toni's breath rasped in her throat. "That's something that does not concern you in any way!"

Mark grinned at her and went back to his seat. Toni was left with the definite impression that the impossible man considered it very much his business. Goodness, how she hated him, with his heavy-handed assumptions and interference! She only hoped she would be so busy, once on the job, that he would have to find someone else as a target for his unwanted attention.

She was still seething as she waited to go through U.S. Customs. For the life of her she could not fathom how she would be able to actually work with a team if Mark Anders was a part of it.

"May I carry that for you, Miss Cameron?"

The resonant question pulled her back to her surroundings. Toni looked up into the solemn face of the Concorde's captain. Without another word he reached down and took her case from her hands. He smiled at her scandalized expression and joined her in the slow-moving line.

"Did you not know captains could envy redcaps, Miss Cameron?" His controlled British voice was amused. Toni could not be sure whether his amusement was caused by his own rather bizarre action or by her startled nervousness. She was certain that lordly captains of international flights seldom stooped to seeing their passengers through Customs.

"May I ask how long you are staying in the States?"

"Why, I—I don't honestly know," Toni sputtered in amazement, not completely sure of her ground. "Several months, I expect."

"Excellent." Fine eyes traced the oval of her face, lingering on her expressive mouth. Toni shifted position awkwardly as she realized he was attracted to her. The captain smiled easily as he interpreted her unrest. "I'd like to see you again, if I may."

"What? No one in London anxiously awaiting your return, captain?" Toni parried lightly. It was strange, she thought with quick perception, how nice it was to be noticed by handsome men. She had truly never realized it before Mark tackled her on the oil rig. Giving the devil his due, she had to admit Mark had opened up a whole new world of enticing prospects for her. She knew that the good-looking man who watched her now was serious in his attempt to attract her. In all honesty, she had to admit she was intrigued by her new awareness, and wondered what it would be like to explore. Toni felt a tremor prickle along her nerves.

The captain grinned. "No one at all. And my name is Mike—Mike Lane."

Toni laughed. "Well, since I will be on an oil rig somewhere in the middle of the Gulf of Mexico, I expect I'll be just a little difficult to get in touch with."

"You must be joking!" He was incredulous. "What would a girl like you be doing on an oil rig?"

"Drilling for oil, what else?" Toni glanced toward the Customs inspector and found her gaze trapped by Mark's intent stare. He was standing behind the inspector, frowning at her. An impatient hand swept through his gold brown hair. Toni returned his hard look, turned her back and laughed up at Lane quite deliberately, driven by some impulse she had no wish to define.

The tall Englishman watched her carefully. "Are you with Anders?"

"Oh." Toni flicked a cool glance back at Mark. "I did not realize you knew him."

"I know him. He crosses with me rather regularly. Are you with him?" he persisted.

"No! Well, yes, in a way," Toni temporized. "We

are traveling together and will be working together."

"I hadn't realized he was employed by anyone."
Lane looked thoughtful. "He seems to do a lot of
moving back and forth. I rather thought him to be
some sort of a high-powered mogul."

"He's high-powered enough, come to that!" Toni
tossed the comment off ruefully as she glanced back at
the spot where she had last seen Mark. "But he's no
mogul. He only works for his wage, as you and I do."

The captain shrugged, dismissed the other man and
got back to his main interest. Toni agreed to let him
phone her. She made it clear that U.P.C. was her only
address at present, but he should encounter no difficulty locating her through the corporation's central
office.

Mike stayed with her long enough to heave her bag
onto the moving belt that terminated at the inspector's
stand. A crew member came then, urging him back to
the business involved in transferring his plane into the
hands of the American crew about to take over. Toni
watched him go, amused and flattered by his evident
interest.

As she cleared Customs, John came by and claimed
her attention. He wished her success in her new job,
promised to find her picture for her and left on the
run. His return flight to London was due to leave
momentarily. Toni watched him go, convinced he
would find her keepsake and restore it to her. She
boarded the ongoing flight to Dallas with much on her
mind.

Mark was waiting for her. He bowed her politely
into her seat, his eyes narrowed against her instinctive
wariness. "May I sit here, Miss Cameron?"

"Haven't I heard that this is a free country? You

may sit where you like." *And it wouldn't do me much good to deny you the right* was her unvoiced thought.

"Since we are to be working together, I think it is time we buried the hatchet." Those hazel eyes gleamed with frosty amusement. "So why don't we take some time and see if we can work it out?"

Toni stared at him. She knew that she was about to have a confrontation she had little inclination to handle. She had absolutely no wish to analyze her feeling of antipathy toward him.

"There is nothing to work out." Try as she would, there was still a nervous edge to the words.

Hazel eyes glinted a warning. "That's not how I read you, Antonia. I seem to irritate you just by breathing the same air you do. Why? By all reports, I am a reasonable man to work with, even if I do have a few objectionable quirks to my personality. May I know why you react so strongly toward everything I do?"

Well, you've asked for it, Toni thought grimly. She let fly. "I don't like you. You are high-handed, arrogant and insolent. Your corporation seems to be quite impressed with you. That is their business. I am sure they must have some method of bringing you to account. In that case, you must satisfy their requirements. However, I am unable to see how we will ever be able to work together on a team." His expression did not change. Chagrined at her apparent failure to shake him, Toni decided recklessly she might as well get it all out. "I happen to take exception to your type. You use people. You maneuver them into position, then get them to act as you want them to act. It is a trait I cannot easily ignore. I don't really see how we can ever work together." Toni finished her diatribe breathlessly, trying to hang on to her departing dignity.

Mark's mouth twitched as he considered her. He was politely attentive, his expression impassive, but Toni saw the laughter hidden in his keen glance. She felt her fingers twitch with a sudden desire to slap him. The strength of the impulse shocked her. She bit her lip and jerked her head around, convinced of the necessity to hide her feelings from his too perceptive inspection.

"Fair enough. I asked you; you've told me." His deep voice was crisp, bluntly scornful. "Are you prepared to do your job in spite of your feelings?"

Toni swung around to face a hazel glance gone cold and unreadable. "Certainly. I am well able to set personal considerations aside and get the job done."

Mark looked her over, nodded decisively. "Right. Let's get on with it, then. May I see those notes you made on the monographs? The rig we will use is scheduled to arrive from the North Sea in about three weeks. We need to have the computer operations fairly well-defined by then. I am interested in seeing what you think the parameters of the specific functions are."

Toni searched his bland and uncommunicative countenance warily because of his unexpected change of attitude. Her instinct warned he had something in mind concerning her, although she could not imagine what on earth it might be. She scowled, wishing mightily that she could understand the man.

Mark grinned at her then, as if her indecision were written clearly in the dark blue eyes regarding him so critically. It was that diverting small bad-boy grin of his that invited her to join in the mischief he had in mind. Toni shrugged and surrendered, her instinct to retreat smothered by the unspoken demand in his manner. As long as she kept things in the proper perspective, recognized his skill in persuading others to his way of thinking and did not put any personal connotation on his ability to arouse her awareness of his charisma, things should not get out of hand. She would see to that, she decided confidently.

For the next hour they studied and discussed the exciting possibility of controlling the siting and drilling operations of U.P.C.'s newest project with on-site computer feedback.

Toni found herself caught up in Mark's enthusiasm and knowledge. He might be a corporate officer, but he had more than an ordinary grasp of the concepts he was trying to develop to create an accurate profile of the conditions below the long-drowned floor of the Gulf of Mexico. He was convinced the proposed techniques would allow oil exploration an accuracy of prediction never before attainable by the industry. By the time the softly slurred voice of the American girl in charge of the passenger cabin interrupted them with instructions to prepare to land, she found that she was working with him in a manner that was extremely comfortable. Another testimonial to his skill at handling people, she acknowledged with a wry twist of her mouth. She pushed up the collapsible table they had spread their papers upon, straightened her seat and fastened her seat belt. Mark did the same and slanted a glance of inquiry in her direction.

"That really wasn't so bad, was it? If we put any real effort into it, we just might make a working team."

Toni bristled, caught the laughter in his eyes and

grinned ruefully. "It was almost painless," she agreed smartly as she laughed with him. Mark tilted his head, lowered those incredible lashes of his as he watched her dimple flash and vanish. He expelled his breath in a gentle sigh.

"Too bad we can't be friends, Antonia. You seemed friendly enough with Mike Lane. Will you see him again?"

Toni shot him a furious glance. "I will not discuss that with you!"

"Just be careful, that's all. He moves fast and he's a lady killer." The curt comment was a pointed challenge to her to deny his assessment of Mike Lane. Toni went rigid at the affront.

"If you say one more word, Mark Anders, about anything in any way that does not concern the job at hand, I shall take the next available flight out of this country. Is that clearly understood?"

"You are gorgeous when you are angry." His lazy drawl laughed at her. "Do you know that, Antonia?"

"I do know that I will not tolerate interference in my private life," she replied hotly. Really, she thought stormily, just when there seemed to be some hope they could work together with a little harmony, he had to throw a wrench in the works. Without a doubt he was the most irritating and impossible male it had ever been her misfortune to encounter.

Mark shrugged gracefully and responded with an urbane twist of his firm mouth. "You have stated your case clearly. I just thought it my bounden duty to drop a warning in that innocent ear of yours. I've had the dubious pleasure of watching him operate. He eats little girls like you for breakfast."

Right. And how many of yours has he eaten, Mark

Anders, Toni asked herself as she followed him off the aircraft. Both men had volunteered the information that they knew each other. She wondered idly about their association as she went through the sliding glass doors into the vast and luxurious terminal of the Dallas-Fort Worth Airport.

CHAPTER SEVEN

THE BEST-LOOKING MAN Toni had ever seen in her life greeted Mark with the boisterous familiarity that only an old and intimate friend would be likely to express.

"¡Amigo!" Black eyes, wide spaced, sparkled with real pleasure. The handsome stranger cuffed Mark on the shoulder, grabbed his hand and shook it enthusiastically. "¡Madre de Dios! Glad you're back, old buddy."

He used the Spanish easily, but his English was standard American, Toni noted as he turned the full focus of his attention on her. His assessment took about three seconds.

As tall as Mark, he threw his arm across his shoulders and shook his dark head in delight. "We'll have to send you away more often, amigo mío, if you are going to return with such delightful companions. How did you find her?"

"Antonia, it is with a great deal of reluctance that I bring our resident Don Juan to your attention." There was a steely thread hidden in the humorous words. "Francisco de la Cruz. Frank, this is Dr. Antonia Cameron, known as Toni to most people, myself being one of the exceptions." For some reason, Toni did not like the way he said that. "She is our offshore operations engineer for the gulf project." Somehow, Mark managed to convey a warning in those innocent words.

Toni ignored him as she gave her hand to Frank. He raised it, touched it with firm lips that were as smooth as velvet.

"How roughnecks have changed. I am glad to have lived long enough to witness the improvement." He raised his head, the soft silky curls that clustered on his forehead and touched the collar of his leather flight jacket a perfect foil for his handsome features. He smiled at her, and Toni felt the full power of his charm.

With quick understanding, she sensed he used his natural charm as he used the air he breathed. A man like this was dangerous to any member of the opposite sex, she thought wryly as she took her hand back. He probably had to beat off women on a day-to-day basis.

She smiled at him carefully. "I can be very rough, as in roughneck, I'm afraid."

"Hmm. . . ." He considered the words, his smooth dark face teasing. "I expect the little lady packs a mean punch, Mark."

"I expect she does. How were things on the West Coast?" Mark's long fingers closed around Toni's elbow in a gesture that might have been possessive. They moved through the vast air terminal, Toni sandwiched between the two very handsome males.

"Everything seems to be in order. I just got back an hour ago. Been waiting for your plane to get in, as per instructions."

"Frank is our chief pilot," Mark explained to Toni. "He has charge of the two company jets and the fleet of helicopters we have. He's a fair pilot in spite of the way he looks."

"I see him safe wherever he wishes to go and how does he repay me?" He heaved a mock sigh and shook his head. "Makes fun of me the first chance I have to impress a lovely lady. ¡*Madre de Dios!*" Frank smote his classic forehead with his palm, looking aggrieved.

Mark dealt with the luggage. An airport limousine sped them around the wide flat roads that looped through the vast airport complex. The men talked about what Frank had accomplished on his trip to the West Coast.

Unheeding, Toni stared out of the car window. Never had she seen such a flat expanse of land. It seemed to go on forever, with very little to interrupt the sweep of the eye all the way to the horizon except for man-made obstructions. The land was green; the air was warm. It was certainly a different setting.

The chauffeured automobile pulled up at the steps of a white and glistening executive jet and stopped. Mark escorted Toni up the steps and into the luxurious interior while Frank transferred the luggage.

Seats that closely resembled comfortable lounge chairs were spaced so that conferencing would be easy. There were several small tables scattered among them in groupings. On one table rested a large cardboard box wrapped in clear plastic. The gaily printed lettering proclaimed it to be an electric train, the best in the world. Beside it, her dainty skirts swirling around in arrested grace, was one of the most exquisite dolls Toni had ever seen. About twelve inches tall, it was a perfectly proportioned likeness of a lovely Spanish dancer. Under the elaborately coiffed black hair, her perfect features hidden by an elegant fan, the doll looked out upon the world through seductively veiled lashes that curved extravagantly up from ivory cheeks. Toni exclaimed in delight as she reached out to touch the appealing creation.

"Do you like it?" Frank dropped the luggage into a rack and came to stand close, his fine eyes glowing with soft pleasure. "I bought it for Karen. The train is for her little boy, Clint."

Toni glanced at him swiftly as she detected a note of defensiveness in his husky and very attractive voice. "Yes. It is truly lovely. Any woman would like it."

Frank glanced over his shoulder, caught Mark's expression and took the little dancer from Toni. "Better put this in a safe spot," he murmured. "I brought it all the way from Mexico City. Be a shame to break it this close to home."

"Yeah." Mark's syllable was cold. "Be a shame."

Frank shot him a hard glance that challenged the censure Toni heard in Mark's crisp voice. He stood there, legs widespread, dark eyes flashing, handsome face as set as Mark's. But his hands on the doll remained gentle as if protecting it.

"Damn it to hell, Mark!" he exploded with soft violence. "When the devil are you going to see that I am in love with Karen? You try my patience, *amigo*. What the hell kind of a friend are you anyway? You should know me better than my own mother. How can you act like this?"

Toni listened in astonishment. The two big men faced each other, her presence forgotten. Tension built with the speed of an electrical charge as they stared at one another.

"Frank, you need to be reasonable. It's because I do know you so well that I feel this way." The attractive creases in Mark's lean cheeks deepened as he controlled some undefined emotion. "Karen's twenty-two. There is no way your feeling for her is going to last, and you know it, down in that black hole you call your soul. She has suffered enough. You know—I don't have to tell you. So knock it off and go chase some skirt you can't hurt."

Toni thought Frank would hit him then. His breath hissed into his lungs through flaring nostrils, and his olive skin whitened dramatically around his mouth.

"You presume too much, old friend!" he rasped bitterly. "A man can only put up with so much."

Real regret washed over Mark's tense face. "Hell, Frank, you know I wouldn't let anything in the world interfere with our friendship. And in the name of that friendship and all it has meant to us, just leave it, will you? I know how you think you feel, but I also know Karen doesn't have a chance against you if you really try to turn her on."

"You can't keep her from seeing me, you know."

"I know. And I wouldn't tell her not to even if I could. All I am asking of you, *amigo*, is to give her space and the time to grow up, the time to mature. You know what I'm talking about. You can stampede her into something she will regret all her days just by looking at her, I think. She doesn't need that."

"She needs me. And God knows I need and want her!"

Mark stared at the other man, assessed him carefully. "I can understand what you are saying." He sighed, then seemed to realize Toni was listening with growing unease. "What say we get this turkey in the air and get on to Galveston? Sorry, Antonia. Shouldn't let my good sense run away with my manners. Sit over there, will you, and we'll get airborne."

Suddenly the fight seemed to go out of Frank. He turned on his heel and went through the doorway into the cockpit. He took the little dancer with him, Toni noticed. She wondered about the young woman, Karen, who had a little boy named Clint.

Frank had forced the issue deliberately, she decided as she fastened her seat belt. He must have left the gifts in sight with the intention of letting Mark know who they were for. If he had expected to get a reaction, he had certainly accomplished his aim. She watched the tall U.P.C. official follow the pilot into the cockpit and lower himself into the co-pilot's chair.

Why was Mark so protective of the unknown Karen? Toni was well able to surmise what the woman's reaction would be to any attempt Frank might make to attract her. But why should Karen's probable response to the handsome Mexican American be of such interest to Mark? Toni was sure he had told her mother and grandfather he had no brothers or sisters when he had exchanged pleasantries with them in the cottage.

And why should he allow Frank's actions to jeopardize what was obviously a long-standing and close friendship? Deciding it was none of her business and certainly not her problem, she turned her attention to the land unrolling under the high-flying jet.

Texas unfolded beneath her in huge streaks of green and brown. The landscape was quite different from the ordered and disciplined patchwork of her homeland. And it was certainly big, Toni decided as they finally landed on the wet tarmac at Galveston Island.

Frank was first out of the plane. Carrying the box and the doll, he turned at the bottom of the steps and helped Toni down with a flourish.

"Welcome to Galveston, Toni. May you like the place as much as we are going to like having you." His black eyes flashed and his smile was endearing.

Mark was right. This man had the power to stampede almost any woman into action she might regret, Toni decided abruptly.

"We leave in two hours, Frank." Mark's crisp directive wiped the smile off the pilot's handsome face. The glance he flung at Mark, a step above her on the jet's stairs, was aggressive, determined.

"Okay, Mark, I'll be here. The crew can refuel. I'm going to see Karen."

Mark watched him stride away. His muttered curse grated on Toni's ears, and she turned her head to look at him. His face was a study of regret and suppressed anger. His hazel eyes glinted, and the strong lines of his face were set in an implacable mold that boded little good for his friend.

But Frank did not seem to hold him in awe, Toni realized. Whatever the conflict was between the two men, perhaps they knew and understood each other well enough to remain friends even though they were in violent disagreement. Would they be able to maintain their relationship, she wondered.

Mark turned away, a case in each hand, and headed for the chain-linked barrier that separated the field from the buildings of Scholes Field. Toni was left to follow. Frank shouted across the intervening distance to say he would see her again. Toni waved. Mark narrowed those gold-flecked hazel eyes of his and raked her with a cold glance.

Although the sun was obscured, the air around her was blissfully warm, full of strange and exotic odors that caused her to respond with delight. Mark's boots rang on the pavement as Toni tried to keep up with him. She realized he was annoyed, but she was too aware of her new environment to be bothered about it.

Even above the sounds of the airport, she could hear the rustle of the palm fans as they whispered against each other in the balmy air high above the terminal buildings. She had never seen palms so tall before.

Toni sighed in contentment. She had certainly made the right decision. Her stay in the Gulf of Mexico was going to be pretty wonderful, it seemed. Even if she had to put up with Mark Anders's arrogance, there was more than a chance she was going to enjoy herself very much from the looks of things.

"Hey, turkey! Over here."

Mark paused in midstride. A broad-shouldered, bronzed giant was bearing down on them. His silk shirt was unbuttoned to his midriff, incongruous in combination with the fleece-lined jacket he wore. Tawny cord slacks hugged the contours of his lean torso and were tucked carelessly into the tops of tall cowboy boots. A cowboy hat sat well back on his tumbled bronze curls. Toni noticed a thick gold chain winking at her from the mat of bronze hair revealed in the V of his shirt. She grinned in spite of herself.

Here was a golden male god if she had ever seen one. She wondered if he took himself seriously. He seized Mark's hand and thumped his back with energy, but his eyes did not wander as he examined Toni's well-shaped person with appreciative enthusiasm.

"Whoo-ee, cousin. You've done yourself proud this time." He doffed his hat solemnly and swept it in a wide and gallant arc as he captured Toni's hand in an enormous grip that was curiously gentle. "Where did you find this little lady, Mark? And how did you get her to come to this poor benighted neck of the world with you?"

"Antonia, this is my cousin and drilling super, Greg

Sims. You'll be seeing a lot of him. He takes a little getting used to, but he is not really as impossible as he sounds. He has had a very lax upbringing and hasn't a manner in the world. But he can supervise a drilling crew, thank God. There was a time when it was feared his only talent was chasing girls."

Toni heard the warning under the careless words. If Greg did he ignored it without any trouble. "Thanks, cuz." His eyes twinkled mischievously. "As long as you realize my talents are many and classify them in order of importance. This lovely little lady could bring out the best in me." His eyes roved again. His approval of what he saw just managed to stay on the proper side of courtesy. He grinned at her. "Surely to goodness, Miss Antonia, I ain't never seen your like in these parts before."

Mark scowled, pushed his hair back impatiently, growling deep in his throat. Greg winked at her. Toni flushed, repressed a giggle at his outrageous comments and took her hand back for the second time that day.

"Careful, Greg." Mark's dry warning cut across her impulse to respond to the breezy flippancy. "The lady is Doctor Cameron. She just happens to be your new boss."

"M'gawd! Not our new offshore operations man!" Greg smote his handsome forehead, groaned dramatically. "Life is getting damned unfair—begging your pardon, ma'am."

Toni's dimple flashed. She could not help her response to the man's easy charm. What on earth had she let herself in for? Mark Anders was quite enough to have to deal with. How could she be expected to work with two of the impossible creatures?

"Just as long as you remember you are a married

man, Greg. Antonia is here mostly because she has other attributes. Her physical attractions are duly noted, but she will be in charge of the exploration team. And I can assure you her very obvious charms have nothing at all to do with the fact that she is occupying the position." Toni listened to the calm statement with a healthy sense of outrage.

So Greg Sims was married! How did that give Mark the right to talk about her as if she were not there? She opened her mouth to protest, but saw the stricken look on Greg's face, her comment arrested by his very evident unhappiness.

"Yeah, Mark," he drawled, suddenly serious. "I need to talk to you about Ginny Lee as soon as you have a minute. She says she is going to divorce me."

"I'm not surprised" was Mark's caustic response as he stopped beside a long white Jaguar. "You've been in trouble with that one from day one." He opened the door for Toni and put her in, attention riveted on his tall cousin. "Do you both a lot of good if you applied the flat of your hand to that good-looking seat of hers and enforced some of your natural rights."

Sims shouted with laughter. "Damn it to hell, Mark. You know what would happen if I got firm with Virginia Lee. You want to get me killed?"

"You need to try it once."

"Yeah." Greg's comment was rueful. "And have her daddy down on me like a ton of bricks—never mind the scarring I'd get from his daughter. There has to be a better solution." Mark shut the door, and the two men moved toward the trunk, their voices blurred to a murmur.

Well, Toni thought. So Greg Sims was in need of advice from his cousin. Mark's scathing counsel might be one way to handle the situation, she acknowledged. Was Mark really capable of physical violence? He seemed determined enough when he wanted his own way. Somehow she could not see him raising his hand to a woman, though. His charm was too easy, too practiced. He probably used it to get whatever he wanted. It was very likely few women could resist it and were happy to accede to his slightest whim, she thought uncharitably. He did possess a magnetism hard to deny.

Seated there, her treacherous body tingled with the vivid recollection of her own reaction when she came into contact with that magnetism. Toni shuddered and glanced quickly over her shoulder, driven by the need to conceal reactions of this kind from Mark. But Mark was paying no attention to her. The men had their tawny heads together as they engaged in a low conversation at the rear of the car. She bit her lip, listening intently to the pleasant harmony of their deep voices in an effort to forget the feel of Mark's strength against her, his delicately exploring hands touching her.

It would be a real relief to get to work and to have her mind occupied so that it did not run around in useless uncontrollable fantasies, she thought crossly. Toni sighed, hoping for the best.

Mark opened the trunk of the Jag, and the bags he carried fell in with decisive thuds. The lid snicked firmly down as the men continued to talk. Toni glimpsed them in the side mirror. They were curiously alike, she decided wryly. Each had a broad-shouldered, muscular frame well over six feet. Leanly built, athletic, they epitomized the ideal male structure. Both had that golden brown hair, Mark being the darker of the two. And of course Mark's discerning hazel eyes differed markedly from Greg's bold topaz ones. But the family resemblance was certainly strong. Even their voices were somewhat similar, Mark's in a lower huskier register. Greg spoke with a decided Southern drawl that his cousin did not share. Mark's voice had a lazy teasing quality laced with a decisive intonation that pleased her ear, Toni admitted to herself. Wild horses could not have dragged the admission out in the open.

As Mark opened the driver's door and slid into the seat beside her, he read her uncertain expression with his usual ease and looked thoughtful a moment; then he grinned at her.

"Are you having second thoughts about working with the two of us, Antonia?" He chuckled at her exclamation of protest. How could he know what she was thinking all the time, Toni wondered wrathfully.

"I can assure you that Greg, at least, is quite harmless, for all his show. He is well and truly married to Ginny Lee. Unfortunately Virginia has been overindulged all her life and tends to have tantrums that are hard to control." His courteous contempt left no doubt in Toni's mind that he personally would not have had the same trouble had he been in his cousin's shoes. "Their fights are legendary, but they always kiss and make up as they undoubtedly will this time, as well."

Toni looked at him with what she hoped could be taken as polite interest. She felt an urge to remind him that his family's problems were of no concern to her, but pushed the impulse away and was conscious of a feeling of nobility. After all, she did owe it to the corporation to try to get along with the man. Mark watched her closely, an earnestness lurking deep down in those hazel eyes.

"I may not be so harmless." The husky murmur touched her, caused her senses to leap. Toni sat up in regal exasperation. Mark laughed. "You are beginning to find your feet, aren't you, Antonia?" He reached down to flick on the ignition, and the powerful car fired. Toni caught the tinge of sarcasm in his tone.

"What do you mean?" she ventured cautiously.

"You do realize, don't you, that I have watched you rather closely in the past few days." He reversed the car and steered expertly into the traffic of the street. "In that time," his mocking challenge continued, "I have seen you meet three men. Not one of them knew what hit him. Be careful, Antonia."

Toni was aghast. "You must be joking! I am quite an ordinary person and I am not given to flirtation with every man who crosses my path." She glared at him, genuinely distressed.

He glanced at her, the steely glint in his regard softening as he examined her stormy rejection of his charge. "Hmm. It is possible you don't know how you affect men, I suppose. In that case you are going to need to use a little discretion, Antonia Cameron. If you don't, I'll find myself fighting all the guys in the crew, trying to keep you out of trouble."

Toni withered him with a look of disdain, and decided the best thing to do was just to ignore him when he was baiting her. She had begun to suspect he enjoyed getting a rise out of her. So she pressed her lips together in a manner that failed miserably to express her displeasure. He leaned forward, inspected her try at contemptuous indifference and grinned.

"Let's get you settled before I manage to fall completely from grace, shall we? You will have to forgive me, Antonia. I cannot seem to resist the opportunity

to tease you.'' The fast-moving car was cruising down
a wide avenue whose center division was planted with a
variety of trees Toni had never seen before. These
made a lacy screen over the wet street, branches etched
against the gray, rain-heavy sky. Mark pulled up to a
stoplight and turned his head to study her quite seriously. "You can be teased so nicely, you know. Your
eyes turn navy blue, and you blush.''

Toni was speechless. She jerked her head around
and stared out the side window. Navy blue eyes indeed!

She had not recovered her coolness when Mark
swung the sleek Jaguar to the curb side in front of a
tall old house. He came around the side of the car to
hand her out, laughter barely suppressed as he met her
scowl. "Let's go meet Ma Ruddy. She takes care of
this place for U.P.C.''

Toni held herself proudly erect and marched beside
him through the gate and down the walk that led to the
attractive dwelling. Set far back in its surrounding
grounds, the two-storied house was encircled with and
shaded by ancient trees. It was painted a pale sandy-
orange color that seemed just right with the long windows and lacework of the verandas circling both the
upper and lower stories. Those balconies were loaded
with potted plants, trailing vines and wicker furniture
with plump gay cushions. The house itself stood high
on a six-foot foundation, in prim isolation from the
velvety green of the well-clipped lawns. Wide steps led
up from the walk to the broad first-floor veranda.

As they mounted the steps, the tall double doors
were flung open. Mark reached the porch entrance, to
be engulfed in a bear hug by a billowy woman of Juno-
esque proportions.

"Mark, honey! I'm that glad to see your ugly mug! Did you break an arm or something? How come you never wrote?"

Mark returned the enthusiastic embrace and planted a resounding kiss on the woman's flushed and pretty cheek. "Had no time, ma." He grinned cheerfully, winking at her. "I met Antonia and spent all my spare time trying to get her to come with me. She's stubborn. It took all my expertise just to convince her."

And with that outrageous statement Mark moved prudently behind the vast framework of the house-keeper. Ma Ruddy shook her head sympathetically as she observed Toni's volatile displeasure, which she was doing her best to keep bottled up. She smiled at the younger woman as a warm welcome danced in her eyes.

"Mark has been giving you a hard time, has he, miss? Don't pay him no never mind. He's mostly harmless." *Harmless! He's the most dangerous man I've ever met!* The errant thought struck Toni as she returned the woman's smile.

"My, what a pretty girl you are!" Mrs. Ruddy exclaimed. "Mind your manners, Mark. Introduce us. Where did you find her?"

"I found her in the middle of the North Sea. I just looked around one day and there she was." His expression complacent, he surveyed Toni with the satisfaction of a youngster who has just found his favorite toy under the Christmas tree. "This is Dr. Antonia Cameron, ma. She is a qualified geologist, a paleontologist and a successful wildcatter. She will be heading up our offshore operations on that next job." He quirked a lazy eyebrow at Toni. She returned his look with one of cool exasperation and decided she

really would have to have a serious talk with him—
make him agree to stop his teasing. Everything he said
seemed to imply an intimacy between them. It was
probably just his way, but he certainly needed to be
aware of the consequences of such careless banter.

Ma Ruddy gave her a glowing smile that was a testimonial to just what Toni feared. There was little doubt
the huge woman thought some sort of intimate relationship had been established, a relationship she gave
a strong impression of approving. Not that Mark
seemed to notice. He slipped an affectionate arm
around the buxom woman.

"Ma Ruddy was the terror of my misspent child-
hood, the horror of my growing years. It's mainly due
to her strenuous efforts that I survived infancy, and it
says a great deal for her strength of character that she
is still around." That proud head of his bent for an instant, his bronzed cheek lowered and pressed against
ma's salt-and-pepper thatch. A fleeting vulnerability
passed over the man's strong features.

"If you've known this one since he was a youngster,
you have my condolences, Mrs. Ruddy," Toni remarked brightly. "You must have been kindness itself
not to have strangled him in his crib!"

The older woman laughed heartily. "I admit many's
the time I was tempted. Yes, lawd, many's the time!"
She turned to cast a laughing challenge at Mark.
"What do you mean you found her in the middle of
the North Sea? What were you doing in the North Sea?
And how did you get lucky enough to find such a nice
girl there? More important, how did you get such a
sensible-looking girl to agree to come to this neck of
the woods?"

"I told her a lot of lies and promised her you would

be here to protect her if she should ever need protection," Mark answered promptly. "Don't you go telling her the truth, either, do you hear? I'm having enough trouble keeping her now I've found her."

"Uh-huh! Well, it kinda seems as if you might just have a little competition in that direction, Mark, m'boy," ma remarked cryptically. She smiled sweetly at him, then turned to Toni.

"Just you come with me, Miss Cameron. I have something for you in here."

She thrust one of the double doors open with a powerful arm and waved Toni into a charming entry hall. It was round and reached to a domed ceiling. Light struck through the dome and illumined the graceful stairway that curved upward to split at a wide landing, which served the doors opening onto the balcony that circled the rotunda. The stairs were carpeted, as was the gracious entrance.

Toni came through the door and stood stock-still. The hall was a breathtaking bower of roses—red roses that gleamed in the muted light pouring down upon them, the heady scent distinctive in the way no other fragrance is. They encircled the room, occupied and hid the surfaces of the tables and sat in proud beauty in great flared pots on the first three steps of the stairway.

Bemused, Toni turned to the older woman, only dimly aware of Mark's deeply muttered sound of scorn. "They are absolutely super," she murmured smiling. "I've never seen anything like this. Where are they from...?" Even as she asked the question, she glimpsed Mark's sarcastic expression. Puzzled, she stared a moment, then intuitively realized before Mrs. Ruddy spoke that the flowers could only have one source: Hussein!

"They're for you, Miss Cameron. Seems some Arab sheik has bought out every red rose in Texas and sent it here. Least that's what the delivery man said, the last load he delivered. He's had a busy day," she commented dryly. "Here's a card. Came in the first load this morning. There have been several loads since."

Toni took the heavily embossed fold of paper from Ma Ruddy's fingers, acutely aware of Mark's sardonic grin, of the powerful fragrance of the massed roses, of the sudden muted ring of the telephone. She hung on to her calm with a desperate effort, but then remembered Mark's caustic remark about the three men she had met and could not help her blush. Mark watched her with narrowed eyes, the lights in them hidden by those ridiculous lashes of his.

Hussein had neatly quoted Keats's comment on beauty, to which he had added a line of his own.

> Beauty is truth; truth beauty,—that is all
> Ye know on earth, and all ye need to know—
> Except you think of me, O Beauty mine.

It was signed "Hussein." Toni lifted her gaze to Mark's face, the hazel glint in his eyes doing little to mask the disdain he so obviously felt. Toni's color mounted, but she was distracted by the man who stuck his head around the frame of a door across the hall.

Tall and thin and homely, he stared at her thoughtfully a moment. "You must be Antonia Cameron," he challenged her. "Phone call for you here. Overseas call."

Toni's first thought was for her mother and grandfather, so she hurried into the den at the man's gesture. The phone stood on a big littered desk in a pleasant, book-lined room. Toni picked up the instrument, conscious of the door closing behind her. She spoke into it, then started in disbelief when a laughing male voice sang down the wire.

"Hussein!"

"Yes, Antonia Cameron. Hussein!" he mocked her. "Did you get my message?"

"Hussein, I have never seen anything so madly extravagant! All those roses, and so beautiful, too—"

He laughed again, interrupting her. "I just wished to assure myself you would be unable to forget me, lovely lady. If one rose tells of love, what, then, does the voice of a thousand say, hmm? Tell me that, lovely Antonia."

His deliberately seductive huskiness lost no power as it traveled across the miles. And it brought to her mind the warm glow she had last seen in his face as he left her. She had not believed Mark when he accused her of attracting Hussein. Worriedly she faced the fact now. There was no sane way to deny the Arabian prince's awakened interest, she realized nervously. What could be done to discourage it?

Toni didn't know but she tried. She took him to task for his extravagance, pointed out it bordered upon bad taste as gently as she could and demanded he restrain himself. He sighed in mock despair, laughed at her discomfort, told her to expect him soon and rang off before she could marshal her forces.

CHAPTER EIGHT

TONI, LEFT WITH THE UNRESPONSIVE TELEPHONE in her hand, stared at it in disbelief.

"Why, you arrogant overbearing—" She heard a sound behind her and slammed the receiver down as she wheeled around, ready to do battle.

"Hussein, I assume you mean?" Mark's mocking hazel eyes were more than a little grim.

Her anger rose. Toni had reached her tolerance level for high-handed males stalking through her life. "How dare you listen to private phone calls!" she accused haughtily. "My personal life is my own and I will not submit to any interference."

Mark's laugh was teasing. "You're sure a pretty sight when you're angry, Antonia. What was he doing, checking up to see if you were suitably impressed by his largess? Quite a gesture, I think." Toni tossed her head high and marched past him. "The call was from Bahrain, eh?" Mark asked nastily. "Do you realize what time of day it is there?"

The phone rang abruptly and cut across his caustic remark. Two strides and he reached it, barking curtly into the mouthpiece. Toni seized the opportunity and escaped back into the passage, her temper just barely under control. He was showing a decided inclination to boss her around, to issue orders as though he had some right to do so.

Was she strong enough to resist his assault on her? It was a question she really must straighten out in her own mind and then begin to deal with. Somehow she had the feeling she was losing control of her own destiny, and she didn't like it—not one little bit.

Ma Ruddy took one look at her stormy expression and hurried her up the stairway with the light-footed grace so often present in the heavy person. Pa, she said, had gone out to retrieve Toni's bags and would bring them to her room. Pa, Toni assumed, was the tall homely man who had called her to the phone. Ma's husband, no doubt.

Ma turned to the right and followed the stairway. Pushing open one of the louvered doors off the landing, she ushered Toni into a lovely bedroom. High-ceilinged, with tall windows draped in satin, the room was done in shades of peach and gold. The bed was enormous, covered with a quilt of the same material as the draperies. The room was well and comfortably furnished. A door opened onto the second-story veranda. There were screens on all the windows and the door. Ma opened another door, showed her a dressing room with vast closets and the adjoining bath.

"Quite often Mark has VIPs staying here," ma volunteered, as if this were his house alone and not the property of U.P.C. "There's no one here just now, though—give us a nice chance to get acquainted."

"And I have serious doubts about that being a good idea," Mark remarked wryly from the doorway. He leaned against the doorjamb and surveyed his housekeeper sternly. "Just you be careful, ma. You'll keep all my family skeletons in the closet, if you know which side your bread is buttered on."

"Oh-ho," she scoffed, obviously unimpressed by

his threat. "Trying to keep this innocent child in ignorance, are you?" She grinned at him good-naturedly, then winked at Toni. "Looking at her, I imagine you are going to find it a bit harder than you usually do to pull the wool over a woman's eyes."

Amen, Toni agreed silently. At least, she hoped ma would prove to be right. Mark straightened and came toward her. Toni's deceitful heart flipped as his hands descended and touched her shoulders.

"This room do for you, Antonia?" She nodded, tried to wrench away. He held her easily, his eyes intent. "Right. I have to go. I'll leave word with Greg to bring your car around and show you the setup. You know how to get things rolling. Do you think you will be able to manage without me?"

"Will you be gone long?" Toni could not have stopped the question to save her life. Mark watched her mobile face with interest.

"I am not sure, Antonia. Do you think you will miss me?"

"I cannot see why I should," she answered pertly. She could feel the heat of him, smell the male fragrance of him. It would be easy to be overwhelmed by his sheer masculinity, easy to give way to the strange demand his closeness aroused in her traitorous body. That demand seemed to have a life of its own; it was getting more difficult to control. But she must find a way to rid herself of his powerful influence over her.

Mark seemed to get a great deal of satisfaction from his scrutiny. Color flared into her cheeks and her eyes darkened. Ma watched quietly, her head on one side, her gaze speculative.

Toni stared up at Mark with an aloof dignity as long as she could. Coolly he returned her look, and at last she could bear it no longer. She dropped silky lashes to the curves of her cheeks, needing to shut out his probing study into the depths of her. She did not know what he was searching for, but she was singularly unwilling for him to find it.

She tried to wrench away and his hands tightened. He chuckled then and closed in on her. His long finger touched her lips. Toni stood as still as a stone. She completely forgot ma was in the room. She was aware only of the man who towered over her.

"I won't be gone long—just to the Coast for a few days. Miss me, Antonia." He issued the command with a husky rasp, a hand tilting her face upward. Unable to move, she had the stunned impression that he was going to kiss her.

He did not. Smiling a crooked gentle smile, he touched the dimple at the corner of her mouth, and then he was gone with lithe suddenness. Ma cleared her throat and moved to unpack Toni's case without any comment whatsoever.

Jet lag caught up with Toni. Almost immediately she slept deeply and dreamlessly, far into the next morning. The house was quiet as she showered and dressed in blue jeans quite a bit the worse for wear. She tucked a red plaid shirt into her jeans and gave her hair a quick brush, not bothering with makeup, eager to get outside into the bright day.

Greg came through the heavy front door as she danced down the curve of the staircase, her booted feet light on the thick carpet. He pushed back the big brimmed hat he wore and ran brown fingers through already disheveled curls, his cheeky grin disarming.

"Doctor Antonia Cameron," he intoned solemnly, "you are a sight for sore eyes." His big hands fell on her slender shoulders as she reached the bottom of the stairs, and he cast a critical eye down her jeans-clad length. "If you don't mind my sayin' so, lady, on you the end certainly justifies the jeans."

Toni laughed up at him. She could not help herself. Never had she met such an ingenuously outrageous man. "You cut that out, Greg Sims. And call me Toni. Most everyone else does." She did not stop to question why she had never insisted Mark Anders do the same.

Ma's caustic tone from the doorway commanded his instant attention. "Mark will have a fit if you manage to insult Miss Cameron first shot out of the box. I s'pose you ain't et yet and are expectin' me to stuff your 'normous appetite?"

"You got it, ma." He kept a lazy but compelling arm across Toni's shoulders as he guided her adroitly past the frowning housekeeper. He planted a resounding kiss on ma's cheek as he passed. "You know I am absolutely unable to resist anything you put on the table. What's for breakfast?"

The room in which Toni found herself was airy and delightful, the white-painted rattan furnishings perfect for their setting. Long windows gathered in the bright winter sun. Green plants were artistically displayed in urns, baskets and pots. The room was full of tantalizing scents. Toni's taste buds responded with a rush. Greg seated her, pulled out a chair and tossed his wide-brimmed hat on the breakfront against the wall.

Ma uttered a sound of disgust and picked it up. "Boy, ain't you ever goin' to learn any manners?"

"Reckon not, ma. That's what Ginny Lee says." In spite of his laugh, Toni glanced at him curiously. There seemed to be a lingering note of sadness in the offhanded comment. Ma caught it, as well.

"That one!" she snorted in obvious contempt. "She ain't got the good sense God gave a goose."

With that rather undignified psychological assessment of the absent Ginny Lee, she swept out of the room. Greg laughed and offered Toni freshly squeezed orange juice from a frosty crystal pitcher. It tasted wonderful. Ma returned with a huge platter loaded with fluffy scrambled eggs, bacon and stacks of enormous, very beautifully browned pancakes. They bore little resemblance to the dainty crepes Toni was accustomed to. She watched in awe as Greg consigned several to the warmed plate ma put before him. He buttered them religiously, then poured a thick syrup over the top. Toni felt her nostrils twitch as the aroma rose from the steaming mass then stared at him incredulously as he shoveled several strips of bacon onto his plate.

"Don't tell me you been deprived of this kind of soul food, Toni."

"Pancakes and that delicious-smelling syrup I am able to understand," she declared quizzically. "But bacon? Ye gods."

"Little lady, pancakes like ma's, with bacon to go along, is fit ambrosia for the gods. Try it. You can take my word as a gentleman and a scholar of all things gastronomical that you will like it."

"Don't take his word for nothing, Miss Cameron," ma warned crisply as she came in with a steaming glass pot of delicious-smelling coffee. "He don't have a bad bone in his body, but he sure ain't reliable sometimes—specially when he's showin' off to someone as purty as you."

"Now, ma, you are going to give this little lady a completely wrong impression of me." Greg's aggrieved protest did not interfere too much with his devouring of the food on his plate. Ma grinned at him fondly.

"I expect Miss Cameron is able to form her own opinions. So mind your manners and behave yourself if you want to impress her."

Toni laughed at the two of them. "I think you had better call me Toni, too," she said to ma as she tackled the food on her plate. "What is this lovely syrup?"

"Maple syrup—the real thing. Mark has it sent down from Vermont each spring."

"I've never tasted anything so delicious. I usually use a little lemon and sugar on pancakes. This is really good!"

"Native North American delicacy," Greg intoned seriously. "A well-kept secret heritage that our ancestors stole from the original inhabitants of this continent, the Indians."

Toni finished her breakfast and complimented the cook.

"Go 'long with you, child. Just ordinary food."

"Yes, well—" Toni pushed back her chair and groaned as she rose "—very many breakfasts of that order and I will begin to resemble an ordinary barrel."

Greg laughed at her and rushed her from the house, his long fingers hooking a set of keys from a pocket of his close-fitting pants. Mark had left definite instructions concerning her keeping, he announced solemnly. And his first duty was to deliver her car and instruct her in its care and use.

A sparkling bright red convertible sat at the curb. It was new, Greg informed her, just one of her bonuses for signing on the team Mark had assembled. He refused to drive.

Toni shrugged a little grimly, her chin at a determined angle. "Be it on your own head," and she slid into the driver's seat. "I'm not only a woman driver, I'm British, as well! Your chances of survival aren't too great."

Greg Sims proved to be an able and patient teacher. Toni spent a profitable two hours learning to keep to the other side of the roadway and conquering the idiosyncrasies of the spirited little red car. It was an automatic, so she was spared the necessity of learning to operate the gears right-handed.

She finally earned her teacher's full approval, and he bought her a hamburger as a reward for a job well done. Toni liked the man and his laughing approach to life. He had a way with words, twisting them into delightful malapropisms in a tongue-in-cheek manner Toni found entirely engaging.

Lesson and snack over with, he took her to corporation headquarters, a huge warehouse facing a vast materials yard. Backed against the Galveston Ship Channel, the ground floor and upper stories of the building were packed with the supplies needed for oil exploration.

Bunkhouses ranged down one side of the hollow goods yard. These were supplied for the men who were far from their homes. Recreation facilities, the cafeteria and a cinema were included in the bunkhouse block, Greg told her. A vast garage and workshop formed the other arm of the square. Vehicles of all sizes, shapes and functions were parked in neat precision along that side.

The center of the square contained an enormous landing pad over which a giant helicopter crouched. Toni and Greg ducked through its shadow. The man dropping down the stairs behind the door Greg thrust open had a glimpse of them both, and had a difficult time delivering the message he carried.

"Hi, Greg." He skidded to a stop, his eyes glued to Toni.

"Yeah." Greg stared at him thoughtfully, waited a moment, then frowned. "Don't pay any attention to this clown, Toni. He's just some dumb working stiff Mark picked up and uses as a geophysicist. His mother named him Johnson Tait Johnson for some reason. We generally call him Sandy—short for sandhog. Has some sort of string of letters behind his name—like Ph.D."

Toni dissolved into laughter and thrust out her hand. "I assume, from the way this man talks, that he must be a friend of yours. I'm Toni Cameron."

"Oh, our new offshore ops off." Her hand disappeared into a paw the size of a small ham. "Very pleased to meet you, Dr. Cameron. You should be more careful about the company you keep, however. One must safeguard one's reputation. It becomes tarnished so easily!" He glared at Greg in mock horror. "Old Glory Hole here is our resident tarnisher." His handshake was pleasantly friendly.

"Some men are just plain unfortunate in those they must call friends" was Greg's aggrieved retort. "With my friends, I surely don't need any enemies."

Sandy laughed and handed him a computer readout. "Mark wants you on the Coast. Right now, from the tone of this."

Greg sobered immediately as he scanned it quickly. "Yeah. I'd better get on my way. I was just about to take Dr. Cameron up and introduce her to that disreputable bunch she is destined to work with. Think you can manage?"

Sandy withered him with a glance. "Get on about your business, buddy. Dr. Cameron has come into safe hands." He tucked Toni's hand into the curve of his elbow and headed back up the stairs a good deal more decorously than he had descended them.

The corporate offices occupied the whole top floor of the mammoth building. The place was modern, airy and comfortable, with wide vistas spreading out from walls that were mostly glass. And those offices were humming with activity. Men and women were deep into particular operations, busy with computers, office machines and the hundreds of tasks any successful drilling project generates. The whole space was carpeted and divided by attractive, sound-deadening partitions through which ran a wide center aisle. Glassed backlit cupboards along the high walls contained rare specimens, art objects, old maps and manuscripts dealing with geology, geography and other aspects of the oil industry. Excellent prints and paintings formed an integral part of the pleasing area.

Sandy guided Toni down the wide passage to the end and led her into a section where a sweet-faced girl presided at a large desk. Across the shoulder-high partition behind her, Toni caught a glimpse of an enormous pair of desks. One was stacked with work, the other clear.

The girl glanced up as Sandy and Toni entered and smiling, rose immediately.

"Presenting Dr. Toni Cameron," Sandy said with a sweep of his arm.

The young woman held out both hands in a welcoming gesture. "I am Karen Prescott, Mark's executive secretary, his personal assistant—whatever. Let me show you around."

Karen led the way to the area containing the two desks. Johnson tagged along, his craggy face alight with benevolent interest.

"Mark wants you to work here, if you don't mind. He likes to have instant communication when the project is in the early stages. If you find you need more space or more privacy in order to think in this madhouse, just ask for a regular office."

The view was absolutely spectacular. Toni moved to the ninety-degree angle of the two glass walls and gazed out over the city. A large sheet of water, either a lake or a bayou, lay off to the left, and beyond it the sun glinted off the control tower of the airport. The beach stretched for miles, with the gray blue of the Gulf of Mexico filling the horizon.

Toni sighed and turned back to the alert girl beside her. "I shan't be responsible for my ability to concentrate in such absolutely super surroundings, you know. I usually work in a less than adequate superintendent's shack on a rig, and even on land most of my working assignments have been carried out in places closely resembling the same kind of quarters. Those shacks are called dog houses because the name fits, I'm afraid."

"Yeah, Mark treats us pretty well when we're doing our head work." Sandy Johnson's drawl was respectfully serious, though his eyes twinkled with good fellowship. "There's a meeting in the conference room in about an hour. Karen can show you around, let you meet the crews already here and then we'll get down to some real work, if that's okay with you."

"Perfectly, Mr. Johnson."

"Call me Sandy." He blinked, recovered from the effect of her smile and vanished.

Karen laughed and took Toni on a guided tour of the facility. The equipment was completely modern, even including a microwave guidance system for use by the big helicopter's pilots when the gulf was shrouded in fog or storm.

"The pilot can take the copter out in weather it is impossible to see through," Karen explained briefly. "It insures the crews can be changed on schedule in almost any kind of weather." She looked extremely thoughtful, and Toni wondered if this ability of a pilot to move in bad weather affected her in some way.

Then she remembered the sharp confrontation Mark had forced on Frank de la Cruz on the trip down from Dallas.

"Who is your chief pilot?" She could not help the question. Frank had interested her, his passionate plea for the right to see the girl called Karen vivid in Toni's mind.

"He's Frank de la Cruz," Karen said briefly, a slight color touching her cheeks, giving Toni her answer. "He's very good and has been with the company a long time, so you need not worry about entrusting yourself to him." Her tone confirmed that she was the Karen that Mark and Frank had discussed on the way to Galveston.

Toni smiled at the other woman, a little surprised at the defensiveness in her voice. So she was involved with the handsome pilot.

"I'm sure he must be an expert to be able to work for Mark Anders," she murmured a little caustically.

Karen grinned. "You've noticed." She pushed open the doorway leading off the wide central corridor at its far end and into the only real room on the floor. "Mark is a bear for work, and he's good. He demands

a high standard from the people he hires and gets it,"
she conceded. "But he's fair and he does appreciate
everyone's efforts. This is the conference room."

Toni had a quick vision of Frank's angry face and
wonder about his involvement with the girl walking so
gracefully ahead of her. Mark had not seemed very
reasonable toward that man. It was really none of her
business, however. She certainly could not see herself
in the position of questioning Karen's assessment of
her outspoken boss. But she did wonder a little at the
forthright demand he had made on Frank to back off
and let the girl find her feet. Karen seemed very poised
to her and not in the least in need of the aggressive protection Mark gave the impression of being willing to
provide.

Karen looked around the conference room, her eyes
shadowed by some unexpressed thought.

"You haven't known Mark very long, have you?
He's a marvelous person," she went on at Toni's head-
shake. "He always has time for anyone he cares
about—and he cares about everyone who works for
him. It's very unusual in these days of big corpora-
tions, I think." She smiled quickly, a shy confiding expression that twisted Toni's heart. "Are you ready to
meet the gang you will be working with?"

Toni laughed at her teasing tone, and realized she
felt more at home with herself and her world than she
had for years.

"I think so," she offered.

"Have a seat and I'll get them in here." As Toni
relaxed into one of the comfortably upholstered arm-
chairs halfway down the long conference table, Karen
touched a button. A muted clamor demanded instant
attention on the other side of the doors. Predominant-

ly men and their secretaries drifted in, smiled at Toni and seated themselves. Karen introduced her and left them.

Toni acknowledged each employee, learned his place on the exploration team and got down to work. They were ready for her. Facts, figures and projections flowed around the table in the order called for. In an hour Toni had the respect of the team, and before the end of the day she was an integral part of it.

It was evening when she drove back to the house where she was to live. She had no trouble at all finding it, for which she was duly grateful. Pa showed her the old stables at the back of the house that was to be the garage for the little red car. Toni parked it and went in for her evening meal, pleasantly tired. Afterward she took a long walk along the deserted beach. The air was warm, almost balmy—unusual for this time of the year, pa assured her in his dry way when she got back to the house.

"Be like this for a little while, then one o' them blue northers will come straight down and freeze the hell out o' us." He slanted a sober quizzical glance at her, the corners of his mouth twitching. "Nothing certain about Texas weather except it ain't certain."

"That's better than having it all bad." Toni matched his soberness. "And I have been in places where it is all bad, unfortunately."

The roses Hussein had filled the front of the house with were still there, given fresh water by ma. Toni talked it over with the housekeeper and made arrangements to have them delivered to the two hospitals in town. Toni found she was embarrassed more than anything else by the Arabian prince's extravagant gesture, and hoped he would not repeat the effort.

The flowers did scent the air nicely, though, she thought as she climbed the gracefully rising stairs on her way to her bedroom. She had refused ma's offer of television, accepted a cup of her delicious coffee and opted for early bed. She found her mind casting back over the day and the events she had experienced.

Karen Prescott, her face flushed as she spoke of Frank de la Cruz, was a memory Toni stopped to consider as she vigorously brushed her hair after her shower. Surely Mark had no right to interfere between those two as he was doing. She again decided it was none of her business and put the thought of Karen Prescott and Mark out of her mind completely, to fall into blissful sleep with an almost tropical breeze whispering through her wide-open windows.

Saturday, she went shopping at a boutique ma directed her to and bought a couple of charming dresses and matching shoes. She drove around Galveston for a while, exploring the island, heartily enjoying the experience. The next day Captain Mike Lane phoned from Dallas.

"How on earth did you get this number?" she asked.

"I have my ways, lady," he told her. "I want to come and see you—on Thursday."

"Oh, Mike, I don't think that's a very good idea. I have to get my team assembled and exploration started. I'm going to be terrifically busy. I don't think I will have any time—"

"You'll have time," he interjected sternly. "See you Thursday." And he rung off without giving her the opportunity to protest.

Well, really! Toni stared at the telephone in disgust. What was the matter with her? Every man she met ap-

peared determined to make an attempt to order
her around, to try his hand at the controls of her
life. It would serve Mike Lane right if she just refused to see him Thursday or any other day. But she
knew she would not do it. She was beginning to
rather enjoy the attention she was receiving from
the unexpected plethora of good-looking men in her
life! Her dimple flashed as she went to find ma
and ask for paper to write her mother and grandfather. She did not mention that plethora in her letter.

On Monday Toni was in the conference room with
Karen. They were assembling data to be fed into the
master computer by the head analyst, Dick Handy.
The door popped suddenly open, and Toni and Karen
swiveled their heads toward it.

The most beautiful woman Toni had ever seen stood
there, surveying them with cold disapproval, the warm
light of early afternoon turning her perfect hair to a
burnished copper.

"Hello, Karen." Her haughty attitude dismissed
Toni at once as of no consequence. "Working for
Mark now, I hear." The sneer in her tone was evident.
"Where is he, may I ask?"

Karen flushed and stiffened. Obviously she knew
the other woman. Toni thought it equally obvious she
did not care much for the newcomer.

"He is away on business." Her polite response was
self-contained. "He will be gone for some time."

"If you are to work for Mark, you will have to learn
to mind your manners, miss. I asked where he was!"
Those cold and lovely eyes passed over Karen with
something like real hate reflected in them. "It will be
best for you if you tell me."

Karen rose with quiet dignity and went to the door. Her glance at Toni told volumes.

"There is no need for Dr. Cameron to be forced to listen to this, Virginia Lee. Will you come with me, please?"

"No, I will not." The woman leaned against the door, her svelte body a sleek statement of attraction. She was clothed in a perfectly tailored pair of slacks that fitted her body like a second skin. They were a lovely shade of cinnamon, as was the daring silk blouse that molded her firm breasts. Her lack of undergarments was apparent where the silk fell away from the rounded contours with which she was richly endowed. Her features were exquisitely formed and in perfect proportion. From the unfastened blouse her slender neck rose in a sculptured column. Her skin was clear as alabaster and positively glowed. And she spared no expense to maintain herself, Toni guessed. She realized who the lady was, but why did she have such a cold look on her lovely face?

The woman looked Toni over, her eyes glittering and frigid. Toni felt astonishment as dislike spread from the lovely stranger to her.

"So you are Toni Cameron. I was wondering what you looked like." Her haughty intonation informed Toni she did not look like much. "It will do you no good, you know, even if you are working with Mark and Greg." Toni, astonished, couldn't imagine what the woman was talking about. Her attitude was bitchy in the extreme, she thought. And what had she done to earn such dislike? She was not to find out.

The woman pinned Karen with green eyes that gleamed with a hard light. "It will be best for you if you learn to answer my questions when I ask them,

Karen. Mark is not going to allow you to be rude to me, no matter how much he thinks he has to protect you." She left them, the expensive aroma of her perfume lingering.

Toni looked at Karen and giggled. She could not help it. Never in her life had she seen a more pompous exhibition. For a moment Karen was startled by Toni's reaction, then she joined in. They laughed until they were breathless.

Toni brushed tears away and turned to Karen. She found herself liking the younger girl more all the time. "Will he?"

"Will who what?" Karen giggled.

"Will Mark tear a strip off you because you dared to put her ladyship in her place?"

"Never!" Karen laughed. "Mark hired me because I am an efficient secretary. Efficient secretaries do not divulge company secrets or the boss's whereabouts to all and sundry. In my book, Ginny Lee Sims is nicely classified as sundry. Hence, no info." And Karen dusted her hands together in a gesture of finality. She grinned mischievously. "As a matter of fact, I'm expecting Mark any minute. Frank radioed in a few minutes ago and said they would be landing in about half an hour."

Toni's heart jerked disconcertingly. She fumbled among the data sheets in front of her, noticed Karen's thoughtful glance and paid strict attention to the task at hand, her mind switching to Mrs. Sims.

"So that is Greg's wife," she mused. "She is certainly beautiful."

"Beauty is as beauty does," Karen paraphrased as she stacked the papers they were using into proper order. "This beauty is ugly indeed by those standards.

And even if she were as sweet as candy, you could *give* her points and still win the prize. Beautiful, stuck-up and stupid just doesn't make it in my book. You are beautiful and a lovely person besides.''

"Why, thank you, Karen.'' Toni was touched by her evident sincerity—not that she agreed with her. The younger woman did not like Ginny Lee. Anyone could see that. And with the fierce partisanship of the young, she was just reluctant to give credit where credit was due. There was no question of Ginny Lee Sims's beauty. Anyone who saw her must be conscious of it. "Let's get these in to Dick Handy so he can start talking to that big computer of his, shall we?''

Toni got down to work with a vengeance. She found herself unwilling to examine the reason for the sudden racing of her heartbeat at Karen's casual announcement that Mark was due back at any moment. So heavily did she concentrate on a mass of seismic detail that she was actually unaware of his presence when he did arrive.

A shadow suddenly fell across her desk, and Toni looked up to find him staring down at her. The light from the windows behind him prevented her from getting a clear view of the expression on his face.

"Hard at it,'' he commented quietly, turning from her to his own piled desk. Toni smiled at him tentatively.

"Yes.'' She waved a sheaf of papers at him. "Have you seen the analysis of these reports?''

"No. Do you think we have something?'' Mark was instantly the cool and driving head of the business he was controlling.

Two hours later Toni surfaced from the in-depth analysis of the reports she and Mark had been working

with. She knew she had spent valuable hours with a
first-class mind, a mind that was able to rapidly classify, collate, analyze and reach sound conclusions. She
found herself thrilled with the man's ability and
respectful of his monumental capacity to absorb
knowledge, then use it. No wonder he was so sure of
himself! In that brief afternoon session, Toni came to
realize that much of what she had thought to be arrogance was just an easy acceptance of his own ability.
In no way was he humble, but she came to realize his
undoubted genius and to appreciate his straightforward approach to each problem.

It was dark when he finally stretched his long body
and gave her a look that glinted with amusement and
satisfaction. "I reckon you might just fill the bill, Dr.
Antonia Carla Cameron," he drawled lazily, massag-
ing the back of his neck with an absolute disregard for
the line of his stylist's painstaking haircut. "You have
a sharp mind, lady."

"Why, thank you, Mr. Anders, sir," she rejoined
tartly. "I aim to please."

"Do you indeed, Antonia?" He left the chair behind his untidy desk with a litheness only the physically fit have. "Then please me and come out to dinner
with me."

"Oh!" Momentarily nonplussed, Toni's mind stumbled, then grabbed at the first excuse presenting itself.
"I couldn't. Ma will be expecting me. She will have
dinner ready by now, I'm sure."

Mark grinned and reached for the telephone on his
desk. Toni knew she had lost the round before ma
had the chance to assure her imperturbable superior
that it was perfectly all right to take Toni out to dinner. She would expect them when she saw them. It

seemed she had planned nothing that would not keep.

"Let's go, Antonia. I'm starved." Toni surrendered to the inevitable, and even offered no protest about needing to change her casual attire.

Funnily enough, by the time they covered the fifty or so miles to Houston Toni was ravenous, too. Mark chatted to her light-heartedly as he raced the big Jaguar through the early dark of the warm winter night. Toni laughed at him, vaguely bewildered at his easy attitude—that he thought nothing of traveling fifty miles just to dine out. She figured the distance was the same as going from London to Oxford. Just for a meal! She told him how ludicrous she found it.

"Fifty-three miles isn't far to go to dinner," he protested with a shrug. "Sometimes I go to San Antonio just to eat at my favorite restaurant down on the river walk. I'll take you some day."

"I think not," she rejoined dryly as he swung the big car into an enormous parking lot. "We shall have to be working too hard for that kind of lark. And I *am* here to work."

"It's only about two hundred fifty miles. Just a good morning's drive." He laughed at her disapproving tone as he assisted her out of the deep bucket seat of the automobile. He shut the heavy door with a decisive thud, keeping her hand captive in his long fingers. Toni glanced at him sharply and he smiled at her. She wondered then if he was in a mood to flirt with her. A small shiver slid down her spine, but she resisted the impulse to remove her fingers.

An hour later she knew Mark was most definitely flirting with her. He had taken her into a vast shopping and office complex he called the Galleria. Glass-roofed with three immense balconies surrounding a huge ground-floor ice rink, it was truly spectacular. Mighty chandeliers dripped crystal lights from the extravagant glass dome. The shops, art galleries, furniture stores and restaurants lining the balconies were attractively set off by porticoed entrances.

But she did not have much chance to linger and enjoy the Galleria. Mark was hungry, and so she was duly led to a beautifully furnished club whose interior soared up the three-story height of the Galleria. The decor was deluxe, the service impeccable and the food delicious. Mark was attentive to the point of arousing Toni's inner warning system to real panic. Other than the warm handclasp as he escorted her to the restaurant, or his solicitude in seating her when they were shown to an intimate corner on the top balcony of the club, he did not touch her; he did not need to.

His smile, his eyes, the timbre of his voice as he spoke to her of the most prosaic things imaginable—all acted as an aphrodisiac, stirring her as she had never been stirred in all her life. Toni fought his skill with a sense of being hopelessly outclassed. Mark did not do one thing for which she could fault him, yet she knew he had set out to make her excruciatingly aware of him as a male.

A male who was stalking her, moreover, with the easy confidence of his own success. His attitude did not seem to suggest any fear that she might find his assault upon her senses in any way objectionable. Toni watched him, reading his mood with extreme wariness. Deep down in her treacherous consciousness resided the flicker of knowledge that she might just enjoy allowing his success.

She killed that thought with a ruthless scorn. She was here to work, not to get involved with the dynamic man who smiled at her with such easy charm across the candles and flowers that separated them.

"Time to go home, Antonia."

His matter-of-fact statement had the power to shake her. What would it be like to belong to this man, to be a part of his life, to really go home with him? As she stood to go, she was again aware of the necessity to remind herself she was here to work—to keep aloof from any tantalizing entanglements. She went with him down smoothly glistening escalators, out into the brisk night with a strengthening sense of resolution.

Mark would have to keep his distance. She, Toni Cameron, was perfectly capable of resisting that lazy charm, that easy unhurried pressure with which he was forcing her to an awareness of his attractiveness. She would just have to see to it! So Toni told herself on the fast run back to Galveston.

She resisted the impulse to relax into the inviting depths of the leather seat, but sat forward, kept her eyes straight ahead and fired crisp technical questions at the man guiding the powerful automobile.

His eyes glinted with a knowing laughter, but his answers to her questions were delivered in an entirely businesslike manner Toni found very reassuring. Indeed, by the time they reached her quarters she had breathed a sigh of relief, sure she had misread his intent.

Ma had left the light burning above the veranda door. Toni hopped briskly out of the car, then turned to thank her disturbing escort.

"I will see you in, Antonia." He fielded her brisk dismissal adroitly. "One must, you know. Ma would scalp me if I should be so derelict in my dealings with a young lady. She has spent a lifetime trying to teach

manners to Greg and me." He rounded the car, his
hand settling firmly under her elbow.

Toni allowed him to steer her up the pathway, conscious of the prickling of gooseflesh down her spine,
down the flesh of her arms. Entirely due to the chill in
the air, she decided with laudable calm. Perhaps she
should follow the lead of the natives of the area and
bundle up. Mark had pulled a rough fisherman's knit
in a creamy natural wool over his turtleneck sweater
when they had left for Houston. Toni wore only a
long-sleeved lightweight woolen shirt in soft shades of
blue and green tucked into the toning skirt swinging
around her legs in a very attractive manner.

She ran up the steps ahead of him, but he reached
the handle of the unlocked door first. He turned it,
pushed the door open and stood aside so Toni could
enter. She did so and stopped short, her heart picking
up its beat, her color rising in quick embarrassment.

The rotunda was full of roses again. Yellow roses,
golden in the light of the high chandelier and the side
lights. Mark swore under his breath, his hand reaching
for her, turning her into his arms.

"Sleep tight, Antonia." His gaze deepened, and
then he kissed her.

Toni could not move as the door closed behind him.
There had been such sweetness in the touch of his
mouth on hers, such a dreamy peaceful quality that
she found herself rooted in place as she considered it.
She sighed, shook herself and went up the wide stairway, completely oblivious to the mass of flowers filling the space beneath her.

Whatever Mark was up to, he was certainly doing it
very well.

Probably a past master in the finer points of seduction, she decided uncharitably as she showered and fell into bed. She drifted into sleep, the fingers of her right hand resting on the location of the soft good-night kiss she had received.

When she came down to breakfast in the morning, Mark was seated at the table, his plate full of a fluffy omelet stuffed with bacon and other good things, his face bland.

"Good morning." He eyed her jeans-clad figure cheerfully, swallowed a mouthful of coffee, then responded to her look of pained inquiry. "We forgot to pick up your car at the office when we came in last night. I came over to give you a lift—and to indulge my need for one of ma's excellent omelets," he offered by way of explanation.

"Thank you very much." Toni realized the matter of the car had not crossed her mind. She slid into the chair opposite him as ma came through the door and put a plate in front of her.

"What are you going to do with all them flowers that A-rabian sent agin, Toni? Same's last time?"

"Yes, please, ma. See what you can do." Toni tackled her omelet and avoided Mark's keen glance.

"He phoned last night, too," ma reported with relish, her assessing glance resting briefly on the man sharing the table with her boarder. "Bout nine o'clock, I reckon. Seemed surprised you were out with Mark." Only ma saw the thunderous shift of expression he instantly masked. She grinned delightedly, turning away.

"Oh." Toni buttered a slice of toast with a dedicated attention to detail. "What did he say?" She had no wish to look at either of them.

"Nothin' much. Only said to tell you he'd be seeing you soon."

Toni's startled gaze flew to Mark's face. He nodded impassively. "That's right. Hussein is bringing in a bunch of those fellows who threw the shindig in London—primarily to assess our whole operation. They won't have to interfere with the work you are doing with the team. You'll be able to get on with that."

There was a veiled challenge in his pleasantly stated fact. Toni stared at him, puzzled. Was he anticipating some sort of problem about her ability to work if Hussein was around?

"When do you expect them?" She kept the question cool, impersonal.

"Arrangements are in hand now, but the final date has not been set. I have to make sure the group is able to contact all the VIPs they have on their agenda. It will be a couple of days before everything is settled. This omelet is delicious, ma."

Toni had a niggling feeling of unease as she searched his calm face for the tension she sensed but did not understand. She decided Mark was up to something, but he was poker-faced. She shrugged and turned her attention to her food.

"May I ask what you did with the other flowers, Toni?" His question was offhand, casual in the extreme.

"She sent them to the hospitals," ma answered as she came into the room with a plate of savory-smelling muffins. "Here. I made 'em specially for you. See you give Toni one."

"Food fit for a king!" For some reason he sounded completely happy, a contented man who had it all. Mark offered Toni one, which she refused, broke one open himself and plunked a slab of yellow butter into it, then sank eager white teeth into it.

Toni remembered the tension she had felt. It had surfaced without any cause she could understand and disappeared the same way. Mark, she decided not for the first time, was a complex individual, not too easy to categorize. And he certainly seemed subject to swift mood changes on occasion.

They finished the meal in amicable silence, bade ma goodbye and went to the big warehouse, to be instantly immersed in the problems they had to help solve.

There was no time for anything but hard concentrated effort. Soon the teams were working far into the nights. Toni would come in exhausted, sometimes able to eat the snack ma left for her in the big and cheerful kitchen, sometimes only able to strip off her clothes and tumble into the wide bed. She awoke early each morning and walked along the silver beach before breakfast.

The flat beach stretched for miles, exposed to the waters of the gulf. The seawall, built to protect the town from the raging waves whipped up by fierce storms, carried the smooth highway that ran the length of the exposed seaside. Palm trees planted two by two waved their whispering fans together far above Toni's head as she strode in the brisk mornings. She felt alive, aware, alert as she had not felt in the time since her father and Kurt had died.

It was a good feeling. Toni embraced it, hugged it to herself and bloomed. Life was good, the world was good and she was undeniably happy. She did not question why. It was just enough to wake up each morning and know that she was.

Her friendship with Karen grew daily. The younger woman was a pet—bright, intelligent and efficient. She worked for Mark with a dogged devotion Toni found slightly disconcerting. Most young women Karen's age were not as interested in their jobs as they were in clothes, the current stars in entertainment and boyfriends. Karen never mentioned these. She seemed single-minded in her desire to do her work well and please Mark. But then, Toni reminded herself, Karen's situation was different from that of many women her age. She had responsibility for a child, Clint, whom she rarely talked about.

Frank de la Cruz had not reappeared. Toni watched Karen, and once or twice wondered about her association with him and her apparent devotion to Mark.

Mark himself remained a puzzle that teased the corners of her mind when she thought of him. She avoided allowing herself to think about him when she was away from the teams of scientists under his control, but it was very difficult to do so when she worked in the same space at the same problems with him during the long hours of the balmy winter days. Especially disconcerting were the times she would glance up and catch him watching her, his eyes masked, his face thoughtful.

He managed to convey the impression of a careful man considering all aspects of some problem he might possibly wish to solve. Toni had not the least inclination to ask him what the problem might be.

CHAPTER NINE

LATE THURSDAY Karen stuck her head around the door of the conference room, where Toni was struggling with a mass of detail that refused to make sense. She announced a visitor. Toni surfaced from the confused and conflicting reports of the seismic survey and looked up to meet the critical gaze of Mike Lane.

She had forgotten the tall captain's threat to come down, and she laughed ruefully and introduced him to a suitably impressed Karen. Karen left, looking charmed, and Mike turned to Toni.

"Laugh, if you wish, my girl—" he leered at her in the best villain tradition "—but be warned. There is no escape for you. You are destined to wind up in my clutches."

"Oh, Mike Lane, you are a fool." Toni came to her feet, and wound up in his arms. She turned her head just in time to avoid a quick kiss.

He held her away and shook her gently, his expression serious under his light laugh. "Scorn me not, Toni Cameron, unless you plan to pay...and pay...and pay."

His long lashes drooped over the sultry intentness of his eyes. He stared at her mouth long enough for Toni to get a clear idea of what he was thinking, then looked away as Mark entered the conference room. Mark shook hands with the pilot and greeted him with cool courtesy.

"I would like to borrow your off. ops. engineer, if I may, Anders," Mike stated mildly. "I have to be back in Dallas before midnight tonight. Sorry to barge in, but I thought she would be through for the day by now." His smile did not hide the challenge.

Mark's glance seared into Toni's rebellious blue eyes, and he shrugged with sheer indifference. "You've been working hard, Antonia. Go ahead and take some time off."

Expecting anything but his agreement to Mike's proposal, Toni clutched at her departing dignity and sputtered, "Th-thanks, Mark. B-but I must finish these reports for tomorrow's meeting...."

"Forget it. We'll manage." He sat down, flipped through some papers, his gesture of dismissal irrefutable. Toni felt an unaccountable urge to apply a sharp palm to that tanned face, which was set in sudden granite withdrawal.

"Thanks, old man," she heard Mike say as she marched out of Mark's exasperating presence. Why she found his unconcern exasperating she could not have said. Fortunately her companion did not give her much time to dwell on the strangeness of her reaction.

She went with him and thoroughly enjoyed herself once she had recovered from her unexplained anger. Mike was a first-class raconteur. He filled the late afternoon and early evening with a good deal of enjoyment and kept her laughing at his tales from both sides of the Atlantic, his various takeoffs, some of the characteristics of passengers he had carried. He was able to do dialogue and dialect, for his ear was good and his sense of mimicry the best she had ever encountered.

It was late when he brought her back to the big house. The taxi stood at the curb while he took his time and kissed her goodbye.

Toni stood in the open doorway and watched him run lightly down the steps. He disappeared into the car and she shut the door on the cool night, her face thoughtful indeed. She liked Mike Lane. She had enjoyed the evening. Why, then, did his kiss leave her so unmoved? She mulled the matter over until she reached her room, then forgot the man without realizing she had done so.

Mark glowered at her when she greeted him the next morning. "Glad to see that English jock managed to take himself off in time so you could get your beauty sleep." The mutter had a vicious edge to it. It pulled Toni to attention.

"I'm sure ma would approve of his manners," she informed him caustically. "Yours leave much to be desired."

Mark tossed a thick folder over the stacks of work on his desk. It landed on hers with a thud. "Here's that report you walked out on last night. It's your responsibility to discuss it at the meeting this morning, and I want them to know exactly what is in it and what it means for cost accounting," he stated flatly.

Toni stared at him, her anger causing her to catch her breath. Never had she been the victim of such an unfair attitude! "Don't you think I am capable of fulfilling my responsibilities? I've put in hours of extra work on this project—"

"Have you? Well, the expectation is that you will go on doing so—regardless of demands your love life might put on you—until such time as the preliminary data is in." His face was uncompromising.

"If you will remember, it was at your insistence that I left this last night. I had forgotten Mike was coming down. I did not plan to go with him." She neglected to mention she had tried to discourage the pilot—hated herself for trying to explain at all. What a thoroughly detestable specimen the man seated behind his littered desk was!

Mark stared at her with hard eyes. "So he's been phoning you, has he?" A flicker of some sort surfaced in his expression, was instantly masked. "Phones every time he lands in Dallas, I presume?"

"Then you presume wrong!" Toni spat at him. She snatched up the report and pulled open a drawer of the desk, throwing her handbag in and extracting a legal-sized pad of yellow lined paper for her notes. She slammed the drawer shut, her eyes a blue blaze as they met the irascible regard of the man seated opposite. "Karen said you would find me a private office if I found myself unable to concentrate here. Please do so," she demanded recklessly. "I am completely incapable of making any decent effort under the present conditions." Only the thick carpet kept her from stamping her foot in anger.

"Where are you going?" There was surprise in Mark's query, an edge of anxiety she did not hear.

"I'll work in the conference room until you can arrange an office for me." Toni stalked out, seething.

The conference was late starting but it went very well. It became clear that the biggest need was for more seismic data, and it was imperative that it be gathered and assessed immediately. Sandy Johnson elected to do some intensive exploration of the proposed site in the small submarine now under contract to the company. Monday was his starting date. It would probably take all next week to finish.

Greg was not at the meeting. He had not yet returned from wherever Mark had sent him the first day of Toni's stay on Galveston Island.

The table was crowded with experts in their respective fields, and Toni enjoyed meeting the whole team for the first time. The collective information they shared from their various disciplines was awesome. She was intrigued by them, absorbed in the depth of the knowledge they were sharing.

Mark ran the conference with easy ability. He expected the best from these experts and he got it. Toni watched and listened, joined in when necessary and came away from the meeting with a growing respect for the man she had so much difficulty getting along with. One thing was certain: U.P.C. knew exactly what it was doing when they put him in charge of this operation. She gave him that, she realized as she reached into her drawer and retrieved her handbag.

It was dark outside. There was a mist rolling in across the island, masking the lights spread out beneath her.

Karen had long since gone home. Toni headed for the passage, intent on doing so herself. Mark caught up with her before she reached the stairway leading to the exit, his hand falling naturally on her shoulder.

"Go fishing with me tomorrow afternoon, Antonia?" he asked in a perfectly normal voice.

Surprised, Toni glanced at him sharply. He had addressed very few remarks to her during the meeting. Several times she had caught his brooding gaze fastened on her. She had ignored him as much as possible, answered queries in a cool straightforward manner, delivered her opinions when he requested them and decided she was right not to have a thing to do with the man outside of business hours. She shrugged off his hand with an irritated gesture.

"No, I don't think so," she informed him. "I would much prefer to choose my own activities and do them by myself." She caught the sardonic lift of his eyebrow. "Or with companions of my own choosing," she added tartly.

There was nothing in her contract that stated she had to be pleasant to one Mark Anders, she told herself rebelliously as she let herself into her car. By the time she reached the house, she had dismissed the man from her thoughts as she looked forward to the pleasure of having a free weekend. Mark had sent everyone home for the weekend. He wanted them fresh and sharp for Monday.

She spent hours in the house on Saturday, chatting with ma. She got her wardrobe in order for the next week, wrote letters and generally enjoyed a relaxed and leisurely day. Then she decided to have a long walk right down to the end of the island. It was late afternoon when she set out after a cheerful word to ma, promising to return in time for the evening meal. But as she ran down the high steps leading from the veranda, Toni rather wished she had not done so. The air was perfect. Warm and moist, bearing the salty tang of the gulf from which it was blowing, it was an almost tropical delight.

She swung along the stretch of beach, her well-shaped legs covering the distance gracefully. The sun shot vivid streaks into the sky behind her, turning the gulf into a flowing iridescent palette. Birds winged and cried overhead.

Lights glowed softly along the seawall to her left, and the occasional car swished along the wide roadway the seawall supported. Passing the great pier that jutted far out over the water, Toni examined it with interest. It had a first-class resort hotel built on it, she knew.

Continuing to stride along in the balmy, sweet-scented breeze, Toni was conscious of a peace she had not experienced in a very long time. It must be the influence of the flat uncomplicated beauty of this place, she decided whimsically. Life was wonderful!

Two small boys tossed a ball into the surf, to have it retrieved by a willing black Labrador. Several men, clad in shorts and little else, passed her with smiles and words of greeting as they pursued physical fitness with typical American dedication.

Toni answered cheerfully, deciding she quite liked the look of firm muscular males moving lithely across the sand. It was a new idea to her. For some reason the whole concept of maleness seemed to have suddenly impinged itself upon her consciousness.

She tossed her head impatiently, then noticed a man sitting in the sand staring out to sea. In contrast to the joggers, he was dressed in slacks, with a leather jacket over his hunched shoulders. His huddled appearance gave the impression he was in pain.

Toni was close to him before he heard her and flung up his black head. It was Frank de la Cruz. He came to his feet, his hands brushing the damp sand from his pants. For an instant he stared at her, anguish written clearly on his sensitive face. Never had Toni seen a man look so vulnerable.

Then his natural charm dropped like a curtain of protection, and he smiled. The transformation was startling. Toni blinked as the full effect of his smile, which warmed his dark eyes, hit her. Her first impression of him was correct. He was the handsomest man she had ever seen. Black curls tumbled above the perfect sweep of his brows. Few people would be able to resist the force of personality this man projected, Toni suspected. And of those who could, none would be women.

He reached out, captured her hand and raised her fingers to his handsome mouth. "Toni! How delightful to see you." He released her fingers and regarded her with expressive velvety eyes. "I am indeed fortunate to have been here on the edge of this cold sea."

"Cold? I find it delightful."

"My Latin blood demands more heat than yours," he told her solemnly, a long finger flicking the collar of his short leather flying jacket. "You probably have noticed by now that the natives, Anglo and Mexican alike, tend to bundle up here—just in case a blue norther decides to visit. You haven't had the pleasure of meeting our sudden cold north wind, I presume. The temperature drops like a stone, and one tends to be instantly quick frozen."

Toni laughed. "No, I haven't yet. I have been suitably warned by everyone I've met, it seems. I take it you are not a native Texan?"

"I, *querida mía*, am a Californian. I am here in durance vile, same as Mark." He protested grandly then regarded her with a soft interest. "Would you mind if I join your walk along the beach?"

"I plan to go as far as the jetty. I would be pleased to have your company if you think you can manage."

"Impertinence from such a lovely lady." He clicked his tongue and swung into step beside her. "My

mama, however, taught me always to turn the other
cheek to the blows of life." He shook his black head in
the light of the overhead streetlamp. His words were
light, but Toni caught a glimpse of moodiness in his
dark eyes. Here was an unhappy man.

She was aware of an inexplicable wish to help him if
she could. She strongly suspected his problem concerned his relationship with Karen and Mark's attitude
toward that relationship. But she was unable to think
of a single way to approach the subject and did not
wish to intrude into an area that might be painfully
personal, so she didn't mention it.

They covered the distance to the end of the jetty in
companionable silence. When they reached it, Frank
stood looking out across the channel toward the roads,
his hands thrust into the pockets of his flight jacket.
Somehow Toni received the impression that he was unaware of the small fishing boats drifting in from the
day's venture.

It was completely dark now, but the boats returning
to berths farther up the Galveston Channel or to the
yacht club were well lit. Toni heard the hoot of the
ferry as it warned its way toward Pelican Island across
the strip of water. She stood quietly beside the silent
man, enjoying the peace of the scene.

Gradually she became aware of the tension that surrounded him. It was potent, a pulsing beat she could
not ignore.

"I did not realize you and Mark were from California," she ventured tentatively when she could no
longer disregard his misery.

"What? Oh. . . ." He seemed to jerk himself back
from some very unpleasant prospect with a real effort.
He turned to her and offered a rueful smile. "I am

very sorry to be so moody, Toni, but I am really going through a bad time. Chances are I won't make it and I cannot bear the consequences if I don't. Yes, Mark and I are both from Los Angeles. We've known each other since we were kids. Grew up together, went to school, college and war together. He's the best friend I have, and it's making a real problem for me."

"Karen?" she ventured.

"Karen," he agreed flatly. "I'm in love with her. In fact, I'm in love for the first time in a misbegotten life. Mark knows me too well. He doesn't believe I'm serious, that I want to make a home for Karen and her child—or that the marriage will last."

Toni was aghast. "Surely it's absolutely none of Mark's business if you happen to be in love with his secretary." Never had she heard of such arrogance.

"It's his business," Frank assured her quietly. "In fact, if I were in his shoes, I expect I'd feel exactly as he does."

"I don't understand."

He flashed his beautiful smile and reached out to touch her cheek. "No, *querida*. And I am not going to say any more. The whole matter is between Mark and me, and it is up to me to solve it."

"Oh, it is, is it?" Toni's color rose with her anger. "What about Karen? Has she nothing to say? And why doesn't Mark help? Is he too good to come half-way, whatever the problem is? Or do you just allow him to order you around in that offensive authoritative manner of his?"

"You make quite an advocate, Toni. Mark has his side to this, too, you know." He made the observation without any heat at all. "For one thing, look at the difference in our ages. I'm the same age as Mark—thirty-five. And Karen has just turned twenty-two. It wouldn't be so bad if I had any claim to saintly behavior, but I haven't. Mark is unable to see Karen as ever being able to control me or meet my needs. What he doesn't know is that she will never have to control me. I adore the woman. I would go to hell and back for her and count myself lucky, but I can't convince that lunkhead."

"Oh, Frank, you shouldn't have to convince him." Toni reached up, caught his handsome face between her slender palms. "If Karen loves you, just take her away and marry her."

Frank lowered his head and kissed her on the forehead, his eyes full of tender laughter, his hands resting easily on her waist.

"I may just have to do that. But I don't want to. I want to marry Karen with Mark's blessing. I want him to be the best man at our wedding. That," he sighed, "would be the best of all possible worlds."

Toni stared up at him, utterly convinced of his sincerity. Frank laughed then, a tight unhappy sound. He threw his dark head up, stared at the low mist beginning to roll in, his face etched for a moment in the glow from the streetlight.

"Fog. We should get back, Toni." He released her and they walked back along the seawall. She glanced at his troubled face, then decided to ask no more questions. Frank was wrestling with a problem apparently only he could solve. He did not need a chattering woman adding to his misery.

Toni was pleasantly tired by the time they reached the central resort portion of the beach.

"Have a cup of coffee with me before you vanish?"

The lonely overtone in the man's voice was an appeal Toni was unable to ignore.

"Just a quick one, Frank." She glanced at her wristwatch. "I promised ma I wouldn't be late for supper."

"Ma Ruddy looking after you, is she?" He cocked a speculative eye at her as he escorted her to a booth in the busy dining room of a nearby motel.

Toni laughed and sat down. "A very good job she makes of it, too. Yes, ma looks after me."

"I see." Frank ordered coffees, his eyes narrowed as he scrutinized her glowing face.

"Private party or can anyone join?" Toni exclaimed involuntarily as she met the hard glance of Mark Anders.

"¡Amigo!" Frank stood and reached for Mark's hand. Mark shook hands with him briefly, raked him with an equally uncompromising stare, then shared the bench seat opposite Toni with the pilot. Frank motioned for another cup of coffee and sat down again.

"Enjoy your day off, Antonia?" Mark asked, a muscle twitching in one tanned cheek.

Frank, his fine dark eyes on his friend's tough face, drank his coffee in a couple of swallows, then rose gracefully. "Thanks for allowing me to join you, Toni. I enjoyed our time together." His eyes caressed her with the unconscious ease of a man who truly enjoyed making the woman he was speaking to feel special. "I have to go now, but I'm leaving you in good hands."

"Call me around eight, Frank." Mark made the request into a command.

"New assignment?" The other man invested his question with a silky challenge. Mark frowned. "Just give me a call."

"Okay, buddy. Will do." He shrugged, turned to Toni. "Mark knows a lot about Galveston. Get him to fill you in, *querida*. Past history doesn't interest me too much." He went without a backward glance.

Toni had the unaccountable feeling she had just witnessed a near explosion. She looked curiously at Mark. Where had he come from? Why was he here?

He was staring down into his coffee cup, stirring the black liquid with dedicated concentration. There was an elusive scent of salt, the faint tang of fish and the sea about him.

"You were fishing?" Toni asked quietly.

"I was. You should have gone. The weather was great and the fish were hungry." He raised his head then, hazel eyes grim. "I asked if you enjoyed your day."

"As a matter of fact, I did." She sought for some way to dissipate the tension rolling over her. Nothing occurred to her. Rattled, she said the first thing that came into her head. "I found Frank on the beach. He walked with me." She knew by the bleak look she received that her choice of topic was ill-advised.

"Did he indeed? I noticed."

"He's a very nice person," Toni protested swiftly. Frank's sincerity as he told her of his feelings for Karen and his need for this man's approval flashed through her mind. Instinctively she knew she must not interfere, but Mark's callous rejection of his friend's probity bothered her. Besides, what on earth gave him the right to meddle in their affairs? "I like him!"

Her declaration came out more strongly than she meant it to. Mark cocked a sardonic brow at her. "And so, my dear Antonia, do literally dozens of others of your sex."

"Why not? I have never met a more charming man."

"I should think not, knowing the sandhogs and roughnecks who are generally attracted to the oil business." He inspected her flushed face grimly, seemed about to say something, then changed his mind and sipped from his coffee cup, his eyes never leaving her face.

"Do you really want to learn a little of Galveston's history?" The cup clattered on the table as he set it down decisively.

"I do." Toni was instantly on the defensive. "But I'll poke around, find out things for myself. Not to worry; you needn't waste your time on me."

"I'm not worried, Antonia." He stood abruptly, waited for her to do the same. "I'd like to take you around tomorrow—show you the town, share the bits I know about it. I can assure you I will not be wasting my time or yours." His words were brusque in the extreme. He stood quietly, waiting indifferently for her to refuse him.

Toni glanced up into those wintry hazel eyes and choked off her impulse to decline the singularly unattractive invitation to spend the day with him. Perhaps, came the errant thought, she might find an opportune time to mention Karen if she went with him.

"Thank you. What time shall I expect you?"

"Early, I think," he returned. "I may have to attend to some VIPs arriving later in the day." He tossed a bill on the table, did not wait for his check. "I'd better get you back. Ma won't like it if you don't turn up in time to eat."

"Oh, dear!" Toni glanced at her watch and hurried along with him. "I forgot I'd promised to be home in

time for supper." She was contrite. There was really
no excuse for lateness in this case.

"So ma said." He strode along silently, apparently
absorbed in thought. After bidding her a cool good-
night he disappeared into the darkness, leaving Toni
with the definite impression that he was glad to be rid
of her. Well!

She went in to her meal knowing with absolute cer-
tainty that she would never understand the man for
whom she worked.

CHAPTER TEN

MARK WAS EARLY the next morning. Toni had barely finished breakfast when he called. She sped lightly up the stairs and collected her handbag, a curiously happy sensation giving wings to her feet. Mark grinned attractively at her and escorted her through the big front door with elaborate courtesy, last night's abruptness gone.

He came to a halt at the top of the steps, a long hand reaching for her in an unabashed possessiveness as a thunderous look washing over his tanned features, only to be instantly masked.

"Just what the hell is he doing here?" Toni barely understood his muttered phrase. Startled, she followed the direction of his gaze, watched a magnificent Mercedes sweep down the street and stop in silvery splendor at the curb. She knew with an inward sinking of spirit exactly who would emerge from the vehicle before the elegantly uniformed chauffeur opened the rear door.

Prince Hussein stepped out into the Texas morning sun, urbane, smiling and very sure of his welcome.

Mark kept his hand on Toni's arm and continued down the steps, his expression cool. "Hussein. I wasn't expecting you until late evening."

"We were able to get away earlier than we expected, so we decided not to waste the opportunity." He smiled engagingly. "Time waits for no one, old friend.

Ah, Antonia.'' He turned the full wattage of his charming smile upon her.

Her full name rolled off his tongue in such a pleasant manner that she decided not to have him call her by the shorter version that most people adopted. She felt Mark's fingers tighten on her arm, then he released her and stepped back, watching with polite interest as Hussein reached for her hand and carried her fingers to his lips.

''Mark, do you know what a fortunate man you are to be able to work daily with this lovely lady?'' Hussein's dark eyes glowed with feeling as he looked deeply into Toni's cautious blue eyes.

''How nice to see you, Prince Hussein.'' Her cool remark put Hussein's attempt to flirt firmly into perspective. ''I didn't realize you were expected today.''

Hussein turned to Mark with a pained expression on his dark face. ''I did not think you would keep my arrival a secret from your delightful assistant, my friend,'' he protested mildly. ''I particularly wanted her to know I was planning to be here soon.''

''I was waiting for final word of your arrival time,'' Mark returned urbanely. ''We're going on a short historical tour of Galveston. Antonia has been too busy to get to know the city before now. Would you care to join us?''

''But yes! What a charming idea! Are we to walk?''

''That's the plan. Where's the rest of your party? Do I need to make arrangements for them?'' Mark sounded like the perfect host.

''No.'' Hussein shrugged easily. ''They are struggling with jet lag in one of those fabulous hotels in Houston. They will be ready to give their attention to business by tomorrow, I think.''

The chauffeur was given instructions and they were on their way, Toni flanked by the two men. Mark's attitude was cool and offhand all day. Hussein kept Toni's hand tucked into his elbow most of the time, but Mark ignored the prince's efforts to monopolize her attention.

After a while Mark made the car detour past the corporate offices. "I have to send a cable that must go at once," he explained as he left them in the silent goods yard. "Be right back."

Toni wondered that he did not invite Hussein up to the top-floor offices, but the prince just smiled in his charming manner and waved away the oil man's brief apology.

"Go, my friend. But I am unable to understand any business that takes precedence over such delightful company." His warm eyes touched Toni's face. "I shall endeavor to entertain our lovely companion while you attend to it, however. Do not worry."

Mark's impassive glance wandered over Toni and he nodded briefly, impersonally. "I won't."

With that he was gone. Toni had the uneasy feeling he was up to something she needed to know about, then decided she was becoming paranoid about the man and his actions. However, he was not an easy man to categorize or understand.

She decided she really must make an effort to get him to talk about Frank and Karen if at all possible. Unaccountably, she really wanted to assist the lovers if she could. The idea of tackling Mark about them was more than a little daunting. Truly, it was none of her business. Yet, if she could help. . . .

"Ah, Antonia, you have not heard a word I've spoken," Hussein accused her. "I'm really not accustomed to being ignored, you know, and you did it even when we first met!''

Toni laughed, remembering the gold coin he had offered for her thoughts that long-ago night in London. Contrite, she discussed at length the merits of the big S-58 Sikorsky crouched in the center of its landing pad.

''It is an efficient machine and versatile in the ways it can be used,'' Hussein commented. ''I only hope de la Cruz will be able to teach my men to handle ours more skillfully.''

''Frank?'' Toni exclaimed, startled.

''Yes.'' Hussein looked a little surprised. ''Mark has obligingly consented to loan de la Cruz for the job. There's little doubt he is one of the best in the business. I'm lucky to be able to get him. He was a bit hesitant about accepting the contract, but today he's told me he will sign on. We had a pleasant chat on the telephone as soon as I arrived.''

Toni gathered her scattered thoughts together. So Mark had consented to loan his chief pilot, had he? And where, pray tell, had Hussein learned enough about Frank's expertise to want to give him a contract for the necessary instruction? She had a very clear impression of Mark Anders sticking his long fingers into the pie.

Of course Frank was not a bonded slave. He could have refused to be shunted into the farthest corners of the earth if he had so desired. To be fair, she had to admit the relationship between Mark and Frank was apparently much deeper than the superficial connections between men who worked together. And Frank had said they were lifetime friends.

If Frank had not wanted to go to the Middle East,

he would not have gone. Still, from the impression she'd gleaned from their talk, she would have bet he did not want to leave Karen. Especially to go so far away! Mark had to have interfered somehow!

Toni cast a scathing glance at the man in question as he chose this inopportune moment to rejoin them under the shadow of the big helicopter.

"I have just been telling Antonia of my good fortune in being able to persuade de la Cruz to instruct my own pilots."

"And what was her reaction to that?" Mark's smile was mocking.

"Did you twist his arm, Mark?" she retorted, stung by the derisive light in his eyes. "Why else would he agree to go?"

"Money, my love," Mark retorted flatly. "Loads and loads of the lovely green stuff. Hussein hasn't any sense at all when he wants something. He managed to make his offer irresistible." The prince looked complacent and Mark sarcastic—at her expense, she realized.

"Oh!" A little ashamed of herself, Toni took the arm the Arab offered and set off on the promised tour of Galveston, a little put out at herself. It was becoming imperative that she get her ambivalence toward Mark under control. Really!

They strolled into the Strand, the district containing the restored fragments of those nineteenth-century days when the citizens of Galveston fully expected it to become one of the nation's largest port cities, inferior only to New York and San Francisco.

"What happened?" Hussein inquired.

"Hurricane," Mark replied succinctly. "A killer came along and wiped Galveston off the map in 1900."

"How large was the city?" Hussein asked, surprised. "Hurricanes can be bad, I know, but they follow a path. How could one hurricane be large enough to destroy a city?"

"Yeah, that's true. But this was a most unusual hurricane. In fact, it wasn't the hurricane so much as it was the tidal wave it created. Let's go up to the observation floor of the Anico Tower and I'll show you."

They went up into the tower that rose high above the flat island. The view was magnificent and unimpeded. The gulf lay beyond the seawall, a vast sheet of dimpled blue, dotted here and there by the oil rigs pumping liquid black gold. Huge ships from every nation inched along in solitary purpose, while other great vessels were docked in the channel, cranes huddling over them like predatory monsters. Small yachts and sailboats plied the channel, too, scattering like snowflakes around an inbound freighter.

"Galveston is practically at sea level," Mark explained. "It was even more so in 1900. That didn't greatly worry the early residents. Nor did the hurricanes. They had survived many by the time 1900 came along, but they had never encountered one of this strength."

He drew a deep breath before continuing. "This one was large enough to suck up the water offshore. If you were outside you were dead. Those under any shelter expected disaster at any moment. Buildings kept collapsing around them. It got darker, the wind got worse, then the water returned with a monstrous tidal wave. Houses and buildings crumpled as if they were made of cards. The flooding tore up the railway bridge' and pushed it through the town like a scythe mowing ripe wheat. It even scoured the graveyard and dumped the coffins and the tombstones all over the place. The devastation was beyond description," he ended quietly.

Toni looked out over the peaceful city and tried to visualize the picture of disaster his vivid words evoked. "Those poor people," she whispered in quiet horror. "Did they stay...the survivors? They must have, of course. Someone rebuilt the city."

"They stayed." Mark watched her face. "They rebuilt. Some folks just can't be told what to do, even by Mother Nature."

The three of them left the tower. As they walked Mark explained the reason behind the peculiarly typical look of most Galvestonian dwellings. "The hurricane filled most of the basements of the original homes with sand even when it left the houses standing. When Galveston was rebuilt the houses were raised up on high foundations—no more basements. And Galveston itself was raised with landfill seventeen feet above sea level. The seawall was built as a further protection."

"It all seems safe enough now," Toni ventured.

"Yes, it does. The only thing is, a hurricane of that force, accompanied by the unpredictable wave and tidal action, has never happened since. I hope the residents never need to find out if they have built better buildings this time."

Chatting amicably, they visited the elaborate Italianate villa that was now restored and on exhibit as an example of the architecture prevalent in the days before the hurricane, when Old Galveston had been called the "Queen City of the Southwest."

They lunched in an old-fashioned restaurant, then generally played tourists.

Hussein was very attentive and charming all day; Mark grew more taciturn and reserved as the hours went by. It was almost dark when he escorted her home and took Hussein along with a firm but determined courtesy.

After showering and eating her evening meal, Toni found she was exhausted. It was the direct effect of the tension Mark had invested in the day as it progressed, she decided crossly. She was on her way to bed when pa said she was wanted on the phone. Half expecting it to be Hussein calling from his hotel in Houston, she was quite surprised to hear Mark's distinctive baritone.

"Antonia, can you be ready to leave with the seismic exploration team early in the morning? Sandy Johnson wants you along."

"Whatever for?" Toni's first reaction was one of blank astonishment.

"You are offshore operations officer. He feels it is essential to have your input as he tries to narrow down the seismic parameters of the area. He wants you with him so he can have instant consultation when he gets new information."

"Well, if he needs me, of course I can be ready."

"He needs you, Antonia. The company car will pick you up at about four-thirty. Sleep well."

Toni shrugged, hung up and went to pack jeans, underthings and her small makeup kit. She considered the springlike warmth of the weather and tucked in some shorts and sun tops along with the only swimsuit she owned. Then, grinning, she added a jacket and woolen slacks—just in case any of those dire predictions came true and she found herself in the middle of one of the infamous "blue northers."

As an afterthought she added her violin case to the small pile in the stuffed duffel bag. Sandy Johnson greeted it with delight when he called for her in the early-morning dark.

"I knew you were an angel sent to relieve my misery the first time I laid eyes on you," he chortled as he heaved her bag into the back of the big station wagon and stowed the violin with tender care beside it. "A lady after my own heart. We will make beautiful music together and mesmerize these clods we are forced to associate with."

The car full of clods greeted this pronouncement with assorted hoots that must have shocked the neighborhood into wakefulness as the men obligingly made room for the lady in question.

"Do you know what he plays—if you can classify those raucous heartrending noises he makes on the thing as a form of playing?" Jon Hendrix, head computer analyst, turned a laughing face to her. "He plays a harmonica, Dr. Cameron."

"Toni." She did not want to be formal with these good-natured men, who were fast becoming a first-class working team. "Aren't you afraid you will offend his more tender sensibilities?" she inquired innocently, joining in the fun.

"Sensibilities!" Jack Thompson, another member of the seismic team, gave a snort of derision that was met with a chorus of approval. "How can a man who plays a harmonica have any sensibilities, much less tender ones? Of course, it is different with us guitarists," he added.

By the time Jack had been thoroughly raked over the coals and reduced to a more proper view of himself, they were trooping up the gangway of the seismic vessel.

It was still dark as the ship moved out of the Galveston Channel and into the waters of the gulf. Toni stowed her things in the narrow cabin assigned to her and went in search of breakfast in the chow hall.

She was unaware of the fact that she had not thought once of Prince Hussein. Nor did she spend any of her time during the next five days considering him, much less the probable reasons for his visit. She was far too occupied with the job at hand.

As Toni had hoped, the days on the gulf turned out to be warm. The men stripped to shorts that were for the most part in various states of disrepair. Toni worked in shorts and shirts or brief sun tops. Everyone was easy, informal.

And everyone was an expert at what he was doing. All the men were American. Toni found herself quite liking the boisterous humor with which they dealt with each other and the problems that arose as the ship quartered the designated area they wished to examine.

They included her in their easy comradeship, watched her a little carefully as they experimented with various mild forms of flirtation, accepted her cool rejection of tentative advances with feigned sorrow and then took her into their close-knit ranks.

The seismic work went rapidly forward. Each day the series of sound waves echoing back from the holes drilled into underground rock, were recorded. Results were measured by microphone and fed into the sophisticated on-board computers, which handled corrections with blinding speed.

Jon Hendrix put his wide-ranging knowledge to work and came up with interpretations that offered intriguing alternatives just begging to be tested. The teams then pursued the location of the best possible drill site with the enthusiasm of true wildcatters.

Their days were filled with work, their evenings with fun. Jack Thompson, Toni and Sandy supplied nightly entertainment. They would tune up on deck, and every man who was not working would gravitate to the spot for the sing-along-cum-concert.

Toni was busy, but it seemed to her that Sandy had little real need of her presence. He assigned her to odd jobs, included her in consultations he could have very well held without her, and she failed to see a great significance in the kinds of advice she was asked to supply.

When she asked him why he had wanted her on board, he stopped what he was doing and looked at her oddly. Toni had the queerest feeling he had to search for his answer to her question.

"Why, I just needed you, Toni. I, er, felt that since you are our ops. off., you should know exactly where we are when we find the anticline."

"I can read a map and figure coordinates."

"Granted." He smiled at her, turned smoothly confidential. "I just wanted you here, Toni. I thought it might give us a better chance of precisely locating our first drill hole bang on target if you helped with the siting. You did bring in your last strike on your first hole down, didn't you?"

Toni admitted she had. "But you know very well that may have been a fluke, Sandy. The odds against that happening again on one of my jobs must be unbelievably high."

"With this new computer profiling technique of Mark's, I am willing to bet those odds are considerably lowered."

"Maybe. I wouldn't count on it."

He shot her a disquieting and strangely assessing glance from sharply intelligent eyes before he went back to his task. He gave the impression of wanting to avoid further conversation. Toni wondered why. Her mind drifted then to Mark, as it had a bad habit of doing if she was not careful. Had he instructed Sandy to take her into the gulf on this week's project? Why would he do that? She dismissed her question with irritation. She was being ridiculous.

They were packed up and pulling back into the mooring at Galveston before Toni thought of Hussein. Surely Mark hadn't just removed her from the vicinity in order to keep Hussein from seeing her? Highly improbable.

She grinned at the idea when the station wagon discharged them in the corporation yard. Sandy insisted the reports be made in person. She and Jon Hendrix had to accompany him. Toni shrugged off her reluctance to face Mark and went up to the top floor with the two men. Ducking into the ladies' room to smooth her hair and use a bit of makeup before going to the meeting, she ran straight into Linda Wells. Toni stared in astonishment at the other Englishwoman.

Linda smiled as she recognized her. "Dr. Cameron, isn't it? I met you in a restaurant in Mayfair one day, remember? I don't recall the name of the restaurant, but I do remember you were there with Hussein."

"Yes. But what on earth are you doing in Galveston?"

"I was Mark's personal assistant in London. I'm now his liaison officer for the new project in the Persian Gulf. I have been here this past week learning the ropes."

"Oh." Toni could not think of anything else to say.

"It's too bad you were out with your team all week.

I would have liked to become better acquainted with
you."

"Yes.... Thank you. Are you staying long?"

"I must leave at once in order to catch the flight
booked for me back to London." She glanced at her
watch, gave a small squeak. "I was due downstairs
five minutes ago. I must fly. Bye!" She picked up a
small case from the floor and hurried from the room,
her lovely face glowing.

Toni ran a comb through her hair, grimaced at her
scrubbed brown face in the big mirror and went down
toward Karen's enclosure.

The girl greeted her with pleasure. "I'm so glad
you're back. Everyone is in the conference room.
Want to see your new office before you join them?"

"New office?" Toni had forgotten her demand.
Karen nodded, her eyes dancing with fun.

"I'll say! It's nice. Mark has had everybody jump-
ing around like crazy getting it ready for you. I think
you will like it."

Toni shook her head in slow wonder. "I really
didn't expect it. I expect I'd best wait to see it,
though."

She went into the conference room. Mark greeted
her coolly and indicated the chair next to his. They ran
over the new reports for two hours.

"That's it, then." Mark leaned back in his chair,
throwing his pencil down. His eyes slid over Toni, then
went to the door as a knock sounded.

Hussein came in. He greeted Mark, nodded to the
others as they filed out and made straight for Toni, the
soft glow in his eyes belying the stern set of his handsome face.

"Antonia, how beautifully browned you are. I have

been desolate. Mark has explained to me why it was necessary for you to go, but my heart has received irreparable damage. And now I must leave for Dallas." His dark features lightened, and those perfect white teeth flashed in an irresistible smile. "Will you come with me? We could at least spend the evening and tomorrow together."

Toni was conscious of the men leaving the room. Sandy looked back over his shoulder and winked at her. She cast an uncomfortable glance at Mark. He hadn't moved. His eyes met hers with such a dark forbidding anger that she bridled, her chin rising in offense.

"How nice of you to ask me, Hussein. I would love to go." She refused to look again at the man who made the muffled sound behind her. "Are you in a rush? I'll have to go by my lodging and make myself presentable."

"I shall be happy to escort you there." Hussein's smile said he was quite satisfied with her the way she was, but was willing to indulge her. "My colleagues all left yesterday for Dallas, but my personal plane is waiting in Houston. It will not leave until we are aboard."

"Goodbye, Mark." Toni walked out without daring to look backward. She heard Hussein murmuring to him as the two shook hands, but she didn't wait.

"Coward," she muttered to herself. It was a relief when Hussein joined her with no sign of Mark at all. Toni went out into the cool air with the curious feeling that she had just deserted a battle she could not possibly win.

Another big Mercedes was waiting at the curb when they went through the automatic doors of the Dallas-

Fort Worth Airport. Hussein's large and powerful jet had made short work of the distance between Houston and Dallas.

On landing, he asked her if she would mind accompanying him while he bought some trifles for friends and family. Assured she would not, he took her to the lavish Fairmount and booked her into a fantastic room, gave her half an hour to freshen up and whisked her off to Neiman-Marcus, a renowned department store. One could buy almost anything here—even a swimming pool full of champagne, Hussein assured her. Toni was suitably impressed. She watched in a kind of horrified awe as he bought the trifles he spoke of so lightly. The total cost was well into the thousands.

Finally Hussein, who had given orders for his purchases to be delivered to his jet, took Toni back to the hotel and insisted she dress in her prettiest gown. The hotel, he informed her, had a noteworthy chef, and the cabaret for the evening included two of his favorite performers.

Toni soaked in the luxurious tub, then lathered her hair under the shower. She wondered what the room would cost her but was not worried. Her salary was such that she could afford the occasional night in Sybaritic splendor.

The dining room was intimate, almost opulent in its rich decor and service. Toni had been plied with compliments, flowers, dark passionate looks and some very excellent viands. Hussein was paying a great deal more attention to her than he was to the fast-moving cabaret on the stage. She parried his attempts at intimacy, flirted with him warily and knew he did not interest her as a man. By the time the cabaret was drawing to a close, she knew he was exasperated with her lack of response. In all honesty, she wished she had not reacted quite so recklessly to Mark's too evident desire to keep her away from Hussein. She should have stayed in Galveston—especially since Hussein did not give the impression of being one who was easily distracted once his mind was made up.

As Toni looked away from her overly attentive escort, she noticed an Arab, his robes flowing, his aristocratic head flung high, searching the crowd, then making his way to the head waiter. The man nodded, gestured and accepted a folded note. Toni watched him come toward them as applause broke out for the entertainers. The band had begun its opening number, and couples were spilling onto the dance floor as the maître d' asked Hussein's pardon and handed him the note.

Hussein held it close to the flickering light of the candle in the center of the tiny table. As he read he scowled. "We must go, Antonia. I am very sorry, but I have received a message I cannot ignore."

He thrust some bills at the waiting man. "That should be sufficient to cover our bill, I think. You may keep the change." By the expression on the man's face, Toni knew Hussein had given him much more than was required. "Come, Antonia. I must make arrangements for your transport back to Galveston, then leave you. I am desolate but I can do nothing else."

"I am perfectly capable of returning to Galveston on my own, Hussein. Please don't bother about me; you must not. Just go and leave me. I will be fine."

By now they had reached the regal messenger. The two men exchanged sharp words in their own language. The messenger glanced unabashedly at her, then stalked away.

"Come, Antonia. I will see you to your room. I am sorry our evening has been spoiled."

"You mustn't think that, Hussein. It has been perfect. I have had a wonderful time. Thank you very much."

He was adamant about seeing her to the room. He collected the key from the desk and saw her into the elevator. "I shall return, Miss Antonia Cameron, and we shall spend a long and uninterrupted time together, if you are willing."

Was she? She did not know. After he had opened her door she offered him her hand. He took it, gave her a glance that should have melted her and kissed her fingers gently.

"Goodbye, Antonia."

"Goodbye, Hussein. Thank you again."

He disappeared into the elevator and Toni went to bed, wondering what the message had contained to make him leave so hurriedly.

Sharp knuckles on the door aroused her the next morning.

"Who is it?" Toni, sleepy, was sure it was very early.

"Room service, miss. Breakfast, as you ordered." The words were muffled through the heavy door. Toni pulled on her robe and went barefoot to the door. Hussein must have ordered her breakfast as he left, she supposed. Thoughtful of him, but why so early?

Her sleepy eye to the peephole, she saw that it was indeed a uniformed employee of the hotel and that a white cloth was draped over the wheeled cart he was pushing. She unlatched the chained door and opened it.

"Good morning, miss." The man's smile was entirely correct. Delicious aromas wafted up from the covered dishes. Toni sighed and went to look for change.

"You should not walk barefoot in a hotel room, Antonia."

Toni jerked around at the drawled comment. Mark was leaning against the doorframe in a pose she had noted before. He was dressed as he had been before, too, in fitted black suede trousers, a black turtleneck sweater and the black suede jacket that suited his wide-shouldered frame.

The waiter crooked a questioning eyebrow at Toni. "It is all right," she assured him in a cool and proper voice. "This man is my boss. Unfortunately he is very short on proper manners, according to all who know him well. But he is relatively harmless."

"If you say so, miss." He took the bills she offered him and tucked them in his pocket. He assessed Mark briefly, and Toni had the distinct feeling he did not consider the oilman to be harmless. But he shrugged and went out.

"Aren't you going to invite me in to share the breakfast I ordered for us, Antonia?"

"You ordered? I thought Hussein...."

"No. I did it. Hussein was in a hell of a hurry. He forgot some of his impeccable manners."

Toni stared at his calm and easy expression. Mark was giving nothing away this morning. She sighed, gestured at the table.

"Well, I expect you will have to help me eat this extravagant spread you have ordered." The table was set for two with crystal, china and cutlery that had the look of silver. A single red rose lay upon the napkin folded across one plate. Mark moved into the room, closing the door behind him.

Toni quickly left to brush her teeth and scrub her treacherous face with cold water. Calmness restored as much as possible, she walked briskly back to her chair at the lovely table.

"May I know what your sudden appearance in Dallas, in this hotel, in my room, is in aid of?" She poured coffee, buttered toast and maintained her poise nicely.

"I knew you were here and that Hussein had to go," he stated mildly. "As I have something I want to show you, I thought this would be a good time to come."

"And how did you know I was at this hotel?" she queried tartly.

"Simple deduction," he murmured, eyes laughing at her. "Prince Hussein has an infallible instinct for the best. This is the best hotel Dallas has to offer."

"Hmm. And just how did you know the prince had to leave?"

"Spies." He leered at her, the laughter in those hazel eyes mocking. "Spies all over the place, ready to do my least bidding."

She laughed without rancor, shook her shining head at him. "You are the most impossible man. What is it that is so important to show me?"

"One of nature's extravaganzas," he murmured. She felt as if he had reached out, touched her caressingly.

Toni stopped laughing. Something in his eyes brought home in full force the intimacy of this breakfast. She swallowed a mouthful of omelet and rose hastily. "If we are going somewhere, I'll just get ready."

"Don't hurry on my account." He smiled with easy charm. "I am in no hurry. . .now." Toni escaped with the sure knowledge that to remain was to invite disaster.

Two and a half hours later Mark turned his powerful XKE into a side road and plunged into a forested area he told her was the Big Thicket of Texas. He guided the car down a narrow, smoothly surfaced road for a mile or two, then turned into a dirt track.

"Close your eyes," he ordered abruptly. "Don't open them until I say."

She looked at him and received a smile of such sweetness that she shut her eyes instantly and thought about the effect that smile had upon her.

Mark stopped the car, opened his door and came around to her side. His hands were gentle on hers as he assisted her from the bucket seat. "Don't cheat. Just hang on to me and keep those gorgeous navy blue eyes closed." His hands on her shoulders, he turned her away from him. She felt the sun on her face.

"Now, Antonia."

Toni opened her eyes to a scene of such natural beauty that it took her breath away. They were standing on the brow of a little hill, a lake nestled at their feet...and the whole rolling landscape was covered with a heavenly blue. The blooms were spread like a carpet under the trees, over the hills stretching to the horizon where the thicket did not interfere with the view.

"Oh, Mark, how beautiful! What are they?"

"Texas bluebonnets, brought on by this long stretch of unseasonable spring weather we have been having. It's a sight not many people are privileged to see. I'm glad you have the chance."

"I'm pleased to have the opportunity to see it. It's fantastic...unbelievable." She turned to him impulsively and hugged his suede-clad arms, her face glowing. "Thank you for sharing it with me."

His intent look told her plainly that he was perfectly willing to share much more with her, but he forbore to say anything; his smile was seduction enough. They walked then, up and down the hills, around the shore of the little lake.

When Mark took her back to the car, he opened the trunk and extracted a big wicker picnic basket. Toni was delighted and not a little astonished at his thoughtfulness.

They ate lazily under the spreading branches of an evergreen oak, talking easily like old friends, all sense of strain gone. Toni packed away the remains of the meal and moved to sit against the gnarled trunk of the tree, her eyes on the blue distance.

"Here." Mark shed his suede jacket and spread it face down for her. Toni accepted the gesture graciously, sank down with her back against the tree, her legs curled under her on the jacket. Sighing with contentment, Mark sat beside her, not touching her.

Silence descended and thickened, broken only by the twittering of the birds, the rustle of the wind in the branches. It was so peaceful, so beautiful, so. . . right. Then suddenly Toni trembled, grew tense as she felt the presence of the man beside her. His masculinity flowed from him, encompassing her with a throbbing crystalline sense of awareness. It was a sense that was fragile, quivering, but as real as the gold and blue of the land. Mark just sat there and waited.

Finally Toni turned to him with a sigh, unable to ignore the purity of the moment, and Mark took her into his arms.

Never had Toni expected to experience such beauty. His kiss was sweetness, fulfillment, enchantment, and it turned into a call she met with eagerness and promise. Mark gasped softly, raised his head and stared down at her upturned face with an incredulous kind of joy, then dropped his tawny head again.

Caution stirred in Toni then. She squirmed, felt something hard press into her tender flesh and reached like a drowning man for the excuse it gave her. "Mark," she protested feebly against his kiss, "something is hurting me."

He raised his head, shook it slightly, came back to earth and read her expression accurately. He moved away then, a man entirely sure of himself.

"Let me see." He moved her closer into the curve of his arm, reached behind her with his free hand, feeling for the offending object. His long fingers dipped into the jacket pocket she had been sitting on, closed over the object that had pressed into her flesh and became instantly still. Toni felt him go rigid and waited for him to remove his hand from the pocket.

"What is it, Mark?" she murmured curiously.

"I'd forgotten it, Antonia." He released her, handed her the leather folio she had lost so many aeons ago in the hotel room in London.

Toni took it, her sense of outrage equaled only by a strange sense of betrayal. Oh, how could he have kept it, allowed her to believe she had lost it?

"You have had it all the time, Mark Anders. You were wearing this jacket when we came from London!"

"My dear girl, I sent John back to London to find it for you, remember?" Something flickered deep in those hazel eyes, something that was immediately masked. "Linda does not mind doing small tasks for me—part of her job. And it did not take up much space in her luggage when she came over."

"Are you saying John found it and gave it to Linda to return to me?" Linda could very easily have forgotten to mention it in her hurry to catch her plane that day, Toni conceded. "Why didn't you give it to me at the meeting?"

His face hardened then, and he rose with that graceful litheness that was so characteristic of him. "I don't intend to continue this discussion, Antonia. Shall we go?"

Chilled by his sudden change of mood, she rose to her feet, carefully ignoring his outstretched hand. She carefully dusted off her skirt, a deep and unexpected regret eating away at her as she allowed her glance to wander again over the idyllic beauty of the place this man had wanted to share with her.

Mark didn't glance back at it as he gathered up the picnic things, threw them in the trunk and slammed it down with a decisive thud. The trip back to Galveston was accomplished in a complete and chilling silence that was far from being companionable.

CHAPTER ELEVEN

TONI FACED MONDAY MORNING with considerable reluctance. She parked the little red car and climbed the stairs, muddled over the problem of how best to treat the dynamic U.P.C. executive. She had decided on a cool and very distant approach by the time she reached the area she had been assigned. A niggling doubt as to her ability to carry through if he should desire to break down such an attitude worried at her. She rounded the barrier to Karen's area with a cool aggression she hoped hid her uncertainty.

"Dammit, you silly goose!" Greg's disgusted voice jerked Toni's attention away from her own introspection. "You know Mark isn't going to do one thing to hurt you! He only has your best interests at heart!"

He had Karen boxed in where the picture windows met at the corner. His big hands gripped the girl's shoulders as he shook her, far from gently. Karen's face was tear streaked.

Toni stopped in astonishment. What on earth did he think he was doing?

"He had no right!" Karen's objection was strenuous. "Frank didn't even have time to come and see me b-because th-that awful Hussein wanted him t-to go right away!"

"Well, Frank called you, didn't he?" Greg's exasperation was apparent, although Toni could not see

Now...bring twice as much romance into your life with a home subscription to SUPERROMANCES™

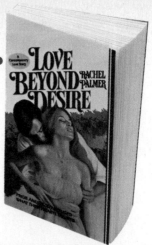

Bring twice as much romance into your life, beginning today. And receive *Love beyond Desire,* **free.** It's yours to keep even if you don't buy any additional books. Mail the card below.

SUPER?OMANCE
1440 South Priest Drive, Tempe, AZ 85281.

← Mail this card today for your FREE book.

- -

A compelling love story of mystery and intrigue... conflicts and jealousies... and a forbidden love that threatens to shatter the lives of all involved with the aristocratic Lopez family.

←Mail this card today for your FREE book.

for the life of her why he was concerned with Karen Prescott's love affair. "Frank isn't about to let Mark or anyone else tell him what to do. You know that. If he went to the Middle East it was because he decided to go. No one, but no one, pushes de la Cruz around."

"I-I know, Greg, but Mark has been so insistent. He keeps on at me as—as if I were a teenager still. And he refuses to believe Frank is sincere, either." She gulped and sobbed at the same time.

Greg looked at her with affection. It glinted in his tawny eyes, lit his tender smile. He gathered her to him, and Karen snuggled into his shoulder as if she belonged there.

"Don't cry, kitten," he admonished softly. "Frank has quite a rep and you know it. If you both are really sure of each other, it'll all work out. He's only gone for a few weeks. It's better to be sure now than sorry after a while...." He noticed Toni for the first time and winked at her over the other girl's head. "Hi, Toni."

Toni stared at him uncertainly. Karen seemed to accept his right to reprove and give advice without taking umbrage. Why? The question passed fleetingly through her mind.

"Oh, Toni...." Karen's little laugh apologized. "I have the blues this morning and they are leaking all over Greg's shirt." She pulled herself away from the tall man and turned around. "Shall I show you your new office? Mark had all your things moved into it while you were gone." She swallowed a faint hiccup and scrubbed at her face with a fluttering hand. "I expect I've made a real mess of my face. Can you wait a sec while I get presentable?"

"Mark got to be too much for you, did he?" Greg

teased her gently when the younger woman had gone. "Karen is having trouble this morning, too." He sighed and turned to the window. "He won't be here this week. She should settle down before he gets back."

"Mark has a tendency to get rather dictatorial," Toni offered dryly.

"Yeah. Well, he's generally right, dammit." His reply was gruff, unhappy.

Had he been right when he offered Greg some ignored and unwanted advice about Ginny Lee, Toni wondered. Greg's attitude gave the impression such might have been the case. He turned from the windows. "Got to go earn my daily bread, Toni. Mark will probably be gone all week, so us wage slaves are going to have to scratch along without him."

"Oh." An odd disappointment washed over Toni. She used considerable energy to deny the fact. "Where has our illustrious leader taken himself off to this time?"

"To Hussein in the Middle East, of course," Greg said with some surprise. "I thought you knew. Mark is extremely careful in his dealings with the Arabs. Those princes do most of their own deals personally, and they expect the courtesy of having the head honcho to talk to. Want to see your office?"

Toni nodded and went with him back down the center of the building. Greg pushed open a door across the aisle from the stairway and stood aside for Toni to enter.

The room had a restrained elegance. It was tucked back into the ninety-degree angle formed by the floor-to-ceiling glass of the two sides. An efficient desk and comfortable chair commanded a panoramic view of the gulf and the seawall. Bookcases and cupboards with wide counters filled the other two walls. A computer was within easy reach. File cabinets containing her projections and work sheets were placed where they would be instantly available.

The whole room was fitted with a wall-to-wall carpet in a soft sage green. A delightful oil painting hung between the cupboards on one wall. It depicted the bluebonnets in the Big Thicket, rendered from approximately the same spot Mark had taken her to.

He had put a lot of thought into this cozy room, she realized. And he must have planned to take her to the Big Thicket all along. Why else would the oil be hanging on her wall?

Had he planned the lovely scene to be the place where he finally seduced her, as well? In all honesty, Toni had to admit to herself he might very well have succeeded if Kurt's photo had not jabbed into her flesh like a prod of conscience. She turned away from Greg to hide the sudden flare of color that crept into her cheeks.

"This do for you, Toni?" he inquired. "Mark really went all out to get it done for you."

"It's quite adequate, thank you." Toni went to the big desk and sat down, her hand running across the satiny finish. "I rather like it."

"Thought you might. Mark said I was to give this to you personally." Greg opened a cupboard door. When he turned he held a tapered crystal vase in his fingers. A perfect rose bloomed in it. It was a deep velvety red set off in an absolutely faultless manner by a frothy sprig of fern. The small card with it contained a message. "Miss me" it commanded boldly, with an "M" for a signature.

Greg grinned at her amazed expression. "Mark said you would know what it meant," he offered as he set the vase down on the corner of the desk. Backing away, he lowered himself into the chair.

Toni thought of the rose Mark had given her in Dallas and her blush came, unbidden. Greg watched the wavering color with interest. He grinned then and brushed his big-brimmed hat to the back of bronze curls.

"Mark has even learned some Arabic." He continued the conversation about his cousin as if it were the most natural thing in the world. "He sounds like a snarling camel when he comes on with it, but they like it."

Toni laughed in spite of herself. "Snarling camel indeed! Greg, you are impossible."

"I reckon so," he agreed complacently. "Part of my undeniable charm. Anyhow, Mark is a smart old boy. The Arabs like it because he has made an effort to understand their language. They don't seem to give a hang if he can't do it well. They are much too polite to laugh at him, and it certainly gives him an inside track."

"I imagine so."

"Hey, young lady, don't sound so sarcastic." Greg sprang quickly to Mark's defense. "Mark just does it as a matter of courtesy. Those Arab princes are as proud as Lucifer. They appreciate an effort like that. Any Arabic is hard to understand if you're not brought up speaking it. Guess Mark has an ear for language. He goes over there and does business on their schedule. Anyway, he's learned a lot about them and it has paid off. 'Course he went to school with Hussein and that has helped."

"I didn't know that." Toni's interest was caught in spite of her resolve to know as little about Mark Anders as possible.

"Yeah." Greg relaxed back in his chair and crossed one booted foot over his knee. "Went to University of Southern Cal together, those two. Mark understands them, as much as a Westerner can, and they trust him. In fact, Hussein almost treats him like one of the family. Their friendship hasn't hurt U.P.C. one bit, but it takes a hell of a lot of Mark's time. He works each deal on a personal basis, and time don't mean a tinker's damn to an Arab. Almost anything can be more important than a business deal. Family, friends, the government."

Toni raised a polite eyebrow. "Speaking of wasting time, Greg, I've masses of reports to get through."

"Yeah, I know, but I don't often get to start off my day talking to such a pretty lady."

Toni tried her best to squelch him with a frosty look. Greg laughed good-naturedly and uncoiled his lean length from the chair.

"Okay, okay." He held up a large hand in a gesture of defense. "I read you, Toni!" A soft knock sounded and he swiveled his tawny head toward the door. "Shall I let 'em in?"

"Please do." Toni's amusement bubbled up.

Greg strode to the door and opened it. Karen was there, anxiety written clearly on her expressive young face. "There's a man to see you, Greg."

The man did not wait to be introduced. He thrust himself forward with an aggressive air. "Gregory Powers Sims?" He flung the words at Greg in a manner that set Toni's teeth on edge. She rose from her place, suddenly uneasy.

"Yeah. What of it?" Greg's easy good humor vanished at the obvious challenge in the man's attitude.

"I'm serving these papers on you. Order of the Superior Court of Harris County." He thrust a legal-sized envelope at Greg.

Greg took it as a reflex action. The man swung around and vanished down the stairs with laudable dispatch. One look at Greg's thunderous expression was enough to convince Toni of the man's wisdom in absenting himself so smartly.

"Oh, Greg...." Karen's choked whisper hung between them. Clearly she expected the papers to be bad news. "What is it?"

"Dunno, honey." Greg stared at the papers he held, a white line around his mouth, his eyes mere slits. "If you girls will excuse me, I'll find out." He headed for the privacy of Mark's littered area.

Karen stared after him a moment, then murmured an excuse and anxiously followed him. Toni closed the door and went to her desk, her curiosity under firm control. She had too much to do even if she had been inclined to question him.

GREG DID NOT SEE FIT to confide in her, but his strange mood worried her all week. He carried a chip on his shoulder in a manner entirely at odds with his usual easygoing style. Any attempt to restore him to his characteristic good humor was met with brusque rejection.

The team suffered. By the middle of the week everyone tried to avoid him whenever possible. Friday, Toni decided she must speak to him. She called him into her office and told him quite frankly he was impossible to work with and asked him what was wrong. "Is it that I am a woman and you find it hard to work with me as head of the team, Greg?''

"Good Lord, no, Toni.'' He rubbed a big hand across his tired face, his stubble rasping. "You will have to forgive me. This has been a hell of a week.''

"It has,'' she agreed. "We've all felt it.''

Greg dropped his tawny head into his hands and was silent. Toni waited. Mark's big cousin sighed gustily, kneaded his eyes with his palms. "Ginny Lee served me with divorce papers on Monday,'' he announced abruptly, bitterness lacing his husky comment. "I just never thought she would somehow.''

Toni watched him, touched. It was evident he had no wish for a separation. "Greg, I'm so sorry.''

"Yeah. Thanks. I should have expected it, I suppose. Mark always said she—'' He caught himself up with a husky sound that was between a hiccup and a sob. Toni's heart went out to him.

"Well, it's happened.'' He straightened in the chair, pulling himself together with a conscious effort, then considered the compassionate expression on Toni's face. "You wouldn't be willing to go to a party with me tonight, by any chance?''

He looked so desperately unhappy that Toni could not refuse him. He gave her a mournful grin and stood, his tall figure slumped.

"I'll make a hell of an escort, but I'll try to cheer up. I have to appear. Thanks, Toni. You make a man's sore heart feel there may be hope in this old world yet. I'll pick you up around eight.''

THAT EVENING Toni finished applying her light dusting of makeup and slipped into the silky dress she had decided to wear.

The bodice clung nicely to the contours of her upper body, hugged her narrow waist and fell in delightful fullness to her slender ankles. The dress was a heavenly shade of blue that set off her golden tan and made her eyes turn a deep and mysterious midnight blue. And she had found delicate sandals to go with the dress. High-heeled, they helped to give her five-foot-two person a bit of height.

A few minutes later she heard Greg come into the hall. Snatching up her velvet evening bag, she tripped down the stairs to meet him, glad to be going out, happy with her new dress, pleased with the way she looked.

Greg was obviously pleased with her appearance, too. Seizing her shoulders, he twirled her around so her skirt swirled about her. He cocked an eye at her and whistled in approval—at least he tried to whistle. A ragged bleat was the sum total of a lot of effort. Toni realized he had been drinking. Rather a lot, she judged from the slight disarray of his spectacularly fitted dress suit.

"Greg, are you sure you want to attend this affair?"

"Got to attend. Mark will have my head if I don't." He rocked back on his heels, the better to take in the full length of the woman in his hands. His fingers tightened painfully on Toni's slim shoulders as he used her for an anchor and maintained his balance. "Besides, I wouldn't miss it for the world. You have got to be the most beautiful woman there. Just wait till the rest of the guys see you. We'll show 'em I ain't dead yet!"

And with that enigmatic remark, he dropped her wrap around her shoulders and marched her from the house. Toni balked at the curb. A powerful American car sat there, obviously one of the more luxurious ones. Maybe a Cadillac, but she could not be sure. The one thing she was sure of was that she did not wish to chance Greg's driving. His tutoring when he had introduced her to driving had been expert but flamboyant. That flamboyance, fanned by drink and frustration, could prove to be downright reckless. She discussed it gravely with the tall man at her side. He grinned down at her with a sweet goodwill, dug into his pocket and produced a set of keys.

"Lovely lady, you are absolutely right. Your wish is my command. Drive!"

And so Toni found herself behind the wheel of the great car, staring at a dashboard that seemed to have enough buttons to control at least a fighter plane. She looked it over grimly, solved the problem of starting the huge thing and soon found herself enjoying complete control of the powerful automobile. Greg smiled benignly and directed them toward Houston, rattling off a comprehensive travelogue as they moved along the dark highway.

The affair was held in an immense and plush private club. Flowers banked the club rooms in lavish disregard for expense. The main dining room was hung with great crystal chandeliers; the tables, covered with expensive china and silver, were like snowy, linen-covered islands set in a thick green carpet as soft as velvet. Toni stood with Greg and looked across the dining room to a ballroom beyond, where the dance floor gleamed invitingly. She could hear the orchestra over the laughter and voices of the crowd in the vast foyer. Everyone had a glass in hand. Hers was soon filled as a gin and tonic was delivered to her; a straight whiskey for Greg. Toni had not heard him order anything, but she took the tall cool glass from the waiter who brought it and thanked her escort for it, wondering how he knew what she liked to drink.

Greg grasped her elbow in firm fingers and stared around the big room. He knew masses of people. Toni gave up trying to remember names, concentrated on the faces and voices and tried to hold her own in the rapid-fire repartee that came from all sides.

Somewhere in the crowd she lost track of Greg. It did not seem to matter in the least. Attentive men intent on entertaining her swirled around her. She found herself with a third gin and tonic in her hand. She was laughing into the sun-browned face of a Texan, who was insisting his heart would be scarred for life if she refused it, when a sudden stillness swept over her. Without thought, she knew Mark was in the room.

She did not have to look for him. Incredulous, she turned her head and met his hooded gaze. He stood across the room from her, close to the entry of the dining area. Toni's breath left her body. She stared at him, her heart literally in her throat, choking her; her response to him was all-consuming. She swayed as the blood drained from her face.

The tall Texan beside her reached for her nerveless arm and steadied her, his other hand rescuing the frosted glass he had just handed her. "Whoa, there, little lady," he murmured, real concern in his twang. "You look like you've seen a ghost." His keen glance followed hers in an effort to locate the cause of her curious reaction. Toni shook her head sharply, color flooding back into her face. The crowd had moved and screened Mark. Thankfully, she took the glass and swallowed a big gulp of the cool contents. She excused herself and fled for the safety of the ladies' room, absolutely aghast at the knowledge thrust upon her by the unexpected appearance of U.P.C.'s chief executive.

In that moment she knew that she was in love with Mark Anders—head over heels, hopelessly, irrevocably in love with a man she was sure she did not even like. Numbed by the fact, disgusted with herself, she sat for a few moments in the ornate lounge, thoughts and emotions whirling in chaos.

It could not be, she told herself fiercely. It just could not be. Such things do not creep up unexpectedly upon one. There had to be some sort of mutual ground, some sort of liking for love to grow. It could not, did not grow out of the rocky and inhospitable soil of dissension. Common sense forced her to acknowledge that it had indeed grown in just such a climate.

"Oh, how could I be such a fool?" she moaned softly. Meeting the startled attention of the group of chattering women just entering the room, she knew she had spoken aloud. She left hastily. She would have to find Greg and ask him to leave, she decided. More than anything, Toni knew she must get away, must have some time alone to cope with this new and devastating self-knowledge.

She got back to the foyer in time to witness Ginny Lee's theatrical entrance to the party.

She stood there, an absolutely stunning figure. Head lifted innocently, eyes glowing with interest, she seemed to be searching for someone. Her shape and her face were exquisite, Toni admitted. The golden sheath that clung to the perfection of her body was a glorious foil for the spun silk of her auburn hair. Wide green eyes, elegantly slanted in the radiant oval of her splendidly balanced features, flashed as they scanned

the crowd. Against the force of femininity she exuded,
her escort was a formless figure, a backdrop for her
beauty. She stood poised, still, searching. Every man
in the room became subtly conscious of that search.
Toni watched them respond.

Ginny Lee smiled, a secretive seductive smile that
accepted the homage granted her and moved on down
into the room, a goddess descending to the mortals
below. Her gown shimmered as she moved, a radiance
that enhanced every movement of the body under-
neath and spoke of the delights it clothed.

What an entrance! Toni sighed, shook her head in
sympathy for Greg and went to look for him. Fifteen
minutes later she had covered all the rooms of the
club. Greg was not in evidence. She had just finished
searching the last of the high-backed, leather easy
chairs in the smoking room when Mark came through
the door, closing it behind him.

Toni stood stock-still, the blood draining from her
head then rushing around her system in a manner leaving her dizzy, intoxicated.

He stood against the door, arrogantly handsome in
black tux and ruffled shirt, laughing at her bemused
expression. "Antonia...."

Her name was a caress on his lips. His voice weakened her knees, caused her hands to clench into fists in
the graceful folds of her gown. Heat washed over her
as she met the smoldering demand half-veiled by those
ridiculously long lashes of his. Bedroom eyes, she
thought, resisting the impulse to giggle hysterically. In
that moment Toni recognized the depth of her trouble,
knew what had happened to unsettle her world during
the past few weeks. Not only was she in love with the
man, but she also wanted him with a hunger so strong
that it threatened her control—terrified her.

She had no time to resist the mad thought, to push it into proper perspective and drown it in scornful contempt, as it deserved to be drowned. He covered the space between them and was close to her then, so close she found it impossible to breathe.

"Did you miss me, Antonia?" The question was husky, seductive.

"Certainly not," she shot back with a passionate desire to hide her new knowledge until she had time to recover from the shock to her senses. "I've been much too busy even to notice you were gone."

"Hmm... let's see, shall we?" Mark's purpose was plain to read.

Toni backed hastily around the big leather chair and tried to put it between them. She found herself deep in the window embrasure, her back against the velvet draperies drawn across it. Trapped, she stared up at him with a wild defiance, unable to say a word. Mark stood over her, his lashes lowered, concentrating on the sweet curve of her lips, on the dimple appearing and disappearing, triggered by the force of her ragged breath. For moments he did not touch her. The sheer power of his masculinity reduced her defenses to rubble, her resolve to nonsense.

Then with a low and gentle murmur, he reached for her. Toni quivered, stiffened and fought the demand of the sweetness that flooded her very cells with ecstasy. Mark muttered a husky reproach against her resisting mouth and increased his demand as he deepened the kiss with a ruthless devastation. Toni fell into the abyss, exploding into passionate intoxication, her being coalesced into one sensitive heartbeat that pulsed and was insatiable.

The door opened and was flung back with a thump that jarred into Toni's consciousness. Dazed, she dragged her soft mouth from Mark's drugging dominance, smudgy lashes a veil over the awakened passion she was powerless to deny.

Ginny Lee simmered in the doorway, but the fiery venom that seared the woman in Mark's arms was quickly masked. "Mark, darling, everyone is hunting for you." The smoothness with which she spoke made Toni aware that Ginny Lee could not have cared less about the implication of the scene before her. "Senator Johns wishes to see you at once. Would you please hurry, darling? He must leave in ten minutes, he tells me. And you know how important the senator is."

"I know, Ginny Lee," he agreed curtly, his attention still on the flushed face of the woman he held. He ignored the other woman's presence, tilted Toni's face up with a long finger whose strength could not be denied and laughed when she dropped her lashes to hide her telltale eyes from his intent probing. He kissed the tip of her pert little nose and let her go. "Stay here, Antonia, please. I have to see the man, but I'll be back."

Ginny Lee watched him go. She reached out and put a restraining hand on Toni's arm when she started to excuse herself in an attempt to beat a hasty retreat.

"Sit down, my dear." The smooth voice did little to conceal a caustic distaste. "I can see that Mark is up to his old tricks, trying to seduce every new kid on the block, as it were. Has he managed it with you so soon?"

"I beg your pardon!" Shocked disbelief held Toni rooted to the spot.

"Oh, you don't need to come on the fine lady with me, you know. I know how these macho males are—and Mark is one of the worst. No woman is safe from

him. Even I, as his beloved cousin's wife...." The
insidious smooth voice trailed off, the glow in the
green slanted eyes unmistakable.

Toni stared into the beautiful face, her own rigid
with disbelief.

"You needn't look so horrified," Ginny Lee
sneered. "It happens all the time, you know. So convenient for us. Mark just sends Greg on a job and then
he can have me to himself." Self-satisfaction lit her
features, giving them a feline appearance. "It is just
lately he has decided he wants all of my time. Why else
do you think I am divorcing Greg? So don't be a little
fool and think Mark has anything more in mind than
to pass a few pleasant moments with someone who is
untried and has passable looks." Her tinkling laugh
was more than Toni could bear.

Wordlessly she snatched up her small evening bag
from where it had fallen when Mark came toward her.
She left the room in as dignified a manner as possible,
refusing to give in to the impulse to launch herself
upon the woman who had just taken the precious ten-
drils of her newfound love and crushed them into
shameful nonexistence. She marched out of the building, uncaring that she had forgotten her wrap.

The chill air hit her like a blow, but it could not com-
pare to the blow her battered heart had sustained that
night. Tears streaming down her face, she took the keys
for Greg's car from her small bag. She hoped that he
would be able to find his way home and would forgive
her for leaving him without transportation. She only
knew she had to leave this place, to find a quiet spot and
sort out her tangled and much bruised emotions.

The parking lot was full. A damp wind tore at
Toni's hair and clothes as she sought to remember

where the car was parked. All of them were so similar, she thought with despair. Then suddenly she found the car. She rushed around to the driver's side and opened the door. Greg was asleep, a drunken sodden mess curled up on the back seat. Toni sobbed with relief and started the big vehicle, reversing out of the parking space and speeding away—away from Mark Anders and his insidious seduction, away from the horrible woman he was having an affair with.

Rain caught them before they were halfway back to Galveston, a blinding rain that finally forced Toni to give up and pull the car over to the shoulder of the highway. It was raining so hard that the wipers had no chance to clear the glass.

Chilled to the bone, Toni finally curled up like a kitten on the ample front seat. She did not expect to sleep, not with the state of chaos her normally well-ordered thoughts were in. But she awoke to daylight, the rain still drumming on the automobile, Greg's tux jacket tucked firmly around her. Toni struggled out of it, ran her fingers through her hair.

Greg was in his shirt-sleeves, snoring gently on the back seat. He awakened as she shifted under the steering wheel, doubled his long length with a surprising agility and slid onto the front seat beside her. He refused his jacket and tucked it back around her.

"Hmm, it's just a little damp out there, isn't it?" His dry remark was accompanied by the rasp of an overnight growth of stubble under the pressure of a big hand. "Gawd, I feel as if somebody pulled the plug and let all my sand run out."

Toni smiled in spite of herself. "Does it always rain with such dedication in this part of the world?" she inquired curiously.

He peered through the window at the barely visible macadam of the road. "Rain? This little shower? Lordy, lady, you should see what happens when it really gets down to business." Toni laughed at the scandalized expression he managed to come up with in spite of his evident discomfort.

"Do you think we can find some coffee somewhere?"

Greg pushed back the ruffled cuff of his disheveled dress shirt and squinted at the gold watch on his wrist. He knew just the place. They spent the next hour and a half in an all-night truck stop. Toni fought the dull ache residing somewhere in the region of her heart and joined Greg in his gay insouciance. He made no reference to Ginny Lee, and Toni could not, either. The scars the woman had inflicted were too raw, too new. She drove on into Galveston later, still not ready to face the issue that ate like a cancer into her peace of mind.

Greg wrapped her in his tux jacket, and they ran through the splashing rain to the house. The door opened as they reached it. Mark stood there, his eyes blazing, his jaw clenched so tightly his lips were drawn back in a snarl.

"And just where the hell do you two think you've been?"

CHAPTER TWELVE

TONI'S HEART CONTRACTED, but she drew herself up to her full five foot two, tossed her wet hair back and managed as scornful a glance as she had ever used on another person in her life. Wordlessly she marched past him on her way to her room, where at least her heartbreak could pass unseen.

A powerful hand brought her to an abrupt halt. Mark glared at her, a wild passion in his slitted eyes. She shivered and jerked out of his grasp.

"Don't you ever touch me again, Mark Anders! And if I didn't have to work with you I'd never want to see you again!" she hissed, her tone blistering with contempt. She faced him, struggling for breath amid the choking anger that caused blood to thunder in her head and deafen her.

He stared at her, his lips thinned, muscles tensed as if he meant to pounce on her.

"Did you understand me?" she lashed at him, not caring whether he did or not. She raced up the stairs and flung herself into the haven of her room, as miserable as any woman in love could ever be, she knew for a fact. And it was all her own fault! Why, oh, why hadn't she had the sense to listen to her inner warning system? It had told her of the danger within hours of meeting that dynamic man downstairs. She had chosen to ignore it, lured into close contact with that fatal charm of his by a wild streak in her nature that had finally broken from her iron control. Her blasted uncontrolled nature had insisted on coming to the States, being around him.

And now she was in love with him! Toni did not need to analyze her feelings to know that what she felt for Mark was entirely different from her love for Kurt. She was an adult now, not an inexperienced girl. There was no way she would ever be able to deny her love for Mark, no matter how reprehensible his character. It was a sobering thought.

Toni was still sober and unsettled when she went to work the next day. She walked through the fresh, rain-scented, early-morning air and climbed the stairs to the offices, not at all sure of her probable actions when it came to dealing with Mr. Mark Anders this morning. She needn't have worried. He wasn't there and neither was Greg.

Greg, Dick Handy informed her later in the day when they were feeding information into his omnivorous computer, had flown out into the Caribbean. The floating rig, *Sea Venture*, was having a rough go in stormy seas, Dick told her. Mark had sent Greg out to help bring her in.

Unbidden, the hateful words of Ginny Lee slashed through her mind: "Mark just sends Greg on a job and then he has me to himself...." Was she with him now? Karen had already informed her Mark was off on one of his business trips and would be gone a few days. Toni threw herself into the task before her in a frenzied effort to kill the pain. The team responded to her driving need by keeping the data flowing in. The parameters that were characteristic of the formations they sought were beginning to take shape.

Toni went home each night exhausted, driving herself until she had no energy left for anything but sleep when she sank into her bed. She would fall into dreamless oblivion, thoughts of Mark successfully blotted out for another twenty-four hours.

Saturday night she worked late. She was the last to leave the office when she finally gave in to weariness. She parked at the curb and ran up the steps. It would not hurt the little car to sit out one night, she thought as she dashed through the door, and straight into the arms of Mike Lane.

He caught her, his good-looking face creased with amusement. "Hello! I really must do this more often if I'm to receive such a super greeting each time!"

"Mike! How did you get here?" Toni had not heard from him and was surprised to see him again so soon. It was a long way from Dallas to Galveston, even as the fast-paced Texans traveled.

He laughed. "I hope that is pleased astonishment I hear in those bell-like tones, beautiful lady. Come to Houston with me, if no one else has designs on your evening?"

She looked up at him, about to refuse, then surrendered to impulse, pushing tiredness to the back of her mind. "It sounds great!" If her nervous little laugh caused Mike's eyes to sharpen, Toni did not notice. "Give me a moment or two and I'll be with you." She ran up the stairs, directing him over her shoulder to wait in the big living room.

Changing quickly into a swirling skirt in a fine red wool, she pulled on the matching sweater, which clung to her, the front a deep V into which Toni tied a red-and-black scarf. She gave her hair a quick brush and ran back down the stairs, her slender feet in high-heeled matching sandals. Downstairs she hunted up ma, properly introduced her to her escort and explained they were on their way to dinner.

"Ain't none of my business, but where?" ma asked bluntly, a faint frown on her good-natured face. Toni, astonished that ma would presume to question her movements, had no time to reply.

"We're going to Houston," Mike cut in smoothly, smiling at the woman with a sure charm. "We may go to a cinema then, or perhaps somewhere and dance. We shan't return until quite late probably." His tone clearly implied that he meant to make the most of those hours.

Ma searched his lean handsome face, then nodded. It was not a nod of approval, just one of reading his intention to have a place in the life of the young woman beside him.

"Have fun—and be careful," she warned as she took in the hired car waiting for them. "I ain't sure these Texas drivers know anything about civilized rules of the road. They take politeness for weakness more times than not and stamp all over you. At least they've been known to try!" She scowled as she closed the door, an odd reluctance to leave them alone all too evident in her manner.

Mike was clearly amused by her attitude. "Who is she? The resident dragon at the door, laid there to protect your virtue, fair maiden?"

Toni laughed with him, not much pleased by the sudden realization that Ma Ruddy might be exactly that. But surely Mark would not have the temerity to put her in a position where her leisure time was monitored—or worse, reported? Her face was very thoughtful as she allowed Mike to guide her into the passenger seat. She dismissed the unwelcome thought of ma's surveillance as ridiculous and turned her attention to her charming escort, determined to enjoy herself.

And enjoy herself she did. Very thoroughly indeed—at least during the major portion of the evening. They ate at the Boston Half Shell, a seafood restaurant that offered incredible masses of gourmet-quality viands from the world's oceans. After stuffing themselves unashamedly, they went on to a film. It was a comedy, and Toni found herself relaxing for the first time in ages, laughing until tears came.

Afterward Mike steered the big car in the direction of a bar some friend had recommended to him. It was a dimly lit rooftop lounge, the habitat of a first-class combo. The cozy room contained a dance floor surrounded by intimate, deeply comfortable sofas built for two, facing each other in pairs across low tables lit by candles. Houston spread out below them, jeweled with sparkling lights.

The lounge was filled with smiling chatting people in expensive clothing. Mike took her to a table, ordered drinks and insisted that she dance with him. Toni melted into his arms, perfectly at home with his smoothly executed dance patterns.

Several pleasant dances later, she walked off the dance floor as the orchestra took a well-earned break. Laughing up at Mike in appreciation of one of his dry witticisms, she ran right into Mark.

His eyesight not yet adjusted to the darkness of the room, he stood at the edge of the dance floor, one arm casually around the waist of a glowing Ginny Lee. He reached with the other and caught Toni as she lurched against him. Light glinted off his hazel eyes, giving them a fiery malevolent glint as he stared down into the amazed face of his offshore operations officer. Toni caught her breath; Mark's arm tightened fiercely a moment, then relaxed. But he did not release her.

"Well, well, what have we here?" His deep drawl was as smooth as silk. For one wild moment Toni entertained the thought that Mark had followed her here deliberately.

He had not appeared in the office all week. Toni had refused to inquire as to his whereabouts, and Karen had volunteered nothing except that he was out of town on business. How had he managed to turn up here?

The fact that he had the too perfect Ginny Lee on his arm sickened Toni, but at least it put the facts in proper perspective. Ginny Lee was with him because Greg was out on the high seas attending to the approaching oil rig! Toni was grateful for the darkness. At least it hid the pain she was sure must be reflected in her face.

"Mark Anders! Fancy meeting you here." Mike's voice was as unruffled as Mark's.

Yes, just fancy that, Toni thought caustically. The pilot reached for her and tucked her against his side with easy confidence. Toni tilted her head, smiled up at him. She was driven by a wild defiance she could not have defined.

"Yeah. . . ." Mark softly trailed the lazy syllable. "H'lo, Antonia. You know Ginny Lee, of course. Virginia, this is Mike Lane, captain of the Concorde."

Ginny Lee's smile was a thing of beauty—and a promise of joy forever, Toni thought tartly. She put a well-groomed and beautifully shaped hand in Mike's, her slanted green eyes warm with approval and that sex appeal that Toni had seen work its wonders on a roomful of men. Toni watched her turn the wattage up, a slow and seductive smile stealing over the perfection of her features.

"I am so pleased to meet you." The low murmur seemed to state clearly that Ginny Lee had been waiting all her life for this moment of introduction to the man holding her hand. "I am absolutely stunned that I should be able to get to know the pilot of that fabulous plane."

"Thank you, Miss Sims." Mike's composure did not seem to be in danger of eroding under her blatant seductiveness, Toni observed, surprised. And the impossible woman was *Mrs.* Sims! Neither Mark nor Ginny Lee bothered to correct Mike's assumption that the woman was not married, and Toni let it go, not willing to be petty. Mike was quite able to take care of himself anyway. "We seem to be blocking the passage," he observed. "Care to join us?"

No! Toni only just managed to choke off the impulse to shout the word. Her aversion to Greg's future ex-spouse had grown to monstrous proportions, she realized to her horror. Yet inevitably, it seemed, the latecomers were seated across from them at a low table in the comfortable lounge. Drinks were ordered and delivered.

Toni managed not to disgrace herself with an outburst, but Mike considered her tight expression curiously and asked her to dance as the orchestra resumed playing. She left the spot with rather undignified haste, relieved to escape from Mark's relentless stare and the undisguised disdain that glittered at her from Ginny Lee's catlike eyes. The cold sick disgust she felt sprang from the knowledge that Greg's wife had been truthful when she had said it was useful for Mark to

be her husband's boss. Useful for him and useful for
Ginny Lee, as well, Toni could now see. Granted, the
Simses were now in the process of getting a divorce.
Still, this had no doubt been the order of things for
some of the time they had apparently been happily
married. Mark would not have to search too hard to
find a good and sufficient reason to send Greg on
urgent business elsewhere, and then have his cousin's
wife to himself.

How vile he was! And how could she ever have fall-
en in love with such a person? It was useless to fight a
fact. She was in love. All the emotion she had so sternly repressed during the past week boiled to the surface.
Dazed by the force of her feelings, Toni followed
Mike's movements without conscious thought. She
was deep in a blue funk when he released her into
Mark's arms, responding to the executive's tap on his
shoulder and his murmured request to interrupt.

Neither man paid the slightest heed to her shocked
protest. Left with the alternative of creating a scene on
the dance floor, Toni gave up and moved stiffly, rigid
with distaste but unable to help herself. Mark held her
close, moved in tentative invitation, felt her resistance.
He punished her then, his arms encircling her in a
manner that stood for no nonsense as he urged her into
compliance with the rhythmic magic of his muscular
frame. Her chaotic emotions suddenly ran out of control, a wild confusion brought on by the wine she had
consumed, the knowledge that she hated the man she
loved, and by the nearness, the feel, the sight of him. It
was all too much for Toni. Her senses went into overload and blanked out on her.

She was left with the absolute enchanting bliss of
moving in complete harmony with the man she loved

to distraction, her only attempt at defense the lowering of black eyelashes to cover the soft dark velvet of bewildered blue eyes. How could she love him so? It wasn't right; she did not want to. But she couldn't help it! What was she to do? Her breath caught in a muffled sound very like a sob. Mark heard it, and a secret frosty smile touched his mouth. He dropped his proud head, brushed his lips across the shining hair of the woman in his arms and tucked her more securely against him as he moved her expertly, sensually, around the floor.

Mike had danced with smooth expertise. Mark combined expertise with creativity in a way that left Toni breathless. The band slowed its rhythm into a dreamy melody. Mark held her close, her flushed cheek in the curved hollow of his shoulder as he cradled her in arms suddenly gentle. Toni floated with him as she followed his intricate movements with an instinctive awareness that caused his eyes to blaze with a fierce aggression. Somehow Toni became aware that the strong heartbeat under her cheek had failed to slow as the tempo of the music changed. She moved gracefully, euphorically, the feel of his body warm against hers.

When the music ceased and he turned her back toward their table, Toni experienced a distinct sense of deprivation. Shocked, she pulled away from the arm that encircled her and marched away on her own, head high. It was then that she noticed Ginny Lee's absence.

Gone to the ladies' room to be sure her beauty was intact, Toni thought sourly. She did not take her seat beside the tall captain. Enough was enough. Better not to risk another close encounter with Ginny Lee's dangerous escort!

"I would like to leave, Mike." She fought down tension, tried for a normal tone. "It's late and I'm tired."

The captain was already on his feet. He retrieved her small bag. "Certainly, Toni. You'll excuse us, old man?"

"Are you headed for Galveston?" Mark asked the question with an apologetic civility that put Toni on instant alert. Mike nodded, gave Mark a level look that anticipated the next question. "Could I beg a lift from you?" Mark actually managed to sound sheepish, Toni noted uncharitably. "I came with Ginny Lee, in her car. I should know better by now. I've displeased her and she has gone off in a tantrum. It has happened before. I'm stranded, I'm afraid. Can't even catch a cab this time of night, so if you don't mind...?"

He kept his eyes on Mike's face and ignored Toni's unladylike snort of derision. The Englishman struggled with his desire to refuse, but surrendered to politeness, as Mark had undoubtedly known he would.

Toni held her temper in check as Lane turned to her for permission. She agreed irritably as she did her best to ignore the impish glint in the teasing glance Mark slanted in her direction. He was too sure of himself!

Toni allowed herself to be escorted to the car by the two men. Mike unlocked the door and Mark helped her in with studied courtesy. Sliding into the seat beside her, he closed the car door. His arm rested across the back of the seat and touched her shoulders. He was much too close!

Toni scowled at him and moved closer to Mike. Mark grinned at her discomfiture, proceeded to engage the driver in conversation. Toni pulled herself erect and maintained a rigid posture all the way to Galveston. But she could not shut out the magnetic effect

of Mark's presence. She was totally aware of his nearness as he sat there in the softly lit darkness, the music
of his voice pleasant to her ears.

As they entered Galveston, he offered the pilot a bed
for the night. "I've plenty of room. You are welcome
to stay." His invitation was innocence itself, yet Toni
had the definite impression he had made the offer for
reasons other than hospitality. There was something
about his tone of voice. . . .

"Thanks very much, Anders. I'll do just that!"

"Fine. We can drop Antonia off, then go to my
place and hit the sack." He grinned at her, teeth flashing white in the light from the dashboard.

Toni had a sharp feeling she had just been boxed
into a corner, but she dismissed the idea as preposter-
ous. Surely Mark was only returning favor for favor?
And yet, came the errant thought, by his offer of accommodation he had made certain the pilot would
have no extra time to linger with her for a prolonged
good-night. When the car stopped, she scrambled
from it. Mike came around the side of the car, joined
her and put a casual arm around her waist.

"I'll just see Toni in. Won't be a moment, Anders."

"No hurry."

Toni said good-night to Mark and moved sedately
up the steps to the veranda, acutely aware of the possessiveness of the firm arm around her slender waist.
She did not glance behind her at the man who stood on
the street in the dark, but she knew he had made no
move to reenter the car. She could almost feel his eyes
on her back as she reached the veranda.

Mike stopped at the closed door, turned her in his
arm, his free hand at the back of her neck as he tilted
her face upward. "I must be back in Dallas before

noon tomorrow, Toni. Have breakfast with me in the morning?" The soft request had a lot of meaning invested in it. Toni remembered Mark's wry comment on this man's ability with women. She shrugged mentally as she met the challenge of his soft demand with a reckless disregard for the consequences.

"I would enjoy that, Mike."

He smiled in the moonlit darkness and lowered his head, his intention clear. On the street below, the car door slammed with an explosive sharpness. Toni jumped, her attention wavering from Mike's expert kiss. And then the porch light came on, blinding in its unexpected brilliance. The pilot swore, tightened his arms and muttered something about the resident dragon. He finished his kiss with a thorough efficiency. Raising his dark head, he touched a long finger to her lips.

"See you. Sleep well."

Toni pushed the door open and went through it without a backward glance. She found ma there, who greeted her warmly. "Thought that might be you out there. I turned on the light so's you wouldn't have to stumble around in the dark. Did you have a good time?"

"Yes, thank you." Toni smiled easily. Resident dragon, was she? Hmm. "You shouldn't have waited up. Good night, ma." Toni started up the stairs, a yawn getting the better of her.

"I didn't wait up, honey. Just came down for a cup of coffee. Did Mark find you? He's just back from the Middle East."

"Mark?" Toni arrested her progress up the stairs in midstride. "Was Mark looking for me?"

"He sure was. He came by here just after you left.

Ginny Lee was here looking for him. He took her and went out. I done told him you had gone to Houston with that there pilot.''

So he had known she was in Houston with Mike! Toni stared down at the housekeeper as another question occurred to her. "Why on earth would Mrs. Sims come here looking for Mark?''

"Ain't no rhyme nor reason to that Ginny Lee, honey,'' she muttered. "That one is just a spoiled brat. No way to account for the things she does. I've no idea why she came here expecting to find Mark, but I do know she goes over the whole district with a fine-tooth comb when she decides to look for him. Always has. A bad'un, that'un. She's got no business sniffing after Mark all the time. Done told her so!''

Toni excused herself and dashed on up the stairs, a sudden acute need for privacy driving her. The thought that Mark had known she was in Houston churned around in her mind. It was possible he had gone to the trouble to hunt her up. Still, she could not see Ginny Lee being agreeable to such an outrageous effort. After all, the lounge high atop the skyscraper was a popular spot. It had to be just a coincidence that he should turn up there with her in tow. Toni slept restlessly that night.

The next morning she went with Mike for an early breakfast at one of the restored restaurants on the Old Strand. On the way back to the house they passed the shining white structure of Sacred Heart Church. Toni had him stop. She said goodbye and went to church. Although she had not attended one for many months, perhaps she could sit quietly and find peace today. It was rather a forlorn hope, but the experience could do her no harm, surely. She walked down the aisle and sat near the front of the church.

When the service was over she moved slowly up the aisle with the departing congregation. A little distance ahead, she thought she recognized the slim figure of Karen Prescott. The crowd was too dense for Toni to gain on the other woman, but she kept her attention centered on the slim young back. She liked the young secretary immensely and would enjoy having a word with her on this bright Sunday morning.

The movement of the parishioners was stemmed for a moment. The tall girl ahead disappeared from sight as she bent down in the crowd. She rose with a child, a little boy, in her arms. Toni found herself staring at the childish replica of Mark. The young hazel eyes were shaded by the same extraordinary dark curling lashes as Mark's. Tawny hair tumbled down his broad forehead. He laughed down at the crowd beneath him. . . the same endearing crooked smile.

Toni, stunned by the unexpectedness of the child's appearance, moved down the crowded passageway, her attention riveted. When she reached the steps leading from the entrance, Karen and the child were already on the neat grass verge of the street. Mark's white Jaguar was pulled up to the curb and the man was reaching down for the laughing child. He swung him high into the air. The little boy shouted with glee. Opening the door of the car, Mark tucked Karen into the seat and deposited the wriggling child on her lap. He rounded the car to the driver's side and slid in.

"Touching, isn't it?"

Toni had not been aware of anyone as she watched the little tableau. Ginny Lee, in a beautifully fitted black suede suit, was standing at her side, a sneer on her perfect features. Her green eyes moved from Toni's mobile face to the powerful car as it left the curb.

"He will never marry her, of course, but he does provide very well for her. Very well indeed...." Toni flushed at the unbearable implication in the woman's words. The green eyes assessed her quickly, a vicious fire hidden in their depths. "He insists the boy must have a father figure in order to grow up properly, so one often sees them together. The likeness is striking, don't you think? But of course it should be. And Mark is not one to care much what others think. He does as he wishes to do. That is what makes him such a unique man. Of course, I understand his needs perfectly. I never mention Karen or the little boy to him. He knows how tolerant I am. Such a tiny slip could never affect what we have between us."

Toni threw the woman an agonized look and sped down the steps into the sunshine, hardly able to believe the anguish that slashed her heart, the pain that knotted her stomach. She wanted to die, quite literally.

How could he? Oh, how could he? Karen was such a sweet person. And that darling little boy.... Tears ran down her cheeks unheeded. Her mouth tasted bitter as gall. And that man, the father of Karen's child, was the man she had thought she loved!

Blindly Toni walked away from the church, away from the crowd, away from Ginny Lee and her poisonous words. She forgot lunch and wandered for miles, lost in her misery and quite unable to come to terms with her own feelings. Every decent instinct she owned raged at her as she recognized the hopelessness of her love for Mark.

She denied that love with a violence born of despair, but there was no way her traitorous body would cooperate with her. She wanted him as she wanted fresh air.

Sometime during the afternoon the wind veered suddenly, whistling down out of the northern plains. Grayness slicked the sky and clouds raced across it with incredible speed. The temperature fell with unbelievable rapidity. The perfectly adequate suit Toni had worn to breakfast with Mike was no protection at all against the numbing chill.

Turning her back to the strength of the bitter wind, Toni was scudded along in front of it. She thanked her lucky stars it was blowing her closer toward her lodgings, for she would have been unable to walk into it.

Blown past a lonely telephone booth, she struggled back to it and sought shelter. Her fingers were trembling, so she was barely able to deposit the necessary coin to call the Ruddys. They did not answer. Desperate, Toni retrieved her coin and used it to dial O. Teeth chattering, she explained her plight to the answering operator. The warm Southern voice replied reassuringly. Toni gave the woman the telephone number printed on the phone and was assured a taxi would be dispatched immediately to the rescue.

A cab pulled up to the booth within a quarter of an hour. She had never spent a longer fifteen minutes in her life. Her flesh felt rigid with the cold and her blood was ice water in her veins. Her head was on fire, her heart a burning lump of pain. Toni stumbled into the taxi and huddled in a corner, her teeth chattering so uncontrollably that she was barely able to give the taxi driver her address.

"Lady, you shore gonna catch your death o' cold.

I'll just turn this here heater up. Here, take my jacket." The man shed his coat and spread it across her shoulders, back to front. He smiled at her and patted her gently before turning back to the business of driving.

Toni returned a fevered little smile, her eyes bright from the temperature building within. "Th-thank you. You are very kind."

"You a stranger to these parts?" He twisted his head around to look at her briefly as he swung the car around and sped back toward the populated center of town. "Thought so," as Toni gave him a pained nod. "Someone shoulda tol' you about these here northers we get this time o' year. A body what ain't expectin' them can downright freeze to death afore you know what's happened."

Toni was too far gone to explain. As they pulled up to the house she fumbled in her handbag for some bills and gave them to him.

"Hey, this is way too much!"

"P-please t-take it. I'm so grateful...."

"Here now." The man hopped out of the car and pulled the jacket she had discarded back around her shoulders. "Just you keep that on till you git in th' house, li'l lady." He put a supporting arm around her and led her up onto the porch.

Toni gave him a watery smile. "Thank y-you again. I'll b-be all right now."

"You shore? You want I should call a doctor or anything?"

"No. Ma w-will take care of me."

He pushed the door open and let her in, taking the jacket she held out to him before leaving. Toni stumbled into the warmth of the hall, grateful to be out of the punishing wind. She stood for a moment, swaying in the warmth of the house. She felt terrible.

Ma and Pa Ruddy were apparently still out. Toni took her throbbing head and her aching heart up the stairs and got into bed, her frozen limbs most uncooperative. It was ages before she was warm enough to drop off into unconsciousness.

CHAPTER THIRTEEN

A HAND SHOOK HER GENTLY, persistently. Toni, in the grips of a raging, fever-inspired nightmare, fought it off, to have it replaced by a stronger, more unyielding grasp. She moved restlessly as she tried to rid herself of the wild dream. Firm hands pinned her to the bed.

"Shh.... It's all right, Antonia. It's only a nightmare, my love."

Mark! Toni instantly recognized his concerned voice.

"She's burning up with fever." Ma's statement mingled with her remembered nightmare. Ginny Lee, monstrous, laughing in callous hatred, had been stuffing Karen and her little boy into some sort of horrid place to get rid of them, while Mark stood by and watched. Toni tried to reach the woman Mark had wronged and her child in time to prevent the tragedy. Her anger at Mark's lack of involvement spilled over with a vengeance as she ran, exhausted, toward them. Toni launched herself at him now, going for the face she suddenly loathed.

Mark caught her hands with a sharp imprecation. He held them easily in one hand and used the other to force her back onto the rumpled sheet. "Ma, get Doc Allen and get him now!" The housekeeper quickly left the room.

"Horrible, h-horrible, despicable man!" Toni muttered as she stared wildly up at her captor. "I h-hate you. Let me go. Let me go!"

Mark took a chance and lifted one hand to soothe her feverish brow, his expression bleak with pain. "Wake up, Antonia! Wake up!" He shook her sharply once more.

"I—I am awake. T-take your filthy hands of m-me." Mark let her go, all color leaving his hard face.

"Did you reach Allen?" he questioned ma as she returned.

"Yeah. He's coming right over."

"Take care of her until he gets here. I'll go let him in." The arctic cold of the words penetrated Toni's throbbing brain. Through the haze of inflamed eyes she watched him go.

He never came back all the time she was ill.

The fever clung to her, burned in her brain, sickened in her body. Or at least, the fever took the blame. Toni tossed on her bed, refused food, felt bad enough to die and hoped that she would. The doctor ma had called came periodically and seemed to be sure of her recovery. He left directions for liquids and medicines but did not insist upon food, for which Toni was very thankful. She was thankful, too, that the flu masked her real illness.

Toni knew she was sick for the love of a man she despised. The flu would pass; her real illness would not.

By Friday the fever had run its course. Toni felt like death warmed over, as she told Karen when the younger woman dropped in to see her late in the day. But she had survived.

"Do you think you will be able to get back to the office by next week?" Karen hesitated as she asked the question.

Toni considered the concerned face of Mark's personal assistant very carefully. A deep sadness for the other's position swept over her, caused her to speak gently. "I expect so, Karen. Why? Is something wrong?"

"Well, Dick Handy had a massive heart attack the day before yesterday." She nodded solemnly at Toni's swift sound of dismay. "He will be all right apparently, but we are going to be hard put to replace him at this stage of the game. And Hendrix fell today and broke his leg." Toni had learned what a valuable man Hendrix was on the week aboard the exploration vessel. The team needed Jon Hendrix, but he was hospitalized.

"He won't be able to do much except headwork for a couple of months, and Mark's gone. He won't be able to be here except for conferences on major decisions. That leaves you with an overload of responsibility, I'm afraid."

Toni searched Karen's pleasant face. She did not show any sign of emotion except concern for Toni, concern for the unfortunate happenings of the past two days. If she missed Mark, longed for him to be here in this time of minor crisis, it did not show. What on earth was their relationship? Karen seemed quite easy about it, whatever it was.

Toni did not know what to say for the moment. She had spent a number of hours in the past couple of days trying to decide what to do. Love she could not deny demanded she stay here, finish her contract and do what she could to disregard Mark's perfidy, his callous use of Karen, his self-serving involvement with Ginny Lee. Pride insisted she leave immediately.

Her conflict tore at her, worsened her appetite, ate

at her emotions with a corrosive strength. She had lost pounds and it was not due to the fever. She knew with absolute clarity that she could never accept the man she loved, but could she give him up?

The thought of doing so cut through her like a knife, choked her and gave her no peace. Dimly she realized that one day she must come to the kind of maturity that would allow her to take just such drastic action. But she knew she was not strong enough to carry out such incisive surgery on her emotions just yet. The sight and sound of him were as necessary to her as food and drink just now. In spite of her need, though, she had almost decided to risk the trauma and go. Karen's delineation of the problems her team faced called upon her innate sense of loyalty and responsibility. She traced the pattern of the quilt covering her with a restless finger, Mark's whereabouts uppermost in her mind.

"Where has Mark gone?" She asked the question without raising her eyes.

"He's in South Africa at the moment. Then he must go to the Near East and on to Australia. He has interests all over the world, you know, and he has been neglecting them recently."

Toni looked up, curious. "No, I didn't know. Why has he been neglecting his other interests?"

"Don't you know?" Karen's smile flashed with delight, but her voice was guarded.

"No. I've no idea." Toni searched the other's expression intently. "Do you miss him when he is gone?"

"Oh, yes!" Karen was entirely calm, it seemed to Toni. "Mark is the most wonderful person around. And Clint, my little boy, is just desolate when his Uncle Mark is gone. But one cannot have everything, you know, and Clint needs to learn that, to appreciate the things Mark does for him.''

"Uncle Mark. Is that what your little boy calls him?'' The likeness of the child to the man was a painful recollection she forced away.

"Of course.'' Karen was matter-of-fact. She dismissed the discussion casually, intent on the problems that had brought her. "If you don't really feel like coming in on Monday, perhaps I could bring the latest computer readouts to you here. Mark has hired a new computer analyst, but it is going to take a bit of time to get him going as a part of your team.''

Toni chafed, then decided to stay and see it through. She put in her appearance at U.P.C.'s headquarters on Monday and found herself pitchforked into the welter of detailed activity massed for her attention. Dan Lewis, the new man, took over the task of heading the computer section with a comprehensive intelligence one would expect in someone hired by Mark Anders to do a job.

BY THE THIRD WEEK IN MARCH the drilling platform was towed into position. Greg appeared onshore, sobered by the strain of divorce proceedings. He was shocked at Toni's thinness, began to address her as "Skinny'' and insisted on dining out with her several times a week, his avowed intent to stuff her like a sausage until she gained back her lost weight. His gay insouciance lightened Toni's grim mood, making her smile for the first time since Ginny Lee had announced Mark's parenthood.

In Mark's absence, Greg was busy superintending the final placement of the rig, flying each day in the big helicopter that commuted to and from the drilling site two hundred miles out in the Gulf of Mexico.

Word got around. United Petroleum Company was getting ready to sink a well.

Men began to drift into the offices: roughnecks, those tough and competent workers that were the core of a drilling team; tool pushers; welders; pipe fitters; warehouse men; cooks—the lot. They were screened then interviewed by Greg and his chief tool pusher, a rugged Australian named Blue Daniels. Men were assigned position, shifts and quarters. They would live on the rig for three-week stretches, celibate, boozeless and responsible for their own entertainment in the vast reach of water to the south of Galveston. The Blue-Chip Sea, they called it irreverently.

Strong men, these—independent and self-reliant, unafraid of man, beast or element. Toni admired and appreciated them, understood the careless amused view with which they armed themselves against the vicissitudes of life as wildcatters.

The technical team worked flat out as the final requirements shaped up. They slaved over their calculations, intent on the mind-bending, tendon-stretching effort to position the tonnage of the mammoth rig precisely over the spot most likely to result in a well filled with enough extractable hydrocarbons to pay for the expensive project and show a decent profit. They were a team welded together by the magnitude of the gamble. Men against nature, they tossed to wrest a fortune from the reluctant generosity of the good earth—or to come up a dead loss. A breed apart, they were not men who liked the taste of defeat. And their leader liked it least of all.

Toni was thinking about this one morning as she

climbed the stairs, thinking about men who worked like demons against time and tide, nature and disaster to make their gambles pay off. Gamblers, all. Gamblers who made a choice, then stuck to it through thick and thin until the gamble paid off or paid out.

She recognized that she had inherited some of that gambling blood, too. With a father and grandfather of the caliber of hers, how could she have missed?

But the biggest gamble of her life was not about to pay off, she knew. And when it petered out, she would just pack up as quietly as possible and leave the source of her turmoil behind. For now, however, she was just going to enjoy her work and the easy camaraderie of the team. And she did, as usual, all that morning.

Her lightheartedness did not last through the day, for Mark had returned.

Toni, unaware of his presence, looked up from the clutter littering her desk that afternoon, and there he was. He watched her color drain away with a closed expression. Toni, who had dreaded this moment, was nevertheless prepared for it. She could not control the onslaught of pain that caused her sudden paleness, but she had her composure firmly in place, her emotions under tight control.

She gave him a frosty little smile and welcomed him back, then returned to the papers before her. She could still read them, she observed with a fierce gladness. Mark stared at her bent head, then told her in a slightly husky voice he was expecting her at a conference in the boardroom in fifteen minutes.

Toni breathed deeply, coolly assembled her thoughts and papers and forced herself to go to the meeting with a clear-eyed icy control that covered her inner turmoil—or so she hoped! With the rig in position, ready to go, all attention was centered on it.

IN THE LAST WEEK OF MARCH the well was spudded in. The race against time and nature had begun. Ian Taylor, who had recently quit Empire Petroleum in London to join U.P.C., stood in the glass cab, his hand on the lever controlling the draw works, one eye on the gauges informing him of his machinery's performance variations.

The Scotsman gave a yell as strident and piercing as a factory shift whistle and started the spin of the rotary table. As the drilling floor throbbed, the roughnecks started the endless process of feeding the drill string, actually lengths of pipe, down while the rotating bit spun its way into the resisting bedrock. The kelly, the top piece of the drill pipe at the center of the rotary table, went into operation, powering the tungsten drill bit as it ate its way into the seafloor. The assembled men let loose an earsplitting cheer that had Ian grinning all over his bluff face.

Mark stood there beside Ian, a wild satisfaction mirrored in his aggressive brown face. Toni, watching him in a moment of weakness she had seldom allowed herself lately, recognized him for what he was. Mark was a gambler, a sure leader among the tough fit men with whom he worked. He was part of a group who shared danger, accepted it, seldom talked about it. Part of a team who mixed muscle, brains and physical effort with dangerous and sophisticated machines. They were a breed of men who tackled the untamable with the knowledge that it could be conquered and shaped by them.

She turned from him, sick with love for him, sick

with her inability to control her feelings. Why me, she raged silently, and why this man? There was no answer. She walked to her shack and got busy with the computer terminal that kept her in touch with all that was going on in the hole being drilled into the seabed beneath.

The next morning Mark left for Galveston on the first helicopter shuttle of the day. Toni was both relieved and upset. Strangely, she wanted him near, wanted to see him, to hear his cool deep voice, his easy laugh. Thoughts of him invaded her waking hours as dreams of him invaded her sleep. These dreams were often passionate and filled with erotic images she hadn't realized could exist in her subconsciousness. The dreams also left her wildly frustrated, throbbing with longing to be near him, to have his arms around her, his body touching hers.

Toni hated herself for the depth of feeling that allowed such fantasies, but was powerless to stop them except by staying awake. This, she found, was impossible to do. So she dreamed and fought her innermost longings with grim determination. She began to lose weight again, but at least she didn't have to see Mark every time she looked up from her tasks.

He was to head the supervisory team that was slated to alternate with hers. When she was ashore he would be on the rig. And she, thankfully, would be on the rig when he wasn't. They were to meet only to confer when the teams changed. She might just be able to settle into work and lose her unhappiness in solving the ever present problems of the task at hand.

Greg caught up with her in the mess hall at noon the next day. He grinned at her, deposited an enormous plate of food on the table and sat down in the chair beside her. "I'm gonna have to watch what I eat," he sighed. "Got to discipline myself or I'll be looking like a wine cask somebody has kicked the staves out of."

Toni laughed, and he looked at her critically as he attacked a mouthful. He swallowed, then gulped down a portion of the coffee steaming in the mug beside his plate. "You look like one of the staves," he told her seriously. "Are you still off your feed, little lady? Gawd, Toni, you worry me."

"I'm all right, Greg. You need not worry about me."

"Doggone it, someone should," he muttered. "Don't know what's wrong with that cousin of mine. I could have sworn—" He broke off, popped a forkful of steak and potatoes into his mouth. Tawny eyes thoughtful, he watched her intently. Toni realized he was wondering about her relationship with his cousin. She colored defensively, rallied her guard.

"Maybe you aren't getting enough exercise."

"Greg, you are a dear, but I've asked you not to bother about me and I mean it. I'm a big girl. I can take care of myself and I'm afraid I don't take kindly to interference, no matter how nicely it is meant." She scowled at him. "I like you very much, but you can't be responsible for me. I shan't allow it."

"Yeah. I know what happened to poor old Mark when he tried that on."

"Poor old Mark.... Well, I like that! Your cousin is the most arrogant, impossible, hateful and immoral man it has ever been my misfortune to meet. There is no way in the world anyone could ever penetrate that thick hide of his and hurt him!"

Greg stared at her in amazement. "Whoa, there, Toni. I didn't mean to get your shirt in a knot." He stirred his coffee, an intense concentration creasing his brown face. His quizzical eyes challenged her. "Mark isn't like that, you know. He's really a great guy."

"Yes, well...champion him if you must. I am sure he can use all the help he can get to offset some of the things he does."

Greg looked at her curiously and changed the subject. "Ever done any sailing, Toni?"

"As a matter of fact, I love to sail." Thankful to dismiss Mark from the conversation, Toni considered Greg politely.

"How about going out with me—crewing my cat?"

Greg had a catamaran called *Sea Breeze*, a sixteen-footer upon which he was practicing to prepare for the world champion catamaran races later in the summer. The competition was to be held off South Padre Island in the gulf. He needed an extra person to crew for him. He spoke enthusiastically about his hobby and insisted Toni would be just right for the crewman he needed.

"But I have never been on one," Toni objected without much conviction.

Just then Ian Taylor stopped by to discuss a technical matter with Greg, so Toni let her thoughts wander as the men talked animatedly.

It was good to see Greg enthusiastic about racing, and she had no wish to discourage him. He had been so withdrawn since his bout in the divorce court. She, for one, had missed the gay exuberance so much in evidence when she first met him. Each time she had seen the drawn look on his face she had burned inwardly, despising Mark Anders and his arrogant selfishness.

Granted Ginny Lee had her faults, but what did it matter as long as Greg cared for her? How could Mark break his cousin's heart with such callous disregard?

Surely there were enough single women available for him to satisfy his macho image of himself? She would never forgive him. Never. And she would never get over the heartache he caused her. During the past few weeks, with Mark always in view, Toni had been unable to deny his effect on her.

By now she had also admitted to herself that she had never been in love with Kurt Grady—not really. What she felt for Mark was as different from what she had considered love for Kurt as the Texas landscape was from the English countryside.

With growing despair she faced the fact that she would never be able to love another man at any time in her bleak future. She was a one-man woman, as her mother was, too. Had she not met Mark, she would have missed ever knowing the soaring heights and abysmal depths of real love. She had convinced herself that her first infatuation was real, and would have lived her life without testing that conviction if Mark hadn't broken down her reserve and forced Kurt out of her thoughts. He had shattered her schoolgirl illusion of love to bits as he forced her into an adult reaction.

She loved him with an all-consuming passion. Her body ached for the feel of him. Her mind ached for communication with him, the communication a woman needs with the only man who can ever exist for her.

And yet her restless intelligence could find no way to compromise and accept him as he was. How was it possible to love a man whose morals, whose actions she found so abhorrent? She didn't know and she hated the weakness in herself, but this self-awareness changed nothing. She still loved Mark Anders.

So, chained to her job by her insatiable desire to be near him, to see him, to engage in work that mattered to him, she stayed. And she suffered agony under the whip of a nature too proud to surrender to her own need.

The past weeks had been hell for her as she fought to keep a cool head and present an indifferent facade to Mark and to the rest of the world. She couldn't have done it if Mark had not changed his attitude toward her.

Since the night her burning fever had mixed her nightmare with reality and she had launched that abortive attack on him, he had sharply altered his manner. The only conversations he held with her were strictly related to business. Cold, precise, he made no attempt to tease her as he had done before. Nor did he try to get her alone for any reason whatsoever. He made no attempt to restore their relationship to the rather shaky intimacy he had worked so hard to establish during the early weeks of their acquaintanceship.

Toni was glad, she told herself fiercely. She performed her duties and went home each night on the edge of exhaustion. She blamed her fitful sleep on her bad appetite, on the amount of responsibility she was shouldering, on everything at hand except her distress over the change in Mark.

Deep in her heart a resolve had been forming. She must leave this place. It was becoming clear to her things were not about to improve. She needed to get away, go back to her home where she might be able to lick her wounds in peace and ultimately get over the flaming passion that was destroying her. She must go once the well came in, but she was not capable of doing so before that last bittersweet moment.

"You will love cat racing!" With a perceptive gleam in those golden eyes of his, Greg intruded on her thoughts as Ian ambled away. "Get your mind off the nasties. We'll try it out on Sunday after the meeting. Okay?"

Toni was agreeable. Progress meetings were held in U.P.C.'s offices every time the operations teams changed. Mark took charge of the meetings. The weekly exchange among the supervisory staff would be extended once the intense workload of these early days had passed. Gradually they would be working three weeks on, three weeks off, as the production teams did. At that time they would enjoy more time off, but this condition was probably weeks away and they all knew it.

AFTER THE MEETING on the following Sunday, Toni sighed with relief as Mark and Blue Daniels, his second in command, herded their crew aboard the big helicopter and left. In Frank's absence the craft was under the command of Sid Lacy, another senior pilot employed by the corporation.

She headed the little red car toward her present home, and once there took a long and Sybaritic soak in an extremely hot bath. She pulled on blue jeans and a snug woolen top, a weatherproof jacket and rubber-soled shoes. She was downstairs waiting when Greg arrived.

Toni viewed the unique craft with exactly the touch of enthusiasm Greg needed. Her offer to help scornfully rejected, she watched as Mark's cousin attached the lightweight trailer containing the mounted craft to the trailer hitch on the rear of his car.

Heading toward the beach on the other side of Galveston, Greg filled her in on the catamaran and its operation. He extolled its speed, its construction, its maneuverability. When they reached their destination, he needed no boat ramp to launch the craft. As he backed the trailer onto the hard-packed sand, Toni found herself in the midst of a horde of onlookers.

Greg made certain she had on her bright life jacket, donned his own and pushed off into the surf, which was high that morning.

"This sling is the butt bucket," he told her. "Sling that li'l ol' butt of yourn in it and let's get moving."

Toni found herself swept along by his irrepressible merriment. She laughed and complied. Greg grabbed the tiller, and they shot through the surf with the blasting speed of a well-launched artillery shell. Toni clung to the rope fastened to her harness, her feet shifting instinctively on the trampoline stretched between the two hulls.

The lashing wind, the rough water, the speed of the hissing twin hulls and Greg's laughing shouts as he managed the bright and brassy sails combined to act upon Toni's frayed nerves like a tonic. They larked around, finally returning to the beach exhilarated, exhausted and completely relaxed.

"Well, how about it?" Greg slanted a quizzical glance of inquiry at her as they packed away the sails. "Want to crew for me?"

"Just you try to have anyone else do it!" Toni laughed her answer as she stripped off the fingerless gloves that had protected her from rope burn. Greg looked thoughtful, then remarked that Mark might not like it.

"Mark has nothing at all to do with me or my life!" came the tart answer.

"Hasn't he?" Greg really did sound puzzled. "I thought you and he had some sort of...understanding." Greg obviously had to reach for the word. Toni frowned at him.

"Certainly not. Whatever gave you that notion?" She dismissed the charge with the full helping of scorn it deserved. "How fast does that amazing craft of yours go, Greg?" As interested as she was in the catamaran, she knew the question was a red herring dragged across his path to deflect his keen questions. No way could she allow him to examine her relationship with the dynamic individual who was his cousin. Her pain was already too great to bear when she thought of Mark. She certainly could not stand to talk about the man, as well.

Greg let the subject go and arranged to pick her up and take her to dinner after she'd had time to change.

That first day set the pattern for the training sessions that followed. When they were ashore they always managed to go out once or twice. By the middle of May they were a team, working together with a rapport that sent Greg into flights of fantasy. He became positive they would win. Toni thought he was rather carried away with the possibility, but she thoroughly enjoyed the sessions anyway.

As May advanced toward summer, the gulf became more unruly. Forty-foot waves and seventy-knot winds were not unusual, but U.P.C.'s *Sea Venture* was built for the home of foul weather, the North Sea. She managed to ride the gales that increasingly packed a hurricane punch, for she was balanced on ballast-filled pontoons that were buried beneath the surging waters almost a hundred feet below the drilling floor. Work went on in twelve-hour shifts, night and day. Greg and

Toni headed operations on the same tour; Mark and
Blue Daniels ran the other. When Mark was away
Sandy Johnson filled in.

Except for the brief conferences they had when the
shifts changed, Mark continued to leave her strictly
alone, his attitude one of cool detachment. Toni told
herself it was the best thing that could have happened.
Now that Ginny Lee was free, Mark was apparently
concentrating on the beauteous divorcée. Not that
Toni really knew—or cared, she assured herself stout-
ly. She was spending tours of two weeks' duration on
the rig now, with an equal amount of time ashore. She
was spared the dubious pleasure of Ginny Lee's presence when she was ashore. Greg's ex-wife did not hang
around the offices while Mark was two hundred miles
out in the gulf, and Toni was duly grateful. She refused to allow herself to wonder how much time Ginny
Lee spent there when Mark's tour was over and *he* was
ashore.

Karen had invited her home to a meal a couple of
times. At first Toni did not go, as she knew it would be
adding salt to her wounds to see the little boy who
looked so much like his father. But Karen was so insistent and looked so hurt when she continued to make
excuses that Toni finally agreed to go over one Sunday
evening.

"Hey, Toni—" Greg pierced her with a keen glance
as they finished up the training stint late that same
Sunday afternoon "—Sissy has been dying to get you
over for supper. Want to go this evening?"

Sissy, Toni knew, was Greg's much-loved sister. He
was always talking about her and had asked Toni more
than once to accompany him on a visit. So far Toni

had been unable to go with him. She had yet to meet Sissy.

"I'm so sorry, Greg. I have a dinner engagement this evening."

"Oh?" Greg cocked an inquisitive eyebrow. "Anyone I know?"

"It certainly is, but I'm not going to indulge you in your tendency to play nosy parker, my lad."

"Shucks, Toni, I'm just trying to protect the family interests."

"What family interests, Gregory Sims?"

"You know...this and that." He waved vaguely, tightened the ropes holding the cat on the trailer. "Just didn't want you to get lost in the tangle of males running around looking."

"Thanks a lot, ol' buddy." She fell into his easy drawl, mocking him nicely. "Ain't nuthin' much you can do to keep me off the streets and outta trouble. I'm a big girl now."

"Yeah!" He popped her into the front seat of his car and stared down at her, a wicked leer on his handsome face. "I have noticed that very thing about you."

Greg had lost much of the gloom his divorce had forced upon him. He worked hard when he was on the rig and was always cheerful there. Since the regular training sessions with the catamaran had started, he seemed to slough off the depression the loss of his wife had forced upon his sunny nature. Toni enjoyed being with him. Their friendship was real and firm, untarnished by sexual overtones. Greg was the big brother she had never had.

He left her now on Ma Ruddy's steps, and Toni

went in to bathe and change for her evening at
Karen's. She really was not looking forward to it,
much as she liked and respected the younger girl. The
small boy's resemblance to Mark ate into her sensitivity, destroying what little peace of mind she'd managed
to attain. But she went.

CHAPTER FOURTEEN

KAREN LIVED WITH CLINT in a neat white house built on the high foundations characteristic of so many dwellings in Galveston. Toni remembered learning the reason for that ungainly-looking type of building on her walking tour with Mark and Hussein. How long ago that seemed.

Karen volunteered the information that Mark had bought the house for her when she had arrived from California six months ago. She seemed completely open about the whole business.

"Mark has been very good to me," she confided as they sat in the cozy living room after the clutter of their delicious meal had been cleared away. Clint, the little boy, helped solemnly with the drying up before being put to bed. A bright and happy child, he chattered away all evening, accepting Toni as an adult he could value, talking to her about his small concerns in a way that tore at her heart.

If only he were not so much like Mark! His appearance damned Mark in a manner no words could have done.

"Clint is the picture of Mark, isn't he?" Toni ventured, twisting the knife in her own heart.

"Yes," Karen agreed with a little smile. "He will be a very good-looking man, I think. He is lucky."

Toni found Karen's acceptance of the situation a bit

incredible. She did not know what to say. "He is fond of Clint?" she finally questioned gently.

"Oh, yes. Mark manages to spend a lot of his spare time with him. He is convinced no boy can grow up without a good male model to pattern himself after. Greg is good about that, too. Between them, they make sure Clint is well looked after."

"I didn't know Greg helped."

"Greg makes a fantastic uncle," Karen responded easily. "Not quite as good as Mark, but more than adequate."

"He calls both of them 'uncle'?" Toni didn't try to hide her surprise at Karen's casual acceptance of her position.

It certainly said a lot for Greg that he was able to help with the little boy. He really must have a great deal of understanding under the carefree exterior he showed to the world. Why had Ginny Lee never found it? Obviously the woman found more understanding elsewhere!

She knew Greg's ex-wife disliked Karen. Perhaps she also took exception to Greg's role of uncle to Karen's small offspring. Toni remembered that bright and disastrous day in front of the church, remembered Ginny Lee's specious explanation for her own tolerance of Karen's claim on Mark. The cold norther that had caused Toni's flu afterward was no match for the chill that now gripped her heart as she sat staring at Karen's bent head.

"No little boy ever had better uncles," Karen went on, an amused smile touching her lips. "I have to watch them both. They each tend to spoil him, though Mark is a much better disciplinarian than Greg. Greg spoils anyone who will let him. He just naturally can't deny a thing to anybody he loves."

Toni remembered the advice Mark had offered his cousin about Ginny Lee at the airport the night of her own arrival. Something about applying his hand to her well-shaped bottom, as she remembered. She recalled Greg's horrified rejection of it, too.

"Perhaps Mark feels responsible for Clint," she offered.

"Yes, he does." Karen smiled with an entrancing innocence. "We are very lucky. Most men would not feel as Mark does. I think I will love him forever. He is truly one of the world's best people."

Toni was stunned by the words. She sipped her coffee; it tasted bitter on her tongue. Toni set the cup down carefully, sick at heart.

Karen was staring into her own cup, so did not notice her guest's abrupt pallor. "I tried to disappear when I learned for sure that I was pregnant," Karen's soft murmur continued, etching words into Toni's heart with a devastating permanence. "Greg and Mark both looked for me, but I had done a fair job of covering my tracks. I took a restaurant job in the California desert. It was in an out-of-the-way kind of place and it was *so* hot. I was ready to be found when Mark turned up." She drank a little coffee and smiled.

"He located me just before I had Clint. I didn't want anyone to know what had happened. Mark talked some sense into my head. He made me go and stay with Ma Ruddy. Then, after Clint was born, he insisted I go to school, complete my training. He sent me to the best business school on the Coast. Ma took care of Clint. Then he put me to work in the secretarial pool in the L.A. office and told me to learn."

"Did you?" Toni didn't recognize her own voice. Karen failed to notice the rasping edge to the words.

"You bet I did." She laughed up at Toni from under dark lashes. "I didn't dare not. I really worked like a dog, but it paid off. I was promoted to the position of personal administrative assistant to the big mogul in Los Angeles in two years' time. It sort of justified Mark's faith in me. Then, six months ago, Mark gave me the chance to come here as his personal assistant. I love it, but it only happened because Mark didn't give up on me. At the risk of being maudlin, I feel like I owe my life and Clint's to him." She looked directly at Toni then, as though it were absolutely vital that she convince the other woman that she was speaking the truth. "I think Mark Anders is the most wonderful man in the world." She grinned engagingly. "Always next to Frank, of course."

Bitterly Toni acknowledged that she got the message—Mark and Karen had an implicit understanding, now. For Mark to have taken advantage of such trust before, to have used it for his own scurrilous ends was obscene. Toni drew a ragged breath. She knew the heartbreak she had felt up to this point was but the tip of the iceberg that encased her emotions and her sensibilities.

How did a man become so crass, so uncaring? And how was Frank de la Cruz able to allow such a man to stand in the way of his own love and desire? Toni knew from her conversations with him, the things she had overheard, that Frank didn't resent Karen's openness about Mark and her relationship with him. And Frank adored Karen's little boy. Unable to understand it all, Toni finished her visit in a kind of numbed vacuum.

She never went back. She was just not strong enough to stand the pressure generated by Karen's loving acceptance of Mark's callous use of her. And the sight of the little boy who so resembled Mark was more than she could bear.

She enclosed her heart in a shroud of icy indifference and went about her tasks, fiercely glad she saw Mark so seldom.

By the first week of June, the bore was down beyond eleven thousand feet. They had a target depth of between seventeen and eighteen thousand if all predictions were to come together and they were to strike a producing well. So far the indications were good that the financial risk U.P.C. was undertaking was an intelligent one.

Mark and Blue Daniels brought their crew in from their tour. Toni heard the rowdy exchange of pleasantries from the safety of her office, but she kept herself busy until the noise subsided. Karen came in to warn her that the joint discussions necessary for the changeover of crew were about to start. Gathering up her papers, Toni pushed open her office door, almost unable to face Mark across the gleaming conference table this Sunday morning.

To her surprise, Mark was standing in the doorway of the large room. He was in deep conversation with John, the cockney who had flown with them from London, the man responsible for the recovery of Kurt's photo.

"Dammit to hell, John, you can do it! I'm trusting you. You can't let me down now." Toni had no trouble hearing Mark's forceful words. He glanced up from his harsh inspection of the Englishman's protesting features and threw a haughty insolent glance in Toni's direction.

"Be with you in a moment, Dr. Cameron." He moved, crowding John away from the doorway, his desire for her to enter the conference room and get out of the way quite obvious.

Halting in her tracks, Toni's anger rose. "I haven't thanked you for finding and returning my photo, John." She extended her hand. The chauffeur took it as he shot an amused glance at his tall boss.

"It was a pleasure, Miss Cameron. Glad to be of service. How are you making out? You look fine."

"I am," she murmured. She dropped his hand and moved on into the noisy meeting room. Muddy Waters, the nicknamed engineer on her tour who had the responsibility for mixing the all-important "mud" without which no modern well was ever drilled, took a sharp look at her face and pulled out the chair next to his. Toni sank down into it with a distinct feeling of relief.

Mark had not wanted her to see John; Toni knew it. It had been more than obvious in his attitude. Why? She wasn't to find out if her impression was valid, of course. Mark came in, gave her a look that was quelling in its coldness and got down to work.

Karen entered the room when Toni was immersed in the reports concerning the latest seismic evaluation of the echoes bounced back from charges set off deep in the bore. "Phone call for you, Toni." Abstracted, Toni took the receiver from Karen and spoke into it.

"Mike! How are you?" She sounded pleased as she responded. Mark turned his head to watch her. She glimpsed a hard anger in his piercing hazel regard, probably because she was holding up the meeting.

"I have been busy," Toni agreed at the pilot's plaintive protest, "and I still am."

"Surely that slave driver you have for a boss will let you have a little time off? I want to see you." Mike sounded determined.

"I'm leaving almost at once for the *Sea Venture*. It's time for my tour. You should have called last week." But Mike had not been in the country for three weeks, he explained. He would come down the next time she was ashore.

"I'll be up on Lake Dallas with Greg." Toni told him briefly about crewing for Greg, preparing for the big race. "The gulf is getting too rough for practicing. Hurricane season is moving in on us down here, and the winds are sometimes pretty strong."

They talked a few minutes more. Toni agreed that she could see him when she was at the lake, as it was only a few miles to the north of the sprawling metropolis of Dallas. She gave him the information he needed to find her, laughed with him and refused to look at Mark. Breaking the connection, Toni took one look at the hard face of the man at the head of the conference table and gave in to the slow-burn of her own anger. With a lift of her chin, she turned to the papers under her hand and got busy with the update on the pertinent information needed if the drilling operation was to continue smoothly.

How dare Mark presume to monitor her spare time or look critically at any man she might choose to date? Over these past several weeks she had convinced herself he was finished with her, other than in areas where her expertise aided and abetted his own ends. At first Toni had felt a panicked relief. But then she had begun to miss his former attempts at seduction. She hated herself for it, but she wanted him to look at her again with that warm and laughing light in his eyes. She longed to have him touch her. And deep in the night she would awaken, her body taut with the need to have his arms around her.

But that he would never know. Surrender was impossible, so Toni marched through her days, performed as she was expected to perform, her love a bitter hurtful weight inside her.

Today she again schooled herself to cover that dull ache with a cold and withdrawn facade. Her cool and competent intellect was in top form despite the condition of her battered emotions. She returned her attention to the meeting with fervor. Karen interrupted the session as it neared completion to hand Mark a late-weather bulletin.

He scanned it, then raised his head. "There's a tropical storm watch on in the Caribbean, guys. Keep an eye on it. It may be headed straight for *Sea Venture*. We'll keep you informed, as well. Lacy wants to be on his way now, just in case." His veiled glance wandered over Toni, his mouth tightening. "The rig is one of the most substantial I've been on, but we can't take any chances." Any chances with Toni, that cool look said to them all. He branded her with that look, marked her clearly as his major concern. Toni's anger flared. How dare he imply to these men, her colleagues, that his interest in her was more personal than employer-employee? And yet he had. She stared at him in real dislike. His smile was sour as he turned and left the room. The men murmured, glanced uneasily at one another and got on with the business of the shift change. Toni simmered, but joined in on the discussion.

She was still at odds with herself as she went to the helicopter pad. She thrust her head through the bright yellow life jacket she was required to wear when crossing the gulf and tapped her bright blue hard hat into position.

"Give me that, Toni." Lacy reached for her soft

roll, her only luggage, as she scooped it up. As she reached for the hand he held down to her, she suddenly remembered her violin. She'd left it upstairs.

"Sid, I've forgotten my fiddle. It's in the office. Can you wait?" He grinned and threw her roll on board.

"Yeah, but light a shuck!" Toni had been around long enough to know the slang phrase meant hurry. She did. The violin was the one thing that soothed her nerves and kept her thoughts from the tendency they had developed to wind themselves inextricably around Mark if they were left unoccupied. It had seen a lot of use recently!

Toni ran up the stairs and through the conference room, because it was a shortcut to her office. The door she had closed was partially open. Puzzled, she stepped through, her feet silent on the thick carpet. She stopped short in amazement.

Mark was sitting in her chair. His elbows were on her desk, his hands in his hair. It had been churned up by strong fingers that were clenched in it now. His profile turned to Toni as she stood in the conference-room doorway, he projected despair and unhappiness in a way that slashed at her senses. She uttered a soft involuntary sound, stretched out a hand, then dropped it hastily as he raised his head. In that first unguarded moment, he stared at Toni with such desperation, such hopelessness that she ached to pull his leonine head to her breast, to soothe him, caress and comfort him.

"What the hell are you doing back up here?" His fierce anger scorched Toni, killed her impulse to offer tender loving care. "Lacy needs to go—now! Every minute he waits puts that copter and the men in it in jeopardy." His lips were drawn into a thin hard line and his eyes blazed at her. A muscle jumped in one lean cheek. He looked as though he hated her and could barely resist the urge to pounce on her, punish her severely.

Toni stared at him, startled. "I forgot my fiddle." She forced the words out in shocked protest against his attitude.

"Get the damn thing—" his mouth was cruel, taut "—and get the hell out of here." Biting the hoarse comment off, Mark flung it at her. Toni muffled a sound like a sob, snatched up the offending violin and fled. She knew with an ache of torment that she would never understand the powerful man who had carved his image on her heart.

TWENTY-FOUR HOURS LATER the weather was deteriorating in a manner that had everyone on the rig as tense as a coiled spring. *Sea Venture*, its giant pontoons buried deep in the water, the ballast tanks full, rode the rough surges as a veteran of North Sea storms should. She was built to keep drilling in weather that would have been impossible for most rigs. The work got much rougher and more dangerous each hour, but it continued.

At dusk U.P.C.'s big helicopter beat its way through the murky turbulence and came to an uneasy perch on the pad high atop the rig. The machine stayed only a moment, then was gone.

Toni was in the super's shack, getting ready to hand over her shift to Greg and Muddy Waters. The door crashed open as Mark exerted his muscle against the power of the wind. He dismissed Toni with a glance, called Greg and Muddy into conference and got down to the business of probable action if the hurricane two hundred miles south and east continued on its present path. *Sea Venture* lay directly in that path. The gale-force winds whipping over them now were the direct result of the great spiral of destruction bearing down upon them at a steady ten or so miles an hour.

Toni tried several times to offer suggestions, positive that *Sea Venture* could ride out anything that was not a direct hit. Mark would listen to her, his face quiet and withdrawn, a bitter sparkle in his hazel eyes as they rested on her. That mobile mouth of his looked cruel, hard. Each time she finished what she had to say, he went back to his own line of reasoning. It was as if he hadn't heard her speak.

Baffled, Toni finally excused herself and went to her own quarters. She stripped and showered, dried herself and slipped between the sheets of her narrow bunk. She lay in the dark, her slender body suddenly racked with a storm of sobbing that was unexpected and disconcerting. She had no idea why she cried. But later, when she fell into an exhausted sleep, Mark's face as she had seen it when he sat in her chair at the conference table kept sliding into her restless dreams. Suffering, enraged, he stared at her through steely, hate-filled eyes. Why should he hate her? Why did he suffer? Her dreams held no answers.

Toni had a bad night. The result was that she overslept, did not pull her protesting body from the sheets until Ian came by. His tough fist on her door, coupled with the foghorn he used for a voice, was enough to insure the end of anyone's sleep. Toni called out that she was awake, hauled herself into her clothes and went to eat and face Mark.

She needn't have bothered screwing up her courage. The unpredictable hurricane had shifted its path and was headed for the Yucatan. Mark was gone. Toni's sense of deprivation was acute, but she ignored it as best she could and got down to the business at hand.

Ian commented dourly Mark's brief and unexpected appearance. Muddy Waters wondered with some asperity whether Mark had doubted their ability to handle the rig and the crew properly had the storm not changed course. Greg just glanced at Toni, a wise and solemn look in those tawny eyes of his. He made no comment at all.

Toni finished that tour in a numbed state. She ate, she slept—if one could call her dream-haunted efforts sleep—and she responded with efficiency to the demands made upon her as offshore operations officer. But she knew part of her was dead, killed by the hopelessness of her position. She began to suspect it might just be the most important part of her.

As she suffered, Greg watched her with a worried look when she wasn't aware of him. He finally decided to take a hand.

"Toni," he announced baldly toward the end of the tour, "you and I have two weeks off after we hand guidance over to that other gang of turkeys. Right?"

"Right," Toni agreed cautiously.

"So do you know what we are going to do?"

He was using the deep drawl of the native Texan by now. Toni's response was a flicker of amusement. "What y'all have on yore cotton-pickin' l'il mind thar, boy?" she came back neatly.

"We are going to pull the cat to Lake Dallas and spend two weeks camping out while we get in some serious training for the race."

"I'd forgotten!" she exclaimed, suddenly cheered. "But camping! I'd assumed we were going to stay in a nice hotel."

He shook his head. "This will be fun, believe me. I'll get a couple of tents and lay on some camping gear. I belong to the boat club on the lake, where all the guys go to train. There's a club house there that serves decent meals, but I've been thinking you might really enjoy roughing it, getting back to nature. You aren't afraid to be alone with me, are you?"

Toni laughed with genuine affection. "No, Greg, I'm not afraid to be alone with you."

"Well," he remarked glumly, "there goes the rest of my self-image. I'm sure going to have to practice up on my allure now that I'm a swinging single again."

"Don't be ridiculous, Greg. You're a very sexy man. Any girl would be proud to have you for an escort." Toni responded at once to the underlying question in his humor. "It's just that I—" She broke off and stared at her feet, unable to complete the thought even in her own mind.

Greg sighed gustily. "Yeah, I know, Toni." Surprisingly, she felt as if he really did understand her turmoil a little. "Our setup probably isn't very flattering, but it sure is comfortable, isn't it?"

And Toni realized it was comforting, extremely comforting, to have a man like Greg Sims as a friend. "You're on," she suddenly decided. "We'll camp at this Lake Dallas of yours and get in a couple good weeks of training...."

THEY LEFT FOR DALLAS as soon as the joint conference had finished. Greg hustled her into the powerful little executive jet the company kept at Scholes Field and took off for Dallas, flying it himself. They were going to have a fantastic time, he assured her excitedly. They were going to spend the days on the lake, the nights eating and carousing. They would spend money as if it were going out of style. And she was going to laugh and be happy.

"And forget Mark," he added slyly, somewhere over the endless expanse of eastern Texas.

"Forget Mark? What do you mean? Why should Mark come into it?"

"Oh, come on! You've been mooning like a sick calf for weeks, and Mark isn't fit for human company." He glanced anxiously at her. "I'm not so sure about you, but I do know my cousin. Dammit, Toni, he's a good guy. How did you get his tail in such a bind? He is living through hell right now, and I'll betcha my bottom dollar you are the cause, my sweet."

"I don't know what you mean." Toni thought of Karen and her little boy, of Ginny Lee's poisonous tongue, and bitterly rejected any responsibility toward Mark Anders. "I'm sorry I'm such a bad companion, but it has absolutely nothing to do with Mark. He doesn't care whether I live or die, as long as I do the job I was hired to do properly. You realize you rushed us onto this plane of yours without even a change of clothing, don't you?" she asked, attempting to divert the keen challenge she sensed in him.

Greg took a good look at her, nodded as if he understood what he saw and allowed the diversion. They were going shopping, he informed her. They would buy a complete set of camp-out gear. And groceries. And they would buy high-stepping clothes, as well. The camping gear they would set up on the lake. The sophisticated gear they would don in the evenings, and then they would do the town. Toni was to have no time for the somber brooding he had been noticing lately— no matter what the cause, he informed her concisely.

He swept her along in his plans and ignored her protests with easy laughter.

There was a powerful rakish car awaiting them at Dallas. Air-conditioned, Toni noted thankfully as Greg rushed her through the heat that blazed down when they left the busy terminal. He slid his long length behind the controls and proceeded with his sketched-in program with verve and energy. In this mood he certainly bore a striking resemblance to another member of his family.

Greg knew how to spend money with flair. He had a bottomless supply, evidently. Toni insisted on buying her own clothes, but that was as far as she got. He loaded the car with expensive and very extensive purchases.

The next day they drove north to the enormous lake. They camped on the shore, Greg erecting the two small tents he had purchased. He furnished them with air mattresses and down-filled sleeping bags, then set up a makeshift kitchen area around a big outdoor grill. Toni's first instruction was in the making of coffee. Her tuition in the fine art of luxury camping went on from there.

Greg belonged to the association that owned the land on which they camped. Colorful catamarans lined the shore, clustered together for pleasure and the serious business of winning races. Toni was subjected to ten days of a unique variety of sailboating. They had hull-flying contests, raced every one the least bit interested in testing skills and held regattas under the strong sun and even by moonlight.

Each night at sundown they went to Dallas. Sometimes they went alone. Greg danced well and was an undemanding partner. Sometimes they went with a crowd. Whichever way they went, the object was to have fun and forget what could not be helped. Toni almost succeeded.

She lived in a bathing suit or bikini and acquired a deep golden tan. She came off the cat late on the second Thursday, wind-whipped hair held back from her brown face by the jaunty yachting cap Greg insisted she wear. A thick coat of white cream lay across her lips and the bridge of her nose—also at Greg's insistence. Bent over, helping Greg heave the light craft onto the flat shore, she heard her name spoken behind her and straightened almost into Mike Lane's arms. She sidestepped him and stood still, remembering the unhappiness she had felt on the day she made this date with him, remembering the cause of that unhappiness.

Mike insisted they go to Dallas. Greg did his best to head the other man off. There was a barbecue tonight, to be followed by a dance. The musicians were counting on Toni's fiddle, he told the pilot. Greg insisted they stay and take part.

Mike laughed quietly and took Toni anyway. She went, subdued and unhappy. He took her for an evening of delightful dining at the Fairmount. The dinner was followed by a first-class, cabaret-style show. Toni tried hard but found her enjoyment inhibited by her unwillingness to encourage Mike. Instinctively she knew his feelings were involved. She liked him too much to hurt him.

But it was too late. As they sat finishing coffee, he became serious, and to her astonishment he asked her to marry him—bluntly, with a need to have a straightforward answer immediately.

"Mike, I—I wish I could, but. . . ."

"But you can't." He ground out the cigarette he

had just lit and leaned toward her, his good-looking face grim. "It's Anders, I suppose."

Toni bleakly returned his penetrating gaze. She did not deny his statement.

"I thought so." He shook his head at her, pain in his expression. "I did ask you, Antonia. The first time I saw you—remember? You were in the Customs line in Washington."

Toni nodded, numb with distaste at having caused this man's unhappiness. Why hadn't she left well enough alone, then? She remembered flirting with him because Mark was watching her with that look on his face....

"I am so sorry, Mike. I—I didn't know...."

"Well, I did. I should have been warned. I did see the way he looked at you, you know. Should have stopped me. It didn't. I couldn't resist you." Fine eyes filled with passion, he captured her slender hands, kissed her fingers. "I fell in love with you the minute I saw you there on the plane. I had to try."

"Oh, Mike, don't!" A tear spilled over, wandered down her brown flushed cheek. He reached up a gentle finger and removed it, tilting his dark head to smile at her.

"I wish I did love you." The fierce whisper was wrenched from her. Mike was such a decent man, she thought with devastating despair. He was not the type to become involved with other men's wives or young defenseless girls. "Oh, how I wish it."

He motioned for the bill and they left. Silently he guided the big car back onto the multilane freeway and headed north. Toni was so immersed in her own bitter thoughts that she did not notice where they were going.

The impossibility of her situation was starkly apparent. How could she love a man like Mark and feel only friendship for one of Mike Lane's caliber? Her heart was a leaden emptiness, her head full of whirling thoughts that solved nothing.

They chatted cautiously the rest of the way to Lake Dallas. Mike guided the car into the parking lot, and the noise of the party drifted to them through the trees.

"Sounds as if they are hard at it," Toni murmured. "Shall we join them? Or would you rather not?"

"I think not, Toni." She was unable to see his expression, but the strain in his voice spoke volumes about his distress. "I'll just take you over and then go, if you'll excuse me." He helped her from the car and kept his arm around her as he guided her toward the rowdiness. Before they reached the edge of the flickering light from the huge campfire he stopped her. Toni turned to him, her face shadowed, regretful.

Mike stared down at her, his features stiff with repressed feeling. "Goodbye, Toni. Remember me sometimes."

His kiss was fierce, filled with longing. He released her with a muffled sound and strode away into the covering darkness. Toni remained where she was until the sweep of headlights through the trees told her he was gone. Then she stumbled wearily through the darkness, keeping to the trees. She could not bear the thought of joining the merrymakers.

What a mess she had made of her life. Engrossed in her own misery, she did not see the man waiting for her until she was within touching distance.

"Did you have a good time?" Mark's question was cold, indifferent.

"It is no concern of yours." Toni recovered from the shock of seeing him with a speed of which she was proud. He was supposed to be on *Sea Venture*, two hundred miles out in the gulf. She moved toward her tent.

"We're leaving first thing in the morning for the Middle East, Antonia," he informed her as her busy fingers fumbled with the ties of her tent flap.

"You are, perhaps." She ducked into her tent, driven by her necessity to shut out of her life the imperious individual talking to her. "I am going to the Gulf of Mexico. I happen to have a job to take care of."

"That's being seen to. You are going with me."

That will be the day, Toni thought rebelliously. Darkness ruined the effect of the glare she winged at him. "G'night, Greg," she called, and caught his answer to sleep well as she pulled down the tent flap. Mark's chuckle did little to ease her tension. How had he known where to find them? Greg must have left word of their whereabouts, she supposed. She was too tired to worry about it!

She kicked off her shoes and got ready for bed without further delay. She did not hear Mark leave and really didn't care if he stood outside her tent all night. Thankfully she was asleep in minutes, her mind blanking as it refused to deal with her tangled emotions.

CHAPTER FIFTEEN

"WAKE UP, LADYBUG!" Greg's command rang out the next morning before the sun was up.

Toni moaned her disgust, but he was insistent. She rolled to her feet and pushed her disheveled head through the tent flap. Bacon sizzled in a pan on the camp stove. The big pressure lantern lit the area. Greg had set the wooden trestle table, she saw. Coffee burbled away in its gay tin percolator, adding its piquant odor to the mouth-watering smell of the bacon.

"Greg, remind me to murder you some day—preferably early in the morning. Justifiable homicide, I think it is called."

"Hop to it, little one. You've got far to go this day."

It was then that Toni remembered Mark. Her eyes raked the camp.

"He's swimming," Greg observed dryly. "Hurry, Toni. You have a plane to catch."

"That, my lad, is what you think," Toni stated tartly. "I'm going with you back to Galveston."

"Honeychile, Mark wants you to go to the Middle East with him. You can't refuse. You are invited to Hussein's wedding the day after tomorrow. It is a special invitation not many Westerners ever receive. Mark stands to lose all kinds of face if you don't show up. You have to go!"

Toni stared up into Greg's agitated brown face, her own eyes darkening with anger. "I don't have to and I damn well won't! Mark Anders can lose his whole bloody face for all I care."

"Ladybug! You ain't taking up swearing?"

Toni pulled her flushed face back into the tent and jerked the flap down. "Go away and don't bother me."

"Aw, Toni, c'mon, now. At least come and eat breakfast and talk it over with Mark. He deserves that much."

Toni didn't bother to answer. Mark Anders deserved absolutely no consideration, no matter what his cousin thought. She spent a couple of minutes struggling with indecision, then dressed quickly, thrusting slim brown legs into faded jeans. She popped a sleeveless striped shirt over her head, scooped up sponge, bag, toothbrush and towel and emerged from the tent still tucking the shirt into the waistband of her jeans. She zipped the jeans over her brief and silky panties and marched to the crude outdoor facilities, battle flags flying. If Mark Anders wanted a confrontation, he was about to have it.

He stood under the limb from which the camp's only mirror was suspended. His face smeared with foam, he was shaving. Clad only in brief black trunks, the lantern light glistening on his smooth tanned skin, he was more than a little spectacular.

Toni felt her nostrils twitch as the tangy scent of his shaving cream reached her. She filled the tin basin near him with cold water and scrubbed away at hot cheeks. By the time she had finished brushing her teeth he had vanished into Greg's tent.

She took care of the rest of her early-morning needs,

then walked down to the water's edge. Staring across
the sheet of water, black in the predawn, she fought
down the emotion she was so unwilling to admit. The
water lapped at her feet. Birds, just beginning to stir,
made sleepy sounds in the trees behind her. Far away a
rooster crowed. Gradually Toni's anger cooled.

So Hussein was to be married. Idly she wondered
who the bride might be. Someone from his own country, most probably. Didn't most Arabian princes
marry cousins? She wasn't sure, but she sincerely
hoped he would be happy with his choice. Hussein
needed a wife because he wanted an heir. Perhaps he
had fallen in love, as well. Wonderful if he had. He
was a nice person and she liked him, but it was strange
that he had invited her to the wedding.

Her limited knowledge of the customs of the area
told her that a wedding was very much a family affair,
especially as far as the bride was concerned. As she remembered, there was little mingling between the sexes
even at such an occasion.

Where did she and Mark fit in? Curious, Toni went
back to the campsite to find out. His explanation
might turn out to be interesting at that, she decided.

Greg served up a plate of bacon and eggs and
poured a mug of coffee, the aroma teasing her. He
filled two more mugs, put two plates beside them,
heaped with his version of a reasonable man's
breakfast, and lowered his lean length onto the bench
by Toni, yelling for Mark.

He came to the table in a dark suit of a cool-looking
fabric. His silky gray shirt and nicely knotted tie of the
same shade looked incongruous in the light of the hissing lantern. He sat down opposite, his impersonal look
glinting as he searched Toni's features.

"Are you planning to wear jeans to the Middle East, Antonia?" The question was faintly derisive.

"I'm not really planning to go to the Middle East." Toni's statement was a flat challenge.

"Sorry, I'm afraid you have no choice. Whether United Petroleum of California continues to profit or not in that area depends on not offending Hussein and his family in any way. He has invited us to his wedding. It's an honor we can't turn down. We'll have to go."

"I thought such affairs were only attended by the immediate families and closest friends in Muslim countries."

"True. But Hussein and I are close friends. We've known each other since college days. And in those years he has learned to trust me. To be truly trusted by an Arab means you become like family to him."

Toni reached for another helping of bacon and considered this. There had been a time when she had thought Mark worthy of that kind of trust, too. She sighed and washed the bacon down with a swallow of coffee.

"I have no clothes fit to wear to the wedding of a prince." It was a feeble effort but she had to make it.

"He has ordered a dress for you from a Paris couturier. It is waiting in the hotel room he has booked for you, along with all the bits and pieces you will need." Mark's easy reply took her by surprise.

"Why would he do such a thing?"

"Because Linda asked him to, I gather." Mark shrugged.

"Linda?"

"He's marrying Linda Wells."

Toni stared at the hard lean planes of the face she

loved so well and hated so much. The suspicion that Mark had thrown Linda Wells at the head of the desert prince in an effort to distract Hussein's attention came to her. It was a singularly disquieting idea. Why had he gone to so much trouble to sidetrack Hussein from his pursuit of her? That the Arabian had been pursuing her Toni knew without conceit.

Toni had not heard from Sheik Hussein since the night in Dallas when he had been called away so abruptly. Not bothered by his failure to get in touch with her, she had never considered that Hussein's interest might have been purposely redirected by the man across the table. What kind of a devious game was he playing?

"Yes, I sent Linda Wells out there quite deliberately." Mark read her thoughts, gave her a quick amused smile. "I told you he was looking for a wife when I first introduced you to him, remember?"

"You sent Linda Wells out there, a lamb to be shorn!"

Both Greg and Mark laughed. "I can assure you Linda Wells is no lamb. And it will be a long day before anyone ever shears her. Linda knows exactly what she is doing and where she is going. If anyone needs protection, it's probably Hussein."

"I hope you know what you are talking about." Toni fixed her employer with a disapproving scowl. "I don't think it's an easy thing for a woman to marry into Muslim society—especially into a family as traditional as Hussein's."

"Linda is aware of that, but she will be a princess and treated royally. And if you are envisioning her cloistered for the rest of her life in Hussein's harem, forget it. Hussein travels the capitals of the world.

Linda will go with him as his wife. The restrictions imposed on her when they are at home will not apply whenever they travel, and I am sure the strata of society she will be moving in will more than compensate her for any limits put on her by the culture at home." Mark looked bored with the whole thing. It was plain to Toni he really was not interested in any trauma his former liaison officer might suffer.

"Besides—" his smile was mocking "—they've managed to really fall in love, from all reports." He glanced at the gold watch on his lean wrist. "We need to go, Antonia. I've booked us on a 747 connecting flight from Dallas to Bahrain."

Toni turned an uncertain gaze on Greg. He winked broadly. "Go on, ladybug. I'll guarantee to keep old *Sea Breeze* roaring away while you go off and enjoy yourself among them there desert sheiks. But watch yourself and don't get carried away to someone's tent."

"That's hardly likely." She breathed deeply, her eyes on the man who watched her so impassively. Toni sighed, something she caught herself doing fairly often these days. "Okay," she suddenly capitulated. "When do you want to start?"

"Now, Antonia." Mark left his seat with a lazy speed. "I picked up your passport from ma. She put a few things she thought you might need in a case for you. It's in the car." Toni felt her temper rise again. So he'd blandly assumed he would have his way, had he?

Long fingers helped her to her feet. She was hustled to the waiting car without time to protest. And what good was a temper when one was dealing with such an arrogant man? Toni shrugged off his hand, but she went.

"I'll pack up here and get the stuff back to Galveston." Greg strolled at her other side. "Don't worry about a thing, ladybug."

"Thanks, Greg. Sorry to leave you with such a mess."

"No problem. When do you figure to be back, Mark?"

"By the end of the week at the latest. Should be in Galveston by Friday or Saturday."

"So long." Greg waved them away and headed back through the trees to the campsite as Mark started the car.

The trip to the Dallas–Fort Worth Airport was a silent one. It was practically a silent trip from New York across the Atlantic, too.

Toni sat quietly, her body tense with an electric awareness of the man with whom she was traveling. She hated herself for that awareness, but was powerless to suppress it completely. Her thoughts scrambled in frantic disarray as her mind tried to cope with his nearness. She met those hazel eyes once in all those miles. His clever, good-looking face remained unreadable. But something hidden in the glinting depths of his glance warned her.... She refused to meet his eyes again.

Mark watched her as she tried to ignore him. His smile mocked gently, as though he were reading her thoughts and knew the extent of his effect on her. By the time they landed in London she was most uncomfortable. She passed quickly out of the jet as soon as the door opened, Mark following smartly at her heels. In the VIP lounge, garment bag over one broad shoulder, her makeup case dangling from his fingers, he gestured with an inclination of his imperious head.

"There's a fairly comfortable ladies' lounge over in the corner," he informed her. "It's best if you change out of your Texas gear now so you will arrive in clothing Hussein's family can deal with. They are still reasonably stodgy in their attitude toward feminine apparel. Take your time. We've a couple of hours before we go on."

Toni avoided his probing gaze. She took the garment bag, murmuring her thanks, and fled toward the woman's rest room. Mark followed her and stopped her before she went through the door, his fingers brushing her sun-browned shoulder. Toni halted in her tracks, frozen by his touch.

"Here." She heard the laugh in his voice. "You may need your toothbrush."

She took the makeup case from him and forced herself to proceed sedately into the ladies' room. Dimly she realized he had almost slipped into his old pattern of teasing again. The ache came. If only he were different!

The garment bag contained two dresses. One was black raw silk with a high mandarin collar piped in white, the other a lovely blue in a smoother weave. Both were ankle length. The other garment there was a loose and beautifully cut hooded cape of a nubbly woven cotton almost as thin as black cheesecloth. A pair of soft black slippers in her size was tucked into the corner of the bag.

After discarding her jeans and top she shook out the raw-silk garment and slipped it over her head. It molded her shoulders lovingly and dropped in enticing folds around her ankles. She donned the black tights she found in her makeup case, brushed her hair and teeth, applied mascara and lipstick sparingly and armored herself to go back out to where Mark was waiting.

Slipping on the comfortable shoes, she swung the cape over her shoulders, picked up her belongings and went out.

Mark met her, his expression cool. "Just the ticket, I'd say."

"You've been shopping?" Toni was curious.

"Yes." His clipped answer was indifferent. "Most women from the West run into difficulty in the conservative Muslim countries because they dress incorrectly. If you'll just pull the hood of your cape over your hair once we land, keep your eyes on the ground and stick to me like a burr, you should do."

"You're joking!"

"I assure you, Dr. Cameron, that I have never been more sincere in my life. If you are interested in avoiding encounters you might find a bit irksome, you will need to be most discreet. And you will need male protection anytime you are not actually inside the walls of a house of some sort."

He shot a glance filled with icy amusement at her rebellious face. "Unless, that is, you would find it easier to fend off the attention of every Arab male who lays eyes on you rather than to stay by my side."

"I think you are exaggerating, Mark Anders, to say the least," Toni retorted flatly. "This is the twentieth century, after all. Those people travel, have television—"

"People like Hussein travel, are educated, read and enjoy the fruits of Western civilization. But meet any Arab, Hussein included, and you meet a man who can't truly rid himself of the notion that a woman, any woman—his sister or mother or his wife—is definitely a female at risk if she sees a strange man." His clever face twisted briefly. "You probably won't be in danger, no matter what you do, but you will save yourself embarrassment if you do as I suggest. A woman unprotected by her man is a woman looking for sex.''

Toni had vague recollections of the years she had spent in the Mideast as a child. He might be overstating the case, but instinct told her he was correct in his assessment. Her mother, she knew, had never left the house without her father or grandfather along. And Joan had always been chauffeured, had never driven their own car while they lived in the desert.

"Thank you. I'll be on my best behavior." She moved restlessly away from him, too stirred by the force of his masculinity upon her raw feelings to want to prolong contact with him.

The jet was being refueled and cleaned. Workers moved over the starkly utilitarian plane with the dedication of bees busy at a honeycomb. Toni stared through the plate glass and ignored the prickle between her shoulders that told her Mark was watching her. Suddenly weary, she sank into the depths of the chair, tucked her feet up beside her on the seat and dropped off into sleep. Toni woke an hour before they landed. Meeting the critical inspection of the man she was traveling with, she wished she had stayed asleep. Mark knew why she had slept the time away. It was in his hard face, in the glint of his intelligent eyes. He recognized her need to escape into sleep, and his shrewd appraisal stripped her defenses away, made nonsense of her frantic attempt to hide her thoughts from him.

Aghast, she didn't try. She beat a hasty retreat to the rest room and stayed there until the captain's command to fasten seat belts came over the intercom. At least, she thought wryly, the interval had allowed her to apply fresh makeup.

Mark slanted a glance at her as she returned to her seat. "Nice," he murmured approving what she had done to her hair and skin.

Toni fussed with her seat belt and didn't answer him. A sincere wish to be thousands of miles away possessed her. As they walked into the modern Muharraq International Airport, located on a smaller island that was connected to the island of Bahrain by a causeway, Toni had learned she was grateful to be back on the ground. She enjoyed flying as a rule, but she had been in the air for over sixteen hours. Not that it seemed to affect Mark. He strode along with her to Customs, energy flowing from him with a strength she was able to feel.

Hussein had sent someone to meet them. They were shown through Customs without much formality and waved through Immigration without any at all.

Mark's glance raked the interior of the big air terminal as they kept pace with the tall Arabian who was steering them toward a private exit. "I don't see Frank," he commented abruptly. "I sent him word we were coming."

"Ah, your pilot," the Arab replied. Toni had not caught his name when he had introduced himself. He was a spectacular figure in flowing white robes. His hair, Toni judged with a swift glance, was as curly as the well-shaped beard that half concealed his determined chin. A headdress, made of the black wool-wrapped cords she was to learn were called *igal*, fell below his wide shoulders in regal folds.

Unwary, she caught the man's eye. Instant humor lit a spark in his dark eyes, and he smiled with a great deal of charm. Remembering Mark's warning, she dropped her lashes hastily and moved closer to her tall employer.

"Yes, Frank is my pilot. He came over on loan to help train men here." Mark's fingers lightly touched Toni's black cape. The tall Arabian understood the slight gesture instantly. Mark was Toni's protector.

"He has been delayed." The Arab's English was precise. "He has sent a message to tell you he will arrive before Hussein's wedding tonight."

"Thank you." Mark's courtesy could not be faulted. "It was kind of you to meet us."

"My pleasure. We wish the friends of the *arusa*, the bride, to be happy while they are here. And I always enjoy our time together, Mark."

"It is kind of you to say so, Faisal. Where are we staying?"

"We have booked a suite at the Marriott for you. It is the newest and best, I think. And your lady should be most comfortable there. The prince is sorry not to have you stay with him this time, but it is the custom here for the couple to be separate until the actual wedding night, when the bride's father must accompany her to the groom's home. Hussein wishes to conform to tradition as much as possible. Miss Wells's family is staying with her at the same hotel. We thought she would be happy if you and Miss Cameron were there, as well. Your suite adjoins hers, Miss Cameron."

Mark nodded his agreement to the arrangements. "Frank is to be at the wedding celebration, then."

"Most certainly. He has become a good friend of the prince in these past weeks. Just through here, please."

Automatic doors slid open, and they walked out into heat that hit them with the force of a blow.

"Sorry to cause you discomfort," the tall Arab apologized. "We have this short walk in the heat to the car."

As they walked, they passed an Arab who addressed Faisal as "Your Excellency." They arrived at a sleek chauffeured limousine into which Faisal directed them.

"Are you Hussein's brother?" Toni asked as the car pulled away, its air conditioner purring silently. She instantly regretted her curiosity. "I'm so sorry," she rushed on contritely. "I didn't mean to be rude."

He laughed, his dark eyes glinting. "You are much too charming to ever be rude, Miss Cameron. It is, perhaps, a natural question. But no, I am not his brother. I am his cousin. Because of the manner in which our country was formed, most of the ruling families are related in some degree. Do you know how we became a country?"

Toni confessed her ignorance.

"Shall I inform you?" He directed the question to Toni, but his eyes sought Mark's approval. Mark smiled slightly and inclined his head.

"I'd love to know," Toni told him brightly, disregarding the sheik's assumption that he needed to get Mark's permission to hold a conversation with her. "Please tell me about it."

"Legend has it that an ancestor became disgusted with the way the tribes in our area warred upon each other. He decided to do something about it. So he organized his tribe into a well-trained unit and set about conquering the region."

"Was he successful?"

"Oh, yes, very successful, apparently. He was a real leader and a great man. And he cemented the tribes together in the only way possible."

"How was that?" Toni responded nicely to the man's sense of drama.

"As he conquered each tribe, he took as wife a daughter or cousin of the chieftain of the tribe. Then he made very sure the young lady was quickly with child. What man can war on his grandchild's father?" Toni laughed along with Mark.

"Thirty years later my ancestor found himself head of all the people of the tribes, ruler of a vast stretch of land, father of a great many children—and very tired." He smiled, white teeth flashing in the mahogany brown of his attractive face. "And he left me with about four thousand cousins, more or less. Hussein happens to be one of them."

He turned to Mark then, and they chatted about the progress of the profiling U.P.C. was just getting under way for the country. Toni merely sat and listened. The car headed steadily for Manama, Bahrain's capital city, near which Hussein lived. She felt a strange anticipation building within her.

CHAPTER SIXTEEN

HOURS LATER Toni stepped out of the shower and proceeded to get dressed for the formal wedding. It was to take place later that night.

Mark and Faisal had departed after she had been shown to the splendid suite occupied by an excited Linda Wells and her family. It included three ornate bedrooms and a lounge the size of a small ballroom. Located right at the top of the beautifully appointed hotel, the suite afforded a magnificent view of the city spread beneath it.

The exquisite bathroom was fashioned largely from marble and fitted with floor-to-ceiling mirrors. Toni was most impressed. She spent a good hour over her toilet, then let the lovely silk-and-lace creation awaiting her on its padded hanger fall around her slender figure in a diaphanous cloud. The sheath of the satin undergarment fitted her like a second skin. She twisted her arm behind her, zipped up the invisible fastening and surveyed herself critically in the long mirror before her.

Good heavens! If the ivory gown she was wearing made her look so virginal and gorgeous, what on earth was Linda's wedding gown like? It must be truly fabulous! She sprayed a cloud of elusive scent around her, slipped her feet into satin pumps that fit her perfectly and went to see the bride.

The elaborate bride's chair held pride of place against the picture windows of the huge lounge. Flower-bedecked, it was raised on a platform at the end of a pathway defined by flowers. Linda would walk down the scented aisle and seat herself in the lovely chair to await Hussein's arrival, Toni had been told by Linda's entranced mother.

Hussein would come down the same aisle accompanied by Linda's father and the male relative of his choice to claim his bride. He would approach her, lift her veil and kiss her as a sign he accepted her as his wife. They would then go back down the aisle together.

Both Linda and Mrs. Wells were completely enchanted by this piece of fairyland delivered to them straight out of the *Arabian Nights*. They had both bubbled over when Toni arrived, talking a mile a minute, interrupting each other in their laughing explanation of the ceremony. Toni had fast become good friends with the excited Linda.

There was to be a feast later in the hotel's sumptuous banquet hall. At least two hundred guests had been invited. Not all would witness the ceremony, perhaps, but the numbers would certainly be swollen by the *mutfarrajeen*.

These, Linda had explained, were uninvited onlookers. Heavily cloaked and veiled, they were permitted to witness all such ceremonies as long as they remained disguised. They were just women who wanted to be present at events out of curiosity. They were tolerated with equanimity and usually arrived early in order to get good seats. Invited guests, it seemed, had no prior rights.

Toni noted with amusement that two *mutfarrajeen*

had already arrived and were perched on the chairs closest to the bridal aisle. She crossed the lounge, the delicate gown swirling around her, and knocked gently on the door to Linda's room.

"Come in," Linda called gaily. "Oh, Toni, how positively super you look!"

"How did Hussein manage it?" Toni asked. "This absolutely stunning creation fits me without a wrinkle."

"I think he had help." Linda laughed, her brown eyes dancing. "I know he phoned Mark before he put the couturier to work."

"Mark! How would he—" Toni broke off awkwardly as the memory of the shopping trip with Mark flooded back. "Oh—" she sounded entirely discomfitted "—that man!"

"When are you going to marry *that* man?" Linda asked casually as she twisted her luxuriant flaming hair up and jabbed a couple of long pins into it.

"Never!" The word flashed out with considerable violence.

Linda swung around on the vanity bench and surveyed Toni's flushed face with evident astonishment. "Never? But I thought.... Didn't Mark tell Hussein...?"

Toni grew very still. What had Mark told Hussein? Linda dropped her eyes and hid her distress, angering Toni more. "There is no way in the world I could be persuaded to marry Mark Anders." The flat statement was fierce. "No way."

"Oh, I'm so sorry, Toni. I didn't mean to intrude. Somewhere I must have picked up the wrong vibration." Linda laughed to hide her flustered retreat. "It's easy to do at times."

And I just bet I know where you went wrong, Toni fumed silently, although the thought that Mark might have given the impression he was to marry her was shocking. What did he think he was about? Or was Linda just plain wrong in interpreting something she had seen or heard Mark do or say? Toni had no way of knowing. She didn't ask, nor did she answer the attractive girl's inquisitive eyes looking at her so contritely. Linda sighed and stood up.

"Well, I've got to get hopping. I sent mom for a nap. Daddy is off with Hussein and Mark somewhere. I probably have a lot of time, but I'm going to need it. Just look at this fantastic veil, Toni. Have you ever seen anything more beautiful in your life?"

Toni took it from Linda's hand and draped it over her fingers. It fell in a drift of sheer loveliness. "It is heavenly," Toni agreed. How wonderful it would be to be as happy as Linda.

"I must go bathe. Will you stay and help me get ready, please, Toni?"

"Just try to send me away."

"Be out in a jiff." Linda vanished into the bathroom.

Toni moved over to the mirrored dressing table, the veil stirring softly in her hands as she walked. How would it look on her own black head, she wondered with a stab of longing. Kneeling carefully on the dressing-table bench, she swept the lovely thing behind her shining head and held it above her hair, not letting it settle in place.

The door to the lounge opened silently, and Toni's arms froze, the veil suspended above her head. Two *mutfarrajeen* peeped at her curiously, eyes hidden behind enshrouding veils.

Toni glanced at the closed bathroom door. At least Linda was concealed from prying eyes for the moment. "I'm sorry," she murmured softly. "I think you must wait in the reception room. This is a private room." She lowered the veil and turned from the dressing table to face the two heavily cloaked intruders.

"Inti min beit meen?" the taller of the two inquired, her voice a rather surprising squeak.

"I'm truly sorry, but I cannot understand you," Toni answered, a faint alarm stirring as they sidled farther into the room, the door to the lounge closing behind them.

The woman repeated the question, peering intently through the masking veil. The shorter one cocked her head on one side and reached out a rough-looking finger to touch the silken, lace-encrusted sleeve of Toni's gown.

She recoiled, startled, then drew herself up and used the tone with which she put rowdy roughnecks into order. "You must leave now." She pointed imperiously toward the door. "Go!" The hooded figures exchanged glances and shrugged at each other.

The short woman beside her moved with the speed of a striking snake. Toni gasped as arms wrapped around her with the tensile strength of steel bands. Adrenaline hit her bloodstream, but the women were too fast. The tall one clapped ether-soaked cotton batting over her mouth and nostrils, trampling the dainty veil underfoot as Toni dropped it.

Toni caught a whiff of the powerful anesthetic just as she attempted to use her indrawn breath to scream. She slumped against the person holding her with a suddenness that almost broke the grip pinning her arms to her sides. The cotton batting fell to the carpet as the two struggled to hold her upright.

Dazed, Toni forced her panic down and remained limp as some kind of garment was dropped over her head and pulled forward across her face as a hood. The cloak fell in ample folds, floor-length, and concealed the white silk gown she wore.

Half-conscious, she realized she was being forced from the room between the two assailants. A cold little corner of her mind demanded she take slow and measured breaths. She stumbled along, dimly aware, conscious of being in an echoing, garishly lit place. And then she felt stairs.

She staggered and felt herself being lifted roughly, flung across a hard shoulder. Her head bobbed painfully, adding to her confusion as the person carrying her rushed down the exit stairs, boots clattering and intensifying the noise ringing through her head.

By the time her abductors reached the ground floor Toni was back in control, her mind functioning with something like its normal efficiency.

The men, for she now recognized them as such, put her on her feet as they halted. A quick rake of dark eyes and the short one knew she was conscious. He jerked back the shrouding cloak and thrust a gag in her mouth, binding it there with quick precision. The handkerchief he used to secure the gag bit into the corners of her soft mouth in a no-nonsense manner. Toni knew she would be unable to dislodge it to call for help even before her hands were caught and tied firmly together in front. The cloak was thrown haphazardly around her once again. She abandoned any thought of resistance and collapsed to the ground.

The taller of the men bit off what was obviously an

imprecation and picked her up. He shot a hard arm
around her and crushed her into his side. The other
man kicked open the door leading from the stairwell.
They hustled her through it, and Toni's heart sank.
Her faint hope that they would have to cross the
crowded hotel lobby died as they moved down a short
passageway and out into the hot night air.

This area was at the back of the hotel and well lit.
The two rushed her toward the parking lot at the side
of the building. As they pushed her in the direction of
an automobile whose engine was throbbing impatiently, a man two cars away slammed his door and stood
up, his glance swinging to look at the hurrying group.

Frank de la Cruz! Toni recognized him in the seconds before she was pushed into the getaway car. With
a muffled groan of despair she threw her head against
the shoulder of her captor and moved it violently. The
masking cloak dropped away with the force of her action. Her shining black hair, the repulsive gag—both
might have been exposed for a flashing instant to the
startled man. Toni fervently hoped so as she wrestled
with the men who threw her into the car.

Had Frank recognized her? The speed with which
the waiting car sped away caused Toni's spirits to sink
further. He couldn't have seen her, couldn't have
known who she was.

Dear God! What was she to do now? And who were
these men; why did they want to kidnap her? She knew
no one in this part of the world except Hussein, and
she didn't know him well enough for it to count in any
way. She sat quietly between the men, numb with a
chilling fright she had never experienced before.

The driver tore through the city. The two men in the
back seat with her paid no attention to his wild driv-

ing. They concentrated on the traffic behind them, keeping their eyes on the rear window as they sped through the town. Muttering to themselves, they issued instructions to the driver that only added to his insanity, it seemed to Toni. She braced her feet against the seat ahead of her and fought to maintain her balance in the swerving automobile.

At last her two captors appeared to be satisfied that they were not being followed. They both turned, joking with each other and the driver, and settled down facing forward. No one was following the car; their actions made that obvious.

Toni knew real panic then. Frank had not recognized her. She was at the mercy of these men whose language she did not know. How on earth could she reason with them, explain to them she was only an innocent visitor in their land? There was no way.

By the time they reached the edge of the city she had come to terms with the fact that there was little she could do to protect herself if the kidnappers planned to do violence to her. She couldn't fight them and was unable to communicate with them. She was entirely at the mercy of strangers in a strange land. Her jaws ached and her mouth was so dry it was painful, since the gag absorbed her natural moisture. Her hands, bound in her lap, were swelling against the cords that held them.

They traveled for ages, until the man to her left leaned forward suddenly and spoke sharply to the driver. Toni watched him glance in the mirror. He slowed them to a much more reasonable speed. In a few minutes she was aware that a car was on the road behind them. It overtook them at a great rate and flashed away, its driver just as obsessed with speed as the man behind the wheel of the car she was in.

The driver spoke then and maintained a pace that was practically a crawl when contrasted to his former headlong rate of progress. Before long the back window was lit once more by approaching headlights. Toni's depression deepened as that vehicle, too, overtook them and passed on into the hot desert night.

Once, a good half hour or so later, a single car came from the other direction and flung itself down the highway, racing onward toward the city behind them. Not long after that her captors' driver pulled up abruptly at the roadside.

The two men in the back hauled her out of the car, held a brief consultation with the driver, then forced her to walk between them up a rough and wild slope. Toni, who had pictured this region romantically as a vista of sweeping, golden sand dunes, was surprised to find herself in what was very obviously mountainous terrain.

The two men knew where they were going. They pulled her along the rough path. The starlight was too dim to offer much help and there was no moon, but they had come prepared. The shorter one produced a torch and shone it along in front of them. The very fact that he did so discouraged Toni dreadfully. Surely he would not have taken the risk of being seen—even by this torch's weak light—if there were any others around! Her spirits sank to a new low as she realized the dreadful peril she was probably facing.

A fifteen-minute walk on the path that continued its sharp climb brought them to a sudden cleft in the slope. The short man grunted with satisfaction, the torch dimly picking out the darker entrance to a cave recessed in the rugged mountain rock.

The other man pushed Toni toward the black gaping

entrance. Seized by an uncontrollable panic, she wrenched away from his restraining hand and bolted back down the path.

He caught her, of course. Hampered by the long dress, to say nothing of the smothering cloak, she didn't have a chance.

He laughed as he dragged her back to the cave. He thrust her into the entrance, his laughter deepening, growing cruel as she stumbled down the sloping, litter-strewn tunnel leading inward. After about fifty yards the cave widened into a good-sized room with a sandy floor. Toni ran to the center of it, her ruined satin slippers cramping her slender feet.

She turned then to face the two leering captors. The short one kept the feeble torch trained on her while the other one advanced steadily, his dark face livid, intent.

Toni backed up slowly, her bound numbed hands raised to use as a club if he touched her. She was no longer conscious of aching or of numbness as she instinctively prepared to battle for her life.

The man approached, menace in his every feature. He reached out and jerked at the cloak, tearing it from her shoulders. Toni swung her clenched hands and hit him on the side of his jaw.

Pain such as she had never dreamed existed shot up her arms and paralyzed them as tears blinded her. Before she could recover, he snatched at her and pulled her off her feet. Toni fell heavily, lay stunned a moment, then erupted into frantic action as she felt his hands on her body.

Sobbing, choking on the gag, she kicked and bucked in helpless determination as he ripped her clothes from her. The sand ground into her back, into her buttocks as she fought him in frenzied horror. He straddled her and forced her down. Toni brought her head up and smashed it into his teeth with a force that split the skin on her forehead as it mashed his mouth. He hit her then, with slapping, stunning, openhanded blows that rocked her head on her slender neck.

Consciousness was slipping away, when suddenly a sound cracked above the ring of the blows he was delivering. Her assailant crumpled, pinning her to the ground as he collapsed on her bruised body.

Toni lay quite still, unable to understand the sudden cessation of violent punishment, the sudden deadly quiet. Warmth spread over her breast, moved across her stomach. She felt it but paid no attention as she found herself listening intently for she knew not what.

A slight movement close by caused her to focus in that direction. The other man was there. He had left the torch wedged in a crevice and trained upon the struggle between his companion and the woman he had planned to rape. The shorter assailant had moved close to the struggle, whether to assist his friend or just to indulge in a titillating bit of voyeurism, only he knew.

He was staring across the cave now, trying to penetrate the darkness beyond the torch. He had a stubby ugly gun in his hand. It was impossible for him to regain his torch without exposing himself to the danger hiding somewhere in the darkness.

Toni stared at the threatening gun. She watched him raise it slowly and move to grip it in both hands.

And then a well-aimed missile hurtled out of the darkness. It hit the man's gun hand with a sharp crack. The pistol fired into the blackness; then her short captor was writhing on the ground, the torch bathing him in an eerie glow as he gripped the wrist broken by the well-aimed rock. His gun glittered as it arced through the air and landed at Toni's side.

She wriggled powerfully and covered it with her body as Frank charged across the sandy floor. After heaving the squirming man to his feet, he dropped him with a chopping blow that hit with the thud of an ax striking home.

In an instant he was beside Toni. He plucked her bruised and naked form from beneath the man whose skull he had cracked with his first hurled rock. He cut her bonds and gently pried the gag from her stiff jaws. Wrapping her in the discarded cloak, he hugged her to his warmth, crooning to her as he reassured her and stemmed her panic.

"Shh, *querida*, don't cry. It's all right now. We must leave here at once."

Toni clung to him as to a lifeline, her hands numb at first. "J-just give me a moment, Frank. I-I'm a little up-upset."

He swore in Spanish. "*Sí*. But I'm wounded and we have to get out of here before either of these bastards wake up and go for me."

"Oh, Frank, what happened?" The question was almost a wail.

"That damned bullet ricocheted and hit me in the shoulder. We need to get back to my car before I lose control. I'm not sure how bad it is. Can't feel a damn thing at the moment, but hitting that misbegotten creep didn't help it much. I wonder where his gun went."

"Under me." Toni felt light-headed, her panic not yet subdued. "It's over there, I think." She couldn't bring herself to look at the man who had accosted her.

Frank released her and stooped over the long form.

He scooped up the gun, then grabbed the man's limp wrist and felt for a pulse. "Let's go, for God's sake. We'll send Hussein's men to deal with these two. They'll both live until they can be picked up."

So Toni went with the helicopter pilot back out into the Stygian darkness. They took the torch with them and made their way back down the hill. As they walked, Frank told her he had followed the kidnapping vehicle from as far away as possible to escape detection. Once or twice he had even driven without lights.

His shoulder was bleeding profusely by the time they reached the car. He was stumbling badly, growing weaker as he lost blood. He leaned limply against the dark shape of the automobile and fumbled in his pants pocket, looking for car keys. Toni's anxiety grew. She glanced quickly up the mountainside.

An animal howled in the near distance. Within a few seconds a dog responded. Toni shivered and doused the light.

"Oh, Frank, do hurry. Those men might follow us."

"Not a chance." His words were so filled with pain she barely heard them. "Open...door. Let me...in. Gear in back seat."

Toni was forced to shine the torch on the car's lock. She tried the keys with nervous haste. When one fit, she sobbed gratefully. It did not turn. She jerked it from the keyhole and stared at it a moment before she realized it was probably the ignition key. Sorting out the one for the lock, she wrenched the door open with a convulsive gasp of relief.

"B-back seat. Gear. Tear up for...for bandage." Frank made a tremendous effort and sprawled into the back seat as she followed directions and opened the rear door for him.

"Got to hurry," Frank whispered. "Bas-bastard driving car will be back."

Of course! The madman who had driven ahead of them to this spot would be returning to pick up his companions once they had finished with her. Had they planned to kill her or just leave her to die after they had assaulted her? Toní shivered as she stripped the blood-soaked shirt from Frank's broad shoulders.

The wound looked hideous. High on his right side, it had torn into his chest and was bleeding profusely. The blood had seeped under the surrounding skin, resulting in a huge, spreading blue black bruise.

Toni tore open the flight bag tossed onto the car floor. T-shirts, work shirts, cotton briefs spilled out. She snatched up the T-shirts and the briefs, knocking his shaving kit out of the bag as she did so. The lid flew open as she touched the catch. He shaved with an electric razor, but he had a pair of strong, curved little scissors tucked away in the case. Toni seized them with a prayer of thanks and demolished two of the white cotton T-shirts in no time flat, turning them around and around as she cut each one into a wide continuous bandage. She tied two ends together.

Then, working quickly, she wadded a handful of cotton briefs and packed them against the wound. With Frank's feeble help, she managed to hold the bandage tight across his chest, pull it over his shoulder and across another wad of briefs placed against the ugly hole in his back muscle, where the bullet had exited. She bound the wound as tightly as possible before she eased him down onto the back seat and tucked his long legs up beside him. She kept out a white shirt and

a pair of trousers and rolled the rest of his clothing
into a pillow that she tucked gently beneath his curly
black head.

Frank gave her a sickly grin and dropped into semi-
consciousness. He was breathing in shallow pained
gasps that frightened her.

Toni pulled on the pants and tucked the white shirt
into them, ignoring the grisly appearance of her own
blood-smeared flesh. Rolling the long trouser legs up
out of the way, she scrambled out of the rear of the
car, her whole body trembling with her driving need
for haste.

Dogs barked again as she did so, and she heard the
tinkling of belled animals through the clear air of the
desert night.

Switching off the torch, she slid into the driver's seat
and thrust the key into the ignition. As she did so she
became conscious of a faint glow of the horizon,
where the road stretched in a long straight line away
from the mountains and back toward the gulf.

Panic hit her, and once again adrenaline acted as a
goad. It was more than possible the approaching car
was the one returning to pick up her abductors!

She twisted the key in the starter and pulled on the
headlights. As the road flooded with light and the
dashboard lit up, her eyes caught the reflected needle
of the gasoline gauge.

It was hovering close to the empty mark. Toni knew
real fear then. She whirled around, knelt and reached
across the back of the seat, her hand gentle but urgent
on the cheek of the wounded man.

"Frank!" To save her soul, she could not have kept
the fright out of her voice. "We're almost out of gas

and there is a car coming! How far is it back to town?''

He stirred and opened dazed eyes. "Too...far, *querida*...." His whisper was a thin reedy sound. "Go...go to the...oasis...."

"What oasis? Where is it? Oh, Frank, don't pass out on me now!''

Heavy lids moved up, wavered as he tried to focus on her anxious face.

"B-back a couple miles...saw it.... Bedouin camp.... Be safe...." Black lashes settled on pale cheeks then, and Frank slipped into unconsciousness.

Bedouins! How safe were those wild desert men? In this case, perhaps the devil she knew was much worse than the one she didn't!

Taking the gamble, Toni quickly put the car in gear and started down the road. The lights of the oncoming vehicle were still smudged against the horizon. She had no idea how far away they were and had no time to look as she drove slowly on, her eyes glued to the roadside as she watched for the oasis Frank had seen as he followed her captors. She realized quite suddenly that the bells she had heard and the barking of the dogs had probably come from the camp.

He had not told her whether the oasis lay to the right or to the left of the road, but she picked up a rough-looking track leading off to the right. She doused her lights and closed her eyes a few seconds, then opened them to see the definite outline of palms marching up the finger of a slope. She turned the car into the track and drove toward the dark silhouette of the palm fans, her headlights once more stabbing through the inky blackness.

Dogs came hurtling out of the night, barking a warning to the camp. Toni stopped the car, afraid she might run over one of the creatures. She glanced toward the road, and saw the approaching automobile was considerably closer now.

The dogs snarled around the car, a menace Toni was unwilling to challenge. Surely someone would hear them and come? Three black shapes appeared just as she was about to start the car and drive closer to the camp. She saw the rifles they carried very distinctly indeed. Would they help her?

A shouted command silenced the rangy animals. Toni rolled down the window. "I must have help!" The urgency in her tone cut through their amazement at seeing a woman behind the wheel of a car. "My friend has been shot."

Arabian tongues rattled around her like rain on a tin roof. Toni put her hands over her ears and cried out in despair. How on earth could she make them understand? They stopped talking with a singular abruptness at her gesture. One man left on the run.

Desperately Toni scrambled out of the car and pulled open the rear door. Frank was deeply unconscious now, the white bandage across his broad chest soaked with blood. Toni looked at him through tears that flooded down her cheeks, unchecked.

Don't die, Frank. Don't die. The refrain throbbed in her head. She turned her stricken face to the two men watching her so alertly.

"Oh, please," she moaned, "do something. Do something quickly."

They responded then. One indicated she should get into the back seat. He ran around the car and jumped in as the other man started it and headed for the middle of the camp. Toni reached out in the darkness of the interior and cradled Frank's cold moist face between trembling hands.

Light flared from one of the black tents. The Bedouin driving pulled up in front of the tent and scrambled out, explanations flowing to the tall man who came from the desert shelter.

He listened intently, then lowered his head and peered into the car at Toni. "You are in need of our help, miss?"

Toni heard the English, impeccably delivered, felt hysterical relief bubble through her and fainted on the spot.

CHAPTER SEVENTEEN

Many gentle hands washed her bruised body, then spread fragrant creams over her abrasions.

Free of blood and dirt, she was clothed in silken garments and slipped between soft sheets that covered the mattress. This pad rested on a beautiful carpet spread over the desert floor. Silken pillows were heaped under her head, some left scattered for her use.

Then, their task done, the women left her. They still twittered like birds disturbed in their nests as they went from the big tent.

Toni had allowed their ministrations, barely conscious of their presence, their chatter. Her mind fogged and disoriented, she slept, to be awakened in the cool darkness by the familiar chop of a big helicopter's blades.

The tent was in darkness, and Toni had difficulty for a brief span of time as she tried to remember where she was. She slept again briefly and awoke to find the darkness gone.

Frank! The events of the nightmarish night flooded back with the strength of a riptide and threatened to submerge her into hysteria. Suddenly the tent flap was thrown back and Mark and Hussein charged in.

"Antonia!" Mark's face was white as a sheet, twisted with anger she heard, agony she didn't see.

"Antonia! Thank God!" Hussein sounded distracted and passionate. He dropped to his knees beside her.

Mark stopped short and stared down at her from the foot of the sleeping pad. "Are you all right?" He sounded abrupt, cold. Toni felt his livid anger and failed to understand it.

She shot him a bewildered glance and managed to clamp a tight lid on her rioting emotions. She turned to the anxious prince and directed the answer to Mark's question at him.

"I don't know yet." She bestowed a tremulous smile on Hussein. "Thank you for coming." She excluded Mark quite effectively from the acknowledgment. "Aren't you supposed to be on your honeymoon?"

"Honeymoon? How could I even get married when you had vanished from the face of the earth? Linda is frantic. We turned the whole city upside down. No one had seen you. We were ecstatic when the authorities received word that the Bedouins had you safely." Hussein threw a grateful look at the other man. "Mark—"

"I helped him look for you," Mark cut in flatly. "I'm glad you are safe. I must go see how Frank is coming along." He turned on his heel and stalked out.

Well! Toni stared at his back, but he disappeared without turning his haughty head. What did she expect from such a man, she asked herself bitterly. To vanish as she had must have caused him to adjust his whole schedule. Inconvenient. No, Mark wasn't in a mood to think kindly of his offshore operations engineer. And he hadn't been for a number of weeks.

Hussein stared after his friend, understanding on his good-looking face. "Mark has been like a madman," he commented softly. "Never have I seen a man so concerned over the well-being of his employee. He—"

"He was only looking out for U.P.C.," Toni interjected sharply, not wishing to hear any more. "He has a reputation for it."

"Antonia, he has been most anxious to find you and to be sure you were unharmed," Hussein objected quietly. "He is probably arranging now to hunt for your abductors."

"He has gone to see Frank," Toni pointed out.

"Yes, that, too. But I do not envy the men who perpetrated this outrage. If they thought to hide from justice, I can assure you they were mistaken in their hopes. Even if I were unable to help him, he'd find them single-handedly. He is implacable."

"I've noticed." There was no charity in Toni's dry comment.

Hussein shrugged, let it go. He searched Toni's bruised face, his fine eyes still hot with anger. "The dogs who have done this to you shall pay." Cool fingers touched her forehead, trailed gently down her cheek.

Engines fired outside the tent and attracted his immediate attention. "I must go, Antonia. The doctor will see you as soon as he checks de la Cruz over. Then you will be taken back to town."

Toni realized with quick guilt that Mark's sudden appearance had made her forget Frank's health. "How is he? He saved my life. S-some man shot him. I was so frightened for him." Toni quivered with remembered horror.

"He'll be fine. Not to worry."

"But why? Why did they do it?" Toni asked, deeply perplexed.

Hussein shrugged, and pain creased his brow. "We can only assume until we pick them up, that they thought you were Linda. I had heard rumors that some of my people did not like the idea of my marrying a foreigner, of sharing my wealth with her. But I had no idea that there was any danger. If I had known...." Guilt was mirrored in his dark features.

"It's all right. It's all over now," Toni cut in reassuringly, already anxious to forget the whole incident.

Mark poked his head into the tent. "Hussein! We're ready to go! Frank says the men were left in a cave nearby. They aren't in any shape to move, apparently, but we better get there right away just in case." He left as abruptly as he'd half-entered.

The desert prince rose regretfully. "I cannot apologize enough for the trauma you have suffered at the hands of two of my countrymen. I must go now to assure they receive their just reward. You no longer have to fear them, Antonia."

"Be careful—both of you," she told him fearfully.

"Don't worry. I have brought many men along to assist us." He smiled reassuringly.

"I'm not afraid. Just a bit battered. Thank you for coming, Hussein."

"I could do no less."

"Hussein—" She stopped, unsure how to say what she wanted to say, then decided on directness. "I'm very happy for you and Linda. Congratulations."

His eyes lit warmly, shone with love. "And I am happy, too," he openly admitted.

If he had ever felt anything fleeting for her, he had forgotten it in his love for his bride, Toni realized with a touch of relief. There was no awkwardness now in Hussein so she felt none about the past, especially the gesture of the roses.

Very sweetly he kissed her hand and was gone. He was, Toni thought, quite spectacular in the national costume of the city Arab. As he strode to the tent entrance the long white robe swirled around his tall figure. The white covering held on his head by the black band added to his imperious presence, leaving her with a distinct impression of majesty.

Outside, several machines roared away into the early dawn. Trucks, Toni judged, from the sound of the engines. Did Bedouins drive trucks instead of riding camels as they wandered around the desert? Did they even wander around the desert anymore? She would ask Hussein, she decided. What a shame it would be to have to give up so many romantic imaginings about legendary desert chieftains. Certainly she would have to abandon some of her illusions after this experience!

She was regretting the lost cultures of the world when the doctor entered the tent. He was followed by an efficient nurse.

"Dr. Antonia Cameron, I'm John Adams, one of the physicians serving the Americans who work here in the oil fields." He grinned. "In the odd emergency I even get called upon to doctor a few others, as well. Ann Rice is my long-suffering head nurse."

He knelt beside her and felt her pulse, while the attentive nurse produced a thermometer and shook it down with sharp snaps of her wrist.

"Let's have a look at you, shall we." He touched her face, eyebrows raised. "Does that hurt?"

"No." Toni tucked the thermometer under her tongue.

"You have the granddaddy of all black eyes," he told her regretfully, "and your cheeks are bruised and swollen. Heart's ticking over properly," he added. "Get that thing out of her mouth so she can talk, Ann."

"You needn't be in such a hurry." Ann waited a few minutes, then removed the offending glass tube and turned it in practiced fingers. "Her temperature is normal."

"Good. Now let's hear exactly what happened." He fixed Toni with a solemn glance.

"May I know how Frank is first?"

"He's going to be fine. Lost a little blood and went into shock, but the bullet was almost spent when it hit him. Ricocheted, he says. Anyway, it hit a rib and was deflected. It tore around and made a hell of a hole as it came out his back, but it failed to penetrate his lungs or hit any vital spot. He's going to hurt for a while but he's a healthy specimen. You were lucky to find this camp, of course. The Bedouins are pretty good at amateur doctoring. They kept him from bleeding to death and prevented him from going into deep shock. Don't worry about him."

"Thank you." Relief flooded Toni's mind. She told him then of her own violent encounter with her abductors.

"Sexual assault?" the doctor inquired laconically. "Did he succeed?"

"No. Frank came, thank God. I don't know how he got there. I was sure no one would ever find me. Frank threw rocks. He was very good. He only threw two, and they both hit exactly where they were needed most."

"He pitched during his school years, he just told me. Good, too. He was scouted by the major leagues, but he decided he wasn't interested in a baseball career." The doctor examined her back then and said it would do until they reached the hospital.

"I don't need to go to the hospital!" Toni protested vehemently.

"I want you where I can watch you for a while, my girl." Dr. Adams sounded uncompromising. "An experience like yours often has traumatic repercussions. You may need a little help to ride yours out."

"I'm not the type to suffer mental hang-ups," Toni told him succinctly. "I'm fine. I just need some clothes and I'll be right as rain."

"Sorry, doctor's orders," he returned cryptically. "And the clothes you have on look great to me."

Toni blushed a little then as she glanced at her silk-clad limbs. "I do rather look as if I've escaped straight from someone's harem, don't I?"

"Get her ready to go, Ann." The doctor issued the command and left.

And so Toni found herself tucked away in a bed in the shining small hospital maintained for the foreigners in Hussein's city.

SHE WAS STILL THERE twenty-four hours later. Linda and her family had visited. The marriage was to take place that night, Linda told her, providing Hussein and Mark returned.

The lovely redhead hadn't seen either of the two men, but Hussein had called her. The lovers had agreed to forego another attempt at an elaborate ceremony. They were to be married as simply as possible as soon as Hussein returned.

Mark and Toni were ticketed on the next return flight of the plane, Linda told her. Both she and Hussein understood that they had to get back and would have to miss the wedding.

Toni's things were brought to her, and she put on the pretty blue silk dress and black cape Mark had supplied on the journey over. Dr. Adams and his nurse took her to the airport in time to catch the flight.

Toni was very glad to hide her wildly colored face behind the anonymous covering of the cloak. Her bruises were spectacular. Various streaks of purply blues, nasty greens and weird browns wove incredibly under her skin. The bump she had raised on her forehead when she used it as a weapon to smash into her attacker's teeth was an interesting addition. She knew she looked awful.

As soon as Toni boarded the plane she made her way to the rest room and changed into shirt and jeans with a sigh of relief. She felt more like herself.

Mark came on board as the flight readied for take-off. "Are you okay, Antonia?" His words rasped against her nerves. How he must dislike her! She dared not look at him for fear of bursting into tears. She felt quite the Victorian miss, awash in a fit of vapors, dying for love of an unprincipled villain. Sniffing in an unladylike manner she still refused to look up at him. Mark made an undignified noise as he sat down, opened his briefcase and got to work.

They did not exchange a dozen words as they flew almost halfway around the world.

With a dull and persistent ache Toni accepted the fact that he was through with her. It was absolutely what she wanted, she told herself fiercely. And it was the only way she could continue to work for U.P.C! So she sat and fumed the miles away, her attention concentrated upon ignoring the man who was her boss.

Once back in Galveston she slept the clock round, then flew out to the oil rig. She still had a week of her tour to do, and she did it with a grim determination that had her co-workers stepping carefully whenever it was necessary to approach her about some problem.

She was in misery.

CHAPTER EIGHTEEN

TONI FINISHED HER TOUR and came into headquarters, dreading seeing Mark again. She needn't have worried.

He was in California, Karen told the team. She wasn't sure how long he would be gone, as usual. Mark's team went out on their tour with strict instructions to keep in close touch with him.

Frank, Karen assured her, was recovered and on his way home as soon as he cleared up the last details of his contract. She positively bubbled as she talked of her love. "Mark has finally agreed with me," the young secretary confided happily. "He's got over that silly attitude of his. We're going to be married soon."

"Why was his approval so necessary to you?" Toni had to know.

Karen looked surprised. "It's because of Clint, of course," she offered. "I could hardly jeopardize his future by marrying someone Mark didn't approve of, could I? And besides, Frank wasn't willing to ruin his friendship with Mark if he could help it. He has always been convinced Mark would change his mind. And now he has!" Karen hugged herself, an expression of sheer bliss sparkling on her sweet face.

This reply only deepened Toni's depression. She had to leave this place, she told herself fiercely.

Greg brought his catamaran back down to the gulf,

as the weather had settled again. Toni trained with him, but found little of the former pleasure she had felt in the strenuous activity.

Sissy, he informed her the first day they were out, was to be married again soon. Toni had never met the girl and paid little attention to Greg's conversation about his sister. She had been married most unhappily, according to the information he shouted over the sound of the hissing waves and the booming sail as they flew across the gulf that day. Toni shouted back what she hoped stood for interested comment, but she hardly heard anything he said.

When it was time for the teams to change, Mark had not returned. Telephones were hooked up and he conducted the handover from wherever he was in California, using the phones for the conference.

His deep baritone betrayed an uncharacteristic strain, Toni thought. He rang off with strict instructions to keep in touch by telephone. He thought the computer analysis and all other test signs indicated the well could be reaching pay dirt at any time. He wanted to know of any change, any shift in the status of progress indicators as it occurred. His instructions left no doubt in anyone's mind that he intended to supervise the final phases of the drilling. Toni's team went out to the rig with a full set of directives.

Her analyst team labored in the computer-filled shack adjacent to the control room. The task of keeping abreast of the welter of information spewed up by the well-monitoring test machines quickly reached the mind-boggling stage. First, the mass of detail had to be analyzed, then categorized and collated. Pertinent information had to be extracted from it—instantly. Everyone worked as if fiend driven.

Then the fast-moving drill hit a gas pocket. It was totally unexpected. The result was devastating. The drill bucked up with a speed and strength that had Ian Taylor turning the air blue with hastily chosen expletives. Activity ceased. They all crowded into the control shack for a conference.

Argument flowed freely as these men discussed the potential and the drawbacks of drilling through the gas pocket. A swift and detailed look at the composition of the mud gave quick insight into the down hole formation the drill bit was cutting through.

Muddy Waters and Greg examined the resulting charts and threw their unqualified votes behind taking a chance and drilling on through the gas pocket.

"There's gold in that there hole," Greg intoned solemnly. "Let's go get it."

Toni, as operations officer, had the deciding vote. "Yes, Greg. But we could set off the gas and fire the whole thing."

"There's a chance we could." Greg frowned at her, not liking to be opposed when he sensed a respectable find. "It's a game of chance we are in, Toni. Ain't an oilman in the world worth his salt who hasn't taken a chance. How do you think U.P.C. has made its billions in just seven years? Just by taking chances where other guys with more money sat on their hands, little lady. What do you say? Shall we shoot for it? I say we ain't gonna fire her!"

Toni considered, sought Ian's opinion. The stocky Scot raised expressive shoulders, grinned at her. "Powerful lot of gas there, Toni. There would have to be to send that drill string bucking the way it did. I have to agree with Greg. We've probably struck it big with both oil and gas from the looks of the analyses.

And we should be able to get through the gas pocket and into the oil reservoir without any trouble.''

"How about Mark? Shouldn't we let him know what we think?"

"Hell, no!" Greg exploded. "He's halfway around the world. We can bring the damn thing in, cap it and hand it to him on a platter in the time it would take him to get here to supervise the next move. The damn hole could fill with water or some such before he could board his plane. We need to move—and do it now!''

Toni gave in finally and agreed to do pressure tests.

Hour after hour the teamwork went on, never faltering, as precise as the pattern of a ritual dance. And as time passed the men who were off duty came to stand around the drilling floor. Drama fairly crackled in the air.

It was near the end of the shift when they finished. The casing was at the selected depth. It had been perforated by a charge device. The top of the testing tool was sealed. The technicians were ready with the assortment of gauges and piping needed for control. Muddy spun wheels, which caused special pumps to carefully apply pressure to the drilling mud. Everyone else concentrated on the instruments under their control.

Pressure built up. Something in the testing device was forcing water that was meant as a cushion up and out of the tubing. Valves spun as men diverted the rising flowing pressure to heaters and separators, then out to the long outboard boom.

Toni stood outside the shack, her feet braced on the rig's deck, her breath caught in her throat as she listened to the rising pitch of sound. One minute it was a rumble, a steady roar, and the next a mind-shattering clap of thunder. A great ball of fire shot upward, intent on melting the tower of the derrick that straddled it.

Toni had no time to react. Her eyes were on Ian Taylor out on the far reach of the big racker arm that he operated. He cursed, then suddenly left the arm to dive toward the waters far below. The flames caught at him as he passed, sent him from her sight with his clothing afire. Stunned, she was rooted to the spot. Men were shouting, screaming all around, feeble accompaniment to the roar of noise from the fired well.

Greg was beside her then. He scooped her up, tossed her over the edge of the drilling platform and followed her into the Gulf of Mexico. Toni sank like a stone, then shot to the surface with earsplitting speed, conscious of flailing bodies all around her. She dashed the water from her eyes, saw Greg next to her and struck out for the tender anchored nearby. As she swam she noted with relief that the two escape vehicles on her side of the rig were both on their way down. Holding thirty men each when full, they ran like elevators down cables. Once on the water they could be detached, then driven with their own power systems away from danger. As flotation units they were unsinkable.

Greg bellowed at her, and she kicked more strongly, moving closer to him. His face was white with shocked disbelief and anguish. He grasped a rope thrown from the boat, clamped her in a rib-crushing hold and held on as they were dragged on board.

It was hours before the confusion sorted itself into an exhausted kind of order. Toni searched for Ian among the burned and wounded on her tender, but could not find him. Horror rode her, clawed at her stomach, closed her throat. She worked frantically among the wounded, fighting off all attempts to make her rest.

Helicopters came, picked up those most in need of attention, hauled them away and then returned for more casualties.

Above them, the fire raged with a roar that muffled all sound. Greg worked like a demon. He commandeered a power boat, swept the area again and again for survivors, brought men to the tenders, then returned to the search. The water was warm but it was rough. The small speedboat smacked through the waves as he drove it like a maniac.

Hours later, Toni looked up as she finished binding a slash that had bared a man's leg bone, and found herself staring at Mark. Fire leaped in his eyes. He reached down and swung her patient into his arms. Turning away from her, the muscles in his back knotted with power, he crossed the deck toward the hovering copter.

"Come with me, Antonia!"

Toni heard the low command and followed him. He handed the wounded man to someone in the cabin of the big machine, turned to Toni and picked her up before she could utter a protest. He held her an instant against the hardness of his chest, then dumped her on the floor of the pulsating machine. His hand rose in a signal for departure, and Toni was airborne before she could call out to him to stay with her. . . .

Once ashore, weary beyond imagination, she stayed in the big corporate offices. She helped Karen coordinate the mass of news coming in, listed survivors as their names became known, made records of the injured and where they were taken for treatment, answered the flood of phone calls, met with the media as they flocked to the scene and sought information. And while she worked, Mark's face as he swung her onto the helicopter, that brief convulsive hug, sat in the back of her mind and warmed her.

Let him be safe, she prayed. *Oh, God, let my love be safe.* Night came, went and came again with no news of him. The blue jeans and shirt dried on her body. She hurried around the big office in a pair of high-heeled sandals Karen kept in a drawer as spares. Her boots were a sodden heap in the corner by her desk.

It was late in the night when news of Ian finally came over the wire. Pulled from the gulf, he had been taken straight to Houston. He was in intensive care, in one of the most efficient burn units in the world. Toni called at once, and as operations officer was able to speak to the doctor in charge. The man was cheerful, quite certain Ian Taylor would come out of the experience as good as new.

"Born survivor, that one," he murmured. "He's been giving me free advice about how to handle all manner of problems. No advice on how to handle him, however." His amusement came over the telephone wire and reassured Toni in a way no words would have done. She hung up, thankful, and went back to work.

In the small hours of the morning Greg appeared. He was fast approaching total collapse. Toni took one look at him, handed the list she was working on to one of Karen's assistants and took him home.

The house was dark. Toni opened the door for the weary man, and wondered as she did so if anyone had told the Ruddys of the fire. Neither of them appeared in answer to her shout.

"Scramble me some eggs, would you, Toni? And I could eat a whole ham, I think. Coffee, too, please. I'll just wash some of this grit off." Greg went up the stairs as if every step were more than he could bear.

Toni started to explain where her room was, but Greg paid no attention, turned and trekked up the left arm at the landing where the stairs divided. Her room lay to the right, but Greg did not hesitate, apparently sure of his ground.

He marched up the left side of the circular balcony, pushed open the second door and entered as if he had been there before. Toni watched him go in. She had never explored the upper portion of the house herself. Ma had told her Mark often had VIPS stay, but none had been in evidence while she had been living there.

Perhaps Greg sometimes stayed here, too, and that was the room he used. Toni shrugged, went into the kitchen and proceeded to hunt up the ingredients for the meal as ordered. Her clothing was uncomfortable, but she would shower and change later.

She had everything almost ready, but Greg had not come down. Sticking her head out of the kitchen door, she could not hear a sound. She went back into the kitchen, turned off the electric coil under the frying pan and climbed the stairs, half expecting to find Greg asleep.

He was not. Toni opened the door to the room he had entered and found herself not in the guest bedroom as she had expected, but in an enormous room that looked to be very much lived in. Dark furniture that bore an unmistakable masculine flavor was scattered with careless charm over a deep golden brown carpet. The coverlet on the massive bed toned exactly with the floor covering, as did the draperies on the floor-to-ceiling windows. Masculine toilet articles were scattered on the big dresser. Photographs in heavy silver frames flanked these: an older man and woman in one; Greg, younger, devil-may-care, in another; and

Karen and Clint, the child still a toddler, in the third.

Toni knew that Mark lived in this room even before Greg stuck his head out of the adjoining bath. He stopped short as he saw her in the doorway and vanished back behind the paneled door.

"Sorry, Toni. I didn't realize you'd come up. Throw me a robe out of Mark's closet, will you? The one on the left." The fact that he had shaved and showered registered dimly upon Toni's shocked consciousness.

Mark's room. Mark's robe. Mark's bath. How could such a thing be? Toni shook her head sharply in an attempt to clear the fog. There must be some mistake.

Moving numbly to the built-in closet to the left of the door Greg had vanished behind, she opened it. It was full of neatly hung menswear: jackets, slacks, jeans. Sweaters, folded and stacked in individual bags, lay on shelves. Slender gleaming shoes filled the racks. A velour robe hung from an ornate hook on the closet door. Short and belted, it smelled like Mark. His tobacco, his cologne, his...fragrance. She reached for it. Then in stunned disbelief she stared into the back section of the closet...at the mink and the lovely gold dress she had worn to that memorable meeting with the Arabians in London. It hung there in all its glory, along with the other gowns she had refused.

Her mind numb with shock, she plucked the robe from its hook, thrust it into Greg's damp hand and fled. Racing back to the kitchen and dumping the egg mixture into the warm pan, she stirred it with no idea of what she was doing. She moved in a vacuum, automatically, as she scooped the fluffy eggs onto the plates she had warmed and added thick slices of browned bacon. She plopped the plates onto the table as Greg came through the door, the short velvet robe belted around his waist. He looked at her curiously, paused to stretch and rub his aching back. Toni sat down at the table, stared at the eggs and bacon, then pushed the plate away as her stomach revolted.

"Took me ages to scrape the grit out of my pores." Greg slid into the chair opposite. His expression was thoughtful. "Sorry."

"It's all right," Toni murmured abstractedly as she reached for her steaming coffee cup. She was frozen inside, unable to think.

"What's wrong, Toni? You look as white as a sheet."

Toni stared at him mutely. Her throat was dry, closed. Swallowing some of the hot brew, she dropped her eyes and tried to form the question that was a serious block to rational thought. Greg pitched into the food before him, wolfing it down without further comment. Toni kept her eyes on the man as he ate with unashamed gusto, on the rich velour of the robe he wore. Her mind refused to register the implications of Greg's request to throw him a robe "out of Mark's closet."

Greg finished and pushed his empty plate away with a sigh. "That should do me for starters." He stirred sugar into his cup, his eyes searching Toni's wan still expression. "You look like hell warmed over, ladybug. What's wrong, Antonia? Tell ol' Uncle Greg."

"Is this Mark's house?"

That he heard the choked whisper at all said something for the acuity of Greg's hearing. He sat perfectly still a moment, bewilderment washing over his good-looking and very tired features. "Yes, it is, Toni. Didn't you know?"

"Know! Know! How am I supposed to know?" The cry was wrenched from her. "Does he sleep here—in that room?"

"I reckon so, my love. Surely you would know that better than anyone."

"Oh, Greg, I don't understand you. I didn't dream this was Mark's house. I don't understand what he has done, why he has brought me here. What is going on?"

Greg searched her wild face. He was very thoughtful indeed. "Toni," he began gently, "do you mean you aren't...." He paused, color washing into his lean and troubled face. He started again. "You seem to be saying that you are not my cousin's...that you are not shacked up with Mark." His embarrassment registered on Toni's shocked senses even before the import of his words. She sat there, her eyes glazed.

"No! Certainly not!"

"Could have fooled me—" Greg's challenge was caustic "—and half the population of Galveston, as well. Mark brought you here. You live in his house. He bought you a car. You are good at your job, but the rumors are flying around that you are extremely well paid—maybe even overpaid for the job you do." His eyes were a little cruel for a moment, then the expression vanished. "What were we supposed to think, Toni?"

"You can't mean what you just implied. This is part of my contract with U.P.C. Mark had nothing to do with it. It was in my contract with the corporation."

Greg considered her with a kind of sad contempt. "Knock it off, Toni. I know, you know, everybody knows that Mark is U.P.C. United Petroleum of California belongs to him—every bolt and man-hour."

Toni grasped the table and shoved back from it. Unsteadily she came to her feet. It felt as if all the blood was rushing from her head. Greg was at her side, his arm firmly around her.

"Easy there, ladybug. Don't faint on me."

Remembering the only time she'd ever succumbed to such weakness, Toni refused to let it happen again. Firmly removing his arm, she folded her own across her middle in a curiously defensive gesture and faced Mark's cousin, her legs straddled in an unconscious stance of aggression.

"I shan't do anything so silly as to faint, Greg. I want some straight answers from you and I want them now!"

"Okay, Toni." He considered her grim expression. "Pour us some fresh coffee and let's sit down, for God's sake. I can't stand very long myself." The man was truly at the edge of exhaustion. He needed to go to bed, not to detail his cousin's sins. Toni knew a swift compunction as she poured fresh coffee, but she overcame it with her need to have the questions that flooded her numbed mind answered at once.

Greg, weary to the point of indiscretion, ran long fingers through his lion's mane and supplied answers to those questions. And more than that, he filled her in on Mark's personal history.

It made a fascinating story that moved Toni not at all. Both boys were orphaned in their early teens. Mark was an only child; Greg had a sister eight years younger, whom he called Sissy. The three of them had grown up in their grandfather's house under his firm guidance. Mark had been serious-minded, eager to learn, while Greg was careless and unable to handle his grandparent's strictness. Grandfather lived in Cali-

fornia but owned a small producing oil field in Texas.
The boys had gone to university together. Their grandfather had died while they were there.

He had left his property to them, with Mark having
the controlling shares. It was only right, Greg affirmed
somewhat bitterly. Mark had always been able to work
harder, longer and with much more efficiency than
Greg could ever hope to do. The oil company they inherited had been struggling when they got it, but Mark
had guided its growth. He had turned it into a billion-
dollar corporation in the few years since then.

"It's all his?" Toni questioned. "You don't own
any of it now?"

"No, I don't, Toni. Neither does Sissy."

"What did he do? Cheat you?" The words barely
got by Toni's sudden surge of horror.

"Don't be ridiculous, ladybug. Mark's not like that.
I married Ginny Lee. She wanted the cash." Regret
washed his tired face. "Mark didn't want me to sell—
begged me not to. He had a devil of a time raising the
money, of course, but he managed. That was five
years ago. U.P.C. wasn't worth as much then. Now I
don't have Ginny, and she has made sure the money is
long gone. So I'm just a working stiff, dependent on
Mark for a job, without a sou to my name. But don't
blame Mark. I should have listened to him."

Toni sat there staring at him. And this was the
woman Mark was probably going to marry. "So she
left you because your money was gone."

"That had a lot to do with it. She would have left
me in any case. She didn't love me. Mark told me that
long ago, but I didn't listen. I've lived to regret it, I
can tell you. Same with Sissy. She demanded her share
in cash and refused to hear anything Mark suggested

about protecting it. That louse she married took it all and abandoned her. Mark nearly went berserk." Greg shuddered. "He makes a bad enemy, but he's a damn good friend and nobody ever had a better relative."

Oh, Greg, if you only knew, Toni mourned inwardly. It was an abomination that Mark should so betray his cousin. But she could see how Greg had been so easily fooled about his wife and his cousin. In fact, if Ginny Lee herself had not been so specific about the relationship, Toni would have found it almost impossible to credit herself. Mark had always impressed her as being ruthless where his desires were concerned, and he was arrogant. But until Ginny Lee had taken such pains to delineate the relationship she had with him, and to point out so succinctly Mark's responsibility toward Karen and little Clint, Toni had never doubted his honor. He had truly not seemed to be the sort who needed to hide his own actions, to be underhanded in any way. From the beginning she had known that he was determined to always have his own way. She had read him as the kind of a man who paid for his own mistakes when he made them, who did not need or want anything that it was not his right to have.

How wrong could a person be, she wondered, and how much deeper did his duplicity run? She would never know. Pushing back her chair for the second time, Toni stood and left the room. Greg took one look at her grim expression and followed her.

"Toni, what are you planning?" he asked with swift insight. "Don't do anything rash."

Toni went into the big room that was used as the den and library, switching on the overhead light as the early dawn was not yet strong enough to illuminate the room. She rummaged in the long drawer of the desk, found a sheet of paper, then fed it into the typewriter that sat on a convenient low table.

"I am typing out my resignation, Greg. I will not stay in this house another hour." Her fingers flew over the keys. "And I am quite sure any effectiveness I might have had in the job I was doing has just ended. Why don't you go to bed? You can use Mark's since you know where it is—or mine, come to that. I shan't be needing it!" The bitter tone of the words blasted at Greg. She reached for a pen on the desk as she pulled the letter from the typewriter's carriage with considerable violence. She signed it and left it on the desk.

"Since this is Mark's house, I assume he will find that!" she muttered curtly as she marched out of the room. Greg switched off the lights and followed her up the stairs, his good-looking face contorted with worry.

"Toni, don't go off half-cocked. Mark will kill me if you go. Listen to me, please, ladybug. Wait till he gets the fire under control and talk to him. Give him a chance!"

Toni turned at the entrance to her room. Anger such as she had never known consumed her, choked her throat, threw her emotions into a raging chaos. "Greg, I am leaving here. Now! I'm sorry if that gets you into trouble with your illustrious boss, but he has ceased being mine. It will please me if you go on to bed and let me get on with my packing." She stopped then. Greg stood beside her, his face so woebegone, so like Mark's that she could not continue her tirade. He just stared down at her. Toni could almost see the wheels turning as he tried to solve the problems her abrupt departure would create. Poor Greg. He was so transparent, so easy—like a big kid. Toni reached up and patted his worried cheek. Capturing her hand, he turned her palm to kiss it.

"Toni, you must not do this. You're planning to disappear, aren't you?"

"Don't be silly! Why should I disappear?" The idea shocked her and it showed.

Greg looked at her keenly. "You don't know, do you? You truly have no idea how Mark feels about you."

Toni stood transfixed a moment, then shook her head. "You are really reaching this time, Greg. Mark has no feeling for me at all." She thought of the past few weeks when he had left her strictly alone. He had barely been polite, speaking to her only when absolutely necessary since that night at the private club when Greg had managed to get drunk. "He may have been attracted to me at one time, but he soon got over that. I do not know why he has gone to the trouble to supply me with this kind of accommodation, or why he has done the other things that lead to your assumption that I am his...lover. I do not wish to discuss it. I shall just leave. So if you will give me back my hand...?" She wriggled her fingers in his grip. A frosty amusement caused her dimple to flash briefly, then disappear, swallowed in the bitterness that riddled her. Greg let her go but went into her room with her.

Flopping down on her bed, he watched moodily as she took her cases from the closet and began to fill them with a haste that did little to assure that the contents would be wrinkle free when next needed.

"You are wrong, you know," he finally ventured. "I have seen Mark look at you," he continued when she didn't answer. Toni winced inwardly as she listened to the same words Mike Lane had used when he spoke of Mark's supposed interest in her.

"Mark is in love with you," Greg went on relentlessly.

"Oh, no, don't say that!" It wasn't true; Toni knew it wasn't. Her hands closed convulsively on the blouse she was folding. She stared at Greg, tormented.

"Sorry to disagree with you, but he is. I've known him all my life. I know him like I know myself." *But not well enough to know about him and Ginny Lee.* Toni could not help the bitter thrust of the thought. "Maybe even better," Greg added bluntly. "He has never been the way he has the past few months." He sighed and watched intently as her color rose. "And you don't even like the poor devil, do you?"

That last soft whisper caused Toni's heart to turn over, shrivel. No, she did not like Mark Anders. But there was no way she could stop loving him. Oh, Greg was wrong. He just had to be wrong. Mark did not love her and never had. Toni turned from Greg and burrowed into the closet. She came out with the last things stored there and flung them into the case. Greg kept his thoughtful eyes on her flushed rebellious face. Toni folded and stacked with a vengeance, then closed the case with a snap. She turned her back on him again and began to scoop things from the dresser drawers.

"You made a promise to me, Toni," he finally said. "I think the least you can do is honor it. I'll be in one helluva bind if you don't."

"Oh!" She remembered what it was. "The championship races next Saturday!" The race was just a week away!

"Yeah." Greg sat up, a shadow of Mark's determination evident on his strong features. "I sure as hell can't train a new person in time for them. I need you.

There isn't anybody else for me to use. And you did promise.''

Toni finished the drawers, went into the bath and picked up her toilet articles as she turned the problem over. Greg pinned her with a relentless glance as she returned to the room. His whole attitude said quite plainly that he meant her to keep her word. And to tell the truth, she wanted to. Crewing a catamaran was exhilarating, a challenge she enjoyed. This race meant a lot to Greg, as she well knew. The time they had spent together had acted as a catharsis for the man, purging him of repressed emotions caused by Ginny Lee's rejection. The physical action had released the stress of the situation, given him a goal to fight for, and it had helped Greg work through his problems. Besides, Toni did think they had a fighting chance to win.

She worked at her packing, her mind busy. Did she have the right to deny him the goal he had strived so hard to reach? Greg lay watching her, his face impassive, his attitude demanding a positive answer.

Toni snapped her last case closed and gazed down at him as he lay stretched out on her bed. He was nearly asleep. Toni shook her head, then decided abruptly that she should not make him suffer just because of her own foolish gullibility. It wasn't his fault she had fallen so easily into Mark's slick setup. She had behaved in a manner befitting a rather stupid schoolgirl. Her own lack of awareness and inability to judge Mark correctly had got her into this. She still did not understand what had motivated the man. It most certainly was not the reason his cousin had given. She was at a loss to explain it, even to herself. But she would go ahead and fulfill her commitment to Greg. She'd help him win the race if possible, then leave this country and its heartbreak forever.

"All right, Greg, I will crew for you next weekend," she told him calmly. "On one condition."

"Any condition at all, little lady. Just name it. Any condition." He watched her with brooding tired eyes.

"You must promise me that you will not mention it to Mark—not tell him at all, in any way."

Greg sat up, reached for her hand and clasped it in a bone-crushing grip. "You got it, ladybug! My lips are sealed. Nary a word to his nibs, Mark Anders."

"I'll be there, then. Tell me the time and place."

They talked a few minutes and made arrangements to meet in Port Isabel the night before the meet. South Padre Island, the site of the upcoming races, was just off the coast near the resort town. Greg would come to the hotel he described. He would arrange her room reservations, he promised.

Toni went to the airport then and took the morning commuter flight to Houston. Once there, she caught the first plane going any distance at all. It was bound for Los Angeles.

She didn't care that she still wore the blue jeans and plaid shirt she had on when Greg had picked her up and dropped her into the heaving waters of the gulf.

CHAPTER NINETEEN

THE BIG JET WINGED its way toward the Pacific. In the dim recesses of her mind Toni recognized that there must be other conditions more traumatic than her own. Human beings suffered all kinds of unpleasant shocks and survived.

Her misery was such that she had some doubt about her own ability to put the loss of love behind her. If she couldn't, what happened then? She wasn't the type to end it all for love. Perhaps she would turn into a bitter withdrawn old lady, keeping herself to herself and snarling at all and sundry. But more than likely she'd just turn into a dedicated surly roughneck, driving hard the men with whom she was supposed to cooperate.

"Would you like a drink, miss?" The pretty flight attendant paused beside her.

"Thank you, no." Toni's grimace was so wry the woman looked startled.

"Sorry!" The hostess started to move on.

"Wait." Toni's command stopped her. "I will have a Scotch." It might help, she thought wryly, though she seldom drank more than the occasional glass of wine with her meal. Or once in a while a beer, if the day was hot and dry and the job dusty.

"Soda?"

"No. Just some ice, please."

The Scotch didn't help. It didn't clear her head of the dull persistent ache throbbing through her with the perseverance of a metronome. She waved away her lunch with a distinct feeling of nausea and closed eyes that ached for a sleep impossible to come by.

The vast and crowded bowl in which Los Angeles was situated did not arouse her interest, as it would have in ordinary circumstances. She listened to the craft's captain as the jet cleared the mountains ringing the enormous West Coast city, but his words barely registered. By the time the plane pulled into the bay assigned to it, Toni was in a fatigue-induced fog.

She hadn't slept for almost forty-eight hours. This, combined with the holocaust of the fired well and the nerve-racking hours spent among the survivors before Mark had dumped her aboard the departing helicopter, were enough to account for her dazed state.

Working the hours that followed hadn't helped much. Apart from her worry about Ian and Mark, she had lived too many hours in a nightmare even before Greg appeared. Then to discover the true depths of Mark's perfidy had been too much for even her realist's mind to grasp.

Already a victim of an inhuman amount of fatigue, the additional stress had overloaded Toni's control. She was in a state of shock; the plane was unloading and that fact didn't register.

The man seated next to the window stood, expecting her to move into the aisle ahead of him. Toni didn't even see him. He watched her a few seconds before he spoke. "Anything wrong, lady?"

"Er...pardon?" Toni looked up, her eyes dulled with weariness.

"Need some help?"

"Oh, n-no thanks." She swung her feet into the empty aisle without realizing she should be leaving the plane.

"This is the end of the line. You need to get out here," the stranger told her, his statement impersonal.

Toni mumbled her thanks and stumbled down the narrow empty aisle before him. The flight attendant on duty at the door looked at her with some curiosity as she bade her goodbye and told her to have a nice day.

Yes, Toni thought in tired confusion, *yes, I must have a nice day. And a nice night. And a nice rest of my life.* Her brief sob sounded curious, like a hiccup.

"If you have baggage, you go this way to collect it." Again the stranger offered advice.

Toni glanced up at him, completely unaware of the image she was projecting. Weary, lost, forlorn and lovely, no young woman had ever looked more vulnerable, more in need of tender loving care. The wrinkled shirt and rumpled jeans didn't detract from her obvious beauty. Never in her life had she cared less about her appearance.

"Have to retrieve my own, if you'd care to let me show you the way," he offered, his manner now a combination of interest and curiosity. Toni's overloaded and exhausted senses registered nothing except his offer to guide her through the confusion of the vast airport.

She went with him down carpeted stairs, down a long escalator, through a long and gleaming tunnel traversed by a moving walkway, then through a series of swinging glass doors, until they finally came to the baggage carousel. The first cases were beginning to eject themselves from the curtain concealing the seemingly endless track upon which the bags were loaded.

"British?" The stranger stood beside her. Toni nodded, watching the incoming bags with the intentness brought on by her unutterable fatigue.

"Coming in from Miami?"

Toni looked at him in surprise. "No. I—I was in Galveston."

"I see." He was staring at her now, but Toni took no notice as she went back to the task of waiting for her case. It was taking an interminable length of time to show up, it seemed to her. The carousel went round and round before her weary eyes. Others reached past her, dragged off the ones belonging to them. Hers did not appear.

The stranger stood beside her, his face alert. If one of the remaining bags on the endlessly rotating equipment belonged to him, he gave no sign. With a sudden small clatter, the electronic sign flipped and announced that this was now the position for the collection of baggage from another incoming flight.

Toni sighed and turned away. All she needed for the nice day the flight attendant had mentioned was to find the place in this huge terminal to report lost luggage.

"What are you going to do?"

"Find my case. Thank you for your help. I can manage."

"I'll tag along. Just in case. . . ."

"Toni!" Firm hands fell on her shoulders, turned her.

Toni found herself staring up into Mike's incredulous face. She closed her eyes, shuddered a little as he took notice of her condition. "My God, Toni! What's happened? You look ghastly."

Mike wasn't a figment of her weary imagination, apparently. She opened unhappy dark blue eyes and regarded him with disbelief. He was staring accusingly at the unfortunate man who had tried to help her.

"Since the troops have arrived, I'll say goodbye." With sour amusement in his face, the stranger turned to the moving carousel, picked up a case that had passed many times had Toni realized it, and disappeared at speed into the bustling crowd.

"Who was that?" Mike pierced her with a stern glance.

Toni shook her head. "I haven't the foggiest idea," she muttered. "Just someone on the plane. He came from Miami." She offered the information in a helpless monotone that caused his scrutiny to sharpen.

"Anders with you?" His dark eyes searched the crowd, then returned to her face. He had not released his grip on her shoulders.

"Certainly not!" She tried a scornful laugh. It left a bit to be desired. She swayed a little and he tightened his hold.

"Why are you here, then, Toni? I thought he never let you out of his sight."

"Don't be ridiculous." Again she managed to turn a sob into a hiccup. "I—he—" She stopped, drew herself up in weary dignity and started over. "Mark Anders has nothing to do with me. I'm going home. Must stay for Greg. Till after the race. Then I'll go. Lost my case...."

In a vague sort of way Toni realized Mike was not in

uniform. A V-neck sweater stretched over his broad chest. White, it was tucked into fitted black trousers that clung to his lean flanks like a second skin. She had never seen him in civilian clothes before. It added to her confusion.

Mike considered her intently as his sharp intellect unscrambled her mumbled explanation. "Right. We'll talk later, Miss Cameron. I take it you are still a miss?" He scooped his own case off the carousel, his tenseness apparent in the movement if not in his tone.

Toni just nodded. She was suddenly too tired to make any further effort to speak. And certainly too tired to pay attention to his sudden look of relief.

"Just you come with me, little one. I don't know what the hell has been happening to you, but I do assure you I mean to find out. Put yourself in the hands of old Uncle Mike and we'll get it sorted out. Right?"

Toni blinked in the bright sunlight as he led her outside the terminal. She blundered along with him across a wide busy roadway and into the cool area of an echoing parking lot. "My case...." She found the energy to protest once.

"Never you mind, ducks." He tucked her into the leather-covered bucket seat of a low-slung car with consummate efficiency. "Uncle Mike is in charge now. It will be seen to." Her view of him lowering himself into the seat beside her was the last conscious sight Toni registered for quite a while. She was sound asleep by the time he inched the long borrowed car into the frenetic flow of traffic.

Some time later she made a vague and very uncoordinated effort to assist persistent fingers that were try-

ing to divest her of various articles of clothing. She
sank into the comfort of cool cotton sheets with a sigh
of relief when restraining hands removed themselves.
Sleep came instantly and deeply.

Toni had been sleeping for a good sixteen hours
when she finally stirred. Full consciousness came with
reluctant slowness. She stretched and rolled onto her
back before she realized she was in a strange bed. And
she had no idea how she'd got there. Carefully she
searched her mind. Then the floodgates opened and
the trauma of the past few days of her life washed over
her. Toni gasped and sat up, electrified.

It was then she realized she was naked. Mike Lane!
In sudden fright, she pulled the sheet up and ducked
under it like a scared rabbit. And like a rabbit, her
nostrils twitched as she became aware of the aroma of
cooking food.

Mmm....Bacon. Coffee. Toast. Suddenly hungry,
she sorted through the savory smells. It must be
morning, she supposed. The large room around her
was full of dusky light. Where was Mike? Her eyes
flew around the room, seeking the man, seeking a
means of escape. She had just located the partially
opened door when he appeared in it, conjured up by
her thought, no doubt.

"Ah, Sleeping Beauty awakens without waiting for
her kiss. As resident prince, I must register a strenuous
objection."

Toni clutched the sheet and stared at him, eyes
frosty. He stood in the doorway, the light behind him.
He was dressed in a short white terry-cloth robe. It
came barely to midthigh and revealed long and muscular legs glowing darkly with his deep suntan. The tops
of his long narrow feet were crossed with the white

straps of the sandals she had learned to call flip-flops while she was in Galveston. His black hair gleamed blue black in the backlighting, and his face was shadowed, unreadable.

Taking a slow breath, Toni asked a couple of questions needing answers. "Where are we, Mike? And why are we here?"

He laughed. "One of the most delightful things about you, my dear Sleeping Beauty, is your ability to go straight to the heart of the issue. Here." He crossed to the foot of the vast bed, picked up a garment and moved to lay it across her sheet-covered form. "We are in the house of a friend of mine. Put that happi coat on and we will discuss why we are here over bacon and eggs. I expect you're starved. The bathroom's just through there." He gestured and headed back the way he had come.

"Where are my clothes?" Toni shot the sharp query after him.

"They'll be back in the morning. They're at the cleaners."

Cleaners? Morning!

What on earth was the time of day? Toni was scrambling out of the bed, her arms seeking the sleeves of the happi coat, when she noticed the digital clock flashing away the seconds and the minutes of the hours with a steady precision. 9:00 P.M. It had been about four when she landed at the airport, she remembered. Probably five by the time Mike put her into his car. Not much sleep, she decided, but she did feel rested.

Not that rest had done much to dull the nagging ache in her heart. But that, she supposed, would be with her for quite a while. Probably as long as she was alive.

Toni shrugged with a resigned little gesture and went into the bathroom.

Feeling even more refreshed, she finally went to face Mike Lane. He watched her as she came across the big living room toward him, his eyes hooded, careful. Toni, clad only in the black silk happi coat, which she had tightly belted, moved with determination. Her bare feet sank into the rich pile of the rug beneath them.

Silently she took the chair he held for her, and just as silently he served her a plate of food fit to tempt the fussiest appetite. Toni was starved. She was also full of uncertainty. She ate with a still attention, her deep blue eyes riveted to the dark handsome face of the man who was eating with equal concentration.

Finishing her food, she picked up her cup of steaming coffee, her eyes still on the man's closed enigmatic features. She found she was painfully aware of her state of near nudity. How she had attained this condition didn't bear scrutiny.

"May we talk now?"

"Are you feeling rested, Toni?" he countered.

"My nap was a good one," she answered. "I feel much better, thank you."

Mike smiled, his glance indulgent. "Toni, you've been asleep just a shade more than sixteen hours. Didn't know that, did you?"

"You must be joking." She spilled a little coffee as she jerked upright in astonishment.

"You were in the last stages of exhaustion when I found you in the clutches of that wolf at the airport. Lucky I came along at the moment I did. You were in no condition to recognize the danger you were in."

"Wh-what wolf?"

Mike explained and Toni listened, her eyes wide with disbelief. "I—I remember you vaguely. But I don't remember anyone else. I guess I was rather... tired."

"Never mind. It's not important." He drank deeply from his mug, his dark eyes searching. "Do you remember why you came to Los Angeles?"

Toni remembered—and how she wished she didn't. She dropped dark lashes over troubled eyes, not willing to meet Mike's probing look.

"Yes, I know why I'm here," she answered with a degree of calm she thought praiseworthy. "I've promised Greg Sims I'll crew for him in the race at South Padre Island next week. I—I have decided to go home, but with the race a week away I thought I might at least see Los Angeles before I go back." She finished in a rush, despising the wave of color she was unable to stem as she attempted to sidetrack the man who watched her so closely.

"You've avoided the real question, Toni."

"I, er, don't know what you mean, I'm sure."

"What has happened between you and Anders, Toni?" Mike's tone was gentle.

Toni glanced up at him. "Don't be ridiculous. There was never any agreement between Mark and me. Nothing's happened."

"Hey, girl, this is your old Uncle Mike you're speaking to. You know and I know you love the bastard, for whatever reason. You turn up here, by yourself, looking as if death hasn't even had the opportunity to warm you over yet, and you have the gall to tell me nothing is wrong—nothing's happened. Come off it, Antonia. Tell me what's going on."

"It's really none of your business." The attempt to put him in his place was ruined a little by her soft sob.

"You don't love Anders anymore?" He risked the question in a bleak parody of hope. She stared at him, bitterly unhappy.

"Don't be silly," she fired back rudely. "I've never loved him." She saw his look and blushed at the lie. "Well, to be fair, I may have been infatuated...."

"Toni."

She met his glance and gave up. "All right, Mike." She spat the words at him, taut with anger. "I am in love with Mark Anders! Period. End of story. What are you going to do about it? Laugh?"

"God, Toni, of course not. Are you telling me Anders doesn't want you?"

"The question hasn't come up, nor is it likely to. Why don't you just mind your own business? Why am I here?"

"You're here because I found you wandering around looking as if the world had just ended. In your condition you were a prime candidate for the first disaster to appear on the horizon. You were weary to the point of unconsciousness, asleep on your feet from the looks of things. What was I supposed to do?"

Toni looked at him, humbled, sorry and completely fed up. She had no idea where she might have ended up had Mike not rescued her. "I'm sorry to be so beastly, Mike. Please forgive me. I am grateful, you know." Again that little hiccup of a sob escaped before she could muffle it.

"Strong Toni... at the end of her tether." His murmured words were wry, for all their softness.

"I—I don't know what you mean." Toni repeated herself without realizing it was becoming a habit.

"And I'm sure you do, Toni." Those fine dark eyes of his were sympathetic, but offered her no chance of prevarication. "It was none of my business, perhaps, but you looked so damned helpless and sad. I called Galveston."

"Whom did you speak to?" Toni's downcast eyelids flew up in real panic. If Mark had answered the phone!

"Don't worry, I spoke to Greg Sims," he said, smiling bleakly. "Gave him a shock he found hard to handle, I'm afraid."

"Yes," she agreed, a sick expression on her face.

"Anders was still out on the burning well. They've managed to cap it, by the way. It just came over the TV as a news bulletin."

"Thanks." The panic and sickness receded a little. "Was—did—is everything all right?"

"No more casualties." Frosty amusement edged Mike's words. "Anders is okay, as far as I know."

"Th-thanks." Toni gulped at her coffee as at a life-giving potion.

"You've got to get a better grip on yourself, Toni." He had turned sardonic, his face hard. "You've worked yourself into a bloody quivering blob. Sims was frantic with worry."

"I'm sorry. He's a good friend."

"Good enough," Mike said, his amusement apparent in spite of the coldness in his voice. "I thought he was going to come right down the phone lines to get at me. Seems he doesn't trust me an inch. When he got over the jolt of realizing you were in my evil hands, he was all for getting on a plane and coming to your rescue. Regular knight in shining armor, that one.''

"Don't," Toni protested. "Greg's a fine person. Don't make fun of him. He's been badly used and I c-can't bear it.''

"Yes, well." He was silent a moment. "He seemed sincere enough in his desire to protect you. And he particularly wanted to protect you from me. Why, Toni?" She shook her head, her eyes miserable. "He's not in love with you?"

Again her silky black head moved in the negative. He drank his coffee, his gaze intent as he tried to apply logic to her attitude.

"I had a hell of a time persuading him it would be useless for him to come to L.A. He was more than a bit upset because I had seen you. I think he was half-convinced we had planned the whole thing. He was very relieved when I finally got through to him that our meeting was entirely accidental.''

He smiled, but he wasn't through. "I had to remind him L.A. is a city of some size, and that he would have the devil's own job finding you in time to rescue you from my evil intentions." He stared at her a moment. "He let it slip you've resigned from U.P.C."

"He did?" Toni whispered.

Mike nodded and got up to pour more coffee into their mugs. "He didn't tell me why you resigned." The statement was a question demanding an answer.

"Do you have evil intentions?" Toni's own demand was meant to distract.

The pilot laughed and let her get away with it. "Probably. I've had evil intentions concerning your person since the first time I saw you. You know that, don't you?"

Toni sighed and spared him a glance that was thoughtful indeed. "I know I'm safe here, Mike—no matter what Greg thinks."

"Let me set you straight right now." Mike's growl held real frustration. "You are not safe. I want you and I want you badly. I shall have you, too—and before you leave this town, if I can persuade you to give me a chance."

Toni stared at him.

"I'm not joking, Toni. I know you don't love me. I know you are convinced you love Anders." He gave her a hard look, his black eyes unreadable. "Fine. I accept that. What I want you to accept is the fact that I want you and I don't give a damn about how you feel about Anders. If you've really decided you aren't going to let him change your mind, then listen to my proposition and give me a fair deal."

"Oh, Mike...."

"Shut up and listen, Toni." He crossed to the sliding glass door that led outside to a patio. "This house belongs to a friend of mine. We were in university together. He's a bigwig in broadcasting and he's in London for the next month. The house, his car are mine to use. He's staying at my flat over there. The day before yesterday, I finally realized what a great idea it was—when I saw you."

He wheeled, came back to the table and stared down at her, his eyes brooding. "I'd planned to stay here for a month, drown myself in Sybaritic pleasures and do my damnedest to forget one Antonia Cameron." He laughed with grim humor. "I arranged my last flight so I ended up in Houston. I caught that plane and ran smack into you. Fate, Antonia. Plain, hard fate. And you were so dazed you just barely recognized me."

"So you rescued me and brought me here."

"Yeah," he agreed, his ruthlessness surfacing in the texture of his voice. "I figured if you were at last ready to get it on with someone, that lucky guy might as well be me."

"Why didn't you? Sleep with me last night, I mean."

His harsh bark of a laugh interrupted her. "Lady, I haven't yet found it necessary to take advantage of someone in your condition. Nope, that's not the way I play."

"And how do you play, Mike? What do you want from me?"

"I want you in my bed!" he said fiercely. "I want you—all of you. I want to make love to you until you give up and learn to love me the way you think you love Mark Anders." Passion flared in his dark eyes. Tension stretched his skin over the lean hard bones of his face. Toni caught her breath as she leaned back in an instinctive effort to escape the blatant masculinity burning at her.

"You—"

"I mean it, Toni. I won't touch you unless you agree, but stay here with me for a week, say. Gamble. It's a chance for you to mend your heart. You know I love you. I know I can make you love me. Will you do it?"

"It's not that easy," she protested. No man would ever be able to take Mark's place.

And yet, her memory whispered, for how many years had she been convinced no man could take Kurt's place? Mark had replaced her girlish love with no effort at all when the time came. Was it possible Mike might be able to replace the man she was now convinced she really loved? Was she basically a fickle person—so easily changed?

Toni licked lips that were suddenly dry. "What are my options?"

"Your clothing will be here soon after we get up. You can put it on and leave, unscathed." His answer was prompt and to the point. "I won't make any effort to detain you or convince you beyond what I have just said."

"Did you locate my case? It was lost, wasn't it?"

"It was; it still is. I have a tracer on it." He straightened suddenly but didn't move away from her. "God, Toni, don't go. Stay with me. Give me a fighting chance."

And just why in the hell not? Any hope of a life with Mark was over, done with, dead as a dodo. Why not take a chance with Mike and see where it led? She liked the man, and it couldn't be all that harmful to do as he asked and give him a chance to prove his point.

Or disprove it. She doubted very much that she would ever find happiness with anyone else, but she had only herself to blame if she never tried.

"Okay, Mike—if you promise not to be hurt when I find I truly am unable to love you."

"I have been warned!" He snatched her out of the chair and wrapped warm arms around her.

"Don't, Mike."

He laughed huskily, sighed, then released her. "Go to bed, Toni, before I forget our gentleman's agreement and disgrace myself," he murmured.

Toni went, but she didn't sleep much that night—or many of the nights that followed.

IN THE NEXT FEW DAYS she tried to find release from
the persistent throb of her heartache. But she found
she was completely out of step with her world as it had
been. She had lost the rhythm, the rhyme so necessary
to one's ability to enjoy life.

Mike Lane did his level best to ease her, charm her,
entice her. He took her to unbelievable curving
beaches filled with golden sand, sun and surf. He took
her up winding mountain roads, through sunlight and
moonlight. He showed her the sights of the sprawling
metropolis and kept her busy every day.

And at night he wooed her with dedication and skill.
They dined and danced in exotic places, sat for hours
on the moonlit terrace of the house they occupied so
chastely high in the Hollywood Hills. Yes, Mike
worked his magic on her.

At least it should have been magic. But it did not
touch the frozen and troubled center of Toni's being.
She decided she was out of her mind not to give in, not
to do as Mike wished her to do.

He was gentle, tender and intense. But his steady
sure insistence didn't arouse her. She couldn't be intimate with him. It was an alien unthinkable thing she
rejected without regret. And before the week ended, he
grew angry. Toni felt his restlessness, his rage, and was
sorry. By Wednesday afternoon she was more than
sorry; she was definitely wary.

All day Wednesday she watched his tension and
frustration mount. They returned to the house quite
late, and she spent some very uneasy minutes fending
him off and denying him access to her bed before he
gave up and stomped into his own room, his temper at
the boil.

Toni slept fitfully, as usual. She was not afraid Mike

would come in and force her to accede to his demands. He had said in the beginning he wouldn't touch her without her agreement, and she believed him. However, she was becoming aware that his delightful charm hid a ruthlessness of character she had not anticipated. His efforts at persuasion were intensifying. In all honesty, she knew his restraint must be costing him a monumental effort.

And today was her last day here. She must tell him no and make it stick. Was she up to it? Wearily, she doubted it. She watched the sunlight dance in the sparkling waters of the pool she could see from her bed, her mind in a turmoil, her body refusing to respond to the need to get up.

"Coward," she finally muttered to herself. The phone rang in the depths of the house. Toni pulled herself from between the sheets as Mike's crisp murmur told her he was up and tending to it. The bedside clock winked twelve-seventeen at her.

Toni sighed and went into the bathroom. The dark smudges that seemed to have taken permanent residence under her eyes were once again in hateful evidence.

Mike rapped briskly at the door. "An acquaintance of mine just called. I'm going out for a game of golf. Will you be all right?" His voice sounded harsh, bitter.

Thank heavens! His absence would give her a much needed chance to think. "Yes, thank you. I'll be fine."

"See you in about three hours, then, and we'll have a talk." There was a direct crispness in his words. Toni knew without being told that her period of grace was over. "Bye, love."

She drank coffee and thought about her position. Was she able to live with a man she didn't love just because he wanted her? Did he really love her, or was his easy charm just plain practiced skill? Her head ached with the effort to make sense of the mess she was in.

She was sure of only one thing. Tomorrow was Friday. She had to catch the plane taking her to Port Isabel in time to meet Greg. She would have to get some sleep Friday night if she expected to be in any kind of shape to crew for Greg Saturday morning. Whatever she decided, Mike must understand her commitment.

She was finishing her coffee when the telephone rang and she answered.

"Captain Mike Lane?"

"He isn't in just now. May I help?"

"I hope so. We have some luggage here we've stored for him. My boss wants to know when the person who owns it is going to arrive."

"You've been storing it?"

"That's right, lady. Generally we don't, but him being captain of the Concorde an' all, the boss said okay. We need to know when the owner will pick it up, though. It's been here since last Saturday, you see."

Last Saturday! The day she had arrived from Houston. "Wait a moment, please." Toni put the receiver on the counter and dashed into her bedroom. She came back with her handbag, searching through it for the ticket and its attached claim check. Mike had returned it to her when he told her he had instituted a search for her case. She found it, fumbled with the phone, then read off the number.

"Yep, that's it, lady. Is the case yours?"

"It is," Toni said, feeling a dull sort of anger. "I'll pick it up today." Toni made up her mind without any effort at all. "May I know where you are?" He gave instructions and hung up.

Toni flipped through the yellow pages of the phone directory, called a taxicab dispatcher and told him where she wanted to go. He promised her a taxi as soon as possible. She got into it thirty minutes later. The note she left on the counter top for Mike was brief.

I've gone for my luggage. Thank you for your kindness. I'm afraid I can't share your kind of world. Good luck.

Toni

She had no trouble locating and picking up her case. According to the chatty attendant, it had arrived on the flight following hers. Mike had asked them to keep it the day she had slept so long.

Toni shook her head, caught a hotel commuter bus and booked herself into a room for the night near the airport. She hadn't much money on her, but her credit card was a lifesaver in this situation. Even though she was sure Mike wouldn't come looking for her, she ordered a sandwich from room service and kept out of sight anyway. She checked out in the morning without breakfast and caught the first connecting flight to Harlingen, then taxied to Port Isabel, a short distance away.

Greg kept the rendezvous but did not allow her to stay in town. A bridge connected the mainland and South Padre Island. In a car he'd borrowed from a friend, he dragged her off to a condominium block his

cronies had rented for the races. The building with
several apartments sat on the edge of the beach overlooking the race site. It was full of partying people,
who absorbed Toni into the ranks with enthusiasm.
She joined in the resultant madness with considerable
reluctance, but was unable to resist the universal
bonhomie. The group went from party to party, from
beach to condo and back to the beach: long-legged,
tanned girls in bikinis and weatherproof jackets;
bronzed laughing men chugging beer, competing with
each other as a way of life. They seemed to be from all
over the globe, yet they were all stamped from the
same mold. Greg said it was the Southern California
look, whether the accent was Australian, South
African or the broad drawl of the American Deep
South. Some even spoke standard English.

The fleet of catamarans for the first of tomorrow's
races was lined up on the beach. The moon shone benignly upon the long dark fingers of the masts thrust
into the sky. The wind sang through halyards and
created its own mournful sea dirge. Bonfires burned
across the stretch of sand, marking the outdoor festivi-
ties that were still going long past midnight when Toni
called a halt and fell exhausted into the bed that had
been assigned to her.

She slept deeply, dreamlessly for the first time since
the rig had fired. When she awoke in the morning her
decision was made. She would crew these races for
Greg, then go home. Once back in Scotland, she would
pick up the pieces of her life and get on with it. There
must have been women before her who were disap-
pointed in love, who never married and yet lived useful
lives. She would find a way to do it. She picked up the
rubber vest and the bulky life jacket Greg had handed

her the night before. Clad in a bathing suit, a thigh-length nylon jacket of a blazing blue and beach sandals, she closed the door behind her and went to look for breakfast.

The kitchen in her section of the condominium was busy. Greg and somebody called "Hack" were frying bacon and scrambling eggs with gusto and skill. Someone else manned the toaster, a great pile of buttered toast on the plate beside him.

Toni accepted a cup of coffee, munched a piece of toast and took a good deal of ribbing as Greg's crew. She grinned back at the brown and healthy faces crowding around, joined in the cheeky conversation in a way that had them roaring. It was on a crest of good-humored laughter that she and Greg finally left the building to find their cat and see if it had drawn for the first heat.

The boats in the race had all been supplied for the races. No skipper there was allowed to use his own craft. The catamarans were distributed by a random draw before each heat, thus assuring that there could be no question a skipper had won because he had used a boat that was in some way superior to the others. The final race was held on the last day of the meet, winners of the preliminary races battling to the finish line.

Greg and Toni had drawn for the first heat. Toni helped Greg rig their assigned boat, shed her jacket and pulled on the rubber vest that offered some protection when the fast-moving craft was skimming the water with rather awesome speed. She was buckling her life jacket over it when some latent sensitivity caused her skin to prickle.

Before she raised her head she knew Mark was near.

A dozen yards away, he had his hand against the mast of a cat. His head was tilted back as he stared upward at the tip of the mast, which was stark against the wind-whipped clouds scudding across the morning sky.

Toni moved. Head down, she heaved against the slender section of the hull next to her, shouting at Greg. He bent over, sent the light craft into the surf and scrambled into position. He immediately became too busy to question her about her sudden wish to be off.

Toni acted automatically from that point on, feeling the cat's demands, responding quickly but not really aware of herself as she danced on the edge of the hull, shifted on the trampoline. Water washed over her, so that at times she was completely submerged. Toni did not notice. Her mind was fastened on the fact that Mark was on the beach. True, he had apparently not seen her. But that didn't reassure her very much.

The wind was high, the water rough. The pace Greg set was blistering. They were an hour into the two-hour race when they slid past the boat that was in second place. Greg let out a whoop and lay into his attack. Toni hiked out and leaned back, straining to counterbalance. The craft responded, skimming like a bird across the blue surface of the gulf.

Then it happened. The wind gusted suddenly, hit a good imitation of gale force just as Greg tacked against an offshore current. The sail caught the blast and they flipped. Toni, far out, felt her foot slip. She was under the overturned craft, caught and held by the trapeze wire, upside down in the waters of the gulf.

Toni struggled to reach her captive ankle as she fought the rising panic that gripped her. She held her breath grimly, twisted like an eel, but the wire did not release. Then Greg ripped away her fingers with impatient hands. She realized instantly that he was trying to rescue her and forced herself to relax, concentrated on conserving her breath. But her lungs were on fire, about to burst.

All at once Mark was beside her, his features distorted by the water and her failing consciousness. Her heart a roar in her ears, her lungs unable to stand the strain, she reached for him as she lost control and water invaded her lungs.

CHAPTER TWENTY

TONI REGAINED CONSCIOUSNESS as suddenly as she had lost it. She was in a dimly lit hospital room meant for two. There was no occupant in the other bed. The lamp at the head of her narrow bed cast a soft glow over the room and the man seated beside her, his face buried in his hands. She turned her head, stared at silky dark hair, which was all she could see of his features. As she watched him, recognition came slowly.

"Kurt?" she whispered in growing disbelief.

The man jerked upright, a puppet on a string. Toni stared, stupefied.

"Toni! Thank God you are okay!" he choked out. "I was so worried." He grabbed her hand.

"You were?" All at once it seemed incredible that this man should have any sort of concern for her at all. "Where did you come from? How did you get here?" Toni moved her hand, took it from his convulsive grip. Dimly she remembered Mark's distorted face as she had seen it when she lost consciousness. More than anything in the world, she wanted to see it now. "Where is Mark?" she whispered.

Kurt Grady gave her a keen glance, knew what she was asking and why. "He sent me in to see you, Toni. He sent a man to find me and bring me here, because he thought that was what you wanted. The man he sent, John Gann, is outside, too. Do you want me to get them?"

Toni digested the information that Mark had found out Kurt was still alive. How had he discovered that, she wondered. "No. Why did you let me think you were dead, Kurt?"

He met her eyes, color climbing into his handsome face, a face that was somehow older, alien. He seemed a stranger to her. A stranger who bore little resemblance to the man she had once thought she loved. "I—I was in love with someone else. In fact, I was already married to her, but no one knew. I just thought it was the best thing to do. I didn't want to hurt you."

"Didn't want to hurt me?" Toni repeated, stunned. "Do you know what the news of your death did to me? I—I've spent years mourning you, remembering you. How could you have done such a thing? It—it was indecent!"

"Yes," he agreed quietly, "it was. I realized it later." Sadly, bitterly he went on. "I wished many times I had just told you. But it was too late by then."

"Did Clive know?" Kurt gave her a puzzled glance. "Clive Atkins. He was on the rig with you and father when the accident occurred."

"He knew," Kurt said, nodding. "He has seen me with—" His pause was short, but Toni knew he had almost mentioned his wife's name, then changed his mind. "With the woman I married. Several times. I think he knew, but he never said. When he came to see me in hospital he was very agreeable to having me disappear, as it were. I'm sorry, Toni. He probably thought it was for the best. I know I did."

"Yes, well, that's that, then." She looked at him

critically, glad she had never come to the point of marriage with this man. "How did Mark hear that you were alive and know where to find you?"

"I don't know how he knew I was still around. Finding me was relatively easy. I'm still working in Alaska. I've been there since the...accident. Anders apparently just put that man of his on my trail, who found me and brought me here."

"Yes, I know Mr. Gann." It was too bad he had gone to all the trouble of tracking Kurt down. She had not the slightest interest in him now. Her lack of interest showed on her expressive face. Kurt considered her for a few moments, then rose, his own expression regretful.

"I can't tell you how happy I am that you did not suffer anything worse today, Toni. Anders is waiting outside. Shall I send him in?"

Toni's firm shake of her head puzzled the man. He stared down at her, pain mirrored in his face. "I regret what happened, Toni," he told her quietly. "If I had it to do over, I would act much differently." He sighed, bent quickly and kissed her in a brief hard manner. "I was too young and dumb to know what was good for me. I made my own hell and suffered through it." He paused at the door and looked back at the slight figure so still on the bed. "She divorced me, you know. Two years ago." His crooked sardonic grin stayed with her after the man was gone.

She was glad to see him go. The wonder was that she could have thought herself in love with him. The years she had spent closeted within herself, unhappy because he was not a part of her life, seemed wasted, useless. She felt no anger toward him. He had used her innocence badly, left scars she knew had changed her personality, but she could handle those.

The thing she could not cope with was her unremitting and consuming desire for Mark Anders. She lay there thinking about it. Mark did not come in. She strangled the thought that she wanted him to. That was just plain ridiculous.

Nurses drifted in and out, checked her progress. A staff doctor came by. He was accompanied by a specialist called in by Mark, he told her. Toni submitted to his expert attention, as if convincing herself she was physically well would take care of her emotional health, too.

She wheezed, heaved, held her breath, shook her head with closed eyes, touched her forefingers together, then did so with closed eyes and performed other little tricks for the man. He pronounced her to be in top shape, which she had expected. But he wanted her to stay in the Port Isabel hospital overnight; she had no intention of doing so.

Toni was going home. She waited until the doctors left, then threw back the bedspread and went in search of something to wear. The bikini and the brilliant blue jacket were hanging in the closet, her beach sandals on the floor. Toni gathered them up, picked up the bedside phone and dialed information. She ordered a taxicab to come to the front of the hospital, put on her clothes and left.

The sight of a young woman clad in nothing but a bikini and nylon jacket did not seem to attract any notice. Toni made her way through the lobby and out into the warmth of the late afternoon. The taxi pulled up as she went through the door.

She gave the man the name of the condominium on South Padre Island and asked him to wait when he pulled up in front of the building. There was no one in the apartment when she opened the door. She could see the catamarans out on the gulf, skimming along in the blue water, the crowds on the shore intent upon them or upon other things of interest.

Changing into a sleek pantsuit with a toning blouse, she brushed her hair into quick order, applied mascara and lipstick with a light touch. In the mirror her face seemed pale under her newly acquired tan, but she couldn't be bothered with makeup. At least she was returning to the U.K. with the kind of suntan she knew everyone would envy, Toni thought wryly. She wondered briefly if the condition of her emotions was as readily discernible as her outer coat of good health, then decided the ache in her heart would never show.

She would make sure it did not. She decided this with a fierce disregard for the depth of her sadness, ran down the stairs with her cases and climbed into the waiting taxi. She caught his speculative glance as she asked to be taken to the airport, but ignored it. Settling into the corner of the wide back seat farthest from the driver, she gave herself up to her thoughts.

The one thing she did not see was Greg. He rounded the corner of the condo as she entered the taxi, recognizing her immediately. But by the time he shouted the driver was on his way. Greg leaped across the intervening space, jerked open his car door and followed. Toni left the cab at Harlingen Airport, and found herself staring up into Greg's concerned face before the driver had retrieved her luggage from the trunk.

"And just where the hell do you think you are going, ladybug?" he demanded harshly as he peeled a couple of bills from the wad in his hand and thrust them at the interested driver. Growling at the man to keep the change, he swung her two small cases up under one arm and grasped Toni in a firm grip.

"Need any help, lady?" The driver placed himself squarely in front of Greg, ignored his thunderous expression and waited for Toni's answer. He was a little fellow, at least a head shorter than the angry man he was so ostentatiously ignoring.

"No, I can handle it. Thank you very much."

Muttering threats that were obviously violent, the little man removed himself. Greg's natural good humor rose to the top, and he grinned, earning the flash of Toni's dimple. "All right, Toni Cameron, let's go get a cup of coffee and you can explain to me just exactly why you are so determined to light a shuck outa here."

"First I buy my ticket. Then we drink the coffee."

Greg assessed the depth of her determination with a swift worried glance. He took her cases to the ticket area without a murmur, waited while Toni found out that the quickest way to get to London that day was to go to Houston, then fly to Chicago. She bought her tickets.

Greg muttered unhappily, checked her cases through and carted her off for a coffee and the talk he was bound to have.

Toni was sure he had betrayed her. She had asked that he not tell Mark that she would crew for him in the South Padre Island races. He had promised. He deserved to lose the championship, she told him severely.

"But Toni!" His protest held the dignity of the wrongfully accused. "I promised you I would not tell Mark you would be there and I didn't! It was just bad luck that he decided to enter the competition. He's the one that got me interested in catamarans in the first place," he went on righteously. "Racing is a hobby of his." He failed to inform her that he had told Karen their whereabouts with the sure knowledge that she would pass the information on to Mark. He managed to look so hurt and put upon that Toni relented. She did like Mark's big cousin. He was a pet, even if he did have some tendencies that were a bit hard to keep in check.

"What happened to me? How did you get me out?" Toni shuddered. "I thought I was well on my way to being drowned."

"You were, my girl. You were." Greg's distress as he relived those tension-filled moments underwater showed clearly in his tanned face. "Mark was skippering the boat that was just about to catch us. He saw us flip and pulled out of the race. He must have reached us inside of thirty seconds. He came down under that boat and almost literally tore it apart." Greg's face, his voice, were filled with awe. "No man is strong enough to tear those nylon lines loose from their moorings, Toni. But Mark did. You should have seen him. He was out of his mind, I think." He looked at her thoughtfully. "I have heard of men being able to accomplish great feats of strength when they are frightened out of their gourds, but that is the first time I ever saw it happen." He stirred his coffee, pierced her with a gaze that would not let her go. "He loves you, Toni."

"No, he doesn't!" the tormented cry rasped out. "He never has. Don't say that."

"Yes, he does." Greg's somber nod was unshakable. "He near killed me once he knew you were out of danger. Blamed me for putting your life at risk. Rightly so, too. Give him a chance, Toni!"

Why not, cried her treacherous heart. *Oh, why not?*

"It's not good for you to run off this way, you

know. For one thing, that well is a crackerjack. U.P.C. is going to be in clover for years from that well alone, now that she's capped and under control. Ian Taylor swears you are good luck to have on a rig. The rest of the guys agree. They want you on the next job." He looked solemn, persuasive.

"Oh, Greg, you don't understand. I could never in a million years stay here. I could never work for Mark again. I—I know too much about him."

"Never is an awful long time, little one. And I've told you before Mark's a great guy. He won't let this happen. You'll see."

"Greg, you are not to tell Mark where I have gone!" she insisted in sudden panic.

"Don't be silly. I'm not going to have to tell Mark anything," he said cryptically, turning his head from her as the loudspeakers announced her flight number. He watched her rise, reached into the breast pocket of the cowboy shirt he was wearing and pulled out a thick embossed envelope. He handed it to her as he walked with her to the barrier. "This is from Sissy. She wants you to come to her wedding."

"She does?" Toni was surprised. She did not know Greg's sister, had only heard about her through his occasional comments. "I won't be coming back, Greg. I shan't be able to attend."

"Take it anyway. She wants you to be there. She feels as if you are almost one of the family, I'm sure."

Toni doubted if she would ever have become used to the odd and rather endearing American trait of including almost complete strangers in the most intimate of family affairs. She would miss that nevertheless, she thought as they came to the barrier. She took the impressive envelope from Greg and stuck it into her handbag. It would be a kind of memento in a way. She had no time to think about it now.

Greg put strong arms around her and soundly kissed her. "Bye, ladybug. I'm gonna miss you around the old ranch. I reckon you won't be away too long, though. Can't see U.P.C. letting the best offshore operations officer it ever had escape." He kissed her on the forehead, then released her. Toni climbed the steps to the aircraft, his prophecy worrying her.

She knew she was never coming back. The thought made her extremely unhappy, but she would get used to it, she vowed silently. After disembarking from the small craft at Houston, she boarded the jet bound for Chicago without any time to spare—and none at all to spend on regrets. She was exhausted when she caught the big British Airways jumbo jet out of Chicago's O'Hare Airport. It was the middle of the night then and Toni fell into a restless sleep. She awoke to breakfast somewhere over the Atlantic and the ache of her heart.

It wasn't until the approach to Heathrow was announced that Toni remembered the embossed envelope she had stowed away in her handbag. She roused herself and reached for it. The least she could do, she thought rather bitterly, was to feel good about the other woman's happiness. Even if she did not know her personally, the very fact that she was Greg's sister should make her want to wish Sissy the best. As a diminutive, Sissy was a little unusual. Toni wondered what it stood for as she slipped a nail under the flap of the envelope and took out the folded contents. A small card was included. It was the invitation to the reception after the ceremony, to be held in the private club in Houston that Greg had taken her to, she noted.

Then she glanced at the Old English script in which the wedding invitation was printed. She never got beyond the first lines.

> *Mr. Gregory Sims*
> *requests the honor*
> *of your presence*
> *at the marriage of his sister*
> *Karen Ann Sims Prescott*

She stared at the words. Karen Prescott...Sissy Sims. Karen Prescott was Greg's sister, Sissy! Toni stared out at the slowly shifting landscape beneath the big plane. No wonder she had the invitation. She knew Karen thought a lot of her.

And Clint has a right to look like Mark, she thought with a sob. The paper crumpled in her clenched fist as she remembered Ginny Lee's insidious implications about Mark's parenthood. "I'm such a fool, such a stupid pathetic fool." The roar of the jet engines as they braked covered the words and kept the man beside her from hearing them, although he had glanced several times at Toni's closed and bitter expression.

Toni grieved silently on the descent. What had she done? She thought back over the past months, her encounters with Mark as clear in her mind as if they had been videotaped and were available for instant replay.

From the beginning he had attracted her. When she thought over his actions and put them together without coloring them with her own reluctance to respond to him, she knew those actions were not what one ordinarily expected from one's employer. He had teased her, enticed her, lured her with that undeniable masculinity of his. He had used his wealth to cosset her, give

her anything he thought she might need. And then, in
the end, he had left her entirely alone. Why had he
done that?

Toni thought of her attitude toward him. Mark
Anders was a proud man, and she had very probably
stamped on his pride with an obtuseness for which she
had no real excuse.

Why had Kurt been at her bedside when she awoke
in the hospital? She knew. Mark had despaired of ever
getting through to her. He had decided to give her
what he thought she wanted. Kurt. How had he found
out the man was still alive? How much trouble had he
taken to bring him to her?

Oh, Mark, she mourned, *is it too late? Can I go
back? What shall I do? What shall I do?* Dithering, she
called Marge when she reached London. Yes, the Han-
somes were very much at home—complete with their
new addition. And yes, if she did not come immediately, Marge would personally take it upon herself to
have one Antonia Cameron purged from the human
race. So get over here! Toni laughed, rang off and
phoned Euston Station for a reservation. She was
quite sure she was about to return to the United States
of America and grovel to the man she could not live
without, but she needed a breather first. She needed to
see her mother and her grandfather. Her spirits lifted
as she headed for Portman Square and her friend's
flat. She would go to Scotland after seeing Marge,
then return to the States.

Marge was exuberant. She looked slim and vital, her
eyes full of sparkle and love. The baby girl was an absolute doll. Toni held the fragrant cooing little bundle,
kissed the small fingers and thought her heart would
break. How would it feel to be as happy as Marge, to

have Mark's child in her arms? Sweetness struck her with the force of a blow. She must go to him soon, make her peace, let him see how much she loved him.

When the child showed signs of hunger, Marge whisked her into the bedroom for a feed. "Won't be a moment, my love. Please stay for a coffee with me. Be a pet and make some, will you?"

Toni went into the smart little kitchen and made coffee. Pouring herself a cup, she went back to the sitting room. Marge and Jim were such a happy couple, well suited to each other, with Jim's quiet good sense nicely balancing Marge's more exuberant nature. And the baby was the cherry on their cake, Toni thought whimsically. They were the kind that let one know marriage was still worthwhile in this topsy-turvy period the world was going through.

By the time Marge reappeared, Toni's earlier depression had completely vanished. Pride in hand, she was going to return to Galveston and march up to him, no matter where he was, no matter the time of day or night, and tell him in no uncertain terms exactly how she felt about him.

And what if he said he was finished with her, decided he'd taken enough from her, wanted nothing to do with her, she suddenly asked herself. Mark Anders wouldn't stand a chance. She'd take him by storm!

Toni reached Edinburgh in an effervescent frame of mind. At twilight she caught the bus that would take her past her mother's cottage. The cozy dwelling lay in its hollow, looking as lovely as ever. Its serenity soothed and reassured her. If she had ruined her life, if Mark did indeed no longer want her, she would come home to stay, she vowed as she went down the long steps to the entrance.

Turning the key in the latch, Toni pushed open the door and plumped her cases down. As she straightened she was struck by the silence of the dark house. She flicked on the light and closed the door. A swift inspection of the main rooms told her her mother and grandfather were absent. Odd.

Toni picked up a case and headed for her room. She turned on the lights in the long hall, walked through the half-opened door to her room and stopped dead in her tracks. Her bed was occupied, the coverlet pulled up over the sleeping figure.

"Mother?" Toni whispered tentatively as she set down the case. The person stirred, then was still. Not wishing to disturb her mother, wondering why on earth she was not sleeping in her own room, Toni tiptoed across to the bedside.

The light from the hallway cast a soft glow into her room. It wasn't Joan who was asleep in her bed. It was Mark.

CHAPTER TWENTY-ONE

TONI'S BREATH LEFT HER BODY in a soft rush. She sank to the floor at the side of the bed, her heart a separate entity that did its best to hammer its way out of its prison. It was very difficult to breathe. She put her hand to her throat, and then, quite suddenly, the tears came. Silently and copiously.

Toni sat on her heels at the edge of the bed, her eyes drowning pools of blue velvet, and stared in disbelief at the drawn face of the man she loved. Again that vulnerable, small-urchin look stabbed at her as it had the first time she had seen him asleep. The long, sun-bleached lashes at rest on his brown cheeks stirred, and Toni found herself trapped by the hunger in his unwavering regard.

Without thought, she was in his arms. She sobbed uncontrollably, strained against him, unconscious of the strength of the hands holding her head, unable to slake her thirst for the passionate mouth moving over hers.

That passion burned her, seared her, called to her as it always had. Her being flamed its answer to that call. Toni became part of Mark, her body the exquisitely sensitive completion of his. She had no existence apart from him as she lost herself completely in the glory of his love.

Her body pulsed to the beat of his heart; her blood

sang an answer to the fierce call of his. She melted into him and became his with an innocent disregard of self. He knew what her surrender meant. "Antonia, Antonia...." Her murmured name was a benediction spoken huskily against her soft mouth. "Are you... sure? Do you know what I am asking?"

She opened her eyes then and looked at him... sultry, driven by the need she had so long denied. Mark kissed her lids closed, his hands gentle as he turned her, removed her clothes.

He touched her then—gentle, knowing, exquisite strokes that sent her into rapture, enthralled and captivated her, made her his forever. As when she had danced with him, she moved to the magic of his rhythm, delirious with the enchantment of his movements, her own the counterpart, the other half of his.

Then he moaned with a suppressed fire and completed their union. Toni gasped, stricken a moment, then answered his demand and fell into an endless valley of bliss that took him with her. Nothing existed for her but the driven supreme power of the man she loved.

Toni did not know when she went to sleep, but she awoke in arms that wrapped her to the man at her side. She was glad enough of the support. She felt as if she might float straight up off the bed if she had the opportunity. As she lay there, hugging the knowledge of the meaning of shared rapture to her, her whole world became infused with glory. She was acutely aware of the small night sounds audible through a partially open window: the movement of creatures outside going about their business, the scent of flowers in the garden drifting along the gentle breeze. The curtains at the window stirred, revealing moonlight. The light she had turned on, aeons ago when she was still a girl, sent its shaft of gold into the room.

And now she was a woman.

She turned in captive arms, intent on her need to see the strong features of the man she had given herself to. Those arms tightened convulsively as he refused to release his hold on her slender form. Hands moved, stroking her more firmly into the lean body that stirred, demanding more of the attention it had recently received. Hazel eyes that caught the light danced with mischief.

"Ah," murmured the arrogant male holding her so closely to him. "What have we here? Hmm.... Oh, yes, I do believe I remember. The woman with the navy blue eyes."

"I have never met a more impossible man in my life," Toni declared, aggrieved. "Do you know that, Mark Anders?"

"Thank God for that. Since you go for the impossible, I would have lost you for sure otherwise." He swooped then to kiss her with rising passion. "And that I could not have lived through, Antonia Cameron. You almost did me in as it was."

"Mark Anders! How could you say such a thing?"

"With absolute authority, my love." His face changed, the teasing light gone. "Oh, God, Antonia. What you have put me through these past months!" He groaned, his lips punishing. "I've barely been able to resist wringing your beautiful neck at times. You've managed to steal a good ten years from my life, do you know that? I've spent days...weeks...absolutely helpless, unable to think, because I was so afraid you would never learn to love me." He raised himself on an elbow, glared down at her in remembered pain.

"You turned me into an emasculated malfunctioning blob, and you acted as if you didn't give a damn." That proud head came down and he planted a kiss on her tip-tilted nose. "Good thing my self-esteem wouldn't take it lying down," he growled, his mood changing as he leered in the most awful manner. "I always knew I'd get you in the end."

"Oh, you did, did you?"

"Well, almost always." Rolling on his back, he reached for a folded paper on the nightstand on his side of the bed. Switching on the light, he thrust the paper into her hands. It crackled in her fingers as she opened it. She kept her eyes on his teasing face, not willing to see what she held.

"Look at it, you witch! Look at the date—documented evidence of my firm intention!"

It was a marriage license, issued in Edinburgh one day last February.

"The day we left Heathrow for Dallas?" she whispered.

"The day we left Heathrow for Dallas," he confirmed. "I came up here that night after our theater party. I had to find out about that guy you were wasting your life over. I put the machinery in operation, then got this little piece of paper. And we are going to use it before the day is over. You shall be mine legally, young lady!"

Toni just looked at him, her future in her eyes. He groaned, his kiss as passionate as fire—a fire that again lit the hidden flame of desire she had successfully dampened for so long. She sank into the sweet valley of bliss, but soon struggled up reluctantly, pushing at his demanding hands.

"What have you done with my fond relatives, impossible man?"

"Oh, God, Antonia, you always pick your moments. How can you want to talk just now?" He caught the determined set of her little chin and sighed deeply. "I wish to register an official complaint—but I'll talk." He ran an exploring hand down the soft curve of her back, buried his face in her silky hair a moment then surfaced with a grudging deliberation.

"Your mother and Jock have gone to Vancouver. They are on a two week-visit to your grandaunt— which leaves the cottage to us for a two-week honeymoon." He grinned endearingly then. "After a very necessary visit to the local dominie, who has been alerted to expect us on short notice, I hereby issue fair warning that I fully intend to spend the balance of our two weeks in bed, sampling the delights my wonderful wife has to offer me."

Toni blushed on clue. "Who are you to marry? Surely you don't expect me to be so foolish?"

"You will be so foolish or you will have a dead man on your hands. I warn you, Antonia Cameron. You've already aged me ten years in the past few months. It has to stop before I'm prematurely senile."

He spent a little time relieving his anxiety, making up for lost time. Toni surfaced, breathless.

"That's to make up a little for the hell you put me through," was his unrepentant comment. "God, how I suffered. First Hussein, then that damn pilot...." He looked strained. Toni touched his lean cheek, unspeakably moved that she could have such an effect on this dynamic individual. "When did you tell Lane it was no go?"

"The last time I saw him." Swift dread rushed over her.

"In Dallas. That's what Greg thought." He kissed her, and Toni made an instant and irreversible decision. Never, never, never would she tell him about meeting Mike in L.A.

"I was very hopeful after that." He managed a severe scrutiny. "But you kept on being as prickly as a porcupine. Why, Antonia?"

Toni remembered why and blushed. "I thought you had...that you were...."

She stopped, miserable that she could ever have entertained the idea that the man who was now regarding her with such a stern and relentless eye could have done such a thing. Her heart had known better. If only she had listened. How much heartache she could have saved herself! But she knew he had to know and struggled on. "Ginny Lee implied that you were Clint's father—that you were taking care of Karen because you were responsible for the child." She wound a hesitant finger in a lock of his hair that had spilled down over his forehead. "I liked Karen. I couldn't bear the thought that you had taken advantage of her, that you were such a ruthless type."

She ceased speaking then, appalled at the cruel expression on the face of the man she loved. His language was fairly explicit. When he finished, she had a complete understanding of his feelings toward Greg's ex-wife. Then he told her of his responsibility toward Greg's sister.

"Karen married a bastard," he growled at her. "He left her, took all her money. She was pregnant, just a kid. I'd been too hard on her and she knew Ginny Lee hated her, so she just tried to disappear. I found her in time. When she had Clint, I had Ma Ruddy look after the child while Karen went back to school—in California. She worked her way up in the organization, and I brought her to Galveston several months ago. That's all."

Toni looked deeply ashamed for her false suppositions. "The plane was approaching Heathrow before I opened that invitation Greg had handed me as I left Texas," she sought to explain, regret filling her voice. "It was then I realized what a silly ass I'd been." She breathed a sigh for the sorrow she had caused, for her lack of faith. "Greg always called her Sissy, never Karen. I didn't know...."

He laughed at her, the most indulgent expression in the world on his face. "Given your lack of information and Ginny's attempt to mislead you, I reckon I'll just have to forgive your lapse this once. Clint does look like me. Genetic throwback, I guess. I was exactly like him at his age. Are you going to mind producing a houseful of replicas? I need them!"

"We'll see, my lad." She tugged at the lock of hair around which her fingers were entwined. "I must remind you I have not yet said I would marry you."

"That is one thing in which you have no choice, my love," he growled with enough intensity to satisfy any female in Toni's position. She squirmed more firmly into place, touched his face.

"Tell me how you found Kurt. I thought he was dead. I could not believe my eyes when I came to and found him at my bedside in the hospital. And you did not even come to see me," she reminded him, also remembering her ambivalent reactions at that time.

"Because you had said you never wanted me to touch you, to see you except as your boss after that party Greg took you to in Houston.'' Bleak coldness, which wiped the glint from eyes that had been dancing with a passionate happiness, told of the hurt he had suffered. "Hell could not have been worse than the agonies I suffered after that.'' He kissed her with severity. "I spent hours figuring how to stay out of your way while I kept you in sight—and I did have Greg around to look after my interests. I knew he would protect my love and keep other guys away until I could figure out what was making you tick.''

"And what if I had decided I was in love with Greg?'' Toni asked teasingly. "What would you have done then?''

"No danger. You treated Greg as if he were your brother, and Greg's attitude toward you did not worry me. Besides, I told him you were mine,'' he finished calmly.

"Hmm, that was something of a gamble. You could have been dead wrong. Greg is a very attractive man. Handsome, personable, fun to be with—'' The rest of the list was lost as he stopped her with a kiss that punished her cheekiness.

"Gambler's instinct, honey. My most reliable trait. I take my chances and know when I'm slated to win.''

"You have an insufferable amount of ego, Mark Anders! What if I had still been in love with Kurt? What if I'd left the hospital with him?''

His expression hardened and a muscle twitched in his jaw. "Grady would have regretted it more than any one thing that ever happened to him,'' he grated, then dropped his face into the curve of her neck, breathed in the fragrance of her skin, his lips soft against her as he spoke. "But he never worried me, sweet, once I found out he was alive and well in Alaska. And that knowledge only came about through a few inquiries that brought the most puzzling answers, which started me digging deeper. Or rather I had John do the digging. The truth 'took me entirely by surprise, however.''

He paused as if reliving the whole crazy discovery and his reason for the search. ''You had been in love with a ghost, but I figured you were much too sensible to continue in that direction once you realized he didn't even have the guts to come and explain his situation to you.'' His breath on the sensitive points of her neck, the softness of his lips on her skin, quite distracted her and made it extremely difficult for her to concentrate on his words.

She sought relief by wriggling, fitting herself more snugly into his embrace. The baritone rumble of his laughter thrilled through her. He relented, raised himself on an elbow and indulgently watched her bemused and flushed face.

''The guy had to be nuts,'' he murmured gravely. ''Only a weirdo would use such an excuse to avoid you—especially when you had already convinced yourself you loved him.'' A faint anxiety shadowed the golden handsomeness she loved so well, then vanished as he read the response she could not hide. ''He settled for a lot less, I understand. But no, I wasn't worried about Kurt Grady. He had settled his own hash. I was pretty sure of my ground where he was concerned,'' he finished complacently.

''You were right, of course.'' She smiled gently. ''I saw him there and felt absolutely nothing. I wasn't even surprised he was alive, once I recovered from the initial shock. He just didn't interest me.''

''So that gamble paid off, you see,'' he taunted.

"I should have had as much confidence in you," she admitted sadly. "I hated Ginny Lee. She made such despicable accusations! Yet I believed her."

He extracted her wandering fingers from his hair, kissed them. "Ginny Lee has always been a trouble-maker." That was a fact Toni had no wish to refute. "From the beginning she went after me flat out. When she got nowhere she married Greg. I did my best to warn him, but she had him snowed. He adored her. And she had her eye on his money, which was a nice piece of change. She divorced him when it was gone. I've never given her the time of day. I did try to talk her into staying with Greg just before the final decree was issued. We quarreled about it the night you and Mike Lane trucked me home from Houston. But I've never been able to abide the woman."

Poor Ginny. Toni thought about it and soon gave up the pang of sympathy. The woman really was arrogant and deserved any setback to her well-laid plan. She turned her attention to more personal matters. Such as the thrill it gave her to rub her hand over the hard jaw that jutted above her. "I thought you were running around with her behind Greg's back, and that she divorced him so she could marry you. In fact, she told me that once in no uncertain terms."

Mark avenged himself for her lack of faith in a manner of the utmost satisfaction to both of them. Toni knew then that the reason for her existence was to love this man whose love was so strong and all-forgiving.

"You sent the telegram Hussein received that time in Dallas, didn't you?" she accused him, murmuring against his lips as he came up for a breath of air.

"You mean when he left and I took you to see the bluebonnets?" His smirk was entirely self-satisfied.

"Nope, I didn't send the telegram. I just sent my Mideast crew some instructions that were, er, badly misinterpreted. It raised quite a fuss on site, I'm afraid. Hussein had no choice. He had to go home to settle the mess. God!" He shuddered against her. "I'll never get over the horror of your disappearance from the hotel room before the wedding. I almost lost my mind then."

"One would scarcely have known. You were beastly to me when you came to the Bedouins' camp."

"I was out of my head. You hated me, and I couldn't trust myself not to grab you up and never let you go until you promised to marry me. If you could have seen your poor bruised little face." He groaned, his arms tightening with convulsive strength. "Oh, Antonia, Antonia. I was sure you didn't want me to touch you." His lean face was bleak with remembered hurt.

She soothed him, her hand gentle on his stubbly cheek. "Did you find them?" She had never asked before.

"We found them." The instant tension in the long body touching hers so intimately told her the man in her arms had no wish to share his memory of the hunt he and Hussein had gone on.

"Why did they kidnap me?" she asked, to divert him.

"They were fanatics—zealots, if you will. Hussein's country has a law that ruling members are not allowed to marry outside the country. In Hussein's case, he had twice married within the law and both women were barren, unfortunately. He is allowed multiple wives, but does not believe in the custom. He asked his king to grant him permission to marry a foreign woman this time and was granted the special favor. The men belonged to a group who were determined not to let this happen. They wanted him to marry within the kingdom. Another cousin, probably."

"So it *was* a case of mistaken identity. They thought I was Linda, Hussein's bride...."

"Yes. They were uneducated men. One Western woman looked much the same as another to them."

"And I was in Linda's room, holding her veil...."

He nodded and stared down at her, his eyes shadowed with pain.

"Why did they take me to that cave—try to—to rape me?"

"In their simple way, they were intent on making you completely unfit to be the bride of an Arabian man. No man worth his salt would touch you with a ten-foot pole once you'd had intercourse with another man. And most especially, a prince could not."

"Were they going to leave me there afterward, tied up, to die?"

"No. The driver of the other car ahead of you had instructions to leave word at the hotel where you could be found. He was to do it that morning. He was caught, of course. And Frank did such a good job of disabling the other two that they did not have a chance to disappear into the desert as they were supposed to do. We caught them before they got far."

Toni moved her head back out of the comfortable hollow of his shoulder and looked at him critically. Abruptly she decided the subject was closed.

"You are thoroughly disreputable, you know," she offered, playfully shaking her head at him. "I understand from unimpeachable sources that it was your house I was sharing in Galveston. Driving a car you bought for me. Being cared for by servants in your employ. And U.P.C. was just a cover for you.''

"Sorry about that, Antonia. But I just had to have you in my house, to have and to hold forever, even if you were not aware of what I was up to.''

"Half of Galveston was apparently under the impression I was your live-in girl friend. How could you, Mark?''

"It was nobody's damn business!'' The hot answer mocked and challenged. "I wanted you there and by God, I meant to keep you there! At least until I could get you to simmer down and see that you were meant for me.''

"Where did you sleep?'' Her curiosity got the better of her. "Greg showered in what he called your room that night after the fire. I was shocked to bits. And then I opened the closet and saw those things I had refused to have in London hanging there....''

Mark's laugh was a little grim. "Yes, well, I hadn't meant you to find those just yet. Greg told me what happened. Your reaction was not unexpected, but I wasn't worried. I knew you would turn up for the races at South Padre Island. Greg had promised not to tell me, I know now, but that didn't mean he couldn't tell Karen, who kindly filled me in.''

"The sly devil!'' Toni pretended to be angry, but it really no longer mattered. She should have known Greg would find a way around the condition she'd insisted upon.

"Anyway,'' Mark went on, "I was planning to explain to you there. Only your boat flipped, a horrible experience I'd never want to suffer through again, and John Gann turned up with Grady. So it didn't work out. You left the hospital without giving me a chance.

When you were in town I slept in a room I have at the warehouse. Mike Lane stayed there with me that time long ago when he came to see you. But why did you run from the hospital?"

"I didn't think you wished to see me. And I couldn't bear the pain of loving you, a man I thought I couldn't respect. Did Greg tell you where I had gone?"

"No, my love. I didn't have to ask. I knew you would come here. So I hiked to the airport and caught the Concorde. I came straight here. It wasn't hard to arrange for Joan and Jock to leave. They've been expecting an announcement from us anyway."

Toni remembered the phone call she had made to her mother before she left London for the Gulf of Mexico in February. What had Joan said? Don't fight your heart. Toni sighed, wishing she had followed that wise advice. Mark smiled at her pensive face.

"Thank God they were on my side all along. And for your information, they did not think much of your former fiancé." He nodded at the question in her eyes. "Oh, yes, they knew he was still alive. But since he wanted to appear dead, they agreed with Clive Atkins it was better to let him bury himself. They didn't realize you were going to use his supposed death as a means of isolating yourself from men—although I'm damned glad you did. Saved you for me. Besides—" and that bad-boy twinkle was back "—they approve of me." His complacency was something to behold.

"How could they resist?" Toni questioned tartly. "There is something about a reckless arrogant gambler who thinks he is a lord of creation whom mere mortals are very susceptible to—"

"Ah, but being the gambler's choice, how can you complain? Do you love me, Antonia Carla Cameron?"

"I love you, Mark Anders." She stroked his hair as he lay against her, her love swelling in her, issuing demands. He turned that proud head of his then and touched the breast his cheek was resting on with lips that were soft as velvet.

With an indrawn breath, Toni gave up her questions. Instead she gave herself fully to the hidden flame that burned within her for this gambling man, a flame that ignited and flared into rapture.

It was a long time before they thought about a meal. Toni was in the kitchen, strips of bacon sizzling, eggs in another pan, when Mark finished his shower and came in, his hair darkened with dampness. He stopped in the doorway and stretched his muscular frame, a smug grin creasing his newly shaved face. A surge of emotion hit Toni, left her helpless a moment.

Mark read her expression, laughed and went to her. He tilted her face upward, planted a sweet hard kiss very expertly on her lips, wiping out her chagrin at his easy understanding of her innermost feelings.

"You enchant me, Antonia," he told her gently. "You have since the first moment I set eyes on you."

"Mmm...and when was that?" Toni responded with some exploring of her own that was vastly satisfying.

"You don't know?"

Toni shook her head.

Mark groaned. "Just as I feared. I step off a copter in the middle of the North Sea, see an angel I know instantly I cannot live without...and she didn't even notice I existed!"

"I noticed you when you tackled me," she offered, buttering the toast with laudable concentration.

Mark groaned dramatically. "God, Antonia, don't

remind me." He stared at her. "Do you realize what you have put me through ever since I first met you? You were almost knocked dead in the North Sea. A hurricane almost wiped you out in the gulf. Then an oil rig exploded under your feet. And to top it all off, you barely escaped drowning in that damn catamaran race. Not to count the three ardent suitors I've had to fight off."

"Two," she temporized, dimple at work.

"Three," he insisted. "Grady would have been after you like a shot if he could have figured a way to claw over me. All that and you dare stand there and not realize how I felt the first time I saw you!"

Toni slipped his eggs onto a warmed plate. Her dimple defied all effort to keep it suppressed. "Oh, aye, Mr. Anders. And would you be having me believe that you fell in love at the very sight of me?"

"I would indeed, Miss Cameron, ma'am. And will you come and eat so we can get that name changed? I cannot abide your single status."

"Greg tells me you are U.P.C." Toni could not resist the last question as she joined him at the table. "Does that mean you alone were responsible for the fabulous contract I could not resist?"

He grinned, unabashed. "It was either that or stir up an international incident and have those famous redcoats of yours landing on our shores, intent on rescue after I had kidnapped you. Come to that, I damn near did anyway." He dove into his breakfast with gusto.

"Yes, I know." Toni considered the top of his tawny head. "Took me off to London, spent money like a drunken sailor, kept me in luxury like some high-priced tart! Minks, model dresses—and that hotel!"

"Uh-huh." His lazy and very unruffled satisfaction with the way things had evolved sent a thrill coursing through her nervous system. "And then I took you to the wilds of Texas where I could isolate you. I turned you over to ma's tender mercies while I figured out a way to rid myself of competition. Oh, God, Antonia." He stood up, reached for her. Exhaling slowly, he pulled her into his arms and buried his handsome face in her hair. "I love you so. Let's go get married."

Toni placed her fork carefully back on her plate, and they went to do just that.

Never had a gambler's choice been more certain.

Now's your chance to discover the earlier books in this exciting series.

Choose from this list of great

SUPERROMANCES!